circa 2000

circa 2000

lesbian fiction at the millennium

edited by

TERRY WOLVERTON & ROBERT DRAKE

alyson books
los angeles | new york

MANUFACTURED IN THE UNITED STATES OF AMERICA.

THIS TRADE PAPERBACK ORIGINAL IS PUBLISHED BY
ALYSON PUBLICATIONS,
P.O. BOX 4371, LOS ANGELES, CA 90078-4371.
DISTRIBUTION IN THE UNITED KINGDOM BY
TURNAROUND PUBLISHER SERVICES LTD.,
UNIT 3, OLYMPIA TRADING ESTATE, COBURG ROAD, WOOD GREEN,
LONDON N22 6TZ ENGLAND.

FIRST EDITION: JULY 2000

00 01 02 03 04 ⓐ 10 9 8 7 6 5 4 3 2 1

ISBN: 1-55583-518-X

CREDITS
COVER PHOTOGRAPHY AND DESIGN BY PHILIP PIROLO.

Contents

Introduction

It's a hazy white-sky afternoon in Los Angeles, in that slow sur-
real week between Christmas and New Year's when everything
seems in a state of suspension, and I am talking on the phone to
Robert Drake. It's midnight in Dublin, where he takes the call.
Robert is my friend and colleague; for the past decade, he and I
have worked together editing nine literary anthologies of work by
lesbians and gay men.

We don't talk on the phone as much since he moved to Ireland
the summer of 1998; we rely mostly on frequent but terse E-mails
detailing the tasks outstanding for these millennial anthologies—
endlessly revised contributors lists, promotional strategies, the night-
mare of obtaining permissions to reprint.

Our conversation today has been more personal—the status of my
ongoing heartbreak over a failed love affair, his missing the longtime
partner he left behind in the States despite his happiness with his
new, young Irish lover. Inevitably, though, our conversation strays
back to work, the strongest thread that connects us.

"Do you realize," he says pensively, "that these are probably the
last anthologies we'll do together?"

The afternoon is bluing toward darkness, and as he asks this, I feel
a pang. Of course I had known it—my burnout with editing and his
relocation to Ireland had virtually assured it—but his articulation
brings home the pathos of this milestone.

I never aspired to be an editor. When I first met Robert in the
summer of 1989, I was working on a novel and teaching creative
writing classes at the Los Angeles Gay & Lesbian Center. My stu-

dents were giving a reading, and Robert came because he'd read about it in the paper.

Afterward, he introduced himself to me, a tall, dark-haired man whose wire-rimmed glasses called attention to a distinctive profile. He was an agent, he explained, interested in representing gay and lesbian writers. He talked too fast, the way agents do, but with more sincerity. "I'm really impressed with a lot of what I've heard today," he told me, "and I wonder if you'd like to work with me."

His idea was to produce a volume of new fiction by West Coast gay and lesbian writers. "Several editors have told me that California is where the hot new writing is coming from." Robert believed I could help him locate some of that "hot new writing," and I agreed to try.

That first volume, *Indivisible* (Plume, 1991), expressed a value that was central to our work together: that the gay and lesbian literary communities could benefit from cross-pollination, that we need to be reading each other's work. This stance confounded the segregated marketing structures of gay and lesbian publishing. When we approached publishers about a second volume, everyone refused us, not because they hadn't liked or respected the first volume, but because no one could figure out how to market it.

We then proposed a series of companion volumes, *His* and *Hers,* coedited by both of us, released simultaneously. In 1998 *His*[2] received a Lambda Literary Award, but Robert was in Ireland, so I accepted it on his behalf.

An inveterate fan of *The X-Files,* Robert used to joke that he and I were the Scully and Mulder of gay and lesbian letters; he is the true believer, writing of the gay community as the "mother ship," while I am the hard-eyed pragmatist worrying about deadlines and systems. What we share is a passion for and commitment to the craft of fiction; over the ten years we've worked together we've striven to establish and fulfill high standards of literary merit, publishing work that stretches its readers from the standpoints of both form and content.

The anthology you hold now was not my idea. The day Robert

called me to propose *Circa 2000: Lesbian Fiction at the Millennium* and its companion volume for gay men, I was cranky and burned out. Although I felt proud of the seven books we had already produced, the sacrificial nature of the enterprise was beginning to wear on me. Reading hundreds of manuscripts, negotiating with authors and agents who seemed to believe we were making a whole lot more money on these books than we ever have (the compensation works out to slightly less than 10 cents per manuscript we read), confronting the seemingly insurmountable difficulty of upping our sales figures with only a minuscule marketing budget—these things were taking their toll on my time, my spirit, and my own writing.

Robert listened to me vent and never disagreed. I knew he was lying when he assured me this would be a project on which we would make a bundle (we didn't); I similarly doubted him when he claimed this process would be so much easier because we wouldn't need to invite open submissions (it wasn't). He still talked too fast, but I let his persuasions wash over me until I gave in. I enjoyed our working process, the way our sensibilities differed—I am drawn to more experimental, craft-based work; he to classical stories and historical settings, more popular themes—yet we still retained respect for one another. I liked the way he'd give in to me when I really wanted a story—or fiercely argued against one. We both gave each other that latitude, didn't insist on consensus, allowed one another to include those works about which we felt passionate.

Our process underwent a change when Robert moved to Ireland the summer of 1998. He'd met a young man, fallen in love, was willing to uproot his entire life to pursue the relationship. I questioned the wisdom of this path, but when he said to me, "If I don't do this, I'll regret it for the rest of my life," I could only wish him well.

On this day in late December, when he reminds me that our work together is about to come to an end, I know I will miss it. I'll miss the great enthusiasm he brings to each project, the irreverence with which he regards the sacred cows of gay and lesbian politics; I'll even miss scolding him for missed deadlines and lame excuses.

What neither of us can know, as the tumult of 1998 draws to a merciful close, is that our work together will be halted by a much more ominous event. That on January 31, 1999, in Sligo, Ireland, Robert will be gay-bashed, beaten unconscious in his own home by two men. That these men would later claim to police they'd been "victims of a homosexual pass" (a ridiculous claim to any of us who know Robert). That Robert would be in a coma for two months, eventually medevac'd home to Philadelphia, still unconscious, or that I would visit him in the hospital in early May, witness my friend and colleague wizened, unable to speak or control his movements. Witness him struggle to lift a baseball cap from his head—each brain function summoned by will, each movement separate as stop-time photography—and to put it on again. That he would cry when I tell him, "I love you."

Neither of us can know how it will fall to me to finish alone our last projects months behind schedule, coaxed but never pressured by my understanding editor. The book you hold now is the product of Robert's vision, our combined selections, and finally my efforts. We sought to feature works by those writers whom we believe will be influential in the coming millennium. There are authors included here who have been prominent in the closing decades of this current millennium: Dorothy Allison, Beth Brant, Rebecca Brown, Ana Castillo, Emma Donoghue, Mary Gaitskill, Carole Maso, Achy Obejas, Patricia Powell, and Sarah Schulman. There are authors whose influence is just beginning to be felt: Elise D'Haene, Larissa Lai, Shani Mootoo, Mei Ng, Gerry Gomez Pearlberg, Robin Podolsky, Jane Thurmond, and Shay Youngblood. And we've included a couple of writers who are at the beginning of their publishing careers—Cynthia Bond, Amelia Maria de la Luz Montes—whose voices promise that we will be hearing a lot more from them in the decades to come.

It's an idiosyncratic roster of writers, heavily dependent on my own tastes. I am certainly aware of absences—two writers who declined permission to reprint their work, the many outstanding writers who could have easily substituted for the ones who are included here with no diminishment of the overall product. Our intention is not to anoint these writers above others, but to say simply, Here are some writers worth paying attention to; here are some voices that will continue to have resonance.

I'm not much given to fixed categories. At least one of these "stories" is in fact an essay; at least three of these authors identify themselves as bisexual. The end of the 20th century has been about the breaking down of fixed categories—of art forms, of culture, of gender, of sexual orientation—the blurring of borders to allow an infinite variety of options for identity and expression. This dissolution brings excitement and possibility, but also confusion, frustration, a certain anxiety. My students, for example, want me to tell them definitively how a short story is different from a personal essay; their foreheads pucker with worry when I say those forms are moving closer and closer together. I know lesbians who are sure that a bisexual woman is nothing like them; they scowl when they read an erotic story they like and I say, "Right now the author lives with a man." Especially in the United States, we want to know, and those fixed categories allow us the illusion—however false—that we do.

How long we can float in this sea of suspended definitions is difficult to predict, and in part dependent on the culture's tolerance for ambiguity. Will the millennium see a move back to rigid definitions and the certainty they promise, or will we continue to dissolve categories until we humans understand ourselves quite differently, until sexual orientation as identity seems a quaint and archaic notion?

If we live long enough, we may discover answers to these questions. Until then, let's revel in art, with all its ambiguities. What this anthology aims to do is introduce you to, or remind you about, a selection of writers whose intelligence, style, and heart may ease our passage into the next millennium.

It is with humility, ever more mindful of the frailty, the ephemeral nature of all things, that I, on behalf of Robert and myself, offer you this book.

—Terry Wolverton

Her Body, Mine, and His

Dorothy Allison

Frog fucking. Her hands on my hips; my heels against my ass, legs spread wide; her face leaning into my neck; my hands gripping her forearms. Her teeth are gentle. Nothing else about her is. I push up on the balls of my feet, rock my ass onto my ankles, reaching up for every forward movement of her thighs between mine. Her nipples are hard, her face flushed, feet planted on the floor while I arch off the edge of the bed, a water mammal, frog creature with thighs snapping back to meet her every thrust.

My labia swell. I can feel each hair that curls around the harness she wears. I imagine manta rays unfolding great undulating labia— wings in the ocean, wrapping around the object of their desire. Just so my labia, the wings of my cunt. I reach for her with my hands, my mouth, my thighs, my great swollen powerful cunt.

Her teeth are set, hips are thrusting, shoving, head back, pushing, drawing back and ramming in. I laugh and arch up into her, curse her, beg her. My feet are planted. I can do anything. I lift my belly, push up even more. Fucking, fucking, fucking. I call this fucking. Call her lover, bastard, honey, sweetheart, nasty motherfucker, evil-hearted bitch, YOU GODDAMNED CUNT! She calls me her baby, her girl, her toy, her lover, hers, hers, hers. Tells me she will never stop, never let me go. I beg her. "Fuck me. Hard," I beg her. "You, you, you…hard! Goddamn you! Do it! Don't stop! Don't stop! Don't stop! Don't stop!"

Jesus fucking christ don't stop.

Don't stop.

I have been told lesbians don't do this. Perhaps we are not lesbians? She is a woman. I am a woman. But maybe we are aliens? Is what we do together a lesbian act?

Paul took me out for coffee in New York and gave me a little silver claw holding a stone. "A little something for that poem of yours," he told me. "The one about the joy of faggots. I've been reading it everywhere." He drank herbal tea and told me about his travels, reading poetry and flirting with the tender young boys at all the universities, going on and on about how they kneel in the front row and look up at him, their lips gently parted and their legs pressed together. Sipping tea he told me, "They're wearing those loose trousers again, the ones with the pleats that always remind me of F. Scott Fitzgerald and lawn parties."

I drank the bitter coffee, admired his narrow mustache, and told him how much I hate those blouson pants women are wearing instead of jeans. "It's hell being an ass woman these days," I joked.

He started to laugh, called me a lech, looked away, looked back, and I saw there were tears in his eyes. Said, "Yes, those jeans, tight, shaped to the ass, worn to a pale blue-white and torn, like as not showing an ass cheek paler still." Said, "Yes, all those boys, those years, all the men in tight-tight pants." Said, "Yes, those jeans, the pants so tight their cocks were clearly visible on the bus, the subway, the street, a shadow of a dick leading me on. Sometimes I would just lightly brush them, and watch them swell under the denim, the dick lengthening down the thigh." He stopped, tears all over his face, his hand on his cup shaking, coming up in the air to gesture. A profound, sad movement of loss. "All gone," he whispered, the romantic poet in his suede professor's jacket. "I never do it anymore, never. Never touch them, those boys. Can't even imagine falling in love again, certainly not like I used to for twenty minutes at a time on any afternoon."

I started to speak, but he put his hand up. "Don't say it. Don't tell me I'm being foolish or cowardly or stupid or anything. I loved the way it used to be, and I hate the fact that it's gone. I've not become celibate, or silly, or vicious, or gotten religion, or started lecturing people in bars. It's those memories I miss, those boys on the street in the afternoon laughing and loving each other, that sense of sex as an adventure, a holy act."

He put his cup down, glared at it and then at me. Indignant, excited, determined. "But you still do it, don't you? You dykes! You're out there all the time doing it. Flirting with each other, touching, teasing, jerking each other off in bathrooms, picking each other up and going to parties. Fucking and showing off and doing it everywhere you can. You are. Say you are. I know you are."

I said, "Yes." I lied and said, "Yes, Paul, we are. Yes."

☐   ☐   ☐

She has named her cock Bubba. Teases me with it. Calls it him, says, "Talk to him, pet him. He's gonna go deep inside you." I start to giggle, slap Bubba back and forth. Cannot take this too seriously, even though I really do like it when she straps him on. Bubba is fat and bent, an ugly pink color not found in nature, and he jiggles obscenely when she walks around the room. Obscene and ridiculous, still he is no less effective when she puts herself between my legs. Holding Bubba in one hand, I am sure that this is the origin of irony—that men's penises should look so funny and still be so prized.

☐   ☐   ☐

She is ten years younger than me...sometimes. Sometimes I am eight and she is not born yet, but the ghost of her puts a hand on my throat, pinches my clit, bites my breast. The ghost of her teases me, tells me how much she loves all my perversities. She says she was made for me, promises me sincerely that she will always want me. Sometimes I believe her without effort. Sometimes I become her child, trusting, taking in everything she says. Her flesh, her body, her lust and hunger—I believe. I believe, and it is not a lie.

When I am fucking her I am a thousand years old, a crone with teeth, bone teeth grinding, vibrating down into my own hips. Old and mean and hungry as a wolf; or a shark. She is a suckling infant, soft in my hands, trusting me with her tender open places. Her mouth parts like an oyster, the lower lip soft under the tongue, the teeth pearls in the dim light. Her eyes are deep and dark and secret. She is pink, rose, red, going purple dark...coming with a cry and a shudder, and suddenly limp beneath my arms. I push up off her and bite my own wrist. It is all I can do not to feed at her throat.

☐   ☐   ☐

I drank too much wine at a party last fall, found myself quoting Muriel Rukeyser to Geoff Maines all about the backside, the body's ghetto, singing her words, "Never to go despising the asshole nor the useful shit that is our clean clue to what we need."

"The clitoris in her least speech," he sang back, and I loved him for that with all my soul. We fed each other fat baby carrots and beamed at our own enjoyment.

"Ah, the ass," Geoff intoned, "the temple of the gods." I giggled, lifted a carrot in a toast, matched his tone. "And the sphincter—gateway to the heart."

He nodded, licked his carrot, reached down, shifted a strap, and inserted that carrot deftly up his butt. He looked up at me, grinned, rolled a carrot in my direction, raised one eyebrow. "Least speech," I heard myself tell him. Then I hiked up my skirt and disappeared that carrot, keeping my eyes on his all the while. There was something about his expression, a look of arrogant conviction that I could not resist.

"Lesbians constantly surprise me" was all Geoff said, lining up a row of little baby carrots from the onion dip to the chips, pulling the dish of butter over as well. He handed me another carrot. I blinked, then watched as he took one for himself. "I propose the carrot olympics, a cross-gender, mutually queer event," he challenged. I started to laugh as he rolled buttery carrots between his palms. His face was full of laughter, his eyes so blue and pleased with himself they sparkled. "All right," I agreed. How could I not? I pulled up the hem of my skirt, tucked it into my waistband, took up the butter, and looked Geoff right in the eye. "Dead heat, or one-on-one?"

□   □   □

"FAGGOT!" That's what he called me. The boy on the street with the baseball bat who followed me from Delores Park the week after I moved to San Francisco. He called me a faggot. My hair is long. My hips are wide. I wear a leather jacket and walk with a limp. But I carry a knife. What am I exactly? When he called me a faggot I knew. I knew for sure who I was and who I would not be. From the doorway of the grocery at 18th and Guerrero I yelled it at him. "Dyke! Get it right, you son of a bitch, I'm a dyke."

□   □   □

I am angry all the time lately, and being angry makes me horny, makes me itchy, makes me want to shock strangers and surprise the girls who ask me, please, out for coffee and to talk. I don't want to talk. I want to wrestle in silence. It isn't sex I want when I am like this. It's the intimacy of their bodies, the inside of them, what they are afraid I might see if I look too close. I look too close. I write it all down. I intend that things shall be different in my lifetime, if not in theirs.

□   □   □

Paul, Geoff—I am doing it as much as I can, as fast as I can. This holy act. I am licking their necks on Market Street, fisting them in the second-floor bathroom at Amelia's, in a booth under a dim wall lamp at the Box—coming up from her cunt a moment before the spotlight shifts to her greedy features. I have tied her to a rail in a garage down on Howard Street, let her giggle and squirm while I teased her clit, then filled her mouth with my sticky fingers and rocked her on my hipbone till she roared. We have roared together.

Everywhere I go, the slippery scent of sweat and heat is in the air, so strong it could be me or the women I follow, the ones who follow me. They know who I am just as I know them. I have ripped open their jeans at the Powerhouse, put my heel between their legs at the Broadway Cafe, opened their shirts all the way down at Just Desserts, and pushed seedless grapes into their panties at the Patio Cafe. The holy act of sex, my sex, done in your name, done for the only, the best reason. Because we want it.

I am pushing up off the bed into Alix's neck like a great cat with a gazelle in her teeth. I am screaming and not stopping, not stopping. Frog fucking, pussy creaming, ass clenching, drumming out, pumping in. I am doing it, boys and girls, I am doing it, doing it all the time.

Revelations (an excerpt from the novel Ruby)

Cynthia Bond

Don' nobody 'round here want nobody's pity. That ain' no reason fo' tellin' nothin'. Naw. If'n we wanted that we'da gone an' planted ourselves in the white folks' backyard. They fertilize with the stuff. Naw. We wants a tellin'. A full, wide one like a river breakin' through. See, sometime a story keep you weighted to this earth. You know that? It weigh in you heavy an' holt down the light air a' a soul. My story weigh me like that. It keep me from risin' proper. I feels that to be true. I feels it holdin' me like rocks tied to a hot-air balloon. I seen one only once. When was that?—'38 or '39? One. It had come to a white folks travelin' circus. This was a richty circus that they didn' even give us not a single day's visit to. Not like they do them others. Them others, they give us coloreds one day. Thursday usually. But by the time I seen that balloon floatin' an' hear that music sailin' over the corn field, well, by then I was lookin' fo' tents raised high, fo' them parades what lace they way through town. Ever' passin' year I would look both with trepidation an' with somethin' else that feel a bit like hope.

☐ ☐ ☐

I 'members that first Thursday I ever seen a circus. It were 1934 in the hottest Texas August God had painted in all a' my eleven years. Ruby was near thirteen when her granddaddy take us. Her mama's daddy—Mister Belle—he what git us them tickets an' tell us to dress like Sunday. Ruby call him Daddy, an' though we cousins, we do too. 'Cause he was sweet like nobody's daddy we knowed. He seemed never to speak, much less yell an' holler—an' when he do put words together, they sounded like a ole song that stayed on the edge a' my remembrance.

So that Thursday Mister Belle give a bitty white man all we tickets he'd bought when another white man come by people's houses sellin' 'em. Pieces a' red apple paper we carry all the way from home to that doorway a' curtain. Mine I'd took to chewin' on the way there, so it were half a' it limp an' dark-red when Mister Belle give it over. But he do it like it were jes' fine an' regular an' every day to have a chewed-on piece a' somethin' to han' over, him lookin' straight into that bitty man's eyes. Mister Belle do that with white folk. Pro'bly 'cause he look so like one. Skin as white as Miss Barbara's. Eyes like a tin a' dishwater reflectin' a thumbnail a' sky. Folks teases Ruby somethin' awful 'bout him. Say her granddaddy a ole white man. Even though they know it ain' so 'cause Ruby's mama come out jes' like him. White as glue.

Ruby, she holt Mister Belle's hand when we go in. She was breathin' deep from the walk. My four brothers run ahead like they ain' got no sense. Almos' knockin' folk down with they foolishness. Mister Belle he ain' say nothin' 'bout it 'cause that weren't his way. Naw…he'd wait 'til after when we was walkin' home to place a few words inside some others an' roll 'em up like a walnut in soft maple candy. Then he'd leave 'em fo' us to take if we please. That was his way a' schoolin'.

Inside the place they was the scent a' wet fur an' flesh, an' peanuts hot an' cookin', an' poppin' corn an' salty salt, an' sweat an' somethin's poop, an' rock candy. All I heared was the sound a' a scratchy band floatin' over people talkin'.

They was colored people there I ain' never seen before. Some po' an' sorrowful-lookin', others look like they preachers an' they kin. Dress all kinda ways. I guess I didn't look too proper, but I sho' wasn't the worst a' them neither. Not like I care so 'bout them thangs. But Ruby, she do, so I stands a little taller jes' fo' her. She were a pretty sight, all high buttons an' that pink bow I tie in her hair tight. We all gets to our place in the middle, not too far back with them no-shoes folk, an' not too close like them bow-tie an' hat-wearin' people. But we sit in the middle amidst that wavin' flag a' colored folk.

I know Ruby like she takin' breath in an' I'm lettin' it back out. We shares the ether a' the world like that. "Mama'd like this," say Ruby. An' I say like I always do, "You gonna have to tell her all 'bout it when she make it back." Ruby look at me soft, then she look away.

It go dark, then it's a spot a' light. First thang we see is a circle put into the earth an' a black moustache man in a tall shiny cap. We all starts to clappin' jes fo' the hat. Then he's speakin' into another circle he be holdin', but can't nobody make out what he sayin' fo' our cheers.

Then they brings out a pinch-face lady on the back a' what they call a elephant. That's one sorry-lookin' creature God put his han' to. Skin slackin' off an' sickly gray, ears hangin', nose draggin' the floor. An' the lady what ride lookin' meaner by the minute, an' her legs be like lumps a' oatmeal. An' what make it worse, she hoppin' up an' down on that sad creature's back. I fell to cryin' when I see the teeny eyes God give it.

Ruby, she feather-touch my cheek. But my brother Julian shove me to stop an' say, "Well Maggie, you finally find you some birds a' a feather." So I hit him like a man. He hit me right back. We hear the crowd say "oooooooooo." So when Julian look up I ball up my fist an' hit him so hard he fall off his seat. He don' bother me after that.

Child, them boys an' we stan' dead still when we see them big stripe cats. Lord, I known in that second how the mouse be feelin' lookin' into them teeths. That white man git his whip out—like that little thang gonna keep them teeth from his neck. I think on Daniel with his head in that lion mouth an' know right then an' there I ain' never gonna believe another word in that book. The white man, he stay in there though long enough to get a cat to stan' on a chair, an' jes' snappin' an' snappin' while he do it. Then out he go.

They was dust or somethin' thick in the air. Like them tents holt in a part a' life an' don' want nothin' stirrin'. It's like they mix up the breath a' day with saw dust an' a twinin' spell—like when you weavin' a newborn's blanket. When you put you wishes in each piece a' thread, an' you hopes in the knots. It were like that in there. Through that thick air nothin' look regular: Men's bodies shrunk into childhood, but they heads stayed grown. Some men's eatin' fire like it's corn bread, others got feet five shoes long. Then the place go dark an' quiet so I close my eyes like I do durin' convection at church.

I look up an' that's when I see all a' them flyin' air people. My eye was caught by the sight. Even though I knowed inside me they didn't even put on the regular show fo' us. Like it seem short an' they don' even bother to smile them glitz smiles I seen in the picture outside the tent. They didn't wave they arms 'round with no relish or nothin'. But still it were a sight. We all be seein' them ladies in them little nothin' thangs they be wearin'. Seein' them climb up them ladders an' hang on string with they teeth. They all seem to have some mighty strong teeth to be doin' all a' that. Lord knows. But I still loves to watch them ladies in them silver tights. An' them capes! Whew, Lord! Them capes was like a million stars all crammed in one itty piece a fabric.

So there they'd be flyin' 'round havin' one a' them ole men catchin' 'em in they hands. I never knowed why all the mens was so ole with they held-in bellies, an' all the ladies be so pretty an' young. Seem like them ladies be better suited catchin' each other. I know I wouldn't trust no man to catch what I be sayin', much less grab holt a body from a way up there. No, Lord. Seem like since it were the ladies left with nothin' to holt to, seem like they'd be the ones who'd know you had to catch holt, cause they'd be flyin' the next time an' they'd want somebody holdin' them.

Anyways, when them lights got to movin' round, an' them drums got to goin', an' they took to swingin', they swing back an' forth. I swear, Lord, the whole a' the place jes' held its breath. Then go that little blond one flyin'. Then she start somersaultin' right there in that air with nothin' but the hard earth 'neath her. Then she reaches out her hands an' she got nothin' to save her from bein' crushed-up bones an' dust but that ole holt-in-belly, big-armed white man. Lord, child, what she do that fo'? Rollin' drums, reachin' han's, shinin' circles a' light, then...then...then...he catch her. Child the place go wild!! Folks standin' an' hollerin' so the white man takin' the money come out an' tell us all to shut up. We git quiet some, but still we screamin' in our hearts.

I figure she got to be some kinda angel to fly like that. She walk out, not even really botherin' to bow good, but she bow good enough fo' me. Somethin' powerful take holt a' me like I ain' never felt before or since. It like to throw me out my seat. I turn an' look, but Julian jes' sittin' there. Ruby jes' lookin' with her midnight eyes. But I can't say nothin' to her. I stan' upright. Somebody yell to sit down. Ruby pull my hand. But somethin' callin' an' I got to go. I start to walkin' from my people. Julian yell out, but I'm quick! An' Mister Belle, he jes' look at me out the corner a' his gray-blue eye an' do somethin' too slight to be called a nod. So down I go, sayin' excuse me, steppin' on toes, leapin' up sawdust stairs, runnin' outta the hooded dark into the halo a' evenin'.

Then I see her. I watches her handin' that cape to the same bitty man runnin' after her. I walk up slow an' when I get close to her I could smell her. She smelled real strong, but different from like how I was us'ta folks smellin' bad. Mama say white folk smell like wet dogs when they sick. An' I could see her hair flat an' oily wet stickin' to her forehead an' cheeks. She was shakin' somethin' awful, an' I see her fall on her knees an' start throwin' up right out there where any-body coulda seen her.

I jes' stan' there. Not sayin' nothin'. Her whole little body retchin'. She stop fo' a minute an' I seen her tryin' to keep her arms from givin' way. Slobber jest drippin'. I scratched my thigh an' she look up.

She say all weak an' mean, "What are you looking at?"

I still didn't say nothin'.

"Come here."

I step 'round that yella mess come outta her. She smell like some-thin' dyin'. It go into me an' I say, "You sick, ma'am?"

"What you think?" she got out, "Don't I look like I'm sick?"

"Yeah, you do."

"Well, I am." An' she throws up again all over my Sunday shoes. Some a' it splatter on my leg.

She turn to me. "I need to get outta the main fareway before anyone sees me."

That's when I realized that everybody else was still inside the tent watchin' the show, an' the little man who had took her silver cape had run off jes' like he'd run to git it.

"Can you help me?" she said.

"Yes'm I can" was all I could git outta my throat. I tried to kick some dust on my shoes, then my little ole self reached down an' picked her up. She were all hot an' damp against me. I got puff up with bein' scared an' thrilled, 'cause sick or no she was still the oniliest lady I had ever seen fly in the clear air.

She pointed me to a torn-up lookin' tent about twenty yards away. We got to it slow-like. Then she lifted up them dust-smellin' heavy curtains an' make her way to a seat. They's a broken-up clouded mirror an' all these circles a bright bright red an' blue an' black an' pink, like I never seen. An' the whole place smell like sweat an' dirt.

"Give me that bucket over there," she say an' point, so I gets it. An' she starts throwin' up again, but this time she ain' got nothin' left in her so she jes' heave up spit an' snot an' sound. I sit an' stare into her.

"Can you pour me some water?" I look, then reaches to my left an' pick up a fade blue pitcher an' pour her some water into a tin cup by it. I han' it over an' what she don' spill she turn up her tin to drink. She holt it out fo' me, so I fill it again an' she turn it up, water slidin' off the angle a' her jaw, her throat movin' up an' down like a fish.

"That towel?" She guesstures an' I get it, then she dip it into a small basin by the colored paints. She presses it 'gainst her forehead an' that's when I get a real good look at her. Lord, was I surprised. I seen that under the sweat an' smell an' them red red lips an' bright bright blue eyes (all streakin' an' misplaced from where they seem to have been originally intended), under all that was a little girl. Little. No bigger than me. Little an' shaken an' sweatin' so, they was long wet spots in strips under her arms an' in the crease a' her hip joint, an' all along her privates an' on her back. Her hands was shakin' so that she couldn't hardly holt the towel. She was gulpin' in huge pieces a' breath an' after a long silent while, she started to cry.

"I messed up the last revolution."

"What?" I say real quiet.

"I messed it up bad. Daddy told me, half-turn then catch. Half-turn then catch. Half-turn then catch. That's how we practiced it. Then I go an' turn a whole one." She broke down again, "I've got to wait a whole beat for him to swing up then back so I had to keep turnin'. I never turned three revolutions...half-revolution then catch, half-revolution then catch...but I turn three. Daddy nearly yanked my arm outta my socket when he caught me."

"I thought you look real pretty up there."

She look up from her sweat an' smeared black blue red face. I could tell now that what I'd been smellin' was the breath an' rot a' fear. She look up at me an' seen me, I think, fo' the first time. I could tell she took in that I was colored, an' if it had been any other time it might a' make a difference, but not then. She look at me an' said. "You think so?"

"Oh, yeah! Everybody was goin' wild about you revelations! They thought you was the best thang in the whole show!"

"Yeah?"

"Yeah! Yeah! How'd you do all a that? It was like a miracle."

"You think?"

"It was the best I ever saw!" I didn't bother tellin' her that it were the only circus I'd ever seen.

"It was my first time."

"Naw!"

"Yeah, Daddy said I could practice on the colored night. This was my first time."

"Well, you was good."

"Yeah?"

Then we start to talkin'. Really she start to talkin'. An' I listens. Every once in a while I could hear the big tent roarin' up a cheer in the distance an' my mind flutter to my people. On Mister Belle holdin' Ruby by the hand. An' I think on the sights them two be takin' into they open eyes an' mouths. Ruby pursin' her lips into a perfect *O*.

I think on my Ruby Belle, still an' dark like Hershey chocolate. I sit here an' I wonder what she be seein'. I think on how smooth an' sweet she smell, how round her belly be, an' them sprouts a' silk black comin' between her legs. Nothin' on top yet an' she almos' thirteen. I had mine comin' fo' two years now since I hit nine. I think on how long it take me to know I loved Ruby like a cleft in my heart. How I first 'members feelin' it at five. How long it take me to kiss her. Yet an' still, fo' all that, I'm glad she ain' here now. I feels selfish like a birthday girl who won't share her cake. Then I sit an' gather up all them stray thoughts, like collectin' yella chicks in the well a' my apron. An' I set my ears an' eyes on this lady. This girl in the chair.

She tell me her name. Irene O'Conner. I tell her mine, Margeret, but how my people call me Maggie or Magpie, 'cause I likes to talk so. She laugh tinklin', then she say she Irish. Which Lord knows I didn't know what that mean. Sounded like somebody sayin', I rich. I rich. I like to say I weren't that big a' fool to be thinkin' that. But I can't.

She take some white cream an' rub it all over her countenance 'til it were all them bright colors mixed together. Then she wipe it all off an' that's when I officially had a meetin' with her face.

She was a little tiny thang. Everythin' about her was tiny. An' while most white folks jes' scared me to no end, she didn't. She told me 'bout growin' up on the road an' bein' born in the circus tent. She told me about New Jersey an' San Diego an' Witchita an' how she wanted to join some Barn Jam Big Big Circus an' travel on trains instead a' trucks.

I think 'bout all them thangs I wants to know, then tell her. Like what it feel like up there? Like what we look like? 'Bout my mama an' Ruby an' Mister Belle. But I don' say none a that. 'Stead I tell her 'bout Marian Lake an' them trees that play the water like a harp with they branches. An' the way them thumbnail frogs pick you sometime to sing to when you visit them. Not nobody else but you. She smile an' tell me how she knowed them frogs woulda pick her mama 'cause her mama had been picked out by God himself.

She told me 'bout her mama fallin' an' breakin' her neck an' dyin'. An' in the retrieval a' it I seen somethin' happenin' inside Irene soul. Somethin' like blood spreadin' into sawdust, somethin' what cover over her like a veil, like how the tale be tellin' itself through her. An' I swear Irene seem hooded in somethin' dark an' quiet, an' she open it up an' cover me with it too. She tole me how she were right there when it happen, an' how the pinkie ring what hit the ground first.

She say that ring always be slippin' off her mama any time a' day or night, an' how it ain' never fit. Say before she was born her papa give her mama it fo' the weddin'—how he ain' never give her no ring a' her own—not no store bought one, not one fo' her special own. No. He can't take all that kind a' time, not him. 'Stead he give her a ole used thang, say it got special meanin' to him. That's all fine an' good, but yet an' still it don' fit her. So he best keep his special meanin' to hisself an' give somethin' to her that will ring the hollow in her heart an' say, "You is what I come here to find." But he don' see it that way; he ain' the kind to take the time to find the circle an' breadth a' her finger.

Maybe 'cause he ain' never give her a proper ring, that's why it were easier to let go a' her in the bright air. Under them red and blue fade tents. Above all them lights. Irene say when the ring hit the ground first it felled right by her stockin' toes an' the edge a' her mama's cape she was holdin'. Holdin' too low, like she'd been told not to, so that it rested on sandy dirt an' puffs a' grainy grass. That ring, she say, make her lift that cape up off the ground, which is why it didn't get much blood on it later. Which is why she wore that cape tonight an' all through practice.

She say that in the seconds a' seein' that ring all a' these thangs crammed into her mind, like how her mama would say, "This weddin' ring is hard work to keep on my finger," an' then she'd laugh, Irene say, throw back her head an' laugh like she was drinkin' cool water, her swan throat movin' jest so. Irene said she never knowed

what that all mean, but that her daddy would get mad an' say, "I'll
get you one to fit when you fit!" An' her mama would say, "Well,
judgment day's not too far off for none a' us Robert an' the devil's
got a ring to fit your nose just perfect!" He'd stan' there sayin' nothin, an' she'd jes' smile, hair like sunset before rain, soft red holdin' a
natural bounce. How her hair would shimmer with her holt-in
laughs then it take to shakin' hard, snot comin' outta her nose, water
pourin' out her eyes 'n' that sun-glow hair make it seem like a rain-
bow a' the spirit was 'bout to break free.

Irene say her daddy'd stamp up dust an' snort an' turn to leave the
room till her mama's laughter tickled him in the small a' his back.
An' how he'd turn 'round cryin' an' smilin' an' say, "Old
Beelzebub's probably fitting me for it now." An' how he'd go over
to hug her an' she'd push him away, an' he'd go again an' again 'til
she'd let him. Then she'd kiss him on the top a' his head.

Irene say she's thinkin' all this an' more when she see that ring.
Then down come her mama an' the gristle an' crack a' bones, some
pokin' through the net a' tights, then come the blood spreadin'
quick into wood, dust an' earth. Then come the sounds a' the world
again; it all rush into her like a nail into wood. Then come the
screamin', then come down her daddy, like a spider down the rope,
then start the music, then go the circle a' light, then go out the
clowns. Then go her mama with prayers floatin' over an' about her
like perfume. Then go her spirit into quiet blue.

□   □   □

Into the cloud a' memory what circle us I say, "She sound quite
somethin'." We sits there soft fo' a time. I watch them clumps a'
vomit an' dirt gettin' set into my shoes. An' I hear the waves a'
whoopin' rise an' fall across the way. I think on how Ruby ain' got
nobody 'cept Mister Belle an' he be what?—85? 86? Old old. An'
how he's more curve each day, an' how the sick spells last longer, an'
how he one time smell a' urine when I come fo' dinner an' Ruby say
he waste on hisself some rare days.

I didn't know I'd stood up to go till I hear Irene say, "You want to see her?"

I stop an' look hard at her in her white little shirt, arms hangin' loose like spokes off a broke wheel...jes' that spindly an' wasted.

"Your mama?" I say.

"Yes, you want to?" An' I had the feelin' she'd not asked the question before now.

I nod yes.

"Daddy doesn't like me keeping this out," she say while reachin' into a knotted wood chest. An' she lift up a frame wrapped in light pink scarf same color as Ruby's bow. Irene pull her chair up close to mine then she unlooses the knot with her tiny fingers. I watch the pink float onto the ground 'tween us.

When I looks up, my Lord. It's like time an' nature done cracked an' splinter the floorboards a' my heart. 'Cause there...in that frame...was Ruby's mama's picture. Same face as the one sittin' in Mister Belle's parlor. I feels sweat breakin' on my temples an' above my lip. Ruby's mama, Charlotte Belle, stared into me behind that glass. I look right back an' feel her eyes catchin' me from fallin'. Charlotte Belle who left her baby an' passed fo' white up north. Ruby an' me, we know the stories all an' every one. How Ruby was still waitin' fo' her mama to send fo' her. How Mister Belle keep a full-mounded plate out after every Sunday dinner in hopes he could set his daughter. Charlotte down before it an' tuck a napkin to catch the leavins. I thinks on how I hear my mama say how Charlotte Belle catch the train fo' New York in the colored car an' leave through the white. My mouth go weak an' I think how nobody's daughter nor mama ever be comin' home again.

"The ring fell first." I hear Irene say.

Then I hear myself say, "Then head first into the floor a' the world." An' we tears they pour like rivers, an' I feels teeny twig arms tight 'round my neck. An' she's cryin' into the shell a' my ear, "Daddy an' I don't cry for Mama." She sing between sobs. An' I holt her tight into the crook a' my neck. I pat her back like I done fo' Ruby all them times an' say, "There, there," whiles I try to steady the wobbles an' catches in my breath. We stay like that I don' even know how long. But by the time I hear people pressin' out into the open with gulpin' laughs an' buzzin' excited talk, I know I ain' gon' tell her. Not her. An' not Ruby. Not even Mister Belle. I ain' about to snatch down the worlds they done built up so high. I pulls back an' kisses her on her cheek to seal the silence. An' she look back at me with eyes red an' wet as the ticket I carried there. "You gon' be alright...?" I say it fo' fact an' I questions it, both the same.

She believe it, an' answer it. An' she nod a fraction, jes' like Mister Belle. An' I see how she an' Ruby carry the same bow in they lip an' the same hope in they eye.

"I best be going."

She nod again...An' we hear the curtains rustlin' with movement. She turn quick an' whisper, "Go, quick! My daddy hates niggers!" An' she pushes me toward the other side...

I guess that's why I slip her pocket comb into my palm when she turn to where her daddy be comin' in.

My knees give out five steps from the curtain door, an' my girl-hood tumble an' slip into the ground. I spit into the earth an' cover it over with my right palm, what Mama say you got to do at the buryin' a' a hope.

I stan', walk an' meet up with Ruby an' Mister Belle in the mist a' night an' people. Mister Belle touch the top a' my head nice like, an' Ruby slip her hand into mine an' we set off fo' the long walk home, my brothers runnin' up ahead bein' tigers an' clowns an' horses. An' me, I kiss palms with Ruby with my right hand, an' play on the comb's tiny teeth with my left thumb. Back an' forth, in time with our steps. An' when we pass by Marion Lake, sho' enough, them frogs start to singin'.

Turtle Gal

Beth Brant

Sue Linn's mama was an Indian. She never knew from where, only that Dolores wore a beaded bracelet: yellow, blue, and green beads woven into signs. Burnt out from alcohol and welfare, Dolores gave up late one afternoon, spoke to her daughter in an unknown language, and put the bracelet around her girl's skinny wrist, where it flopped over her hand. She turned her face to the wall and died. November 4, 1968.

Sue Linn watched her mother die, knowing by instinct that it was better this way. Better for Dolores. But her child mind, her nine-year-old mind, had not yet thought of the possibilities or penalties that lay in wait for little girls with no mother. She thought of her friend, James William Newton, who lived across the hall. She went and got him. He walked Sue Linn back to the room where her mother lay dead.

"Lord, lord, lord, lord," the old man chanted as he paid his respects, covering the still-warm woman with the faded red spread. His tired eyes, weeping, looked down at the child standing so close to him. "Go get your things now, little gal. Bring everything you got. Your clothes, everything."

With his help, Sue Linn removed all traces of herself from the darkening apartment. James William made a last, quick search, then told the child to say good-bye to her mama. He waited in the hall, his face wrinkled and yellowish. His hand trembled as he reached into his pants pocket for his handkerchief, neatly folded. He shook the thin, white cloth and brought it to his eyes, where he wiped the cry, then blew his nose.

Sue Linn stood beside the bed she and her mother had shared for as long as the girl could remember. She pulled the spread from her mother's face and looked intensely at Dolores. Dolores' face was quieter, younger looking. Her broad nose seemed somehow more delicate, and her dark lashes were like ink marks against her smooth, reddish cheek. Sue Linn felt a choking move from her stomach up through her heart, her lungs, her throat and mouth. With an intake of harsh breath, she took a lock of her mother's black hair in her small fist. She held on, squeezing hard, as if to pull some last piece of life from her mother. She let go, turned away, and closed the door behind her. James William was waiting, his arms ready to hold her, to protect her.

Together they opened his door, walked into the room that was welcoming and waiting for their presence. African violets sat in a row along the windowsill, their purple and blue flowers shaking from the force of the door being closed. Sue Linn went to touch the fuzzy heart leaves, wondering once again what magic the old man carried in him to grow these queer exotic plants in the middle of a tired, dirty street.

James William put aside the bag filled with Sue Linn's belongings and told the child to sit in his chair while he went to call the ambulance. "Don't answer the door. Don't make no sounds. Sit quiet, little gal, and I be's back in a wink." He hugged the child and went out the door.

Sue Linn sat on James William's favorite chair, a gold brocade throne with arms that curved into high, wide wings. She stared out the window. She looked past the violets, past the ivy hanging in a pot attached to threads, dangling fresh and alive in front of the glass. She looked onto the street, the avenue that held similar apartment buildings, large and grey. Some had windows knocked out, some had windows made bright by plastic flowers. Some had windows decorated with a cross and JESUS IS MY ROCK painted on from the inside. The Salvation Army complex stood low and squat, the lights beginning to be turned on, bringing a softening sheen to the beige cement. The air was cold, the people on the street pulling their coats and

jackets closer to their bodies as they walked, hunched over in struggle past the Chinese restaurants, the grocery, the bars, the apartments. Cars made noise—the noises of rust, of exhaust pipes ready
to fall off, of horns applied with angry hands. Buses were unloading
people, doors opening to expel faces and bodies of many shapes and
colors. The avenue seemed to wander forever in a road of cement,
tall buildings, people, machines, eventually stopping downtown,
caught up in another tangle of streets and boulevards.

James William walked down the three flights of stairs to the pay
phone in the lobby. He called the operator to report the dead
woman, walked back up the three flights of stairs, his thoughts jumping and beating against his brain as his heart lurched and skipped
from the climb. When he entered his room the child turned to look
at him. "They be here soon, child. Now we not lettin' on you here
with me. We be very quiet. We lets them medical peoples take care a
things. We don't say one word. Ummhmm, we don't say a word."

He came to the window and watched for the ambulance that
eventually came screaming to the curb. Two white men, their faces
harried and nervous, got out of the ambulance and entered the
building. A police car followed. The cops went into the building
where the super was arguing with the medics.

"I don't know nothin' about a dead woman! Who called you?
Who did you say she was?"

The officers hurried things along, the super angrily getting out his
keys. "If it's 3D, then it's that Indian. She's all the time drinkin' and
carryin' on. Her and that sneaky slant-eyed kid ain't nothin' but
trouble. Who did you say called in? Nobody let on to me!"

On the third floor cops, medics, and super formed a phalanx
around the door to 3D. Knocking and getting no answer, they
unlocked the door and entered the room. Up and down the hall,
doors were opened in cracks. Eyes looked out, gathering information
that would be hoarded and thought about, then forgotten.

"Anybody know this woman?" the cops shouted in the hall.

Doors closed. Silence answered. One of the cops pounded on a
door. A very old woman opened it, a sliver of light behind her.

"Do you know this woman in 3D? When was the last time you saw her?"

Her dark brown face resettled its lines as she spoke. "I don' know her. She was an Injun lady. One a them Injuns from out west, I guess. I don' know nothin'."

The officer waved his hand in disgust. He and his partner started down the stairs, their heavy black shoes scratching the steps, the leather of their holsters squeaking as they rubbed against the guns.

James William stood, his ear pressed to the door. Sue Linn continued to stare out the window. There were sounds of feet moving away, sounds of hard breathing as the body of Dolores was carried down the three flights of stairs and into the cold November twilight.

James William Newton turned from the door. He was eighty years old. He was a singer of the blues. He was the Prince of Georgia Blues. He was Sweet William. He went to the kitchenette and put the kettle on to boil. He moved slowly to the cupboard, taking out a pot and settling it on the tiny stove. Everything surrounding Sweet William was small and tiny like him. The table, covered in blue oil-cloth, was just big enough for two. Little wooden chairs were drawn tight to the edge of the table, waiting for his hands to arrange the seating. The one window in the kitchenette was hung with starched white curtains trimmed in royal-blue rickrack. A single wall was papered in teapots and kettles, red and blue splashed on a yellow background. The wall was faded from age but still looked cheerful and surprising. A cupboard painted white held thick dishes and the food. Rice, red beans, spices, cornmeal, salt, honey, and sugar. A cardboard box placed on the cracked yellow linoleum contained potatoes and onions, the papery skins sometimes falling to the floor, coming to rest by the broom and dustpan leaning against the teapot wall.

On the first night of Sue Linn's new life, she watched Sweet William work in the kitchen, her eyes following his round body as he walked the few steps across the linoleum, taking leaves out of a tin box, placing them in a brown pot, pouring the whistling water over the tea. He replaced the lid on the teapot, removed a tea cozy from a hook, and placed this over the pot. The child, ever fascinated by Sweet William's routine, his fussy kitchen work, his hands dusting and straightening, felt comforted by the familiar activity. Often James William made supper for the girl. Cooking up the rice, a towel wrapped around his fat waist, mashing the potatoes, adding canned milk and butter. Sometimes, there was ham hocks or chitlins. The hot, pungent dishes were magic, made from Sweet William's hands and the air and salt.

James William sang quietly as he busied himself with the pot of soup. His eyes grabbed quick looks toward the chair and the thin, golden child who watched him with blank eyes. Little folds of flesh covered her eyelids, which rapidly opened and closed. Sitting like that, so still, her eyes blinking, blinking, she reminded the old man of a turtle he'd seen a long time ago home in Georgia.

Poking around in the marsh, he and his friends had found a spotted turtle upside down, struggling to put itself right. He had picked up the turtle and looked at its head pulling in, eyefolds closing over the eyes in panic, opening, closing, staring at him. He had set the turtle on its legs, where it continued on. The boys had laughed at the creature's slow journey. James William remembered the turtle, remembered his friends—the sweetness of them. Memories like this appeared in a haze. When they came to him, he clutched at them, holding onto each moment—afraid he would never see them again. He stood in the kitchenette and recalled the day of the turtle. He called forth the weather, so hot and lush, you could hold the air in your hand and feel it wet on your skin. He called forth the smell of the marsh—a green smell, a salty smell. He recalled the reeds, pulled from the mud and stuck between their lips, the taste of bitter grass mingling with another taste of sweet—like the stick of licorice his daddy had once brought him from town. He tried to call forth his friends, their names, their brown-and-tan colors, but the memory was fading. Yet, he remembered the black skin of Isaac, his best friend of all. Remembered when Isaac held his arm, the thin fingers spread out looking like molasses spilled against his own yellow, almost white-looking arm. Isaac.

"Isaac?"

Stirring the soup, he sang bits of song culled from memories of his mama, church, and memories of the band—Big Bill and the Brown Boys. Tunes spun from his lips. Notes and chords played in his throat, starting somewhere in his mind, trickling down through his scratchy voice box, coming out round, weeping, and full. Sweet William sang, his face shifting as he wove the music in and out of his body. His head moved and dipped. His shoulders jerked and shrugged to emphasize a word, a phrase. To Sue Linn, it was as pleasurable to watch Sweet William sing as it was to listen. His words and music were almost always the same words that came from a heartache, a home with no furniture.

"Lord, what I gonna do with this here child? Now listen up, girl. You gonna be my little gal. We be mama and little gal. We be a family. Ummhmm, anybody ask, you be mine. It ain't gonna be easy. Old James William here, he gots to think of some heavy talkin' to fool them peoples what be snoopin' around here. Them government types. Yes ma'am, James William gots to think of some serious talk. Lord! Old man like myself with a child. A baby! I tells you, you know I never be's married. Leastwise, not no marriage like the government peoples thinks is right. Just me and Big Bill, movin' with that band. Me bein' a fool many a time over some sweet boy what talks with a lotta sugar but don't make no sense. But that Big Bill, he were some man. Always take me back, like I never did no wrong. Yes ma'am, I be a fool for a pretty boy. But I always got a little work. Workin' on them cars sometime. Child, I swear the metal in my blood. I still hear that noise. Whoo, it like to kill me. That noise, them cars hurryin' along the line, waitin' for a screw here, a jab there. But I worked it. I worked it. Yes I did. And me and Big Bill, we make a home. Yes we did. We did. And before the sugar and the high bloods get him, we make a home. We was a family, that fine man and me. Ummhmmm.

"Now look at her sit there with them turtle eyes. She can't talk. Now listen here, baby. You mama at rest now, bless her sorry little 'fe. You got you another kinda mama now. I take care my baby. You 'a so peaceful now. With angels and the Indians. She make that transition over ummhmm. She be happy. Now, I gots to make this here turtle gal happy. You gots to cry sometime, child. Honey lamb, you gots to cry! If you don't grieve and wail, it get all caught up in you, start to twist your inside so bad. Girl! It hurt not to cry. You listen to this old man. Sweet William, he know what he talkin' 'bout."

I sing because I'm happy
I sing because I'm free
His eye is on the sparrow
And l know he watches me.

The old man began his song in a whisper. As he ladled out the soup into bowls, he switched from hymn to blues, the two fitting together like verse and chorus. He nodded his head toward the child, inviting her to sing with him. Sue Linn's thin voice joined James William's fat one.

Heaven's cryin', seem like the rain keep comin' down
Heaven's cryin', seem like the rain keep comin' down
That heaven don' let up
Since my baby left this mean ole town.

They sang together. They sang for Dolores. They sang for Big Bill. They sang for each other. Blues about being poor, being colored, being out of pocket. Blues about home—that sweet, hot, green-and-brown place. Home was a place where your mama was, waiting on a porch or cooking up the greens. Home was where you were somebody. Your name was real, and the people knew your name and called you by that name. It was when you left that home that your name became an invisible thing. You got called new names—*Nigger, Bitch, Whore, Shine, Boy*. It was when you left that home you started to choke on your name and your breath, and a new kind of blues was sung.

The old man came from the kitchen and picked the child up in his arms, set her on his lap in the brocade chair; covered them with his special afghan, and the two rocked and swayed.

"She like a bird, no weight on her at all, at all. I *do* likes a rock in this old chair. It help a person think and study on things what ails us. Yes ma'am, just a rockin' and a studyin' on them things."

Sue Linn's tears began. Soon she sobbed, the wails moving across the room, coming back in an echo. James William sang, crooned, wiped her eyes and his with the dry palms of his hands.

"My baby. My turtle gal. Lord, I remember my own mama's passin'. It hurt so bad. She were a good woman, raisin' us ten kids. My daddy workin' his body to an early grave. It hurt when a mama die. Seem like they should always just go on bein' our mama. You mama, she try her best. She were a sad woman. She love you, little gal. And I loves you. We be a family now. Big Bill! You hears that? A family. Sue Linn Longboat and James William Newton. Now ain't they gonna look twice at this here family? I tell you. I tell *you!* It be alright, my baby girl. It be alright."

Sue Linn stopped crying as suddenly as she had started. Her thin face with the slanted eyes, small nose, and full lips subdued itself. "But Sweet William, I hear people talk about heaven. My mom didn't believe in it, but where will she go now? I don't know where she is. And sometimes…sometimes she said she wished I never was born."

The girl stared into the old man's face, trusting him to give her the answers. Trusting him to let her know why she ached so much, why she always felt alone and like a being who didn't belong on this earth. His skin was smooth, except for the cracks around his eyes and down his cheeks, ending at the corners of his mouth. His eyes were brown and yellow and matched the color of his skin, like mottled corn, covered with hundreds of freckles. He had few teeth except for a startlingly white stump here and there. When he opened his mouth to sing, it looked like stars on a black map. His lips were wide and brown. His nose was flat, the nostrils deep.

"Baby, I don' know 'bout no heaven. My mama truly believed it. But I thinks this here story 'bout pearly gates and all is just a trick. Seem like they ain't nothin' wrong with this here earth. The dirt gonna cover your mama and that be alright with her. She miss the sky and the wind and the land. Told me plenty a times. Seem like, compared to that heaven where the peoples hang playin' harps and talkin' sweet, this here earth ain't so bad. You mama, she be mighty unhappy in a heaven where they ain't no party or good lovin' goin' on. Seem like that heaven talk just a way to gets the peoples satisfied with the misery they has to bear in this here world. Once you gets to thinkin' that a reward waitin' on you for bein' poor and colored, why, it just beat you down more. You don' stops to think 'bout doin' somethin' 'bout it right here, right now. Ummhmm, them white peoples, they thinks a everything. But there be a lot they don' know. Everything don' always mean *every thing!* I do believe Dolores more at rest in the brown dirt. And lord, child, from jump every mama wish her children never be born sometime! That's a fact. Ummhmm. Honey, she love you. She just too full a pain to remember to *tell* you.

"It just like me and Big Bill. Why, they be days we forgets to say, 'Big Bill, you my onliest one. James William, you sure one fine man.' Then you gets to thinkin', *Hey, this man don' love me no more!* And you gets afraid to ask, 'cause you thinkin' that's *his* duty to remember. Then you gets mad and sad all together and it get all mixed up and then you speakin' in shortness and evil kinda ways. You forgets that everybody be carryin' his own pain and bad things. The disrememberin' be a thing that happen though. We be foolish, us peoples. Ain' no way gettin' 'round that; seem like, if we be perfect, we be like them white peoples up there in that heaven they thinks so special. Yes, yes, we be in that white heaven, with the white pearly gates, and the white robes, and the white slippers. Child! You ever think 'bout heaven always bein' so white? Lord, child! Whooo!"

He laughed and laughed, hugging Sue Linn tight, his chest rumbling in her ear. She laughed too, even though she wasn't sure she knew the joke. But it made her feel better to be sitting in Sweet William's lap, her head pressed to his heart, the afghan of bright colors covering her coldness and fright. She used to laugh with Dolores. Mostly over Dolores' mimicry of the people on the street or in the bars. She had almost become those people, so good was she at capturing a gesture, a voice, a way of holding her body. There was no meanness in the foolery; just fun, just a laugh, a present for Sue Linn.

"Now, my turtle gal, this old colored man be talkin' more than his due. I says, after a song and a good cry, they am' nothin' better than hot soup and peppermint tea. I thinks I even gots a little banana cake saved for you."

They unfolded from the brocade chair and went to the table. The tiny, round Black man of light skin. The tiny, thin girl of gold skin and Indian hair, her body wrapped in the afghan crocheted by Sweet William's hands. As James William poured the tea, his white shirt dazzled the girl's eyes. She watched his short legs walk slowly to the stove, his small feet wearing the felt slippers he never seemed to take off. He was wearing his favorite pants—grey flannel with handsome pleats and small cuffs at the bottom. He was wearing the only belt Sue Linn had ever seen him wear—a wide alligator strip with a buckle of solid silver round and etched with the words FLORIDA EVERGLADES. It had been a gift from Big Bill so many years ago; the date and reason for the gift were lost in James William's memory. He only remembered Big Bill's face as he handed the belt to Sweet William, the pale mocha of his skin flushing and reddening as he pushed the tissue-wrapped gift toward James William, saying, "Here, honey. For you. A gift." James William's starched, white shirt had cuffs that were turned back and fastened with silver-colored links, a red stone gleaming in the center of each piece of metal. Sue Linn stared at the stones that seemed to signal on-off-stop. Red means stop....

She had learned that in school when she started kindergarten. That was four years ago. She was in third grade now, a big girl. She liked school. At least, she liked it when she went, when her mom remembered to send her. When Sue Linn felt safe to ask Dolores to braid her long hair without making the woman cry. When Dolores was in a good mood from having extra money and bought Sue Linn plaid dresses, white socks, and shoes that were shiny and had buckles instead of laces. She talked loud at these times, talked about how her baby was just as good as anybody, and anyway, she was the prettiest kid in school by far. Sue Linn had a hard time understanding this talk. Everyone in school wore old clothes and shoes with laces. It didn't make sense. Maybe it had to do with the picture magazines that showed up around the apartment. The people on the shiny pages were white and stood in funny poses. They wore fancy clothes and coats made from animals. They looked like they were playing statues, which Sue Linn had played once with the kids at school. It was a scary feeling to stop and stand so still until the boss kid said you could move. She liked it though. It made her feel like she was invisible. If she were really a statue, she'd be made out of wood or stone—something hard.

Sort of like the statues at the place her teacher, Miss Terrell, had taken them. Miss Terrell called the giant building a museum and said the statues were sculptures. She pointed out one made by a Black man. She took them to see a display case that had Indian jewelry resting on pieces of wood, only Miss Terrell called it Native American art. Sue Linn thought of her mother's beaded bracelet and stared at the glass cases. It made her want to cry for a reason she couldn't even begin to think about. She remembered the Indian case for a long time after. She told her mom about it, and Dolores said it would be nice to go there; she had gone there once, she thought. But they never talked about it again. No, Sue Linn was not a statue. She was bony and covered with soft, gold skin and black hair that was coarse and reached below her shoulder blades. She practiced statues at home, standing on the worn green couch, trying to see herself in the wavy mirror on the opposite wall.

"Getting stuck on yourself, honey? That's how I started. A grain of salt, honey. That's what we need to take ourselves with. We're just bones and skin, honey. Bones and skin."

The child thought her mother much more than bones, skin, and salt. She thought Dolores was beautiful and was proud to walk with her on the avenue. The day they got the food stamps was one of the best days, for a while. Dolores was sober on those days. She would sit at the card table making lists and menus. Dolores labored hard on those days, looking through her magazines, cutting out recipes for "tasty nutritional meals within your budget." Sue Linn stayed close to her mother on days like that, fascinated by Dolores activity.

"How would you like chicken vegetable casserole on Monday? Then on Tuesday we could have Hawaiian chicken. I found a recipe for peanut butter cookies. It says here that peanut butter is a good source of protein. Would you like Dolores to make you cookies, baby? Maybe we could make them together." Sue Linn shook her head yes and stood even closer to her mother. Shiny paper with bright colors of food lay emblazoned on the table. Sue Linn was caught by Dolores' words, her magic talk of casseroles and cookies. Writing down words that came back as food. Food was something real yet mysterious. Food was something there never was enough of. Sue Linn ate a free lunch at school. Always hungry, eating too fast, not remembering what she ate, just eating then being hungry again.

Each morning Miss Terrell asked if anyone had forgotten to eat breakfast, because she just happened to bring orange juice and graham crackers from home. Miss Terrell must be magic because there was always enough for everyone. Miss Terrell was black, almost pure black like the stone set in the school door proclaiming when it was built (1910) and whose name it was built to honor (Jeremy Comstock). Marble, yes, that's what Miss Terrell called it. Black marble, that was Miss Terrell's skin. Her hair was cut close to her head and curled tightly against her scalp. James William's hair was like this, but more bushy, and his hair was white, while Miss Terrell's was black with a red cast in the sunlight. She wore red lipstick, sometimes purple to go with the dress with white and pink dots on the sash. Her clothes were beautiful. Blue skirt and red jacket. Green dress with gold buttons. Her shoes were red or black shiny stuff with pointy, pointy toes and little wooden heels. Miss Terrell was tall and big. Some of the boys whispered and laughed about Miss Terrell's "boobs." Sue Linn saw nothing to laugh about, only knowing that boys giggled about sex things. She thought Miss Terrell's chest was very wonderful. It stuck out far and looked proud in a way. When she told this to Sweet William, he said, "Child, that Alveeta Terrell be a regular proud woman. Why wouldn't her chest be as proud as the rest of her? You lucky as can be to have proud Miss Alveeta Terrell be your teacher!"

One time, and it was the best time, Miss Terrell had come to school in a yellow dress over which she wore a length of material made from multicolored threads of green, red, purple, yellow, and black. She called it Kente cloth and told the class it was woven in Africa and the people, even the men, wore it every day. She said she was wearing this special cloth because it was a special day. It was a day that Black people celebrated being African, and even though they might live in all kinds of places, they had come from Africa at one time. Then she showed them a map of Africa and traced lines running from that continent to North America, to the West Indies, to South America, to just about everywhere. Amos asked, If Africa was so special, why did the people leave? Miss Terrell said that the people didn't leave because they wanted to, but because these other people—Spanish, British, American, and French—had wanted slaves to work on their lands and make things grow for them so they could get rich. And these same people killed Indians in North America to get land. And these people had captured Africans as if they were herds of animals. They had put them in chains and shipped them to lands where their labor was needed. Some Africans had died trying to escape, some from hunger, thirst, and disease, but some had stayed alive to reach the new land that was a stranger to them.

The children pondered on these facts before raising their hands to ask questions. Miss Terrell answered in her sure voice. She knew everything. She told them about Denmark Vesey, Nat Turner, John Brown, Crispus Attucks, whose last name meant *deer* because his mama had been a Choctaw Indian. She told them about Toussaint-L'Ouverture, about the Maroons in Jamaica, about Harper's Ferry. She told them about the Seminoles and Africans in Florida creating an army to fight the U.S. soldiers and how they had won the fight! Sue Linn's mind was so filled with these wondrous facts, she dreamed about them that night. And it came to her in the dream that Miss Terrell was a food giver. Her thoughts and facts were like the graham crackers she laid out on her desk each morning. They were free to take, to eat right at that moment, or to save for when one got really hungry. The next morning, Sue Linn copied down her dream in the little notebook she carried with her everywhere: "Miss Terrell is a food giver." She told Sweet William, who agreed.

Food stamp day. Dolores making something out of nothing. What did it mean? Everything meant something. This she had learned on her own, from the streets, from being a kid. She wanted to talk with Dolores about this, but was too shy.

Dolores was ready. Sue Linn puttered at the table, stalling for time, prolonging the intimacy with her mother. Sue Linn was not ready for the store. *It* happened every time. Dolores got sad. The store defeated her. It was a battle to see how far down the aisles she could get before giving up. The limp vegetables, the greenish-brown meat, the lack of anything resembling the food in the magazines. Sue Linn sensed it before it happened. The faint shrug of Dolores' shoulders, the shake of her head as if clearing it from a dream. Then they proceeded fast, Dolores grabbing at things that were cheap and filling, if only for a few hours. The little girl tried calling her mother's attention to funny people in the store, or some fancy-packaged box of air and starch. Anything, *please, please,* to get that look off her mother's face. That look of fury and contempt. That look of sadness and loss. They would end up with a few things like bread, canned corn, and, maybe, hamburger. All her food stamps gone, they'd put the groceries away, and Dolores would go out and not return until the next day with a few dollars and a raging headache.

Dolores picked up her lists and stamps, placed them in her purse, a beige plastic bag with her initials stamped in gold letters: D.L., DOLORES LONGBOAT. She went to the wavy mirror and with her little finger applied blue eye shadow because "you never know who we'll meet." She brushed her black hair until it crackled with sparks and life across her wide back. Dressed in too-tight jeans, a pink sweater frayed and unraveling at the bottom, her gold-tone earrings swinging and dancing, she defied anyone or anything to say she didn't exist. "Let's go."

Sue Linn took hold of her mother's hand and stared up at Dolores, as if to burn the image of her mama into her brain, as if to keep the scent of lily-of-the-valley cologne in her nose. The brown eyes shaded in blue looked down at her child. Dark eye watched dark eye—two females locked in an embrace of color, blood, and bewildering love. Dolores broke the intensity of the moment, cast her eyes around the apartment, committing to memory what she had to come home to. Tightening her hold on Sue Linn's hand, she said once again, "Let's go." She set the lock and the two went out into the street.

☐   ☐   ☐

Sue Linn's eyes closed with this last memory. Her head nodded above the soup. James William rose from the table and pulled the bed down from the wall. Straightening the coves and fluffing the pillow, he made the bed ready for the child's tired body and heart. He picked her up and carried her the few feet to the bed. Taking off her shoes, he gently placed the girl under the blanket and tucked the pillow under her head. He placed the afghan at the foot of the bed, folded and neat.

James William Newton—Sweet William—went to his chair and sat in the nighttime light. He could see a piece of the moon through a crack between two buildings across the street.

"Ole moon, what you think? I gots this here child now. Them government peoples be wantin' to know where this child be. Or is they? Seem like the whereabouts of a little gal ain' gonna concern too many a them. Now, I ain' worryin' 'bout raisin' this here turtle gal. It one a them things I be prepared to do. But Moon, we gots to have a plan. I an old man. This here baby need me. Yes, ma'am. There gots to be some providin' to do. Big Bill? Is you laughin' at me? It be a fix we in. Ummhmm, a regular fix. Big Bill? I needs a little a that talk you always so ready with. Honey, it ever be a wonder to me how a man could talk so much and *still* make sense like you done! I sittin' here waitin' on you, honey. Sweet William, he waitin' on you."

He sat through the night, refilling his cup many times. His memories came and went like the peppermint tea he drank. His lips moved in conversation and song. Sometime before dawn he laughed and murmured, "Thank you, honey. You always was the bestest man." He drank his last cup, rinsed it, and set it upside down in the sink. He settled his body on the blue davenport, the afghan pulled up to his shoulders. He looked one more time at the sleeping child, her dark hair hiding her face in sleep.

"Child, sleep on and dream. Sweet William, he here. Me and Big Bill take care of our baby, turtle gal. You be alright. Yes, ma'am, you be alright."

He closed his eyes and slept.

Bread

Rebecca Brown

For breakfast there were two kinds of rolls, white and wheat. We would get a basket of eight and there would be one, and sometimes—but only very rarely—two wheat ones; the rest were white. The white ones were long and looked like short croissants straightened out with four or five sections. We could see where they were wrapped around. They were white with thin butter glazing that made them yellow or gold or brown on top. They were in sections, and we could eat them in sections, tearing off a bite at a time and spreading a knot of butter on the soft open end we'd just pulled off. There was orange marmalade too, but I liked them more with only butter. The wheat ones were round around the top and sides but flat on the bottom. They didn't have glaze but were round and had specks of grain in them. They weren't as soft inside or in your mouth, or as sweet. We could just eat them; they weren't in sections and didn't have glazed caps to peel off or raisins to pick off. We could only tear them like a loaf of bread. They were small and fit in one cupped palm.

There was only one different way to eat them and there was only one person who did it that way.

It was you.

You never talked about it and no one ever talked about it in front of you, but everyone saw and no one dared do it like you. If someone else had started it, everyone would maybe have done it or felt they could have done it. Probably no one would have noticed it as something special if anyone else had done it.

But you had started it. It was yours and no one else's.

☐   ☐   ☐

Someone would bring the basket to the table and put it in the middle. Everyone would reach for a roll, a white one, and when everyone had one, there'd be one left; you'd take it. It was always the last one, the wheat one. You'd lean forward in your chair and reach your right arm over the basket and flex your whole hand around it and pick it up and put it on your plate and put your napkin in your lap. Then someone could start the butter around and we could eat.

You would slice the one brown wheat roll through the side like a knife into a stomach. You'd cut the top from the bottom and sometimes the knife would catch and there would be a pileup of dough at the end where you split the top from the bottom.

You sat at the end of the table with your back toward the window that looked out into the yard. Sometimes I could see steam rising against the window from your just severed roll. I'd watch you put the two portions on your plate, bottom and top down, the exposed, soft insides up. You'd slice a triangle of butter from the yellow rectangle on the common plate and press it to your plate, then a tiny spoon of marmalade. Then you'd pick up the bottom half of the roll in your right hand and butter it with the knife in your left. Then you'd put that half down, pick up the other, and spread marmalade on that. Then you'd put the knife down, pick up the bottom half in your left hand and put the two sides back together. Then you'd put it, assembled, back on your plate, wipe your hands on your napkin and pick it up and bite into it. Your teeth were straight and slightly yellow.

☐   ☐   ☐

If there was ever more than one wheat roll, we'd argue over it because it was special, but also because they were better. If there were two wheat rolls, we'd all, all of us except you, rush to grab one of them. None of us ever dared touch both of them because one was reserved for you. Whoever got the second one smiled and was smug, and everyone else just took a white one.

We took turns bringing the rolls to the table. Sometimes people would volunteer out of turn to get them so they could touch the extra wheat roll, if there was one, and claim it before anyone else at the table had a chance. But you never had to do that. You never went to bring the rolls. When there was another wheat one whoever got it would eat it, tearing off pieces bit by bit, like a white one. No one could eat them the way you did. It was your way.

☐   ☐   ☐

Our table didn't talk at breakfast. We were usually one of the first tables dismissed because we finished quickly because we didn't talk. You didn't like to talk in the morning; we didn't either. Sometimes you would look up from where you were sitting by the window at another table across the room if someone was talking loud or a group was too energetic.

Once you stared over at two girls telling a story to the rest of their table. One girl was thin and blond. Her fingers were like sticks and she kept snapping her skinny hands in the air to illustrate her story. She slapped the table and jumped around in her seat. Her friend was fat and very pale except for red cheeks. They interrupted each other, correcting each other and laughing. Their whole table was laughing with them: The fat one mimicked the accents of the people in the story. She puffed out her cheeks and lowered her fat double chin into her neck and spoke in a drawl. The skinny blonde screeched a narration. People at other tables were looking at them and trying to listen. We did too. The fat girl slapped her hands to her chest above her breasts and swayed her shoulders back and forth in a parody of her character's gestures. It was a good story and everyone was watching. I turned to the girl to my left to ask her for the butter, but I didn't ask because when I turned, I saw you.

You were sitting perfectly still, your forearms solid on the table in front of you on either side of your plate. You were staring at the two girls at the table. You hadn't eaten but one bite of your wheat roll. Your face was completely still. You were utterly silent.

I was ashamed.

I nudged the girl on my left. She was smiling at the story and she smiled at me, almost leaning over to say something. But when she saw my face she quit smiling. She opened her mouth to say something to me but I nodded at you. She looked at you, then dropped her head and snatched up her soft white roll, snapped off a section and stuffed it in her mouth. She kept looking at her plate. She ate another bite before she realized she hadn't put on the butter or marmalade. She buttered the next piece, but the knife slipped and she dropped it on her plate. It crashed and she grabbed it with both hands. Her hands were shaking. We all glanced at her but everyone else turned back to the story.

I nudged the girl on my right and nodded at you. She looked at you and stopped listening to the story too. She nudged the girl at the other end of the table and kicked the girl opposite her under the table. We stopped paying attention to the story.

The story went on and on. I tried not to hear it. I tried to listen to the inside of my ears, the crinkly sound when everything is quiet, or just the sound of my chewing. I tried not to hear the girls, but I did.

Our whole table had stopped looking at them. Some of us stole sideways looks at you. You were still staring at them. It was a long, loud story. The fat girl was getting louder and the blonde was getting more animated. They had the attention of the whole room.

Then you did it.

The skinny one threw her hands in front of her to punctuate a point and knocked a cup of coffee on herself. She jumped up and screeched. Everyone at her table flinched and moved. Two girls on either side of her put napkins on her hands and arms where the burning coffee hit. They rushed her out of the room. Everyone else turned to their table and stared. People from different tables leapt up to get the Head Prefect and the Housemistress. Some other girls had gone to get the cleaning woman. Everyone looked up. Everyone flinched.

But you stayed still.

Our table still stayed still.

Then, when everyone was watching the aftermath of the accident, you began to eat again. You didn't say anything. You lifted your arms from the table, daubed your hands on the napkin in your lap and picked up your butter-marmalade wheat sandwich. You brought it to your mouth and at least one person from every other table went over to that table to ask what had happened and if everything was all right. But none of us did. We all tried to eat our rolls like you. We all looked at one another quickly. We looked at everyone at our table except you. You didn't look at anyone.

You willed the thing to happen. I knew. No one else knew, but I did. You knew I did.

We all felt ashamed.

I felt ashamed. I wanted to say, "I didn't mean, none of us meant—"

After the coffee was cleaned up things were quieter. You liked it more. You don't like conversation at breakfast, and you never liked it if someone else wanted it.

We all felt ashamed. We all wanted to be forgiven by you. You did-n't look at any of us.

That girl got blisters on her hand. After that, we were all more careful.

☐   ☐   ☐

You sat at the end of the table. The seating was arbitrary. No one was assigned. We just established ourselves in time. Technically, one would think the other end, opposite you, was the head because it was in the center of the room and closer to the head table where the Head Prefect or Housemistress sat, but the end you sat at was the head because you were there.

You sat at the head of the table in front of the window that over-looked the yard. I sat in the middle seat on the side of the table to your right. In the morning after breakfast the sun came in and lit you up from behind. Before someone put the lights on, and it was a little dark outside, your shadow went across the table a short way. When the lights came on, it disappeared.

☐   ☐   ☐

One day there was a two-day period when there were no wheat rolls. You didn't eat white ones and we took the basket back at the end of breakfast with one white roll left in it. You didn't say anything about it. You just looked at the basket and didn't take a roll. No one else said anything about it in front of you. After breakfast, though, we talked among ourselves about it and made plans to go out and find wheat rolls for you if they didn't reappear soon.

We thought you were so strong to not even comment on their absence those two days. We talked about it for days, then long afterward. We admired your acceptance of the situation but reasoned that the position of being the one to eat the wheat roll every day went with the ability to deal with its absence. You had something we didn't have. You knew how to deal with things.

You were our heroine.

☐   ☐   ☐

Every day they'd give us either buns for morning break or biscuits. Bun days were better. You wouldn't touch biscuits; neither would any of us. Buns had raisins and were soft. There was a thin layer of shiny glaze on top. They were soft and white around the sides but brown on the bottom from the tray and beige to brown to dark-brown on the top, like shellac. When we tore them open they were soft and white inside with raisins. We counted the raisins. We did it because one day you did it and the next day you suggested we all do it. We did it every bun day and started keeping tally, even when you weren't there. We reported to you when you came back. Sometimes someone would cheat. No one ever told you about cheating. It wasn't your business, but it was an issue between us. But I know you knew about it anyway. I bet you were pleased with it.

What was good was to take a small bite from the edge and break the surface and make an opening and then, poking and folding one finger into the warm inside, pull out a thick wad of pure soft bread. We made shells; we hollowed out the insides with a finger, and what was left was the shiny brown top and white sides and brown bottom and one hole in the side. Sometimes we found shells where someone had made one and left it.

We could also eat buns bit by bit, eating the top first, because often there was a thin pocket between the brown shellacked top and the white inside. If there was a bubble on the top, we could put a fingernail in and peel it off and either eat it in pieces or wait until the whole lid was peeled off, then eat them together. Then we could eat the soft part or give it to someone who liked that part if we didn't.

You taught us these ways. Even if you didn't think of each of them, whoever did presented it to you and you dismissed or accepted it. If you accepted it, you'd teach it to us. You never said whose idea it was if it wasn't yours, and in your presence no one ever said, "That's my idea." We didn't want to boast in front of you. But sometimes among ourselves, one of us would say, "That was my idea."

□   □   □

But we didn't listen to anyone else. You were the person who mattered. You were the person we loved.

□   □   □

Before every meal we had prayer. After everyone was in the room and at their table, the Head Girl or Housemistress would call on someone to say the prayer or say it herself.

The prayer was the same every meal. Only one person said it, and no one had to say it with her. The prayer was, "For what we are about to receive may the Lord make us truly thankful." Everyone said "Amen" and sat down or rushed up to the counter to bring back the food. If it was breakfast, one person from every table went up to get the rolls and then someone from the kitchen, sometimes the fat girl but usually her mother, wheeled out the cart with the pitchers of coffee. The coffee already had milk in it. They had it that way because without, it would make us nervous.

One morning I got there early and was washing my hands in the sink and the fat girl smiled at me. She was pouring the milk into a big pot of coffee. There was another pot of coffee without milk. I said, "Can I have some?" She smiled at me and I picked up the cup from the counter and scooped it into the hot steaming pot. The cups were glass. There was no pattern on them. They were old. The glass was thick and I couldn't see through it. It was rough from so many washings. I scooped it into the pot of black coffee. When I looked at the coffee through the cup, it was thin and brown. I tasted it and it burned my tongue. It was terrible. She poured bottles of milk into the pots. She broke the silver circle seals on the bottle lips. She punched her fat thumb into the center and broke open one side of the seal then she peeled it off and scooped the cream off with a spoon and put it into a dish. Then she poured the white milk into the coffee in the big silver pots. I threw the terrible coffee into the sink and rinsed the cup and put it back on the counter. She picked up the cup and washed it with soap and water. She waited until the water from the faucet got steamy, then she got a dish mop from the tray and scoured the cup. Her fingers got pink. I thanked her for the coffee. Then I left the kitchen and went into the dining room and waited for breakfast.

☐　　　☐　　　☐

We had prayer before every meal. The Head Girl or the Housemistress would say it herself or call on someone to say it. They could call on anyone. They did it that way to make sure everyone was paying attention to prayer. Some people didn't. Some people wouldn't listen or said it quickly to get through it. They rarely called our table, though. There was no need to. You were at our table.

It started this way.

One time she called on Philippa Rogers. Philippa Rogers did not believe. She skipped service each Sunday. The Head Girl said, "Rogers," and everyone bowed their heads. Philippa Rogers said the prayer. She said, "For what we are about to receive, may we all be truly thankful." We heard people pause for a second before we scooted our chairs to sit down or rush to the basket of rolls.

You didn't sit down. Everyone scooted their chairs and two people started from their tables to go get their baskets of rolls. You stayed standing. You didn't move. You said out loud, "That's not right." Everyone stopped. Everyone looked at you.

You stood at your seat. Your left hand was open and your curved fingers were near the table and your fingernails tapped the edge of the table. The fingers of your left hand stretched and tapped the table 1-2-3-4 like castanets. Your right hand pressed the table. The fingers of your left hand tapped the table: little finger, ring finger, middle finger, index finger. Your right hand was clenched in a fist.

You only said it once. Everybody looked at you. Then everyone looked at their plates. You looked at Philippa Rogers. Your face was hard.

I heard you breathing.

You snapped your head back then lowered it. You closed your eyes and everyone looked at you.

Two girls at our table lowered their heads. Three girls at the table in front of us lowered their heads. Two girls at Philippa Rogers' table lowered their heads. When everyone's head was bowed, we heard a scrape as Philippa Rogers leaned too heavily on her chair, lifting two of its legs off the floor, and it fell back to the floor. I looked down at my hands. My head was lowered and I saw my hands clenching and my knuckles going white. I tried to see around me without moving my head. The girl to my right was clutching her napkin. I closed my eyes and didn't see anything.

Philippa Rogers cleared her throat and said, "For what we—" Then we heard her swallow.

We heard the noise her throat made when the saliva went down from her mouth. She exhaled quickly through her nose, then said, like she was out of breath, "For what—for what we are about to receive, may the Lord make us truly thankful."

No one moved.

Then we heard you slide your chair out. We raised our heads. Your chair scraped across the floor and you sat down and scooted yourself in. You put your forearms on the table, on either side of your plate. You looked at the girl at our table whose turn it was to get the rolls. You smiled at her.

She jumped up quickly to get the rolls. We all sat down. When the rolls came we ate them quickly. During the meal someone at Philippa Rogers' table dropped a plate. You didn't look up. You ate your wheat marmalade roll.

You were beautiful.

☐   ☐   ☐

On Sundays we were required to go to church. We could go to whichever church we wanted to, but we had to go somewhere. The Housemistress or Head Pre would ask us where we'd been to make sure we'd gone. Also they would make spot checks at churches. They'd go to a different church every week to make sure people were where they said they were going to be. Christ Church was only two blocks away, and St. Philip's was three. There was also St. James and Parish Church and all the denominations. People went to different ones to keep from being bored. We could go to the early service at 7:30 and be back for breakfast or go to the later service after breakfast at 10:30. Everyone went to the later service because Sunday breakfast was at 8:45, fifteen minutes later than the rest of the week, and we liked to sleep in.

On Saturday nights everyone would ask everyone else which church they were going to and make plans. Sometimes we took turns and four of us would sign out as though we were going to a church but then only two of us would go and the other two would do something else like shopping or going to Devil's Chimney or the

Sandwich Bar, and if the Head Pre or Housemistress came to that church and asked where the other two were, the two in church would vouch for them and say they were sitting behind the pillar or in the bathroom. No one went to church by themselves.

Except you. You went to both services every Sunday. You went to St. Gregory's 7:30 service every Sunday by yourself. St. Gregory's was far away, and you had to take a cab. Every Sunday morning at 7:00 a black cab pulled up by the front door of our house and you were waiting for it. You stood inside the tall bay window to the left of the door. You held the heavy beige curtain back with your left hand, and your right hand held your shoulder purse. Your fingernails shone. You did your nails the night before.

The cab drove into the driveway and stopped, but you were out in the driveway before he was even at the door and you'd wait for the cab driver to open the door for you and you'd get in. As you slid into the backseat, you tucked your coat beneath your hips. You wore shiny black shoes with wide high heels. You never wore them any other time except to St. Gregory's on Sunday.

One time I woke up early to go to the bathroom, and when I stood over the sink by the window washing my hands I looked out and saw you get into the cab.

Every Sunday after that I saw you from the bathroom window. I leaned on the white sink by the window to watch you. My feet were cold on the concrete. You wore your Sunday shoes. You never saw me.

☐   ☐   ☐

Monday to Friday from 8:00 to 4:45 we wore our uniforms, and from 8:00 to noon on Saturdays. At 4:45 class was over, and we could change in the hour before we had to be back in the library to study or we could wait until right before dinner at 7:30, but we couldn't be in our uniform at dinner. If shoes were too high-heeled or not polished, we couldn't wear them. In the morning on the way into prayers the Pres stood at the door into the auditorium and looked at our shoes. They made sure they were polished. If they weren't polished, we were dismissed from prayers and docked an hour of free time or had to report to the Head Divinity Mistress for extra divinity lessons. We got the Ones and Twos to polish our shoes. They liked doing it for us, and they'd compete for who got to do whose shoes. They tried to get the Pres' first, and everyone competed for the Head Girl. She awarded her shoes to different Ones and Twos to give more of them a chance. She always had her shoes done the best because she had all of them compete for her. Her shoes were the best of anyone's.

Except yours.

You did your shoes yourself. At first the Ones and Twos competed for your shoes like they did for the Head Girl's, but then they stopped. No one else in our form did her own shoes. We were too old, and the Ones and Twos wanted to do them for us. But you did. You did your shoes yourself. You did your shoes better than anyone.

☐   ☐   ☐

To leave, we had to have it planned in advance and have our parents come or write permission and say where we were going. We had one weekend a month, plus half-term and Saturdays and Sundays. You were away more than anyone. No one else went as much as you. Your father came and got you every Saturday at 1:00. The first week of every month you spent the weekend at home. Every weekend after that you spent the day with him on Saturday and came back in the evening. On Sunday you went to church in the morning and sat in your room for the rest of the day. In the evening after supper you came out and talked with us. You spoke with everyone the same.

One time you came back with a huge white box. Your father left it in the calling room when he dropped you off. It was Saturday evening. The box was huge. The Head Pre called a house meeting. You opened the box, and there was a huge Black Forest cake in it. It was at least three feet by two feet big. I'd never seen a Black Forest cake so big. I'd never seen a Black Forest cake half as big. It was gorgeous. Around the edge of the box on the inside I could see a rim of brown where the oil and cream had stained the white cardboard. There was dark-brown and regular-brown frosting. There were six rows of cherries. Someone from the kitchen brought a knife. You cut the cake. You asked someone from the kitchen for some napkins. She brought them. I was standing near you. She handed me the napkins. I put them on the table by the box. You picked up a piece of cake. I picked up a napkin. I handed the cake and napkin to the girl in front of me.

We did this for the whole house, thirty-six pieces of cake, plus two for the mistresses and three for the kitchen. We saved some pieces for people in the morning. You and I ate after everyone had their piece. The cake was good. The frosting was thick and smooth and creamy. The inside was brown sponge soaked with cherry liquid. Everything was moist and sweet and heavy. None of us had ever tasted anything so wonderful. All of us felt wonderful. No one asked you what it was for or where it came from.

We remembered that day forever. The next day we told all the other houses about it. Some people from other houses said things to you, like they'd heard about it and wished they had been there, but no one asked you about it.

We talked about it forever. Someone said your father owned a bakery. Most people disputed this: Your father was too much of a gentleman. We didn't know why the cake had come.

Then the rumor started that it was your birthday. No one asked you and no one thought to ask the Housemistress. We didn't ask about your mysteries.

I started the rumor.

□   □   □

On Sundays I woke up early, every Sunday except the first Sunday of the month. I watched you from the bathroom window. I watched you with your shoulder purse. I thought of your shiny black shoes and your high black heels, getting into the cab on the way to St. Greg's. My feet were chilly on the cold concrete. Then I went back to bed.

In the morning they rang a bell half an hour before breakfast. I
tried to be up earlier than the bell. I put on my robe and went to the
bathroom. My robe was long and fake-velvet dark-blue. It was soft
and in a minute warm over me. I never put on slippers. If I was early
there was hardly anyone else in the bathroom. In the bathroom were
four toilet stalls and five sinks with mirrors over them and windows
between them. Next door was a room with four little rooms with
bathtubs. I went to the bathroom and washed my face and brushed
my teeth. By the time I was finishing more people would be coming
in and I would nod good morning if my mouth was full of tooth-
paste or say hello, and sometimes I wouldn't know who I was saying
hello to if my eyes were closed under soap. People were sleepy-look-
ing and in their robes. Some people didn't talk at all because they'd
just woken up and some people were in talkative moods.

When I finished in the bathroom, I went back to my room and
got dressed. I undid my robe and it fell to the floor and I was naked.
My uniform was hanging over the back of my chair by my desk. If it
was cold I'd jump around and try to make my blood go faster with
my hands and inhale through my teeth, a "ssss" sound, and wring
my hands. I put my shirt on first. It was white and long-sleeved and
I buttoned it all the way up, even the sleeves. It was straight around
the bottom with no tail. I pulled on my underpants. They were uniform too. Then I put on my skirt, thin if warm, thick if cold. It
zipped up the side and was plain. Then I put on my tie. I stretched
the tie in my arms over my head then put it behind my head on my
shoulders. Then I dropped it and pulled my hair out from underneath it. I tied the tie. The tie was green with red stripes going down
it diagonally. It was the house tie and had a scarf to go with it too,
red and green. It was very ugly. If it was too cold it took my hands
a long time to tie it. Then I put on my sweater. I almost always wore
the thick one, not the thin one, because if it was warm I didn't wear
one at all. I pulled it over my head. When it was on I pulled my hair
out from the sweater and straightened my tie and reached my hand
up under my skirt to pull the shirt down and straighten it. Then I sat
on the bed and picked up the socks on the chair and put them on.

They were thick and soft and wonderful dark-green. I liked them. I bunched them up over my hand and made a tight ball of my fist and put my foot into the little opening at the end of my palm. My feet were freezing, even more than my hands, and sometimes I'd just hold on to my foot with my hand to try to make it warm. I put my foot in the sock and pulled the sock over my foot, then stretched it up my calf to my knee, smoothing and straightening on the way up then I put on my shoes. They were brown and plain and low. They were our uniform shoes.

Then the bell was ringing and I went downstairs for breakfast.

☐   ☐   ☐

For breakfast there were two kinds of rolls, white and wheat. There was butter and orange marmalade and pots of coffee. There was a box on the shelf on the wall by the door and everyone grabbed their napkin from the box and took it to the table. After the meal was over we put them back. Everyone had their own box, their own napkin. They were white and stiff and rolled into a cylinder and stuffed in tiny boxes. We got them washed once a week with the laundry. By the end of the week the box was full of wilted, dirty napkins. There was only one napkin that was never wilted or dirty.

It was yours. Yours was always perfect.

☐   ☐   ☐

On the first Sundays of the month, when you were with your father, you weren't there to eat the wheat roll in the basket. On those Sundays we'd rush to be the one to get the basket of rolls. We looked forward to seeing if we could get the wheat roll.

We talked a lot on those Sundays. We talked about you and wondered where you were and what you were doing. Then we just talked about where we were going to church and what everyone was doing. We were often very rowdy the first Sunday of the month.

□ □ □

The Night of the Cake we got to stay up half an hour later. The Housemistress smiled and said she realized we were all too keyed up to get to bed at the regular time, so she'd let us stay up until eleven, providing she didn't see too many tired faces in the morning, and if someone wanted to go to sleep before eleven, no one was to stop them. We finished eating our cake way before then but we were all so thrilled we couldn't sleep or study. We just stood in the calling room talking. When the Housemistress said we had to leave we went to our rooms and talked. We talked until 11:00, and then, even after she had called lights out and did her rounds, some people snuck into their friends' rooms and stayed up late talking. The next day everyone was in a particularly good mood, though some in fake good moods because they were tired but had to fake it for the Housemistress.

I went to bed at 11:00 and stayed in my room.

I lay in my bed with the lights out and looked outside. I saw the orange light of the street lamp through the dots of rainwater on the window. There was steam on the window from the cold outside. The leaves looked orange and bronze in the light of the street lamp and sent out shoots of orange into the air. I heard traffic going by and people walking and laughing quietly.

I thought about holding the napkins you put your cake on and everyone else eating theirs before we did. In my mind, I pretended we were doing it again. I wanted to tell someone, but someone different, not the people going to each other's rooms. I stayed in my room and looked at the bronze-leaved trees and listened to the traffic and people walking until I couldn't hear them anymore. Then there was no noise coming in from the outside. I closed my eyes and fell asleep.

□ □ □

Sometimes I saw you in the bathroom before breakfast. You were always completely dressed. You never left your room without being completely dressed. You came to the bathroom completely dressed and washed your face and brushed your teeth in full uniform. Your shoes were always polished.

You were always perfect.

I was in love with you.

□ □ □

When they were taking people for a special scholarship, you were one of them. It meant you went away lots to be interviewed and look at schools. It meant you missed breakfast because you'd leave after lunch one day and come back the next day for lunch or supper. Your space was empty at the table. Your wheat roll just sat there. We were afraid there could be a mistake and you might just come in late and what would you do if you didn't have your wheat roll? We were very careful.

□ □ □

One time Fiona Donovan asked me if I would ask you something for her. Fiona Donovan had been raised poorly. She had no social sense. She wanted me to ask you if you would help her with her Applied Mathematics prep because she had been out for a week. Everyone knew you were the best at Applied Mathematics. I told Fiona Donovan she was a fool. I said you had better things to do with your time than help someone with their problems when she could get anyone to help her and what were teachers for anyway? Then, she said, "Well, couldn't I just ask you?" and I said, "Why me?" and she said, "You're the one who helped the Night of the Cake." I said, "Sure, but that's nothing." She said, "Everyone knows she told you it was her birthday the Night of the Cake." I looked at Fiona Donovan. I didn't say anything. I had made it up. You hadn't told me anything. I said to Fiona Donovan, "Yeah, well, so what? It's no big thing if it's your birthday. Why shouldn't she tell me?" I said it as nonchalantly as I could. I was thrilled. Fiona said, "Well, she doesn't say things like that to anyone. You must be her friend." I said, "Well…"

I tried to sound secretive and humble. I didn't look at Fiona. I was proud. Fiona said, "Well, couldn't you just ask her—" I snapped my face up at her and said, "Don't be ridiculous. She doesn't spend her time with just anyone, you know." Then I walked away.

I pretended you had told me it was your birthday. I imagined you said my name. We were standing by the table holding our pieces of cake in our hands. You had cut a piece of cake and put it on the napkin I held. You said my name, and then you said, "Today is my birthday." I listened to you and looked at you and you were beautiful and it was your birthday.

☐ ☐ ☐

For breakfast one person from each table went up after prayer to the counter and picked up a basket of rolls for the table. The person getting the rolls would put the bowl and plate into the basket and carry them back and put them on the table and take the bowl and plate out of the basket and put them on the table. We all got our rolls and passed the butter and marmalade around.

☐ ☐ ☐

One day—it was a Monday after you'd been to St. Greg's—you weren't at breakfast. You were out somewhere looking at a school or being interviewed for a scholarship. We knew you wouldn't be there and your place was empty. I looked at your empty chair and the wheat roll sitting in the basket. We all ate our breakfast and at the end I took the basket back to the counter and the fat girl who poured coffee with her mother saw me and smiled. She saw the wheat roll and looked at me. I said not everyone was at our table. She looked at the wheat roll again. She shrugged her shoulders and picked up the wheat roll then picked up the basket and turned to put the basket away. As she turned, I saw her pop the wheat roll into her mouth. She did it like it was nothing. My mouth fell open in awe. I stared at her.

The next day at breakfast you didn't come again. Someone brought the rolls to the table and there was one wheat roll and you weren't there. Everyone helped themselves to a roll. I was the last one. There was one white one left and the wheat one. I reached for my roll. Then I paused, hand in air over the basket. I didn't turn my head, but I tried to look at everyone else. The butter was going around and people were eating. We didn't wait for everyone because you weren't there. I decided. I withdrew my hand and started again.

I leaned forward in my chair and reached my arm over the basket and flexed my hand around the wheat roll and picked it up and put it on my plate. I put my napkin in my lap and someone passed me the butter.

I sliced the wheat roll through one side, cut the top from the bottom and put the two portions on my plate, bottom and top down, insides up. I sliced a triangle of butter from the yellow rectangle on the common plate and pressed it onto my plate, then a tiny spoon of marmalade. I picked up the bottom half of the roll and buttered it with the knife. I put that half down, picked up the other, and spread marmalade on it. Then I put the knife down and put the two sides back together. I put it, assembled, back on my plate, and wiped my hands on my napkin. Then I picked it up with both my hands and bit.

I felt the tiny crunch as my teeth broke the surface and went into the soft inside. I tasted the warm brown taste and the knotty texture of the grains and specks of wheat. The texture was tougher than the plain white rolls. It didn't taste as sweet in my mouth, but did taste more full. I could feel the slick texture of the butter and the sweet one of the marmalade between the layers of bread. The marmalade was almost gritty it was so thick. The white rolls were bland compared to this. I was happy.

Then you were there. You stood directly opposite me. I saw you and stopped chewing. My mouth was full of roll but it felt dry like I was going to throw up. You stared at me for a second then passed on to your seat. You moved so gracefully, like your feet didn't touch the ground.

Everything in my mouth felt full. I felt like I had already thrown up and it was in my mouth. I looked around at everyone else. Some people were staring at me but most people were staring at their rolls or plates and wouldn't look at me. The girl to my right made a gesture to pass the basket of rolls to you. There was only one roll in the basket, a white one. I was eating the wheat one, your wheat one. You didn't shake your head, but almost. She took her hand back and put it into her lap. She didn't pass the rolls to you.

My mouth tasted like vomit. I swallowed. The roll sat on my plate with one bite taken out of it. I looked at my plate, then closed my eyes. Then I looked up at you. You drank your coffee and looked at nothing. Then you smiled.

You were so kind and forgiving.

Then you looked away and drank your coffee in silence, not looking at anyone.

I tried to drink my coffee, but I couldn't. I didn't try to eat the roll.

I took the basket back at the end of breakfast. The one white roll was left.

☐　　　☐　　　☐

The next day at breakfast, after prayer, you touched the girl to your right, whose turn it was to get the rolls. You didn't say anything. You didn't need to. She sat down. Everyone else did too. I wanted to say "No," but I couldn't.

You went to get the rolls.

All of us were silent. You'd never been to get the rolls before.

You brought the rolls to the table. You took the plate and bowl and put them on the table. You stood at the corner of the table, two people away from me, the corner closest to the counter on the opposite side of the table from your seat. When you'd taken the plate and bowl out of the basket, you didn't put the basket on the table.

Here's what you did.

You offered the basket to the girl on your left, my right, and she took a white roll. Then you offered the basket to the girl on your right, and she took a white roll. You moved around the table and offered everyone a roll and everyone took a white one.

You'd started with the girl on my right. I was going to be the last one.

When you came to me, I reached up to take the last white one, but you pulled the basket back. I said, "What are you doing?" You didn't answer. You reached your right hand over the white roll as if to take it out of the basket and put it on my plate, but you didn't. You took the white one out and held it in your hand. Then you turned the basket over on my plate. The wheat roll fell on its side then fell upright.

"What are you doing?" I whispered.

You put the empty basket down in the center of the table. You sat down. You turned to the girl on your left and held out your hand. She passed you the butter. You had a white roll on your plate. It looked deformed in front of you. You had never eaten a white roll before.

I looked at the white roll and felt spit in my mouth.

I couldn't eat. My stomach felt hot like there was a bubble in it. My mouth was full of water.

The butter was going around and everyone was buttering their plates and their white rolls. When the butter came to me, it stopped.

I looked at you and said, "What are you doing to me?" I said, "Why are you doing this to me?" You didn't look at me. You tore off sections of your white croissant roll. Everyone else looked at their plate or roll.

I looked at the girl across from me. I said, "What is she doing?"

She didn't look at me. She only looked at her white roll.

I looked at everyone. Everyone was eating white rolls. You were eating a white roll. No one looked at me. Nobody would look at me.

I sat there and I couldn't move. I closed my eyes.

Inside I saw the color of your St. Greg's Sunday shoes.

Again, Like Before

Ana Castillo

This city belongs to us. It was the first thought I had when we landed. It belongs to us despite the hard rain and the fact that I have been locked in my hotel room all evening. I stare out of the window, at the rain, and listen to my "neighbors" in the room next door discussing something very important in Chinese or in Vietnamese or in some other language beyond the range of my meager comprehension of communication.

I left you a message on your machine two hours ago.

I did not think of this as your city until we landed. It was still daylight, but the rain made it hard to see your city, the streets that you see everyday. After I got my room I leaned against the doorway for a while since it was stuffy inside. A Hindu delivery man walked past me with a pizza for the people next door. He eyed me up and down. I smiled at him, I don't know why. After he delivered his pizza he eyed me again as he passed me once more, and just as he was about to turn the corner he stopped and turned back. "How much?" he asked me. He was standing objectionably close, close enough to smell his pores. "What?" I said.

"How much?" he repeated.

Understanding then what he meant, I turned away from him. I was repulsed. "You'd better hurry along," I said without looking at him, "my husband's on his way."

He hesitated as if he knew I was lying, but then decided that "no" was no for whatever reason, so he did as I asked. I looked down at my dress. Perhaps it was too short, the décolletage too revealing. My hair, perhaps. All of me, too…No, I dismissed the thoughts, the excuses, that is, that society gives a woman for such unsavory encounters.

I remember when you made my hair up just like yours. By chance, when we met our hair was the same length, cut the same, long layers of curls. Mine were from a permanent, yours were natural. After our shower and shampoo you applied globs of sticky stuff from aerosol canisters to make my hair stiff and full like yours. You dressed me in your expensive clothes. We went out that night. There was a "gentlemen's club" you wanted to show me.

We were the only two females in the place. Two minutes after we sat at a table, a young man in an Armani suit leaned over from the next table and whispered to me, "Do you girls know what kind of place this is?"

Without looking at him, but staring in front of me, as I did with the Hindu pizza delivery man earlier, I responded, "Do you know what kind of girls we are?"

It was one of the worst evenings of my life. Well, not my life. But of my summer here with you. The entertainment for that evening was a chanteuse. Now there were three of us. A singer who sat on the piano and did her best with a repertoire of Broadway show tunes and in between told jokes that, of course, being a gay bar, had to be gay jokes. I don't know why I say "of course," but you know that what God gave me in other ways He deprived me of with regards to a sense of humor. So as the evening progressed my bad mood grew worse. Seeing *us,* however, *together,* she could not resist the temptation and spontaneously improvised her whole performance at our expense. Did we have our hair done at a two-for-one? Were we *engaged?* She jumped off her piano and with mike in hand came over to us beneath a spotlight in the otherwise darkened room. "Excuse me, dear," she said, leaning over to me, "is that *aftershave* you have on?"

I grabbed her by the back of the neck and kissed her hard on the mouth. When she pulled back she tried to laugh it off but retreated to the safety of the piano, telling the audience she would make sure she would sit in such a way that neither my "girlfriend" nor I could get a "view" under her dress.

When the show was over, you said, "Why did you say yes when she asked if we are engaged?"

"Why not?" I said. I finished my second and last drink. Two was my limit, you said. Two drinks for me. None for you. The benefits one gets from being with someone who has already gone through recovery include involuntary recovery.

"But we're not," you said. You were pouting. The guy in the Armani and his friends were enjoying our argument. They eavesdropped on us, drank Moët & Chandon, and it was all great fun.

My second and last drink finished, the only other female in the whole place a misogynist, and you, mad because I didn't want to marry you—"Pay the bill," I said, and then, "I'll see you later." I got up and got my jacket from the coat and hat guy and went out to catch a cab.

It was our city, our summer, and I hated it. I can let myself remember now, sitting here listening to the rain, wondering if you will get in tonight and get my message, if you will call, and if I will care whether you do or not.

It was your money, your Greek Orthodox parents in the suburbs holding the pulse strings, your gay brother who came to check up on you saw me there, and stayed.

Okay. He was only twenty-two, had never been with a man (not a woman either for that matter), and I have no right to assume he is gay. The fact that I walked into the dining room one evening and found him sitting on his married companion's lap trying to spoonfeed him I suppose was one of those cultural-difference things that he was always insisting that I didn't understand about you and your family.

By the same token the fact that he came in one afternoon with his married companion, while we were making love with the bedroom door open, was equally ignored. You know, one of those In-the-Afternoon-Greek things.

Now, IF you were, you know, like *that*...he would have had to beat you, again, as he had the year before when he suspected it. So, no, of course you weren't. And I? *I*? What was *I* doing there with you? I was part of the family, like his married friend whose wife apparently was still in Athens having a baby. We were all part of the family, until the end of summer.

If you don't call, I don't care, you know. But if you don't call I know it's only because you're away, on vacation with your family, perhaps. I know that everything here with you is the same. Everything. While the end of that summer caused a part of me to perforate and it ripped off as soon as I got on the plane. I took your credit card number that morning, called a travel agent, and made the reservation. While you were in class I was making my way to the airport. I thought of using your credit card number and charging a watch for myself at the airport, but I did not because I am a fair person.

You were not.

You promised me a round-trip ticket but wouldn't let me go. And your punk brother saying hypocritically to me, "Stay, Celeste! Why do you want to go so soon?" Well, who had invited *him*? He came one weekend with his married friend and the two camped out in the living room permanently, or at least until I left. "Isn't that my sister's cross?" he asked, fingering the gold crucifix on the eighteen-karat-gold chain you had put around my neck that morning before you left for class and I was still half asleep in bed. "Yes," I said. Then added, "Your sister gave it to me this morning."

Surely he understood friendship, I thought. Hadn't he told us how he had spontaneously given his own watch to his married friend because he did not have one and could not afford it, being in this country all alone looking for work and his wife in Greece having a baby? Friendship. You know, like two guys who sleep embraced in the spoon position on the floor every night. One married, one looking for a *wife*. You know, friends.

"Get rid of these guys or I'm leaving," I demanded every night and every night you laughed. "He's my brother!" you said.

"There's something weird about all this," I insisted.

"What? Do you think my brother could be gay?" The thing was, you were *really* asking me. I didn't know what was going on. And it got more that way the evening a certain woman called you, a "friend of the family" as your brother referred to her because she spoke Greek, but you and I knew she was after you. Your brother took the call since you were in the shower. *"I know she wants to go out with me!"* he whispered to me with his hand over the mouthpiece. "Give me that!" I said. He pulled away, and with the telephone clutched to his chest, he ran into the bathroom and locked the door.

The next thing I knew he had given the phone to you while you were in the shower. I could hear you shouting over the water, "What? Who? Oh, hi! How are ya!"

The brother's married companion who didn't speak English was standing outside the door by then, both of us staring at it and hearing you and your brother talk, sometimes in English, sometimes in Greek, together and on the phone and laughing, and then it sounded like he too was taking a shower.

I asked you about that later. You said it was no big deal in your rather large family. Surely this was not a cultural misunderstanding. By this point I decided it was me and my own prudish upbringing where adult siblings were too uptight to bathe together.

No, that was not the reason I left without telling you. No, my darling whom I once desired so, at least for one summer, it wasn't two ostensibly straight men sleeping together on your living-room floor and spoon-feeding each other at the table. It wasn't your brother coming into the bedroom without knocking and his friend always watching us from the doorway. It wasn't that we ate at some of the best restaurants in town but you always chose when and where and if we would go at all. It wasn't my two-drink limit. It wasn't the gifts you gave and took back when I wouldn't say I loved you, when I wouldn't say I'd marry you, when I wouldn't stay forever, in your apartment, in your city.

It wasn't how you always shut the lights out, got on your knees before a big framed picture of Jesus the Good Shepherd on the wall to say your prayers before getting into bed to make love with me.

And it wasn't those things about you and me there with you that summer that are too despicable to recall in this lifetime, but which will surely be recalled for us in some way in the afterlife for being so despicable and having nothing to do with love at all.

There it is. There's your call. I'll let it ring and you will surely call back again. And if I don't get out of here, sometime in the middle of the night you will come over here. You'll suspect I am out, and you will wait in the lobby and hope to catch me. Catch me, as if I had surely been out committing a violation against you, my sin of insisting on existing without you.

If I don't move quickly, you will move even more so and there will be no escaping you. Perhaps I should get another room. Call a cab. Find an all-night bar. I can't stand the thought of it; you'll come and in minutes you'll be crying, making those little donkey-like noises when you start to hyperventilate and cause a scene. We'll be forced to get an ambulance and spend the night in an emergency room. Then your older brother, the doctor, will appear. And he'll see you, red and half-strangulated by your own mucus, and see me and ask no one in particular since you won't be able to answer, "Who's this?"

And I'll have to tell him and look away, repulsed by the fact that he doesn't care who I am but has asked simply to have better reason to dismiss me.

No, it's too much. I should never have let you know that I was here. After all, there was no reason to tell you. It was just that we landed and I was sucked up by the tentacles of this, your city, and your name and that summer that were all inseparable, and I called as soon as I put my bag down on the bed in this room. You must have heard that I've married. That isn't *the* reason why I shouldn't have called, but it is a reason why I shouldn't have called because you will surely reproach me for it.

You'll write something meant to make me feel terrible on the bathroom mirror again in your crimson-red lipstick just before you leave, like, "Why did you ever bother to call in the first place???" And I'll spend an hour trying to wipe it all off so that the maid won't think badly of me tomorrow.

But how could she think badly of me when it is you who is capable of doing such things? Like going through my phone book and ripping out all the pages with names of people you didn't know and who were therefore suspected of being romantic liaisons. No, that was not the reason I left you either.

I left you because I simply did not love you. I left you because I grew bored with your long, black eyelashes. I left you because your money was a nuisance in my life. Above all, summer had ended and I left because that is when I said I would leave, and I did.

Which is what I had better do now, again. Or perhaps not. It doesn't matter. If you want to come by, speeding in your little car in the rain, getting my room number, pounding on the UP button, then taking the stairs, do it. It is your night, your city, your money, your hotel for all I know. Nothing about you matters to me now. And all of this here, that I am in, is you, again, like before.

Excerpt from Licking Our Wounds

Elise D'Haene

Hospice \'häs-pis\ *n:* a place of shelter for travelers.

The sound of my boots on dried beach stone. Followed by a drawn-out stony wheezing, like Sister Kizzie panting Jesus and holy face cream. Peter's lungs. This was the sound. The first thing he said to me on the phone was this: "I thought you forgot that you were my executor." He said, "ek'sikyoot-er," the one who carries out the death penalty, not, "ig zek'yater," one who carries out the provisions of a will. I didn't correct him, and I didn't forget my promise: I'd be there for him, in the end.

Leonard, the nurse, was happy happy happy to see my face, the face of Peter's designated primary caregiver. KS lesions were feasting on Peter's lungs, CMV clouded his eyes, and mounds of lymphoma sprouted like cauliflower under his armpits and at the base of his neck. Other than that...Peter was refusing to eat and would barely drink enough water to keep a cactus alive. The staff at the hospice resorted to puncturing his veins with needles that catered liquid food and beverages. He kept pulling the needles out, causing infected blood to splatter the walls and the staff. He was considered "uncooperative." I talked to Leonard and then went into Peter's room and locked the door behind me. His bedside table was strewn with get-well cards and a vase of fresh daylilies. A card said, "I love you, Peter. Christie." My angel friend started sending flowers wrapped with herself after Eduardo died. She couldn't come face-to-face.

I had to blink several times when I first laid eyes on Peter. Like slides, the faces of Tom, James, Doug, all of them, came into view. It was the sunken, ashen, skeletal look, and the stunned disbelief staring back at my own thinly disguised shock.

"Hey, Peter. I see the Karen Carpenter diet is working like a charm." I sat down on his bed. He grabbed my hand and smiled, like a very little boy.

"Maintaining my girlish figure, which is more than I can say for you, cowgirl."

"I've been snacking on sugar instead of women. Donuts do not break your heart."

"Mia, I was scared you forgot about me. I've missed you." Our eyes locked. It was a collision of disbelief mixed with equal parts of hopelessness and love.

"Peter. Do you want to die?"

"Yeah, cowgirl."

I talked to Peter about his prognosis. I talked to him about the hospice staff. "Peter," I said, "you've got a reputation around here as a big pain in the ass. They are all afraid you are going to sue them. You know lawyers." He liked that he had a reputation and that the staff feared him. It seemed that this knowledge gave him a smidgen of power, and when your body has been conquered, a pinch of authority helps. I told him that from now on I would be in charge. Don't piss off this old bulldagger. That's what I said. He hacked out a laugh. Before I left for the night, he asked me to sing to him, in a deep voice like Elvis, like I used to do with my brother Fritz and when I did my Elvis impersonations at the White Trash parties. So I sang, *"Oh baby let me be / Your loving teddy bear / Put a chain around my neck / And lead me anywhere. / Oh let me be / Your teddy bear."*

I called Peter's doctor, the Chipmunk, and found out that he'd dropped out of AIDS medicine and moved to Wyoming with his family. Peter's case was being handled by Dr. Helena Carter. I had her paged, and the first question she asked was what were Peter's wishes. Not life wishes, like I want to make a bijillion dollars, have two houses, one on the ocean and one in the mountains, and a lover who worships my spit. She was talking about death wishes. Do not resuscitate. Do not plant a device, like a trained bystander, into my heart. Stop dripping fluids into my blood. Peter's death wishes were well-documented. As she kept throwing out treatment options, I kept tossing back dosages of morphine. "High dosages of morphine will shut down his entire system," she said. I didn't want to completely alienate myself from her, but I asked her how long she'd been treating patients with AIDS. There was a long pause, and I kept trying to think of that joke about Carter's liver pills. I'd have to call my dad. We agreed to meet the next day at the hospice.

Men's Adam's apples seem to bounce like a ball when they suppress feeling. It's as if the fragile little lump of sadness is just too weak to get around that apple. I think it's why men clear their throats, hard, when they talk. Making sure that they can slam-dunk those annoying feelings back into the hoop of their guts. My dad's Adam's apple has gotten bigger and bigger over the years. I don't know if this is just a natural part of a man's aging, like how their noses extend, taking up more room on the face, or how their ears seem to swell and both sprout hairs like stubborn weeds. I think my dad has just been collecting layers and layers of gristle to keep his throat clogged. He doesn't know any better.

When I talked to Peter, it was as if his Adam's apple were being dribbled by a pro basketball player. I wanted to palm his throat with my hand and stop him, mid bounce, hold on long enough for that sorrow-lump to push through to his mouth. It's easier for women: We don't have such a large mass of cartilage in our throats, so the passage from our guts to our lips is much clearer. Maybe that passage is too clear, and that's why women seem to slam-dunk their feelings all over the place. All I know is, after I left Peter's room, my lumps heaved out of my gut like cannonballs and I had to pull off the freeway and sob for a while. I remembered a moment months earlier when Peter and I embraced in front of the ReadyTeller and I kept saying to myself as I squeezed, "Don't die, don't die." As if somehow, by my saying this as I squeezed his chest hard and listened to his heart booming silent grief, that somehow, magically, my silent prayer would erase all infection from his body. Peter has more infected cells than Carter has little pills. That's the joke.

I was treated like an arbitrator between warring nations when I arrived at the hospice the next day. Angela, the day nurse, was fed up. She pulled me into the backyard and told me that Peter kept masturbating in front of the staff and that this was unacceptable, especially when the female staff tried giving him a sponge bath. Roland, the hospital administrator, then joined Angela and me in the backyard and asked if I thought Peter was suffering from dementia and perhaps that is why he keeps pulling out his IV needles. He was having a hard time finding anyone willing enough to work with Peter. "We don't want any legal trouble." They invited me to move into his room until the end.

I flung open the door to Peter's room like a drill sergeant. "Peter, I'm gonna pickle your pecker if you don't start pawing in private! Get it?"

He had that look in his eyes, like a little boy, right at the moment the fat old teacher's butt hits the pointed tip of the tack.

"Hey, cowgirl. You sure do got your undies in a bunch." My eyes were drawn to the floor, where deep-brown urine streamed from the hose connected to his penis into the plastic bag.

"You're getting a roommate today."

He shut his eyes stubbornly and barked, "I don't want anyone in here with me."

"It's not just anyone." I leaned down and planted a big wet one on his lips. Then I whispered into his ear, "Peter, Peter, it's a pussy eater."

His eyes got big and wide. "You're gonna stay here with me, Mia, really?"

Suddenly he grabbed my neck, pulling me close to his mouth, and he whispered frantically, "You've got to stop them. They're trying, all of them, they're trying to kill me. Help me stop them. Please. Please!" I stared into his eyes and the little boy was still there, but there was no mischief left; it was a little boy who hadn't learned yet that nightmares about spooky monsters under the bed aren't real. The problem was, I couldn't just crawl under the bed and assure Peter that he was safe, lift the covers back and say, "See, there's no spooky monster." His body knew the truth. He broke out into a sweat, began shivering, then closed his eyes and fell into an agitated sleep. His muscles twitched and his lips kept moving. I sat, dazed, and watched as his Adam's apple bounced and bounced and bounced. That's why Peter kept pulling the needles out of his veins. He's fighting for his life. I'm the allied forces, but I don't have any weapons powerful enough. I'm scared.

□   □   □

"The MRI showed significant, irreversible atrophy of the brain." This was Dr. Carter's first sentence. Followed by a seemingly endless chemotherapy protocol to address the pesky lymphoma problem, massive doses of whatever antiviral medication Peter could stomach, and maybe a combination drug therapy to bolster that immune system. She was calling in an oncology specialist to handle the chemo and radiation. How did that sound to me?

"Like dropping another atomic bomb on Hiroshima."

"Excuse me?" she said. So far Dr. Carter hadn't looked me in the eye, talked as if Peter weren't in the room, and had this annoying habit of clicking her fingernails. Click click click. Our eyes met, and I could see that she was nervous. She seemed like a bright, well-bred, well-balanced gal from the Midwest who'd studied hard, didn't date much, and was considered an achiever. Someone who had clear goals and met those goals. Someone who'd said when they were five years old that they wanted to grow up and be a doctor and help sick people like Grandma. I imagined her parents had lots of framed photos of her smiling, smart and sweet. That click click click gave her away, though, revealed an insecurity, a fear, a frayed edge to the perfect tapestry of her life. I liked her for that. Her fingernails really went at it now because Peter started palming his dick, and she did her damnedest to lock eyes with mine. If I were really sadistic, I would have started tweaking my nipple on the spot. Instead, I smiled and led her out to the backyard.

She started that clicking again, so I just took her hand in mine and held it firmly. "Dr. Carter, Peter is going to die. The important thing is that he isn't in physical pain and he doesn't suffer. That's what I want to discuss with you." We had a long, long talk and got real chummy when we discovered that we were both from Michigan and that her parents lived about two miles from mine and our fathers belonged to the same Kiwanis club. We swapped Michigander stories and agreed that we missed the change of seasons and especially the fall, when you could drive to a cider mill, pick a bushel of apples, eat warmed donuts, down endless amounts of sweet cider, and finish off with a gooey caramel apple that made the dried autumn leaves stick to your hands. By the end of our talk, she agreed to the morphine drip, no oncologist, and minimal use of medications, but only after a full blood work-up. Just to be sure. Then I said, "Peter's got more infected cells than Carter has little pills." She laughed and told me her dad's always telling people the same thing about her brains. One more thing: By the end of our talk, Helena had stopped clicking.

☐   ☐   ☐

Peter's too young to die. All of them are. Too young for this kind of fear, and it's a fear too big for a lullaby. That's what I needed, though, a song, a string of words, like a poem, or a motion to lull Peter's fear, to calm and soothe. When his morphine was increased, it was like a tender lullaby for a body fretful and in distress. As if Morpheus himself entered through the veins, conjuring up dreams in the blood, into the marrow, floating from one troubled cell to another singing, "Hush little baby don't you cry." But once the arms of Morpheus began to weaken from the weight of Peter's body, then the demons returned. Peter was like my infant, because I would wake up and I'd be at his bedside even before my dreams had lifted from the pillow. Four to six A.M. was the most active time at the hospice, the anxious twilight when a gradual pall seemed to cover the inhabitants throughout the house. I could hear Leonard frantically moving in and out of rooms, calling for his aide to bring fresh linens, wrestling with a growing fever by carrying a patient into the bathtub and pouring ice cubes into the water, or trying to unclog terrified air passages by vacuuming up phlegm. For Peter, this was the time when he and I wrestled with demons of hallucination, of an atrophied brain gone awry, sometimes so scary, I'd peek under his bed just to make sure. These were our nights.

☐   ☐   ☐

Mercy. Peter and I had a bad night. Leonard gave me a bottle of liquid Valium at 3:30 to inject into his veins until he calmed down. I felt like David and the spooky monster was Goliath who appeared as Peter's father. It was as if I were witnessing a child being beaten and bloodied and I was standing by just watching. My attempts to soothe couldn't penetrate the phantom fist of a raging father as it smashed the pleading face of a little boy trying to cling to his dad's thigh. Peter kept crying, "Please, Daddy, stop. I didn't mean to. I'm sorry." I rubbed his brow, his cheek, saying, "You're safe, sweetie, you're safe." I was boxing, and the shadow was winning. This went on forever, it seemed, until I emptied the bottle into his arm and let a few drops land on my tongue. Goliath finally fell at sunrise. At ten A.M., when I opened my eyes and looked over to Peter, he was staring at me with a big smile and said, "I want a man." It was ironic that the kindness of an atrophied brain is forgetting. And here I was being handed the gift of remembering. The moment I saw that glimmering, horny, and hungry look in Peter's eyes, I felt lifted and struck like a bell. I climbed into bed with him and we were like schoolgirls passing secret notes in class. We shared our most wicked and twisted sexual fantasies, and when Angela came in to change the bedsheets, Peter grabbed my tit and moaned and groaned, and Angela did the fastest about-face I'd ever witnessed. We didn't have to behave; we'd killed Goliath last night. Peter slept the rest of the day.

☐   ☐   ☐

The man in the room across the hall died. His name was Roberto. His mother said the rosary as the priest delivered the last rites. I stood at Peter's door while they carried Roberto out, his body zipped up in a bag. I'm glad Peter is sleeping. Like a gesture as ordinary as licking my lips, a prayer formed in my head. May his soul rest and all the souls of the faithful departed, through the mercy of God, rest in peace. Angela looked at me, brushed a hurried tear from her cheek, then changed Roberto's linens. Another traveler was arriving today.

□   □   □

Helena brought me a caramel apple with chopped peanuts. They were Macintosh apples too, slightly tart and crunchy. If my taste buds were a choir, they were booming the "Hallelujah Chorus." We sat in the backyard together, silent as we hungrily licked and crunched and sucked our afternoon treat under the hot August sun. When we finished, I turned on the garden hose and both of us gulped down streams of cold water. Then we talked. Peter didn't have any more helper cells. They deserted, packed up, and left no forwarding address. We would increase the morphine slowly, depending on his physical discomfort. His liver was departing as well. When Helena talked medicine her voice was as confident as a handsome quarterback. Even when she discussed death, it was like the final call in a playoff game. I figured she learned how to do this from a textbook. Otherwise, she was as shy as the fluttering petal of a discarded wallflower. The click click click abated only when I brought up Michigan.

□   □   □

He was bronzed, chiseled, thick-chested, and except for the dirt under his nails, he could have been on the cover of *GQ*. His blue jeans were bleach-stained with precise frayed holes revealing snatches of skin and bulge. They hung loose around his taut waist and butt, and I imagined that without effort or thought he could step right out of them. His chest was exquisite, as if carefully carved by a master sculptor, hard and smooth. One lonesome silver ring pierced his right nipple. Wisps of shiny black hair escaped from the bandanna wrapped around his head. In his face was hunger, not for flesh, but for food: a panicked salivation across the lips and the tense stare of a gnarling appetite. After circling the block a few times, I drove up and rolled down the passenger window. He didn't approach. His eyes kept darting back and forth, surveying the boulevard like the referee of a tennis match. "Excuse me?" I said, aiming my voice like a precise arrow, hoping the scruffy drunk lumped on the sidewalk behind him wouldn't stir. He ambled slowly toward my car, palmed his cocky bulge, then bent down and said, "I don't do girls."

☐   ☐   ☐

When Leonard came in at five this morning to check on us, he didn't say a word. He came up from behind and put his hands on my shoulders, began massaging, pushed his thumbs firm into the hard marbles of tension in my neck. I was leaning over Peter. He was calm and cooing, fondling my breasts, pawing at them like a well-fed baby. I kept wiping at the yellow bile that dribbled from his mouth as he cooed. Little shudders of release ran down my body from where Leonard pressed, and I felt a strange comfort in the strength of his muscled arms loosening my weary flesh. Peter clutched my tit and pulled it toward his mouth and suckled through my T-shirt. I didn't pull away. Leonard whispered, "We all want mama in the end." As I offered my breasts to Peter, they seemed to swell with phantom milk. And I was thinking, *I wish I could capture this moment on film, the familial ease of kindred spirits.* We were a perfect trio of queers, so at home on the landscape of the body, united in the language of survival, the tongue of flesh, the dialect of stroke and suck. A language that crosses borders easily.

☐   ☐   ☐

I'm feeling blessed today. Had to suction out Peter's mouth and throat three times so far. Phlegm and bile. Lungs wheezing and crunching. Gave Leonard a manicure and a pedicure, used deep-Bordeaux nail polish and teeny tiny silver stars. He does drag on Friday nights. Helena increased Peter's morphine, then we had lunch. She feels like a long-lost pal from home. Invited her to Leonard's show next week. She clicked a few times then said yes. Peter was talking with Tom last night. Maybe Tom has finally come to take Peter away to that place on the other side of space and time. From what I could gather, they were speaking the secret language of old lovers. I couldn't get a word in edgewise. Felt lonesome.

□   □   □

I fell asleep reading about the AIDS quilt, then had this dream about Mother Earth, and she was so cold and tired that all of her children began sewing a huge blanket for her from the bits and pieces of their lives. And I had my tiny swatch to offer, but I couldn't find any thread, so I kept searching and searching and finally realized that a string of white cotton was in my pocket. A single strand from Cup's shirt. So I carefully aimed one end into the eye of the silver needle, tied a knot at the bottom, and began to sew.

□   □   □

Mr. "I don't do girls" was called Tony on the streets, but his legal name was Chester. He was twenty-two. He said he remembered Peter and wondered why he hadn't heard from him. He ordered a double cheeseburger, french fries, a dinner salad, a chocolate shake, and coffee. I ordered a dinner salad. Tony didn't know his HIV status, wasn't interested in fact, and was working the boulevard hoping to save up money to record an album.

"What kind of songs do you sing?"

"Ballads, sad ones, romantic ones, the old stuff mostly."

"Like, *Romance finis/ Your chance finis/ The ants that have crawled down my pants finis?*" Tony eyed me like I had just dribbled food down my chin.

"No, old stuff like *memories, may be beautiful and yet...*"

"Oh, *that* old, huh?" The waiter asked if we'd like dessert. I went ahead and ordered peach pie with vanilla ice cream. What the hell, I could drop dead any moment. As he chewed the last bite of pecan pie, Tony stretched and yawned and rubbed his belly. The silver ring around his nipple jiggled when he moved, and it was hard for me not to stare at it. He agreed to come by at midnight. I dropped him back off at his corner, and before I pulled away he palmed his cock again, bent down and said, "Peter the lawyer, right?"

☐   ☐   ☐

I borrowed Leonard's manicure and shaving kit and spent the rest of the evening preparing Peter for his date. I sponge-bathed him with a mixture of water, rose oil, and aloe vera gel. I clipped his nails carefully and had to skip his left foot because the buildup of grunge and fungus was permanent around the nails and between the toes. I trimmed his sideburns and left his face scruffy, the way he did when he'd go on the hunt for a man. As I ran the washcloth behind his neck, I felt the bulge of lymphoma; it felt like a bone and was as big as a lemon. I was struck with how accommodating skin is, stretching to capacitate abnormal growths from inside. I carefully wiped his penis, and he lifted his balls for me as I ran a stream of warm water around them. "I can't feel a thing, cowgirl."

"I know what you mean." I told Peter to just use his imagination. We listened to an old tape that Tom made of classic Motown, and every so often I could see Peter's foot tap to the rhythm, trying to dance. Leonard helped me slip some faded black jeans over what was left of Peter's legs and hips. He wanted to wear his blue button-down silk shirt. First we had to unhook his IV in order to get his arm into the sleeve. Then we put his lizard-skin cowboy boots on and crossed his legs for him, posed him so he had the appearance of a self-assured lover. Once we were done, Leonard kissed Peter and said, "Girl, if only I were single." I set up some candles around the room, and Leonard brought in a bottle of champagne. Then we waited. At around 11:45, Peter asked me if I was sure Tony really wanted to see him. I'm sure, I said. Inside I was chanting, *Please show up, please show up, please show up.*

Leonard opened the door like a staid butler and announced the arrival of Peter's guest. "May I show him in, sir?" Peter nodded. Tony had on the same jeans with a neatly pressed white dress shirt and spit-shined black boots. His hair was slicked back and his skin was lightly spiced with the scent of patchouli oil. He carried a single red rose delicately between his thumb and forefinger. I wanted to hug him, even though I could tell the red rose came from the bush in front of the hospice. As I left the room, Tony bent down and kissed Peter, fully on the lips, while Peter's foot danced to Aretha singing *"Answer my prayer...say you love me too."* I closed the door.

Tony came out to the backyard and said that Peter was asking for me. I was floating just above sleep, sitting in a lawn chair lulled by the sounds of traffic and the hovering police helicopters patrolling the night sky. I followed Tony into Peter's room. That look was in Peter's eyes, and I leaned down and whispered, "There's no monster under the bed." He wanted me to stay while he was with Tony. "I want you here, don't leave, okay?" Maybe Peter wanted me there so that I could sew this swatch of his life into my memory and keep him alive. Tony just shrugged his shoulders, like no big whoop, and so I sat on my bed, hugged my legs close to my chest, and rested my chin on my knees. A single candle flickered on Peter's bedside table. The shadow of the daylilies filled the wall and looked like the arms of worshippers stretched toward heaven, making a joyful noise unto the Lord.

After kicking off his boots, Tony unzipped his jeans, and they fell to the floor as easily as a silk slip. He flexed his buns like biceps, his ass so unlike a woman's. There wasn't one extra pooch or tuft of skin on him, nothing to press, to feel the shape of flesh change and dip under the weight of your body. Every inch and corner of Tony was just like a brick. He began gliding his hands on Peter's chest with sure and certain brush strokes, easing right over the hard lesions as if they were just minor bumps in the road. He pinched Peter's nipples, then bent to lick and bite, and then kissed Peter, teasing with his tongue, over and over like hide-and-seek. When he fingered the top silver button on Peter's jeans, Peter clenched his wrist and stopped him. He was staring at Tony's cock, willing it hard under his gaze, then groped and clutched as if trying to grab a rope extended toward a falling man. He tugged and pulled and seemed determined to make Tony hard under his grasp. Tony's cock was a leash that yanked at Peter's desire, jerked it out of him like a pulled tooth. He mustered up enough energy to move to the very edge of the bed and leaned toward Tony's erection coming at him like an arrow. I closed my eyes and buried my head into my pillow and just listened to the slippery sound of saliva and sucking and heard Peter groan like a man heaving the discus.

A long time passed, and I fell asleep, cradling my legs like a lover. When I finally looked up, Tony was lying silently on top of Peter. I just stared at them and watched as the shadow on the wall slowly dissolved to a solitary, lone worshipper. The tiny tongue of flame sputtered, then evaporated, and a single thin blue line of smoke rose to the ceiling, and I imagined grabbing on and flying up, way up, dreaming and flying, like my brother Joseph told me to do so long ago. Dream and fly. This seemed the only thing to do, in this moment, when I'm yearning for a simple evening kiss before slumber. The kind of kiss that graces a child's forehead or woos lovers, assuring safe passage through the night.

☐   ☐   ☐

Tony and I were back at the same restaurant, this time eating piles of pancakes with fresh strawberries and mounds of whipped cream. We clasped legs under the table like high school sweethearts. His white shirt was wide open and loose, and he lazily circled his pierced nipple with his finger as he lit a cigarette. The coffee shop was packed, the tables filled with boozed-up bar queers tossing tired-old-queen jokes back and forth like a beach ball at a stadium. Tony and I didn't talk to each other, just laughed along with the crowd, and then Tony looked out to the boulevard and said he had to get back to work. He refused payment, but I paid for breakfast and slipped twenty bucks into his pocket when I hugged him. "Consider it my contribution to the arts," I said. I sat in the booth and watched as he stripped off his shirt, tied it around his waist, and leaned against a telephone pole. The moment he palmed his cock a burgundy Jaguar pulled up, and Tony disappeared. Then I sat back and just listened to the clamor of queers speaking the language of survival, and just like the shadow of worshippers, making a joyful noise unto each other.

The Fox on the Line

Emma Donoghue

Any other June, we would be in Hengwrt by now. I would be waking up with the white-topped mountains ringed around me. Cader Idris, where the giant once sat, would raise its shoulder between me and all harm. Sitting under the snowy cherry tree, I would keep one ear cocked for the brook that sounds so much like a woman singing, you have to lay down your book and go and see.

But we are trapped in London, waiting to make history.

Keeping a diary is a monstrous waste of time. But I cannot seem to help it. Without words, we move through life as mute as the animals. Of course, I burn these jottings at the end of each year. What I should keep instead is a daily memorandum of Fà and all her works. Posterity will not interest itself in me; I am only her Mary.

On the first of June 1876, then, our Society held its first General Meeting at the Westminister Palace Hotel, Lord Shaftesbury presiding. Cardinal Manning defied the Pope and spoke in our favour. Resolutions in support of our Bill were passed with the utmost enthusiasm.

I break off here to remark that it cannot go on: the evil, I mean. We spill their blood like water. There is so much we could learn from them—devotion, patience, the fidelity that asks no questions. The men of science say they pick only the useless ones, but who is to decide that? And what are we to think, we old maids who have so often heard ourselves called *surplus*?

☐   ☐   ☐

It stands to reason that those who assault nature will suffer at her hands in the end. I read these stories every other day in the *Times*. A boy was beating a plough horse with the stock of his gun. It back-fired and took his arm off.

Do I sound uncharitable?

It has been a long year.

☐   ☐   ☐

Every week our Bill creeps a little further through the House, progressing like a pilgrim under the flag of Lord Carnarvon. I try to steady my heart. I work a little every morning in my sculpture studio at the bottom of the garden. My hopes shoot up and down like a barometer. But we walk by the Thames when the sky has begun to cool, and Fà ends each evening by convincing me all over again. The great sacrifice she made last year, when she laid down all her other causes and writings, will be rewarded at last. Every newspaper supports our Bill. The Queen is reported to be most impressed by its wording.

In the veterinary schools they reckon on sixty operations for each horse before it is used up or dies of its own accord. The professors set students to do things that have been done a thousand times before, that could as easily be done on corpses. They practice finding nerves. They burn the living horses, make them breathe smoke and drink spirits, pull out their guts, carve off their hooves, pluck out their eyes, peel back their skin. Still living. If that can be called living. My hand shakes on the chisel when I think of it.

Fà has on her bedroom wall a text that her great-grandfather the magistrate had on his. *Deliver him that is oppressed from the hand of the adversary.*

☐   ☐   ☐

I am attempting a cocker spaniel in brown marble. My master when I trained in Rome was John Gibson—a Welshman, but a Greek in soul. He always encouraged me to be mythological, and I did once try a Niobe, but the swell of her marble breast disconcerted me. I cannot believe in anything I have not seen. All I make these days are dogs and horses.

Kitty brings the letters to me as soon as they arrive, so I can remove the hateful ones. I can tell by the handwriting. They call Fà a stirrer-up of sentimental old women, despite the fact that there are rational people of both sexes in our campaign. If they only knew how little of an extremist she is; she laughs at faddy vegetarians and hunt protestors. All she means to do is control a necessary evil—to minimize pain, to make the men of science accountable. They call her a squeamish coward, but where is the courage in what the vivisectors do? Boys pulling wings off flies.

The day our Bill becomes law, no experiment whatsoever may be performed on a living cat, dog, horse, ass, or mule, nor on any other animal except (in almost all cases) under conditions of complete anaesthesia from beginning to end. The reign of terror is almost over.

I wish we were in Wales. It is easier to believe in a state of nature there.

☐   ☐   ☐

No news.

Last year we passed by Llangollen and visited the pretty house where the Ladies lived. It is said they never slept a night away from home. Nothing parted them; nothing disturbed them. They supported no causes. They took no part in public life. They did nothing; they were ladies in the old sense. They looked no farther than the ends of their aristocratic noses.

Shall I confess? Sometimes I long for such a life. A narrow, private existence, as Fà would call it; a limited life. House and hearth and daily bread. Like Rosa Bonheur and her friend, when we visited, with their horses, goats, sheep, monkeys, donkeys, lapwings, and hoopoes! I can imagine us at Hengwrt with our animals around us, well-fed and tended, and no thought of all the others. No memory of all the viciousness of the world.

Fifteen years ago we made our bargain. A trip to Wales every summer, but Kensington all the rest of the year. Meetings, dinners, petitions, debates, dinners, appeals, circulars, dinners, calls, printings, meetings, dinners. There are things to be said on platforms; things to be said at tea-tables. And things not to be said at all.

A lady lion-tamer put her head in a lion's mouth last week, and he bit it off. If a lion attempted to put his head in my mouth, I expect I would do the same.

☐   ☐   ☐

Lord Carnarvon has been called away from London to his dying mother. She lingers; he has been gone for a fortnight now. Meanwhile our Bill lacks a midwife to see it through the House. Fà rages at Carnarvon for what she calls his dereliction of duty. But how is the poor man to choose? On one side, the muffled cries of hundreds of thousands of creatures; on the other, his mother. It would drive anybody mad.

The slightest things set us ajitter, at this eleventh hour. On the way home from chapel I panicked at the bray of an ass. Yesterday I snapped at Fà over the grocer's bill. She asked if I would prefer her to earn a thousand a year or do God's work on Earth?

If we cannot love each other through times like these then what we thought a rock beneath us is turned to shifting sands.

☐   ☐   ☐

She was on crutches when I met her. Summer in Rome; I was working on a model of my little Arab horse when Charlotte Cushman was announced, with a visitor. To think of a time when it was not familiar, that warm bulk, lurching across the room! Miss Frances Power Cobbe. She told me very cheerfully about the doctor who had left her crippled. I asked her to come riding on the Campagna. I was merely being polite; I never thought she would come.

She wrote me poems which were very bad but softened my heart. She boasted that not only had no man ever wanted her, but that she had never wanted any man. She said that love was the highest law, and that the Bedouins had rites to solemnize the mutual adoption of friends.

I went home with her three years later. I took her to Wales. She said "Hang the doctors" and threw away her crutches, and we climbed Cader Idris.

☐   ☐   ☐

If I shut my eyes, I am in Hengwrt in our dark-paneled dining room, our little Rembrandt girl looking down at us with serious eyes. It cannot be long now. I have sent word that half a dozen rooms should be aired for our arrival.

I chip away at my spaniel, but it lies awkwardly on its marble rug.

Fà is shut up all day with lords and bishops and men of influence. I must order a good roast for dinner.

I remember Hattie Hosmer in her smock and cap, climbing the scaffolding around one of her giantesses. "Art or marriage, Mary," she used to remark, "it's one or the other."

☐   ☐   ☐

Still no news.

I lost my temper twice this afternoon, though I kept my lips together and Fà never noticed. Would she like me better if I were a dumb beast?

We try to stick to our routines. We are always in bed by eleven o'clock. We have few friends, these days. Half are lost to us because of bitter arguments over the cause. Even our beloved Harriet St. Leger looked up from brushing her great black retriever and remarked that she could not understand us. "My dear girls, a dog's just a dog!"

But she is wrong. A dog, pinned down in a laboratory, its nostrils full of the stink of phenol and its own blood, is more than a dog. It is the whole sin of our race in miniature.

Nowadays I see vivisections everywhere. In the heels that deform women's feet, for instance; in the corsets that grip our lungs. "If we dress like slaves," Fà says, "no wonder men enslave us." I have known two women who died of having their ovaries removed, quite unnecessarily. I have heard whispers of another fashionable operation, where a part is cut away that is not diseased at all. The surgeons do it simply to kill passion. Simply to make women quieter. Simply because they can.

□   □   □

Three thousand doctors have signed a Memorial to the Home Secretary, protesting at the insult we do their profession by attempting to subject them to legal control. They propose amendments to every word in our Bill. A crowd of them marched into the Home Office and slapped it on the desk.

Fà got to the letters before me this morning. She cried when she read one accusing her of wearing a feather in her hat that was ripped from a living ostrich. Such an absurdity! A woman who for half a century has worn only the plainest homemade suits. I made her laugh about it, over caraway cake. I called her a slave to fashion.

Does she guess? Does she see through me? The truth is that I long for this Bill to pass not so much for the animals' sake as for ours. For this battle to be over, and the two of us come safe home.

I read in the *Times* about a fox who saved his own skin. A pack of hounds was on his heels when he suddenly turned in the direction of the railway and lay down on the line. An express was approaching at a fearsome speed. Unwilling to see their hounds cut in pieces, the huntsmen had to call off the pack. The fox stayed on the track until the train got within ten paces, then slipped off into the countryside.

Knowing when to go, that's the trick of it.

☐   ☐   ☐

No word from Lords Carnarvon or Shaftesbury. No news of the
Bill. July has come in dank and windy. Fà is irritable as always when
bad weather keeps her home; like a dog, she needs her constitutionals.
    I have been addressing letters all morning; my hand is a claw. I
have copied out Fà's table of arguments and rebuttals till I am hearti-
ly sick of them all and can no longer remember which ones I am
meant to believe. I dread the next meeting of our Society, the
motions and counter-motions, the pompous, desperate repetitions.
Perhaps I will pretend to have taken chill.
    What am I doing here, in the anteroom of a public life? I was born
to live tucked away in a quiet green corner of the world, with my
stones and my chisels, under the wing of Cador Idris. That is my true
habitat. If I had known my own mind fifteen years ago—if I had met
and joined my life to a different kind of woman—
    I will burn this page before dinner.

☐   ☐   ☐

As the poem goes, *I have looked coolly on my what and why.*
    Because when Fà is away mending the world, she writes to me
every evening, and keeps every letter I ever sent her in a big box.
    Because greed for cake is her besetting sin.
    Because she lumbers along precipices and laughs at the drop.
    Because her head, as measured by a skilled phrenologist, is twen-
ty-three and one-quarter inches in circumference.
    Because nothing quells her. When she heard that Ruskin called her
a clattering saucepan, she roared, "The better to boil his head down
to size!"
    Because she thinks every girl should be taught how to hit a nail
straight.
    Because she is such a bright light that no one peers behind her at me.

☐   ☐   ☐

Justice and Mercy have gone from the Earth.

The Bill has been read in the Commons. We barely recognise it. It has had its throat cut, the life blood drained out of its veins. It is a shadow of itself now, a mockery, a twitching monster.

It no longer protects animals from vivisection, but vivisectors from prosecution. It allows anyone to apply for a license to do anything to any animal. It says a scientist is under no obligation to put a suffering creature out of its misery unless in his opinion that suffering is likely to endure long.

Fà leaned against me, when the news came, and her whole weight bore down. "Mary," she said, "what have we done?"

At times like this I wish we shared a bed, as some friends I knew in Rome used to do. Then I could hold her all night. Fà has always joked about her body, calling it Kensington's own grotesque. She doesn't understand that I love every pound of flesh.

□   □   □

Late August, and we are in Wales. The Parliamentary Session is over, and the summer, and all our hope.

The Vivisector's Charter is passed. It is the first time I have ever cursed the Queen. We always thought Victoria was on the side of the animals; we always said she had a tender heart. How could she have signed her name to this?

Hengwrt does not seem as beautiful as it was last summer; we have missed the best of it. Or rather, all its loveliness is at a little distance, as if behind glass. The Rembrandt girl's eyes puzzle over us.

Fà never looks up. She is busy writing the bitterest letters I have ever read, to those of our supporters who have melted away. I have begun again on the business of circulars. I print them and post them and eminent people sign them and return them and I compile a list of the signatories and send it to other eminent people. *Circular* is the right word.

The damage is done, but we go on; nerves are cut, but still they feel. An unpopular cause has its own momentum. It bears down on you, blind and urgent as a train. Qualms are no longer permitted. We have set our faces the way we mean to go. There is no more room for nice distinctions, reservations, doubts, normal life.

Another story for my scrapbook. An old man went hunting rabbits with a ferret and was found buried days later, halfway up a collapsed rabbit hole.

Of course, saving them may kill us too.

☐   ☐   ☐

Lord Shaftesbury writes to say that the Act is better than nothing, and should be given a chance. Mr. Gladstone assures us, again, that his sympathies are with us—but will sign nothing.

Some we once called comrades have given in entirely. We burn their letters. Why waste our breath pleading for reform? We will settle for nothing now but abolition. Government is corrupt. Men of science are liars. We will address ourselves to the hearts of the public with a simple message. No living thing should be cut open to satisfy human curiosity.

I say "we," because I am as one with Fà in this.

I persuaded her to spend the afternoon in the garden, for the good of her health. The shrubs are dreadfully overgrown. She cuts the best flowers to send away to the friends we have left. I hold the basket and she wields the knife like a sabre.

This evening I looked at my plate and felt queasy. Now I begin to consider the claims of the animals afresh; it seems to me that vivisection is only the outermost skin of the onion. Whatever about the rest of Mr. Darwin's views, he has proved that we are closer to the lower kingdoms than we ever suspected. God has made us all of one stuff. And I wonder now why, if Fà and I will not fish for sport, on principle, we still dine on salmon. Why I sit here in boots made of calfskin, holding a tortoiseshell comb, on a cushion filled with down, on a horsehair stool.

These thoughts make me dizzy. I have not mentioned them to Fà; she would tell me I was getting hysterical.

But where does it end? We have fenced in the creatures of the world, made them depend on us like fearful children. We cannot seem to live without their labour, their milk, their skins. What would it mean to tear up this dreadful contract? How could we begin all over again?

☐   ☐   ☐

From Fà's window you can see the little churchyard where, in time, we will lie together. Our souls, I hope, will be in a better place. *They shall not hurt nor destroy in all my holy mountain, saith the Lord.*

Until then I will do nothing, say nothing to divide us. Fà always says she cannot abide a lie, but I think a little discretion is necessary if two lives are to lie alongside each other as quiet as cutlery in the drawer. So I will never let her suspect: my disloyalty to the cause, the weariness that comes over me as I gum down another envelope, the utter indifference with which I set it aside for the post. I will keep my treachery locked up in my heart.

I am making her a cat in alabaster for her fifty-fourth birthday.

Last spring Fà took a solemn vow never to go to bed at night leaving a stone unturned that might help to stop vivisection. My own oath is a more private one. To stand by her in this doomed cause, as in everything else. And with my last breath—because for all her girth and aches, she is sure to outlive me—I will urge her to keep up the good fight. Yes, that's the phrase she will want to hear. I will say it not because I believe, anymore, that she or anyone else can save the animals, but because she is most herself in battle. Like the Cavalier in the old poem: She could not love me, loved she not honour more.

The Rubbed-Away Girl

Mary Gaitskill

My sister Daphne is 42. I am 43. She is married with children, and she also works. I live with someone and I work. We don't visit each other very often and when we do, we are quiet. We don't say that much to each other, and what we do say seems incomplete or muted. I think mean things, and I think she feels my thoughts.

Daphne was once beautiful in the way of a common flower: It's easy to overlook, but once you notice it, it seems better than the fancy kind. I used to stare at her, thinking that no one could be more beautiful, even if they were models or movie stars. I think she felt those thoughts too. Once when we were both in high school, Daphne and I lay on the bed we shared, reading. The sun was so thick that the room seemed dry and viscous at the same time. I turned to Daphne to say something and saw that she had fallen asleep, her face on a folded, faded blue pillow, her lips opened, one knee bent up to her chest so that one hip stuck up. I took in the blue and mauve tones of her skin and lips, the glinting brown of her hair and dullness of her short, blunt eyelashes against her radiant cheek. Her beauty almost shocked me. Fascinated, I grazed her lower lip with my finger. She frowned an innocent sleep-frown and licked her lips, bumping my finger with her tongue. She almost smiled, then went more deeply into sleep.

But now she looks exhausted and brittle, as if she has collapsed inside, leaving her skin stranded with nothing to support it. Like mine, her face is lined; like mine, it sags. She seems weak and enervated, even though I know she's not. Sometimes I'm mad at her for losing her beauty and then I'm mad at myself. Daphne is dutiful and she's kind; she makes me feel selfish and ashamed, and yet determined to cling to my selfishness like it's the only way I'll survive. We never lie in bed together and read.

It seems strange to me now that we were, as teenagers, still sleeping in the same bed. It seemed natural to us because our mother shared the same bed with both her sisters well into their teens. The frame and headboard of the bed shared by Daphne and I had belonged first to our grandmother, then to our mother, and it exuded beneficent matriarchy. It was a massive and handsome stained oak piece painted at the center with a pastoral scene so faded it was barely discernible—the outline of a plump arm, the ghost of a wide-rimmed hat, a flying scarf, a rose bush, the fluttering frock of a rubbed-away girl on a rubbed-away swing shimmering through a nasty scrape in the varnish.

Daphne inherited the bed when she moved into her first apartment. She slept in it by herself and with a half-dozen boyfriends until she was thirty-five years old. That's when she got married. When that happened, she dismantled the bed and kept the head and foot boards in a basement storage room. It's possible that she's even thrown it away by now and that she didn't think to tell me. The last time I saw the pastoral scene, covered with dust in the basement, it was so faded that it looked like the wood had been defaced with some crude substance. It did not look like it had been specially painted with a wonderful scene to take little girls safely into sleep.

□   □   □

One of the first pictures ever taken of Daphne was taken with me, and it still sits on her dresser in a cunning plastic frame shaped and painted like a coiled cat. We are two and three, and I am grabbing Daphne with both arms while she flails and buries her head against me, resisting me and clinging to me at the same time. I am smiling in ignorant triumph. She looks blurred and stunned.

One of my first complete memories is of Daphne and I, at two and three, lying with our heads at opposite ends of the couch and our

feet pressed together, wildly pumping our legs, laughing and screaming "Two twos! Two twos!" until our mother ran in and said, "Stop
it! You'll make yourselves sick!"

As we grew older, we were constantly together, almost ignoring
our younger sister Margot. We played games that spanned the course
of days and sometimes weeks, for which we arrayed whole villages of
toys across our room so that we could enact ongoing stories. (We
didn't completely ignore Margot; we would occasionally put one of
her stuffed animals on trial, find it guilty of something and toss it out
the window while she screamed.) We could spend whole afternoons
sitting on the floor of our shared bedroom feverishly drawing characters and then telling their stories in crayon scenes, which we took
turns drawing. I remember us moving at a contemplative crouch
through the wild strawberry patch in back of the abandoned hot-
house next door, picking berries with a rhythm so deeply sympathetic it was as if the movements of one physically propelled the
other. I remember holding hands as we ran up an inconsequential
hill, drunk with the joy of our arms and legs and the fact that we
could move them. I remember playing a game that consisted of me
chasing her around the yard, whipping her with a supple branch
while she whinnied like a horse. I remember our tickle fights, which
I would always win, not because I was stronger, but because when
Daphne straddled and tickled me, I would scream so desperately that
she would just give up.

☐   ☐   ☐

With Daphne I felt an emotional fullness I have rarely felt as an
adult. I have never felt more intimate with a lover—and really, if you
stretch the term, Daphne and I were lovers. In the guise of "practicing" we, eleven and twelve, stripped naked under cover of night and
embraced beneath the maternal auspices of the phantom pastoral
romp, rubbing our little groins together until the bed springs
creaked. Because I had rudimentary breasts, I would always play the
woman—which was, for us, the position of honor. Daphne would lie

between my opened legs with her legs together and her hips thrust resolutely forward, chivalrously supporting herself on her elbows as she made love to me with a gentle rocking motion, every now and then pausing to ask uncertainly, "Is it in?" Afterward, we would kiss and she would touch my breasts with theatrical reverence while I turned my head in an expression of doomed abandon. We would giggle and joke, inevitably banging into the cheap air conditioner that jutted from the window next to the bed, heightening our fun with the thrill of being heard and caught.

Gradually these sessions fell off with the mutual goodwill or our former tickle fights and then stopped altogether.

☐   ☐   ☐

Then I started high school. All at once I had what our mother called my "problems." I had been a good student, and suddenly I almost flunked everything. My friendships disintegrated. I abruptly grew four inches and, with grim inexorability, added two more as the years progressed. The unexpected height—I was all at once taller than my mother—caused my narrow frame to droop strangely, my ribs and pelvic bones to protrude. I didn't have the grace to carry it. I was funny-looking. I stayed up all night crouched by the radio in the dark, writing poetry and reading fashion magazines. I would go to sleep in my clothes so I wouldn't have to spend time getting dressed in the morning. My mother took me for free therapy at a state-run clinic. That was okay with me, as it meant I skipped a couple of classes a week.

But Daphne lost respect for me. I didn't realize this until I published a poem titled "Lemons Under a Teakwood Tree" in the newsletter put out by the state-run clinic. I was proud of the poem, and I read it to everybody at dinner. Later that week, I dug Daphne's diary out of her underwear drawer and read it while eating from a bag of candy. I did this every now and then, and it didn't occur to me to feel bad about it. But I did feel bad when I read what she thought about my poem. She wrote that it was stupid and pathetic and it made her feel sorry for me. She wrote that I thought I was so great for having it printed in a mental hospital paper. I went into the closet and lay under a pile of clothes and cried so loud everybody in the house could hear me. She said it was my own fault for reading her diary, but I thought she knew I read her diary and that she'd written those things in there on purpose.

But sometimes we were friends again. Sometimes when one of us bathed, the other would come into the bathroom to keep the bather company, sitting on the closed toilet, playing the radio and talking. I remember one time in particular. I had read something by Henry Miller at the library which I had Xeroxed and brought home for Daphne. It was about a man having sex with a woman he didn't like who had, for some reason, come to visit him wearing nothing but a garter belt and stockings. She gave him a bath, and then he had sex with her while thinking about how horrible she was. When they were finished, he told her that he liked her cunt, that it was the best thing about her. The story he told scared us and bewildered us, so we were sarcastic about it. Daphne splashed and clowned as she made fun of Henry Miller. She stood and bent over like the woman in the story, except she exuberantly squatted and peeped from between her legs and made a funny face. The water ran in rivulets from her wet pubic hair, her smiling eyes were all for me, her sister who loved her, mean diary entry or no.

Who else has she ever done that with? I mean, in the bathtub, with a funny face, in the middle of a literary conversation? I wonder if she even remembers? And, if she does, how it makes her feel. I think she might feel embarrassed. I am not embarrassed exactly. I am uncomfortable because the memory engages my emotions more fully than I am used to. It makes me feel titillated in a way I can't categorize. It makes me feel queasy too. Because in some way it illustrates Daphne's frequent, tacit agreement to submit to me—an agreement which often entailed her mild contempt based on our secret knowledge that I was the weaker one. She, after all, let me win at tickle fighting because I couldn't stand to lose. She gave me the honor and drama of the woman's role, but she fucked me.

□　　　□　　　□

I flunked out of school when I was seventeen. My parents accepted my decision to drop out in a way that was both sweet in its toler-
ation and infuriating in its assumption of defeat. I lazed for a few
months then got a job at the concession stand of a small theater,
serving candy and popcorn and primary-colored drinks from droning dispensers. After work I would stuff candy bars in my purse and
go to meet my boyfriend Ed in the parking lot of the hardware store.
We would drive to the playground of a deserted elementary school
on the edge of town, the broken turn signal of Ed's old car flickering at hysterical hyper-speed at each turn. His friends would be
there, and we would smoke and drink together, seated gangling and
overgrown on the iron instruments of play, our shadows intermin-
gling with those of bars and spans of metal and chain, our car doors
open so that our tape decks could blare.

We didn't do anything on the playground but talk and drink and
smoke. Still, weird energy seeped through all our gestures: Slowly a
girl would comb her hand through her hair, then collapse the hand
palm-out against the side of her neck, woefully crumpling her fingers, then jerking the hand into her lap as if remembering something
shameful, then reaching for her can of beer, her ringed hand weakly
coruscating as she lifted it slowly so that she could bring her cigarette
to her lips before she drank, all the while talking and talking so
quickly, rocking herself, her ankles locked tautly together for lever-
age. And everybody would shift their hips, play with their hair, pull
at their lips, clap their hands, collapse in on themselves with giggling,
then suddenly flex erect, chest and pelvis thrust frontal. All movement was soft and mute in the gray tenderness of the street lamp
light, even when somebody chased somebody across the playground
and playfully slammed him on the asphalt. The music from our open
cars surged through us in gross currents and came out refined
through our small, special movements. It was as good as going out
to dance—better really, because we were too shy to dance.

I was especially friendly with a girl named Sheila, a small, royal creature with dark, sensuous circles under her flat, bitter eyes, narrow hips and tiny breasts. And I was fascinated by a girl named Denise and her boyfriend, Jeff. In our group, they were the best, and Denise was even taller and thinner than I. Her austere fleshlessness gave her round face, heavy-lidded eyes and frenetically shaped hair a chic grotesquerie. She slouched with her shoulders pulled down and back and her pelvis thrust forward, her stance authoritative, yet also sad and humane. As if you could show her your baseline gracelessness, your embarrassing noises and odors, and not only would she understand, she would admit you into the aura of her fleshless glamour. Her boyfriend Jeff was also slim and slouching, with an affable, pouchy face and sweet little lips that he pursed and nervously bit. He wore long sweaters in shapes of relaxation, and suede loafers with tiny chains spanning the arches, which we saw as indicating his special tastes.

I remember them partly because of their glamour and partly because of an incident that stuck them in my mind as examples of a certain sort of horribleness that no one, apparently, was exempt from.

One weekend one of Jeff's friend's parents left town, and he gave Jeff a key to the house so that he and Denise could have sex in his bedroom. Unfortunately, on the second night, a vigilant neighbor who suspected a break-in called the police who then surprised Jeff and Denise. The cops cuffed the naked kids and then stood there and laughed at Denise's body. They even called the back-up cops in the car outside to come in and laugh. After they stopped laughing, they questioned the couple, every now and then pausing to snicker at Denise's chest. Apparently they believed their story because they just took the house keys and released them without telling their parents.

All their skinny glamour laughed at! How bewildering it must've been—or maybe not. Maybe it was what they expected, even agreed with, in the secret part of them that pulled their shoulders forward and down.

But if their slouching shoulders expected to be humiliated, Denise's stubborn pelvis thrust up against it in defiance, and her defiance was strong enough to carry Jeff. They were back on the playground the next night, where they perched on the teeter-totter and made jokes about handcuffs. Everybody was very delicate about it.

But when Ed and I left the playground and drove to a quiet place to have sex, I brought Jeff and Denise and Sheila with me. I didn't exactly think about them, it was more that I felt them, especially when Ed and I made love. It wasn't like a sexual fantasy—I didn't want to have sex with them, at least not all of them. But their imaginary presence in the warm car made me feel safe and ardent in a way that Ed by himself did not. The feel of them made me feel more loved and loving, in a way I would not ever put in words.

I would get home at around four, crawling into the big bed I shared with Daphne, inhaling her warmth as I lifted the light summer blanket, firmly planting my back against hers, letting the breath of her deep body take me into sleep.

I'd wake alone in the afternoon. The days were a grand torpor of late breakfast and long phone calls to Ed. When the family sat down to the dinner table at night, my father would point to the side of the table where Daphne and Margot sat and he would say, "These girls want to be part of this family. They want to contribute something." Then he would point at me and say, "You aren't contributing anything." Daphne and Margot would lower their heads. I would scowl.

I began to resent Daphne. It was unfair and I knew it, and my knowledge made me ashamed, which made me resent her more. I was keeping my own diary during this time, and it is, among other things, a record of my peevish, furious resentment. In it, I described the time Daphne and I took a drive to the mall and, on the way, took some of our father's mail to the post office, which he had asked us to do. He'd specifically asked us to take the mail inside the post office instead of using the drive-by mail box on the curb, because he'd read that pranksters sometimes poured glue or pitch or even more ruinous substances into mailboxes. We made fun of his fears on the way to the post office, but when we got there, Daphne insisted that we park and take the letters into the post office instead of disobediently dropping them into the drive-by box.

"But he won't know!" I protested.

"But if he did, he'd be upset," Daphne answered.

I maintained an annoyed silence all the way to the mall, and in my diary I spent a page heaping violent sarcasm on Daphne's obeisance.

Another time Daphne thought to buy a stuffed animal for the birthday of a sad, fatherless little girl we both baby-sat for, and I criticized her in my journal as a do-gooder. To her face I said, "You're nice like a TV person." She flinched so imperceptibly only I could've seen it. Then she assumed the same expression she wore when my mother came upstairs and asked her to "act as a buffer" between her and our father—which meant that she wanted Daphne to amuse and soothe our father and so keep him from picking a fight with our mother.

At the end of the summer I quit my job at the theater and took one at a small packaging plant. It was slow-paced assembly-line work, mostly putting products inside boxes as they ground by on a conveyor belt. It paid well, and after about seven months I moved out of my parents' house and into an apartment with Sheila. My immediate memories of that short-lived time are: lifting my feet to wash them in the bathroom sink because the tub was backed up. Sitting on our tiny fire escape with Sheila, tipping our chairs back luxuriantly as we ate tins of frozen cheesecake for dinner. The burst of purple lilac in the yard below. Getting up at 7:00 in the morning to eat cold cereal with Sheila before we went to work. The dirt on Sheila's bare heels as she paced the kitchen waiting for the coffee to be done. At night, the people from the playground would come to the apartment, and what had been so mute and tender in the lamplight became startling and loud. People yelled at each other. The music was a blunt instrument. Denise sat regally spread-legged on the edge of the couch, a ring mistress of loudness, cutting lines of coke with martial precision, her fingers rigorous and expert. Ed suddenly got mad about something Jeff said; Denise screamed and Ed punched Jeff in the face. He fell with one pointy little foot twisted under one skinny calf. Denise stood up so fast she knocked the table over, she and I fell on Ed and we lurched sideways, Ed numbly groping the air. A boy from Pittsburgh pulled Jeff to his feet, knocked over

Sheila's goldfish bowl, stumbled back and ground a little dancing
fish into the floor. Sheila moved around the room, agitated and chat-
tering, her bitter eyes sparking deep inside as she yelled, "No! No!
That's not cool! That's not cool!" The body of the little fish, mashed
except for its poor staring head, was still there the next day when we
got up for our cereal.

□   □   □

I visited my family once a week. I would sit with my parents and
watch TV as Margot passed through the room like a ghost and
Daphne did her homework at the dining-room table. My mother
would laugh and comment on the television characters, and my
father would go along with her comments halfway, like he thought
it was stupid to be talking about TV people but that at least she was
making the effort to talk. When Daphne went up to her room, I
would go with her and we would lie across the bed and talk. She had
decided that she wanted to go to college and become a therapist. She
was getting A's in school. She was volunteering at an old person's
home, although she quit when one of the old people bit her. She
carefully filed her nails and shaped the cuticles. She used pale-pink
fingernail polish that was almost transparent. She would apply it with
intense concentration and care, like it was one of the things keeping
her on the path to college and therapist school. She would apply her
polish and listen to me talk about Denise and cocaine and Ed and
Sheila and Jeff getting punched and the crushed goldfish. I think she
liked to hear me talk about those things. I was doing something
messy, and she was doing something neat. It made sense, like when
I was three and she was two; I was the one to grab her and she was
the one to flail. Like I was the one to chase her around the yard with
a little branch and she would run and whinny, even though she knew
she didn't have to run from me at all. I didn't have to tell her things
I knew she would find ugly and stupid, but I did. I even made them
sound more that way than they were.

The summer came. It was so hot in the apartment that Ed and I brought the couch cushions out on the fire escape and slept on them under a sheet. We woke with the sun warming our eyeballs through their lids, the inside of our mouths sore and sweet with residual alcohol. By the time the summer ended Ed and I lost interest in each other. I took a GED high-school equivalency exam, sold my car, and moved back into my parents' house. My father walked around alternately scolding me for dropping out of high school and praising me for taking the GED. Then they just accepted me. I enrolled in the local community college. Daphne, who had graduated high school, enrolled too.

Since there was only one car in the household, our father drove us to the college on his way to work. We would walk across the parking lot to the campus, close together, our steps small but intent, our movement forward but also inward, as if we were walking deeper and deeper into ourselves. At the end of the day our father would pick us up in the parking lot and take us home, usually stopping at the A&P for groceries. We would tell him about our classes and teachers. We could tell he was very proud and pleased that we were both in college, and secretly, I was glad to have given him that pleasure. When we arrived home it was often with a sense of unity and satisfaction that felt so good we sometimes went nuts and ran around the house imitating chimpanzees shrieking and pretending to scratch our heads and armpits. Our father started it. Part of the fun was that he would just start doing it and then just as suddenly stop. "Well, I feel better now!" he would exclaim. Then he'd go get a beer. It was as if to say that, under the daily things that got us through the world in one piece—school, work, grocery shopping—we were sweet, friendly animals that wouldn't hurt each other.

Except that we did hurt each other. College scared me at first. I flunked science; even remedial writing class was hard for me. Daphne took advanced classes and got all A's. I told Daphne I hated her and that if she became "more successful" than I did I would kill her. When I said this, her expression left her face so swiftly it was almost as if she had disappeared. She left the room.

We had a reconciliation that was partial and tense. She said, "Well, if you want to feel like a success, you're doing the right thing by going to college. Because you're smart, and eventually your teachers will know it." Her expression as she said this was careful; I had, after all, not taken back my threat on her life.

She was right; after the first semester I started to get A's too. I went to a big university sooner than she did. But I don't know if either of us "became successful." The idea of it makes me sick. I threatened to kill my sister for it. I didn't mean it literally, but I did mean it some way. I thought there was something she might take from me, like there was only one thing and if she got it, I couldn't have anything. It was the thing in the photograph from when we were two and three; I'm hugging her, there's love in it, but I'm also saying, This is mine. She's letting me say it, but only because she is little and she doesn't feel like she has a choice.

But then there's the time we put the bottoms of our feet together and screamed, "Two twos!" Or ran up the hill together or picked the strawberries. Then we didn't have to fight over anything; there was an endless supply, and the more she got, the more I had. We could roll it back and forth between us. When we were older, and we lay on the bed and read together, we weren't rolling it back and forth anymore, we were planting ourselves deep inside it and drawing it up into us. The more the one got, the more the other had.

I know that feeling is still there in us, that inside we both remember it. But it's at the inside of a labyrinth with too many hallways, too many complicated turns. At that inside place, music is playing. We can hear it through the walls, but we can't quite make it out. Maybe that's why, when we're together, we're quiet and don't say much. We're listening, carefully.

Excerpt from When Fox Is a Thousand

Larissa Lai

"When a fox is fifty years old, it acquires the ability to change itself into a woman. At a hundred it can assume the shape of a beautiful girl, or that of a sorcerer...At that age the fox knows what is happening at a distance of a thousand miles, it can derange the human mind and reduce a person to an imbecile. When the fox is a thousand years old, it is in communication with heaven, and is then called Heavenly Fox, t'ien-hu."

—Hsuan-Chung-Chi

I'm going to tell you the first story of my birthdays. Moon calendar birthdays. Soon I will reach my thousandth. A thousand years is a long time for a fox to live, especially now in the age of science, when it is common knowledge that canine life spans average less than twenty European-style years. It has been a long wait and bus-stop boring, especially for someone as restless as me. The worst part was the first fifty years, trapped in an aging dog's body. My hair started dropping out in clumps when I was about twenty-eight. Even the most feeble rabbits managed to escape my dull teeth. I ate mushrooms and moss and grew as thin as a Taoist ascetic and bald as a human baby.

My fiftieth birthday arrived in the cold dark, just when, hairless and blind, I thought I couldn't hold on any longer. My birthday enfolded me in human arms and granted me the first of my transformative powers, the ability to change into a woman. But I was given no choice as to what kind of woman. I was given a body discarded by an older fox who had just passed her hundredth year. There was nothing wrong with her, really. She was as young as the smell of fresh rain and newly tilled soil, but had the face of a poisonous mushroom: red with white spots and spongy. Her hair roped like the matted old man's beard that hung high and green in the leafless branches of swamp trees. Someone said to me later that there is nothing more beautiful than the modesty of the plain, but I think I had to live it first. In the meantime my sensibilities were driven by the same conceptions of beauty as everyone else's. And there would be no bargaining for chickens in the day market with a face like this.

At first, I refused to approach her. I spent much more time in my rickety canine body, so repulsed was I at the thought of becoming her. After a while, I discovered I could animate other corpses, not for long periods of time and seldom on more than one occasion. But in a more handsome body I could cause more trouble in a shorter period of time, so it was worth it. After a few winters had passed, however, my affection for her grew, the way the flavour of wood and sweet voices grows in young wine after it has been sitting in the barrel through the passage of several seasons. I discovered that she had a great capacity for mischief, or, rather, my own was greatly increased with her as my disguise. Howling like an attic ghost, we frightened rich families from their meals, and I ate better than I had in forty years.

My fur grew back, red and thick as butter, and my eyes glittered again like resurrected stars. She put on weight, although she never appeared much healthier.

☐   ☐   ☐

A blood-hot day in summer. The air is liquid and hard to breathe, and I am filled with a restless frustration that burns along my spine. Whether I take animal or human form, the mosquitoes hover about me, a host of lesser angels. Each one lights a small fire on my skin that itches like hot peppers. I think of each spot swelling as big as a second head and bursting with pus and infection. I think of scratching the itch right down to the bone. I bite furiously at a particularly aggravating one at the base of my tail, biting harder and harder, trying to push pain into clouding over the all-consuming itch. What finally distracts me from the itch is an idea. Turning it over in my head like meat on a slow barbeque, I sleep off the hottest part of the afternoon.

The sun begins to drown in the liquid air, and the evening becomes cool enough to move through. I walk into the closest village, my unwashed hair smelling of complicated nightmares, and my red face puffy. My feet are bare and muddy, and my clothes hang loose like scar tissue. I haven't yet found a place to steal new ones that will fit.

The first house on the edge of the village is a mansion surrounded by a high white wall. Beyond is a garden full of trees that can talk and flowers that smell of honey and spices. I speak to a man who guards the gate. He is small inside a clean but baggy uniform.

"I would like to speak to the lady of the house."

"She's too busy to speak to you."

"Then tell her that an old lady has a gift for her." The man calls through the gate and another man peeks through an eyehole. There is the whispering of leaves. The gate opens. The second man leads me through the garden and the trees chat noisily. He doesn't answer them, and I don't want him to think I'm crazy, so I don't either.

The mistress of the house is sitting in the courtyard drinking tea and eating pastries.

"A few scraps for an old lady?"

"You lied about why you wanted to come in. Go away before my husband catches you and gives you a good beating."

The second house on the edge of the village sits on a small plot of land. A few meatless-looking chickens scattered about the yard peck disconsolately at the limp earth, as likely to get a gullet full of mud as of worms. For a moment, my mouth waters, more at the incredible good fortune of such an easy theft than at the kind of meal these birds would make. I coil my body, ready to spring, and then uncoil again, finding myself constrained by my own human limbs. I look at my hands, the well-articulated if warty fingers. The chickens will have to wait. I refocus my eyes and notice a woman has been sweeping the walkway for quite some time. She is thin and her arms are knotted. She might still be young, but there are thick streaks of gray in her hair, sprouting wiry, a warning from the gods. Her face is pale, and her eyes are flooded with muddy tiredness, like a river delta after too much rain. She sweeps in brisk, sharp strokes.

"A few leftovers for an old woman?" I am careful not to come too close, in case she notices how ugly I really am.

"Please," she says, rushing to the broken wood gate to let me in. She takes me by the arm, oblivious to the smells of the forest in my hair.

It is no warmer inside the house than outside, but she loads the stove generously with wood from an almost-empty wood box. From a large basin she fills a kettle with water and sets it on top of the stove. She waves me over to a warm spot and disappears back out into the yard. I gather my bones into the warmth, allowing my body to sink into it. From outside, where the mountains have swallowed the bleeding sun, there is the sound of chickens babbling terrified nonsense, then a sudden silence. She comes back in, holding a lantern that floods the room with warm yellow light in one hand, and the limp body of a chicken in the other. It seems even scrawnier than when it was alive. She sets the lantern on the table. In the yellow light, feathers rise in a cloud around her hands and scatter at her feet like dirty snow. Her fingers move in a rapid, even motion, as though she were playing some strange instrument from a place far away. I dissolve into the music, let the open windows fly away.

The presence of a third party jolts me back. It is a tall woman, perhaps three or four years older than my host. Her hair is long, and black as the thick darkness gathering right up to the ledge of the windows. Her skin is smooth and translucent as a veil, but her eyes are lightless. I think I know her from somewhere, but I have never met a blind person before, so I dismiss the inkling.

"Your sister?"

"My late husband's concubine. She's blind."

"Yes."

"They say the blind have voices like angels."

"Is it true?"

"She sings like a peach tree in full bloom."

"How could your husband afford a concubine?"

"He couldn't. I stole my dowry back and bought her myself."

She smiles as she sinks the featherless chicken into the kettle of boiling water. As the chicken cooks, the blind woman opens her mouth and a lilting tune like a cascade of ripe fruit pours out.

Although there are no spices in the chicken and rice she serves me, the intricate flavours of the blind woman's song makes these dishes suitable for much less humble immortals than myself. We eat quietly until the dishes are half empty.

"We don't get many visitors here," says my host.

"You have been very generous."

"I suppose you don't live in the village."

"Not exactly."

"Then you don't know what they say about us there." The blind woman kicks her under the table, accurately, by the look of things. "They say we murdered our husband."

"Did you?" I remember once coming across a man's body in the dump, the head hanging at an absurd angle. Not being human, I wasn't very much disturbed by him and continued scavenging.

"What do you think?"

"Don't listen to her," says the blind woman. "She's so excited that we have a guest that she doesn't know what she's saying. Sometimes she gets a little silly after dark. She's a great believer in ghosts. Go to bed, love, I'll clean up."

"I'm not silly! That's what they say. Go into the village and ask around if you don't believe me."

"Just ignore her," whispers the blind woman, and I could swear she's winking at me. "Won't you spend the night? I'll make a place for you by the stove."

The younger woman goes to bed. I watch the singer moving about the room, with the fluidity of intuition that no sighted person could match. She rummages through a chest for blankets, and as she begins the work of making a bed, I know why she seemed familiar. She is a well-practiced housewife. I want to ask her how she became blind, but don't dare.

"You married again," I said.

She raised an eyebrow. "Beg your pardon?"

Of course she wouldn't recognize me in my pimply body. "Weren't you once married to a man named Tam?"

"No." Too sharp to be true. "Never."

But she doesn't have to tell me.

I let her finish making a bed for me. Filled with chicken, rice, and music, there is a warm lethargy curdling in my bone marrow. Sleep caresses my tired back for perhaps an hour or two, until I am awakened by the sound of two women breathing in unison. I smile to think of them curled together on the narrow bed in the other room. When they are finally quiet and their breathing evens to the pace of sleep, I slip under the door of the bedroom like a gas. They are a tangle of limbs, still moist with sweat.

I look at them as little as possible, to respect their privacy, as I approach the basin of water in which they have washed. It smells of sweat, wood, cut grass, smoke, chicken feathers, and roses. I blow on it once and a gold sheen ripples across the surface suggesting seashell-pink, blood-crimson, midnight-blue, peacock-green, and then evens out again. I blow again and the water becomes viscous, pure gold but with the sticky, globby consistency of crude oil. I blow again and the basin is filled with small gold coins. Pleased, I revert to my four-legged self and leap out the window.

Artemis could hear the music booming before she even turned the key in the lock of the little bachelor suite where she had lived by herself for the last two years. With the music making its own company inside the apartment while she stood alone outside, she felt more than ever as though she didn't really live here. It was a problem she never could describe to anyone. How her own home never felt like hers. She was here almost every night now, as her nocturnal visits with Eden became less and less appealing. She would come in the front door and wonder how to make it suit her better. It wasn't so plain as to be impersonal. There was lots of light in the main room, which did triple duty as a place to eat, sleep, and live. It was dominated by a double futon that folded into a couch during the day. Over it lay a piece of Indian fabric in green and white. There were posters on the walls of bands that she listened but had no particular attachment to. Cotton dhurrie rugs in blues and greens were scattered across the worn hardwood floors. But none of these things grew on her. She had them merely because she did not know what else to put there. The only thing about the place that appealed to her was the assortment of objects scattered across her windowsill, largely the products of her secret heists, containers and fragments of things: the fake box of the True Cross; the little ivory statuette she had bought the same day; a human shinbone; pictures of an Asian family she had bought at a garage sale, having no idea who any of them were; a small glass case with four brown, crumbling butterflies pinned to a green background she had lifted when the biology department was moving into new premises; a little pewter pillbox she had found one dawn with Eden in the ashes of a burnt house.

It was odd to come back to hear the place come alive without her. The moment she opened the door, the smell of hot oil wafted out. In retrospect, she realized she should have been more worried. It could have been any stranger in her house. Soul II Soul was on full blast, and someone was frying shrimp chips in the kitchen. Artemis dropped her knapsack and peered around the corner. Oblivious to her arrival, Diane was dancing and singing along with the tape as she dexterously wielded a pair of long chopsticks, moving from the pot of hot oil to the plate on which she was building a mound of large, pink, wavy chips layered with wads of paper towel to soak up the grease.

"How did you get in here?"

Diane danced over waving a fresh chip between her chopsticks and lowering it playfully to Artemis' mouth. "Climbed up the trellis and came through the window. You should really get locks for them, you know."

"You climbed up the trellis?"

"Those darn rose thorns got me pretty bad, but other than that it was easy." She was clearly pleased with her own daring.

Artemis was delighted in spite of herself. "You're so crazy." She slumped down at the kitchen table. Diane got a bowl, pushed some chips into it and set it down in front of her.

"Eden ever give you any of those pictures?"

"Yeah, last week. There's some for you too. I told him I'd pass them on." She got up and fished them out from a desk drawer, and put them on the table. "Watch out if your hands are greasy."

"I just want to look. Oh god, how goofy."

"It was kind of a goofy idea."

"I look like I'm in some kind of drag," said Diane. She leaned over an image of the two of them sitting back to back smoking long white cigarettes like truant schoolgirls. "Do you know where he got those costumes?"

"From his father."

"Does he have a lot of them?"

"I don't know. He says his father stashed a lot of stuff." Artemis could not have said later why she didn't tell Diane about Eden's recent gift.

"Bet they're worth a lot of money."

Artemis noticed something flare in the kitchen behind Diane. "The oil!"

Unattended, with the blue gas flame still raging beneath it, the oil Diane was using for deep frying had caught fire. The room filled with smoke. Diane rushed over to rescue it, jerking the pot off the stove. The burning liquid moved up in a long, slow arc, slapping across her face. She dropped the pot automatically, her hand flying up to meet the burn. The pot fell over her, its contents splashing over her arm and chest and stomach. As she backed away from the stove, she slipped and fell to the floor. From the living room the music continued without missing a beat.

Artemis was at the sink. With cupped hands, she splashed water over her friend.

"You're supposed to use cream or cold oil." Diane's voice came out a raspy whisper.

"I've never heard that before." Artemis continued to throw water over the human heap on the floor until a pool of cold oil and water spread around Diane on the cracked tile. "I'll get you a towel. Do you think you need an ambulance?"

"No, it's not that serious." Diane rose slowly, wincing where burnt skin caught against the cabinets. She took the towel and dried herself slowly. "I should be going."

"You can't be serious. You should see yourself."

Diane ambled over to the hallway mirror. She examined the long red mark down the side of her face. She pulled the wet sleeve of her T-shirt away from her arm, surveying the streak's path down her shoulder. Water dripped from her hair and her clothes onto the floor. Artemis shut off the tape deck.

The only clean clothes Artemis could find were a pair of jeans she could no longer squeeze into and a never-worn T-shirt her parents had brought back from a tour of China the previous year. They had offered to take her, but she had courteously refused, saying the trip did not interest her. They brought the T-shirt back anyway, with two stone dragons facing each other on the front, and the name of the tour company on the back. She pressed them into Diane's hands and went into the kitchen to clean up and leave Diane her privacy.

In the narrow kitchen, she mopped the wet, oily mess off the floor and dumped the pot into the sink. She scraped the plate of soggy chips into the garbage. Then she poured glasses of 7UP, took the undamaged bowl from the table, and, balancing carefully, juggled all this into the front room. The TV was on at a low volume. Diane sat cross-legged on the futon, wearing the clean, dry clothes, and swaddled in the depths of the quilt Artemis' birth mother had left for her.

"Where did you find that?"

"On the shelf in the closet up there. Is it okay?"

Artemis had completely forgotten she had stored the thing in her place at all. Her adoptive mother had made her take it when she moved out, although mercifully allowing her to store the chest and padded jackets in the house. The smell of mothballs wafted around the room. It bothered her. It called up myriad things she had no name for, and didn't particularly want to know about. But she couldn't think of a way to say so to Diane so she just nodded her head. "Of course."

On the television, a young Vietnamese girl wearing a transparent pink plastic raincoat roller-skated around a steaming bathtub in the middle of a large warehouse.

"Don't you ever wonder who your real parents were?" Diane asked.

"No. I don't."

"Not at all?"

"I guess I've never really thought about it. I never knew them. They didn't want me. So what's to wonder?"

"Don't you wonder about where you came from, who your...people were?"

"I know who my people are. My mother and father, Eden, you, my friend Mercy, I suppose, even if she drives me crazy sometimes."

"I mean the people who know your history. The people who will care about you even if they don't know you."

"I don't know. I really don't think about it. Look, here's some 7UP. And these chips managed to escape the fracas." She paused. "Things move and change a lot from generation to generation. I am no less who I am for where I've ended up."

"I just don't understand how you can't be curious."

In a different scene, wearing a white vinyl coat with huge buttons and high black boots, the TV character walked into a record store. She carried a portfolio under her arm. She wandered down the middle aisle of the store, into the jazz section. Glancing furtively around to see that no one was looking, she slipped a record into the portfolio's secret sleeve. Some honey-rich voice trapped flat against black vinyl. As she moved toward the door, the clerk asked to see her port-folio. He drew back the cover, revealing photographs of the girl, stark naked, gazing precociously into the camera as her black hair swirled about her. He turned through several similar images until, red-faced, he could look no more, and then handed it back to her, even though he was sure he had seen her slip a record somewhere between the heavy leather covers.

In 1258 I fell in love with the Chinese princess who was sent as a tribute to the Prince of Persia. She let me touch her foot. I held it in my hand, fragile inside a tiny embroidered shoe shorter than the length of my palm. The secretive shoe was enough to make me pack my bags and pursue her across the reaches of the new Mongol Empire. She was interested in me, but not half as interested as she was in being tragic.

When it was cold in the mountains, I blew warm breath into her hands. When it was hot in the desert, I blew cool air into her ears. We passed a carving of Buddha as big as a whole village. We passed dark caves where thousands of sutras were hidden. We were almost accosted by bandits except that I smelled the sweat of the thrill before attack on the wind and rushed the whole retinue into hiding. After two years and the deaths of seven horses, we arrived at Jamal al-Din's marvelous astronomical observatory at Maragha, perhaps six months from our destination. There were astronomers there from all over the empire: Some with strange pale faces and light hair; some with the bulky bodies and thick beards of the northern tribes; some clearly from the south, who were so small that beside them the little princess became a towering giantess. One of these small men sat down with us and late into the night explained the mathematics of the Cowherd and the Weaver. Everyone nodded off except me, being a nocturnal type myself, and very much interested in the mechanics of the stars.

The princess had long since become bored of our simple cama-
raderie. She talked passionately of her plan to run away. She would
not meet this prince, never mind how much shame it might bring
upon her father. The following evening she climbed the highest wall
of the observatory and jumped. To her surprise and consternation, a
young star watcher below caught her. He thought a goddess had
descended from the heavens. She had fainted dead away and thus
could not inform him otherwise. When she came to perhaps an hour
later, he was sorely disappointed to learn that he had caught not a
goddess but a mere princess in his arms. In embarrassment, we cut
our visit short and began the last stretch of our journey the following day.

She decided she would settle for the melancholy life of a captive
in a foreign land. It wasn't as good as dying, as it required consider-
ably more patience. But when we arrived in the Persian capital almost
a full three years after our departure from Khanbalik, the prince himself had passed away. His son was a practical man, more interested in
silk, gunpowder, and paper than he was in women. The gift of a
Chinese princess was refused. She was to embark for home as soon
as fresh horses could be found.

He told her about his evenings as if they were something magical,
a journey into a forbidden country. It started after a man called
Angel hanged himself. Eden had seen him just two nights before
with his boyfriend. After Angel died, Eden started cruising the strip
on Homer Street where young men sold themselves. He would go
and talk to them, and sometimes they would sit with him in his car
and touch him, and not even charge, so Eden said, because he was
young and handsome just like them.

She saw them sometimes in the early evening before the sun went
down, if she was walking up from downtown to cross the Granville
Street Bridge. There was one who was there all the time. He was tall

and lanky with a lean face and glazed eyes that scanned the street restlessly up and down. Intent on his work, he did not see her at all as she marched past, stealing surreptitious glances.

She believed that Eden could make the night into something she herself could not. A place of magic and illicit secrets that revealed themselves only to him. It created a well of longing in her she could not understand, nor make an object of, the way he seemed able to. But the seams in the illusion they had built for themselves were beginning to give.

"Come to the bar with me tonight."

"But it's men's night."

"We'll fix you up. Come on. It'll be fun to see if we can get away with it."

They cut a sheet into strips and flattened her small breasts against her chest. He slicked her hair back and tucked it under a skull cap. Loose jeans, a baggy T-shirt, and men's shoes her size he had picked up at some fancy vintage clothing store.

"Well, you don't look too sexy, but you do look like a boy," he said.

"They're going to be able to tell if they just look at my arms," she protested, holding out a skinny wrist, fist clenched.

"Lots of Oriental boys are very slender. They won't bat an eyelash."

She looked uncertain.

"Bet you anything some rice queen tries to pick you up!"

The doorman gave her a slow once-over that made her cheeks flush. He nodded at her, and she had the distinct feeling he knew but had decided not to say anything. The bar was packed and redolent with the animal smell of men. They towered above her. She never felt tall walking down the street, but here she felt like a dwarf in the land of giants. There was not the mediating presence of women to make a gradation between them and her.

They pushed their way to a table at the back where Eden had some friends. Tom, who had come to her place with Eden for drinks once, recognized her and winked. She winked back. Eden pushed her a bottle of beer and someone offered her a cigarette, which she was about to take when Eden leaned over and whispered. "Don't. Your hands will give you away." It was true. She looked at them and marvelled at their smallness, like a child's. She had never really thought them extraordinary before, but now, looking at her companions' large hands as they drank and smoked and gesticulated, her own seemed wonderful and strange.

Eden pulled her onto the dance floor, and some of the other guys from the table came too. Under the pulsing lights she melted into the music, closed her eyes, imagined her body as boyish as she could and hoped her hips wouldn't give her away. When she opened her eyes there was a man staring right into them. She stared back crossly, but instead of being embarrassed the man just smiled and continued to stare.

"Someone better teach you how to cruise fags properly," yelled Tom above the music, "or you're going to find yourself in trouble."

"Yeah, no shit. So what do I do?"

"Well, that guy is going to be over here any second now. I'm sure you'll think of something."

"Tom, come on. This isn't funny."

"You don't think so?"

She couldn't read his eyes. Was he amused, or was he angry that she had invaded a territory not meant for her and wanted to see her get her comeuppance? She looked around for Eden, but he had gone off a song-and-a-half earlier with a man who looked like Rutger Hauer. The man with the stare was maneuvering slowly through the crowd toward her, inching, sussing out the situation. She glanced nervously at him from moment to moment, wanting to know where he was, where she could run to.

"Don't keep looking," said Tom. "He'll think you're interested."

The man crossed the path of an old friend, who grabbed him playfully from behind, and they danced together the way old pals do, hamming heat and passion with a kind of affection that has long since moved beyond those things. Not that they didn't look for action elsewhere. In the meantime, Eden resurfaced.

"Can we go now?" Artemis asked.

"She's chickening out," said Tom.

"Were you giving her a hard time?" Eden asked him, getting protective.

"Of course not, Daddio."

They moved on to a bar that had once been gay, but had slowly been infringed upon by heterosexuals until gay people stopped going there, at least for the most part. The man who looked like Rutger Hauer came with them. In the back seat of the car, modestly concealing her activity beneath her coat, she unbound her breasts and shook her hair loose.

It was hard to find a table, but after several turns around the bar, they finally found a spot at the counter overlooking the dance floor. A waitress came by and Eden bought a round of beer. As he pushed a pint down the table to his new friend, there was a look in his eyes that made Artemis disappear entirely from the room so that she was shocked by her own absence. A look of longing. A look of conspiracy. Caught up in her own sudden invisibility, Artemis did not feel the gaze of the woman dancing on top of one of the four pillars that delineated the dance floor. If she had cared to look she might have seen a well-muscled stomach undulating smooth as water beneath a little T-shirt cut off at the midriff, and small dark eyes watching her every move. Small nose twitching.

Someone else was watching too from across the dance floor—a young man with dyed black hair offsetting his pale face. She looked back with ease because it was so much less complicated than the man who had thought she was a man. She only half welcomed it. The unnatural darkness of his hair, while appealingly glamorous, concealed its true colour, and she thought of it more as a lie than as a secret. As he approached her, a kind of relief flooded her veins.

"Dance?" A single word tossed up in the smoky air.

She laughed because no one did that anymore at this bar, asking you to dance. If you wanted to dance you just got up and did it. She was not sure if he knew this and was flying rebelliously in the face of the not-so-new convention, or if he was a recent arrival from the suburbs who was still living light years behind. There wasn't any point sitting here with Eden and old Rutger, she thought, so she followed him to a place under the black lights.

At two o'clock, when the lights went up just as surely as Cinderella's coach turned into a pumpkin, he handed her a matchbook with his name and phone number on it. "Call me for coffee?" Under the strident yellow lights, his skin looked sallow. His eyes were red and the dark hair greasy.

☐   ☐   ☐

Diane called several days later. A week had passed since the burning incident.

"It's all peeling. Looks disgusting."

"Will you come see me?"

"Doctor says to stay home and rest. He thinks the accident was the result of some nervous disorder."

"That's ridiculous."

"That's what he says."

☐   ☐   ☐

She didn't call the matchbook man until a week later. She and Eden had made plans for dinner, and she called at the appointed time, but Eden wasn't there. He had been doing that a lot lately, making dates with her and then standing her up. Exasperated and restless, she dialed the number on the matchbook.

He lived in the basement of his mother's house. He was waiting at the door when she arrived.

"Don't mind the posters and stuff. My mom's into some hippy feminist shit. She thinks she's cool, but she's kind of crazy." There was a poster for the Vancouver Folk Music Festival and a number for demonstrations and conferences on the walls. In the kitchen was a calendar with bright full-colour photographs of bare-breasted brown-skinned women with an explanation in tiny letters underneath saying what they were doing and where this activity fit in the cycle of their lives. She followed him down the stairs beside the fridge.

"I used to live on my own, but a poor person can't support himself out there these days, you know. Only the capitalist pig-dogs."

"Yeah, I know," she said.

"My mom's all right. She's a little crazy, but she doesn't hurt anybody."

The basement was sparsely decorated and cold. There were two guitars on stands in a prominent place against the front window. There were posters on the walls of bands like the Gang of Four, The Clash, Art Bergman. The futon lay open and unmade. There was nowhere else to sit, so she sat there.

"You want a beer?" He had a little bar fridge containing nothing but. He handed her one and then came and sat next to her, put his hand on her breast and tried to kiss her ear.

"Hey, not so fast."

"Isn't this what you've come here for?"

"No, I don't know. Not like this."

"Like how, then?"

"I don't know. I thought we could talk, maybe."

"What do you want to talk about?"

Later she couldn't have said why she felt compelled to tell him things she had never spoken of before. But they tumbled from her lips as if of their own accord: the unexplainable airless nights on Eden's bed; her fascination with his disappearances; the feeling that she was being watched but never seeing by whom or from where; the whole mess with Diane, the burning, the old quilt with its thick odour of mothballs; the single, never-again-mentioned kiss; and how Diane was beginning to drift away. And then the man in the men's bar and not understanding what had driven her to go there in the first place, except that it was more than a vicarious curiosity about Eden's life.

"You ever sleep with a woman?"

"No. Why?"

"Maybe you should try it." He leaned toward her and kissed her mouth. His breath was thick. His hands were cold and clumsy. Only his dark hair was reassuring, but when he undressed his pubes and armpit hair were a brilliant and alien golden-red that glinted in the pale beam of the streetlight coming through the squat window.

She left him without waiting for morning to come. Truth in the dark was one thing; under the scrutiny of the sun it was something else again. She didn't want to wake and gaze down the length of their bodies, to observe her own blue, bony limbs flush against his sallow ones with their fine coat of red down. She did not want to breathe in the stale smell of the night's contact or feel the sweat of his sleep running between her breasts. She returned to her own apartment, where the ghost of Diane lingered, even though almost three weeks had passed since the burning accident.

I have big feet. In this century, I'm glad to have them. It makes it a lot easier to balance in these heels I've got, shiny red leather dreamt into a perfect shape. For a while, it was a problem. I spent weeks on end in the graveyards waiting for lily-footed dainties to pass away before their time. I could go nowhere with the long paddles left to me by the poetess, although they served her perfectly well in her own time. But starting with the courts of the khans up until very recently, I might as well have worn an *olisboi* beneath my skirts as gone about on my obscenely masculine feet. It fact, it was around the time of that first visit by the young Venetian and his two uncles that I stopped visiting male scholars except in those very temporary bodies I found in the hills and managed to animate for a night or two. I focused my attention instead on the courtesans who wrote beside the river under the full moon, or the nuns who sat out in the courtyards with their ink blocks after the rest of the clergy had gone to bed. They were puzzled by my lean, squarish jaw and plain dark robes that betrayed nothing but my amusement with the game of dressing. What seemed to relieve and reassure them was the sight of my feet, their phallic length. And then it was "Tea, elder brother?" Or "A game of rhymes, perhaps?" If they discovered later that I was a woman after all, by then it did not matter so much.

But occasionally I made errors. One night, passing through a neighbourhood near the Western market, I noticed a young woman sitting by a candle in the window, brush poised in her elegant hand. I was tired and hungry: On my way, in fact, to visit the Saracen cloth trader who kept a yard full of plump chickens. The old rooster, great-grandfather to the eldest of the hens, was randy again. I could hear his unfortunate love of the moment squawking in consternation. The woman glanced every now and then out the window, and the longing in her eyes was more than I could resist. I reknotted my hair, smoothed my robes and approached the door.

"Oh!" she exclaimed, evidently surprised to see me. "Are you his brother?"

I was puzzled for a moment, until I realized that she was not the lonely scholar of this sad little house, but merely some prostitute or courtesan, waiting for a man to return. Of course, I was disappoint-ed, but then I should have known to trust my knowledge of this city by now. I knew every scholar, every priest, and every nun of every faith that was practiced in Chang'an. There were many, believe me. Some strange ones imported from way beyond the Gobi Desert. The priests worshipped their god as though he were the only one that existed, in spite of the evidence to the contrary right in their own neighbourhoods. I could never understand this, but humans are often a peculiar lot. And then I thought, *If she holds a brush, she can write. What does it matter if she doesn't own this little house?* It was a pleasant and convenient place to haunt, old as the city itself and cov-ered in climbing trellises.

"His brother, yes, exactly," I said, so as not to disappoint her.

"You'd better sit down, then. I'll get you some tea." Tea was all these people ever drank anymore. I don't know whatever happened to good old barley water, but I suppose tastes change with the times. It was much too hot and nearly burned my nose, which remains sen-sitive to sun even until this day. I was more than a little surprised when she noticed. Most humans do not have such a keen eye.

"Perhaps you would prefer to drink wine?"

I nodded gratefully. She took a bottle and two cups from the cupboard and poured generously.

"Are you clever with couplets?" she asked.

"Not as good as my brother," I answered. I have never been particularly given to modesty, but in this case I thought it might round out my disguise. Especially given her uncannily keen eye.

"Well," she said, "my work is not so sophisticated that you should have trouble." She pushed the scroll toward me. On it was written:

The order of nature is never fixed
The west is moving, the east cannot be still.

Clearly she was disturbed by the visitors in the court of the khan. It was true he listened too willingly to their advice and bestowed too many gifts upon them. His scholars met their priests, who spoke of the one god as though it were a bag into which they wished to stuff everything they had learned of the Middle Kingdom.

I picked up the brush and after considerable thought wrote:

The nature of order is never still
It moves not with the wind but with will.

"Very good," said she, "although that end rhyme smacks suspiciously of Western influence."

"I have lived in their company for much longer than you," I said.

She shook her head. "You should not pass judgment on things about which you know nothing."

This remark made me raise an eyebrow. With her literary skill, there was already more to this woman than met the eye. But how extraordinary was she?

She smoothed the fine hairs of the nib against the ink block, added a few drops of water, and worked them through the ink until the brush was saturated again. Then she wrote:

A strange guest visits the walled city.

and pushed it back. This was clearly a test, although I couldn't be sure what she was testing for.

I wrote:

Ordinary ghosts roam the streets.

"Ah," she said, "are you afraid of death?"

"Not at all," I replied.

The sheets are white, the streets are quiet.

The guest is more afraid of wine than spirits.

It took me a while to finish this one, but when I was done, I made the last stroke with a grand flourish and accidentally dropped the brush. Quick as a fox I was under the table to retrieve it, brushing my hand against her dainty three-inch foot as I did so. She was still blushing when I surfaced above the table again. She giggled when I leaned forward to kiss her, took my hand, and guided me toward the bed.

"I hope my brother does not come back soon."

"If he does, I hope he will have the good sense to hide himself among the trellises for a while."

I cannot tell you now what made this such a hurried thing, since I am usually a creature of breath and careful pacing. But at the same moment we placed our hands in that telltale place between the legs, and I discovered that she had something that I had not, and she discovered, since I had no *olisboi* with me that night, that I lacked something which she had. Being good-natured creatures, we both fell to laughing and went on with what we were doing.

When I finally got up to leave, she gave me her dainty embroidered shoe as a token of the evening, and I went home dreaming of all the possible disguises the future held.

"I haven't heard from you in weeks."

"It hasn't been weeks, just ten days or so. I've been busy. What have you been doing?"

"Reading. Playing Space Invaders."

"You should try to get out. Meet people. Ming says that people

who stay home all the time are more prone to high blood pressure
when they get older."

"Who's Ming?"

"It's not her real name. Her real name is—uh, I forget—Charity
or Patience or something awful. She says being called Ming makes
her nervous, but it suits her so much better, don't you think?"

"How would I know? I've never met her."

Artemis grew afraid that Diane would disappear altogether into
Ming's world and never come out. Instead of looking for a summer
job, she spent the long afternoons in the games arcade playing Space
Invaders. As the aliens rained down on her head, she imagined Diane
trapped under debris in a fort below the screen, and fired heroically
from the gunner's position all afternoon. Sometimes it was the
church she stepped inside, slumping into one of the back pews and
breathing holy air. Christianity did not particularly interest her, but
she imagined the church to be a stone temple from the time of the
Greeks with light streaming in through the high windows, and a
marble altar with a stone bowl for the blood of the sacrifice.

Once, standing in front of the altar, she imagined a man's blood
gushing over her hands. She hurried out into the wet street with cars
rushing by. She heard the long sigh of bus doors closing. She ran to
catch the bus. The driver opened just one of the folding doors to let
her in and then pulled quickly away from the curb while she stood at
the fare box counting change. She counted a dollar twenty and had
to do the last five cents in pennies while her wallet threatened to spill
its entire contents onto the floor. Finally, she had the right coins,
dropped them down the chute, snapped her wallet shut, and turned
to scan the bus for a seat. There might be one in the back. She wob-
bled toward it, knees bent like a skateboarder's, when the driver suddenly slammed on the brakes, cursing under his breath at two cyclists
who cut in front of him. Artemis lurched forward and fell into the

soft lap of an Asian woman who was growing out her dyed blonde hair. The dark roots reached her ears, and from there her hair was blonde to the chin. Artemis was sure she had seen the woman before. She didn't know where, but the sensation of that last act of looking came to her so vividly that she said "Hello" before apologizing for her loss of balance. The woman smiled, and in a rich voice that was almost otherworldly she said, "Don't worry about it," as her warm hand half-lifted Artemis back to standing. Artemis thought she smelled chicken on the woman's breath, but she couldn't be sure.

Diane was sitting on the front steps of Artemis' apartment building with a knapsack and two stuffed shopping bags beside her. A bedraggled but defiant Diane, with a long red streak, from which skin was peeling, still marring her perfect face. "I got kicked out of the house. Ming would have taken me in, but it was too awkward to ask her mother. Do you think I could stay with you for a while?"

"Why did they kick you out?" Artemis asked, trying to conceal her feelings of delight mixed with relief.

"I couldn't pay the rent. I don't know what the big deal was. It was just a sublet. Stupid white girls can afford it. So what do you say?"

"Of course, come on in." Artemis picked up both shopping bags, and they climbed the stairs to her little one-room suite. She would have Diane to herself now. She didn't even stop to feel hurt that Diane had asked Ming first.

Diane curled up on the bench in the seat by the window, and her thin body became small, no longer a young woman's, but a child's. Artemis put rice on the stove, crushed garlic, took sui choy out of the fridge, and began cutting. This was what she could do now to keep Diane's attention, and it was easy, meditative. The cabbage fell easily in long diagonal slices under her hand. It felt both familiar and foreign at the same time. As a young teenager, she had hated these tasks. Her mother had made a point of teaching her to cook Chinese. She had always resisted those lessons. She resented them. Her hand had been clumsy beside her mother's practiced one. "Teach me lasagna instead. Teach me chicken pot pie," she would complain, but to no avail.

From the window seat, Diane watched, murmuring approvingly as Artemis plunged into the serious act of cooking, slivering beef into paper-thin slices like flower petals of flesh and pouring on sherry and soy sauce so it would be tender when cooked. She threw the crushed garlic into a small puddle of hot oil in the cast-iron pan. From the corner of her eye she tossed a quick glance in Diane's direction, ready to absorb the comfort she felt seeing Diane curled so small and fragile against the window. But Diane was not there. Above the hissing of the oil, Artemis could hear her, laughing with Ming on the phone. Diane was still on the phone when Artemis had finished cooking, and laid each artfully arranged dish on the table. She stuck her head into the main room.

"Dinner," she said in her mother's voice to the back of Diane's head, which faced away from the kitchen toward the entrance. Diane threw up a hand, at once an acknowledgment and a dismissal. It was a good fifteen minutes before she came to the table. She heaped her plate with food, not really looking at it, and ate hungrily.

"Ming and I are going to a women's bar tonight." She did not extend the invitation.

"Your first time?"

"We went last week. There's a woman there who likes me."

"Oh?"

"I guess you're studying again tonight, huh?"

□   □   □

They used bookshelves to divide the room. On her side, Diane tacked up a poster of Tracy Chapman posed in the conscious act of thinking, promotional posters for a couple of recently produced independent films, and some snapshots of friends. Her futon lay unmade, the shape of her restless sleep demarcated by the indentation in the mattress and the human curves of the crumpled sleeping-bag-turned-quilt with its batik cover. She was seldom home, but her presence filled the apartment now, the way nothing up to that point ever had. Artemis' little heap of talismans on the window sill diminished against the bright summer light that poured through the panes. She found herself always alert for the sound of Diane's key in the lock, even late at night as she sank into sleep.

One night, alone with the flicker of the television, she took the smocks Eden had given to her down from their hiding place high up on the closet shelf. She shook the red smock Diane had worn out to its full length. It wavered in the air neither dead nor alive. The smoothness of the fabric as she held it at arm's length from her body suddenly made her skin crawl. She rolled it up quickly and returned it to the bag. She pushed the whole bundle back into its place on the shelf.

She came home late on a sunny afternoon, having spent so long sitting in the back pew of the church that the pastor appeared and invited her to Sunday's sermon. She had muttered an embarrassed refusal and hurried home.

She pushed the door open and nearly knocked over Diane, who was posing in front of the mirror on the bathroom door. Diane had on a short, black, crushed-velvet frock that fit her torso closely and then flared out in a short skirt.

"Do you like this dress? Ming gave it to me." She sashayed into the living room and back toward the door with a grin that was both self-mocking and self-satisfied at the same time. And innocent too, something that pulled on Artemis' wrists where the pulse was making her feel less afraid of abandonment than she might have otherwise, and somehow protective. Diane was almost back at the front door when she stumbled and fell, clutching her stomach and gasping for air.

"What's wrong?" Artemis threw down her bag and flew to where Diane had collapsed.

"Nothing, I'll be fine."

"You don't look fine. Let me help you to bed." Artemis touched her arm.

"No, leave me. I just need to lie here."

"What is it?"

"Trouble with my stomach. It's nothing. Don't worry." She got up and half crawled, half staggered to her bed and collapsed there.

Artemis thought she noticed some bruising along the inside of Diane's legs.

"Why don't I call an ambulance?"

"No. Don't." She doubled over again, and suppressed something loud and animal that rose visibly from her belly to her throat. Her expression, combined with the burn scars that lingered on her face, created a forlorn whole.

"Diane, for fuck's sake. Tell me what's wrong."

"A miscarriage," she whispered. "I had a miscarriage this afternoon, and Saint gave me the dress because he felt guilty. Don't tell Ming. Don't tell anyone. My family can't find out."

□   □   □

The following morning Diane was up early, frying bacon and brewing coffee. Artemis got up and ate with her, and so they wiled away the morning the way they might have mere weeks ago, before Ming had appeared.

"My rasta friend Tony is coming by later to drop off some weed. Hope that's okay with you," said Diane.

"Have I met him before?"

"Well, he's not really my friend. He's not really a rasta either. Too white, too upper-class. Never been to the Caribbean and can't get the British Properties out of his accent. But be nice to him, okay?"

"Why?"

"He gives me a good price."

Tony arrived in the early afternoon, enveloped in a cloud of marijuana smoke and patchouli. Artemis slouched over the kitchen table as she had since breakfast, reading a novel set in an Italian villa. Tony plunked himself down beside her.

"What are you reading?"

"It's called *Alope's Robe*. It's about the discovery of an ancient moon temple in a small Italian town."

Diane pulled up a chair. "I don't know why she wants to read that stuff."

"There are worse things, girl. Jah say we should read what moves us."

"Somehow I'm not surprised to hear you say that, Tony," Diane retorted.

"Girl, sometime you should listen to what I tell you. Wouldn't do you no harm."

"Doubtless. Did you bring any weed?"

"We'll get to that, child. Did I tell you about the time Ronnie get busted for growing hydroponic in his mother basement?" He didn't wait for an answer. "Well, Ronnie mother go to London for six month to see she new boyfriend. Ronnie think that plenty time to get a crop going, and she have such a fine dry basement…"

Diane looked out the window while he talked. She played with her hair. Tony rambled on with no signs of stopping. After fifteen minutes of Tony's unbroken chatter, Diane gave Artemis a strangely conspiratorial look, excused herself from the table and left the house altogether. Tony did not stop his story to acknowledge her departure, but merely shifted his address to Artemis. He had her cornered for the rest of the afternoon.

He was still there when supper time rolled around, and Artemis' stomach started to rumble. She didn't know how to be rude.

"You hungry?" she asked.

"No, girl. I should be going."

"Suit yourself."

There was a knock at the door. Perhaps Diane had forgotten her keys? It was Saint. "Diane in?"

"Saint, my man!"

"Get out of here, Tony. Hasn't your mother got supper on?"

"Diane took off," said Artemis.

"She said she might have some things to interest my father. I think she was hard up for cash."

"Diane don't have nothing to sell anyone," said Tony. "She broke though. I can tell you that."

"I might have some things to interest your father." Artemis immediately wondered whether she was being too impulsive, but it was out now, and what use would she have for those creepy smocks anyway?

"I'm on my way there now," said Saint.

Artemis went to the closet and took the bag out without bothering to look inside.

"I'll come with you."

"Great," said Saint.

Tony said, "I guess I should be going anyway."

☐   ☐   ☐

The house was set back from the road and largely hidden by a tall hedge of shiny green leaves over which a profusion of morning glories climbed, the innocence of white cups disguising their intention to choke their host. Saint spoke into a voice box beside the gate, and after a moment the wrought-iron gate, with spokes that curved and curled between straight iron bars and ended in sharp, unexpected points, swung open. Artemis knew it was some simple electronic mechanism that allowed a person inside the house to open them by remote control, but there was something about the hedge and gate that transported them to another place in another century, so that the swinging could just as easily have been a result of magic as of science. The grounds were not as meticulously kept as she might have expected. Roses that had passed their peak of perfection some time ago now hung sadly from thorny limbs, the hip eyes at their centres just beginning to glow. To some, a few bright petals still clung weakly. But every flicker of colour that remained, no matter how feeble, burned with life against the backdrop of the massive house itself, which towered like a tremendous stone in unsettling jet-black. It seemed to have risen out of the earth, neither natural nor unnatural, its turrets pushing up out of the trees that surrounded it, as if competing with them for sunlight. The house was immense, all spires and gables, trimmed with curls and circular engravings. In the two black turrets were long stained-glass windows, indicating two circular rooms with high ceilings. The lines of the glass circumscribed yet more roses, pink, yellow, and blood-red.

"Don't mind my old man," said Saint. "Collecting is his life. He runs an auction once a month—it's the most talking he does. So he talks very fast. If you don't understand what he says, just ask me. I'll do what I can."

Artemis walked on flagstones up to the door—reverently, as though something were sleeping inside. She gripped the straw handles of the shopping bag. The smocks rested there, uncomplaining.

"Don't let him talk your ear off," said Saint. "He'll try."

A woman answered the door, evidently the housekeeper. She was a large woman, with a dignified face, the most prominent feature of which was a sizable but nonetheless elegant nose. "Mr. Hawkesworth is waiting for you in his study."

The foyer had once been grand. Two staircases angled off in opposite directions, reversed their courses at the first landing and met again at a balcony that overlooked the door. The balustrades were elegantly carved of some dark wood that Artemis could not identify. Against every possible wall leaned various antique tables with elegantly carved legs, scattered with small curious objects. Each table had a theme. One contained miniature dollhouse chairs, each worked in meticulous detail: some daintily carved wood, others richly upholstered in brocades embroidered with the teeniest leaves and flowers. The chairs were not of the same proportions: Some were meant for larger dollhouses; some were so small they could have collectively furnished a walnut shell. Another table overflowed with objects of deception: a papier-mâché elephant that opened at the neck to reveal a candy box; a tiny slipper that was actually a hat pin holder, from which spiked long silver pins that ended with a bright jewel or a baby's head carved from ivory. Yet another table was covered with clocks ticking away the hours of history as they had for god only knew how long; others had stopped, clinging to some distant moment of glory or sorrow in the past that was now remembered only with numbers—five after nine or that dubious minute before midnight. Still another was adorned with the exoskeletons of various rare and exotic marine creatures—turtles, oysters, and corals in odd geometric patterns, all browns, yellows, off-whites, pale autumn colours suggesting red here and there only in the faintest whispers. Artemis could have examined these things for hours, but the silent pause in the foyer had already grown far too long.

Saint took her hand. "Don't let the old lady catch you gawking." They walked into a cavernous study.

The floor was strewn with flowering carpets that absorbed the sound of their footsteps as though with the intention to erase their presence. Among the leaves and petals, tigers prowled, snakes slithered, and little people galloped on horseback, ancient instruments of war taut in their ready hands. The walls were papered in scenes of old China, mandarins and courtesans reclining under breezy pagodas while gardeners trimmed peonies and labourers lugged twin buckets of water on poles across their backs. Above the visitors, from wall mounts, the heads of exotic animals presided, stunned eyes staring down at them with the sagacity of the dead. The place positively hummed with artificial life, objects ordinary enough in themselves made strange through the act of collection.

Among these things sat Mr. Hawkesworth, a tiny man with large water-blue eyes and thin lips from which proceeded a constant stream of words and numbers. He sat perched behind a carved oak desk against the study's far wall.

The volume of old Hawkesworth's mutter increased slightly. Artemis could not make out a single word.

"He's asking you what you have," said Saint.

Artemis felt suddenly sorry for the little rolls of fabric in her bag, as though they were alive, as though she were delivering them to an unknown and unpleasant fate. Reluctantly she drew the smaller one out of the bag and unfurled it before the old man's eyes. He beckoned her closer. He took the garment in his long bony hands and scrutinized it with an almost pornographic gaze that made her shiver. The mutter rose again.

"He wants to see the rest," said Saint.

If she had dared she would have turned and run, but she remained frozen where she was and opened the second garment out, along with the accompanying pants. He took them in those hawk's hands. She cast her eyes to the flowered carpet so as not to see the long fingers wandering over the fabric, the small bright eyes missing nothing.

"He says they are excellent examples of their type," said Saint. "He wonders if you come from an aristocratic family."

"They were given to me by a friend."

"He says the quality and condition are exceptional. He would like to offer you nine hundred dollars for everything."

She gasped at the amount. She had had really no idea what to expect. "Is that good?"

"I think so. Of course, he wants to be able to make a profit if he decides to sell them, but it seems as though he intends to keep them for his own collection. He has quite an impressive wardrobe of Oriental garments. One robe used to belong to the last emperor's concubine."

"I see."

More than anything she just wanted to get out of the airless room and forget about what she was leaving behind altogether. She looked the old man in the eye and nodded agreement. Later, walking back down the garden path, with a cheque in Hawkesworth's looping, twisting hand burning in her pocket, she wondered how such an ordinary man as Saint could have proceeded from the body of that man and any woman.

He parked the car in front of her apartment building. She thanked him for his help, and was about to step out of the car when he grabbed her wrist. "Invite me up."

"I'm afraid. Diane will be sleeping."

"If she's there, I'll go."

"Maybe another time."

The door was quiet as she inserted her key into the lock. It clicked open loudly. The blinds were up. The apartment was empty. Or rather, all of Diane's things were gone from it: the futon, the posters, the books, the strewn clothes. Her shape did not linger, not in the bed clothes, nor in the faint soap and lemon smells of the bathroom, nor even as a ghost in the full-length hallway mirror. She was gone. On the walls a few of Artemis' own uncomfortable posters remained. Here and there were furnishings that she had bought, the things that never seemed to belong to her.

The only thing of significance left was the old blue quilt her birth mother had left for her. It had been fluffed out, neatly folded, and left in the window seat. She sat down there. She tugged at the even folds and pulled the quilt around her, letting the smell of mothballs waft into her lungs. For the first time the pungent odour was comforting.

"Saint. She's gone. Do you know where she is?"
"I haven't seen her."
"It's so empty here."
"Do you want me to come by?"

She let him lie down beside her. She let him touch her because the same hands had touched Diane, carried a part of her with him now. Buttons and zippers slowly came undone. A heap of clothing built gradually on the floor. They held each other in unfocused arms. Rocked back and forth like a wooden horse with stunned eyes. On the verge of sleep, she came, her mind fixed on the image of an old sleeping bag on a sagging futon, preserving a curved indentation, the curling question mark of the spine.

"The Garden of Eden. Adam speaking."

"Very funny. Is Eden there?"

"He's sick. He ate a rotten apple."

"Ha, ha. Will you put him on, please? It's important."

"As long as you're nice to him. He really isn't well."

"Hello."

"You sound terrible."

"It's just a hangover."

"I called to say you were right."

"About what?"

"About one of us leaving. It's going to be me. I'm going to Hong Kong next week for the rest of the summer. My father got me a job in his friend's import/export business."

"You can't leave."

"Why not?"

"Because—because so much is happening right now."

"Yeah, and I need to get away from it."

"Come and see me before you go."

"I don't know if there will be time. I'm giving up my apartment and putting everything into storage. I have to pack."

"Will you write me?"

On a return trip to China via Hong Kong, I spot Artemis in the market and realize for the first time that her gait is measured and cautious the way the Poetess' was nine hundred years ago, when she stepped outside her aging father's gate the last time.

The ones who are born overseas are always obvious. She thinks that as long as she doesn't speak, releasing a poor accent or wordless open-mouthed silence, she is safe, invisible. But her eyes betray her terror of being spoken to. In the mornings she is already on the bus when I get on. I feel her eyes snare me as I drop my coins into the fare box, so I purposely take a seat directly across the aisle from her. Now she will have to look at me. Her eyes go down, and she does not look up again until I ring for my stop, get up from my seat, and leave through the rear doors. She gets off at the stop right after mine and trudges up to her office.

It's not so much that she is small as that she walks as though she were. Having lived so long in the land of giants, perhaps it's hard to adjust. In fact, she's of average height compared to the citizens of this city of tall buildings and high finance. At least, that's what kind of city it is to them. To her, the tall buildings and shiny cars are mere overgrowth, a disguise concealing the past. This she glimpses when she peers into the backs of shops or steals up certain side streets where the cobblestones have not yet been paved over. Her eyes are like mine, quick and dark. She has learned how to conceal in their depths anything they take in. A woman with a prominent dowager's hump hobbling up the street in an old-style suit. The brown, calloused hands of a vegetable peddler. She knows these are the things that a Western tourist would see. This disturbs her. Is she trying to prove to herself how quaint and archaic these people are, even the ones who have managed to disguise themselves in three-piece suits and well-cut dresses? Or is she merely looking for shadows of herself, glimpses of a truth beyond the dull surface mirage of twentieth-century life in any city? She does not know that beneath every mirage is another mirage.

The search for shadows makes her hungry. Always keen for a hunt.

This makes her dangerous, at least to me, an old fox of the once firmly established Hu family of Chang'an, the capital of old China, now living in the cold outreaches of the British colonial legacy. Especially now that I am alone and tired of my solitude.

And here in Hong Kong, less than ten years before the colony returns to China, who is to say which of us is more out of place—she whose parents knew these streets as children, or I who have not been here for five hundred years?

At lunchtime she comes out onto the steaming streets with other office workers and goes to the noodle shop or else the Japanese bakery in the basement of the Matsuzakaya mall. This time it's the noodle shop. She orders wonton or fish-ball noodles in a clumsy accent. Once when she went for lunch late, the restaurant was nearly empty and a group of bored waiters gathered around her and asked, "Japanese?" "Korean?" She said, "Ga la dai yun," and they all reached out to marvel at her hair as black as theirs.

Today she is buying mangoes in the street market from an old woman in a straw hat. She knows how to choose them, pressing the yellow skin, gently testing for the right balance of firmness and tenderness. The old woman tells her she looks like her lost daughter and gives her a special price even though she doesn't understand a word. In the street she slits the yellow skin with her pocketknife, and peels it back like a banana. Oblivious to whether or not anyone is paying attention, she bites into the sweet flesh and lets the juice run past the side of her mouth.

I get careless and let her catch a glimpse of me in the hawker's market. Perhaps she knows I'm watching for her and is watching for me too. She's rummaging through a cart of clothes with Liz Claiborne labels, holding a denim skirt up to her body and tugging on the elastic to see if it will go around her waist. I cross the street a block away, cutting across her field of vision. She looks up. Later, going behind the hawkers' stalls in an alley, I hear her speaking grammatically jumbled Cantonese with a watch seller, but I stay hidden until she is gone.

Artemis takes an elevator to the top of one of those fancy hotels. She gets out at the revolving restaurant at the very top and is seated by a harried waitress struggling to be polite, at a lonely table by the window. The man she intended to meet is dead—an old tea merchant who had been friends with her adoptive father when he was a young man studying ancient trade routes in Asia. She will meet his daughter and his blind wife, who used to sing tragic roles when she was younger. The old woman has lost her voice now. The body has fallen out of it, leaving only a ridiculous falsetto that her old ears can barely hear. They arrive just minutes later, the daughter pushing an empty wheelchair, the old woman hobbling on a cane. She stumbles over the crack between the moving and the stationary sections of the restaurant floor.

"She won't use the wheelchair. She loves all the new hi-tech things, except the ones that will actually improve her life." And then, sheepish at this blurted-out display of emotion, the daughter tries again in a more even, amiable voice. "Hi, I'm Leda."

The old woman says something in Chinese, as the waitress helps her sit down.

"She wants to welcome you back," says Leda.

"Back?"

"She knows you've never been here before. But she means it as a compliment." Like her namesake, interposing her body between the human and the divine, Leda spans the gap between cultures. "She says the West is a very strange place. She hopes you will find life here more ordinary."

"More ordinary by the day," Artemis assures them.

Leda offers to take Artemis to a resort in the New Territories. Artemis meets Leda, her cousin Shirley, and two of Shirley's coworkers at the Star Ferry. She is happy because they all speak English. Inside the ferry terminal, they follow smooth hallways to the subway station. She likes the way the seats are built for people her size, even though she has to stand this time because the train is so crowded. At one station many men and women in business suits crowd onto the train. At another there's a large group of factory workers. She finds herself thinking things she thought she would never think. "No wonder the government is so strict about border control..." She wishes she could forget that she is Chinese too.

She gets wedged up against the glass at the front of the car. Voices flood like water into her ears, displacing air. The steel pole she clutches is beginning to sweat. She imagines long fingers wriggling through her rib cage to grab her lungs and squeeze. A thin breath dribbles out of her lungs and she gasps to snatch it back, but the greedy fingers squeeze tighter and all that goes in are the familiar voices she doesn't understand. She is growing pale. The fingers snake into her belly. Grow double heads. Maybe forked tongues too. They writhe. She leans forward. A clot of vomit rushes into her mouth, but at that moment the train stops, the doors open, and the people rush out.

They flood through the brown doors of a brown train station in the hills. It would have been nice, an American-style bathroom, white tile floors so well-disinfected you could lick them, a claw-foot tub waiting like a porcelain womb, a wide-basin sink with hot and cold water running crystal clear as a mountain spring in the land of the immortals. And a pristine white sitting toilet that could flush away all those messy bodily unmentionables. The single bob of a handle and it all swirls away to some unknown, unthought of, and unremembered place, to be replaced by clear, lovely water.

But this is almost China, soon to become China again. One of those nearly forgotten places in the hills. Unlike those fancy hotels for Westerners, the rich, and the overseas Chinese, there is no gray woman mopping away the parts of people that they themselves are afraid to discuss, or holding out white towels smelling of lemons. There is just a dry sink, a bare light bulb, a wet floor, and a hole in the ground that smells unhappy.

When Artemis comes out, Leda says, "Maybe your digestive system hasn't adjusted to being in a foreign country yet," laughing kindly behind an accent as perfect as American denim.

Artemis smiles and says, "I guess not." They have missed a bus waiting for her, but no one seems the least bit reproachful. Still, she finds herself feeling bad, and the night is hanging by a thin thread, threatening to tumble out of the sky at any moment. They stand together on the curb outside the station talking about Shirley's new boyfriend, who has just bought a motorcycle.

"Crazy, the way traffic is these days," says Leda.

Shirley laughs. "I'm not that serious about him anyway. If he dies in an accident I'll just go find another one. There's lots where he came from!" She looks at Artemis. "You got one?"

She has just received a letter from Eden detailing his various summer flirtations. "Sort of," she says, "but not really."

It's cool inside the bus, air rushing through the open windows as the serviceable but hardly elegant vehicle bumps over potholes two or more at a time. By the time they reach the resort the eroded hills have drunk all but the last drops of blue from the sky.

It's the way she imagines a nunnery to be. She knows that it's too plain to resemble one really, five identical buildings with undecorated high white walls and a slanted roof made of long black bamboo poles. They are led into one building by a perky young woman with short hair wearing a green polo shirt. There are thirty beds in the big hall laid out in three rows of ten each. She's glad there are still beds left by the window.

When they get to the dining hall, it's already packed full of office workers and their families. She recognizes a man her father's age as a draftsman who works on the floor above her. She nods her head in his direction. "First holiday in twenty years," he tells her later. She finds it strange to sit around a table with strangers and share a meal with them, poking chopsticks into the same dishes of rice noodles or pork and vegetables, but at least they belong to the same profession.

There will be a thunderstorm tonight, and I will pay the first of many visits. The dark is heavy as she walks back toward the building. Although it's cooler than in the daytime, the air is viscous as honey and the night is as dark and smooth as hair. She has no choice but to take it into her lungs and let it flood through her bloodstream. With each inward breath her blood grows thicker, until it is as rich and dense as the dark. The night ripens. The first drops of water descend just as they reach the door of their building.

By the time she has washed and climbed into bed, it is raining

steadily. Thunder muttering in the distance. In the sleeping hall the
air is still tight. It is hot, and mosquitoes buzz incessantly except
when they stop to insert a tiny pin into her skin, take a single drop
of blood, and leave her feeling hot and itchy and irritated. She tries
to seal her entire body, heavy with night air, inside the sheet, except
for a tiny hole to the side where she puts her nose. Sleep is just passing a gentle hand over her face when the first flash comes. The room
is startled blue for an instant. The growl that follows doesn't come
until perhaps ten seconds later, trembling over the hills and smashing into her ears. How could everyone else be sleeping? A whole
room full of women and no one stirs.

The next bolt bites closer. I feel more confident now, strong
enough to nudge sleep aside and lean gently against her back, careful not to conjure up memories of the train ride, as she tries to curl
away from the storm.

Either she doesn't notice me or she pretends not to. A torrent of
rain passes over like a wide-winged angel and moves on to the next
hill, black blades pounding. The air is thicker than ever. If she does-
n't come out from under the sheet, she will choke on it. The next
bolt of electricity explodes right over her head, banging in her ears
like the Mongol army galloping into China's ancient capital. I put
my hand on her shoulder and gently pass it over her body in a gesture of comfort. The sky is descending in liquid torrents.

A memory rushes at her, arching through the dark. It comes from
when she must have been two or three years old. As she lay on a
white camping cot in an empty house, lightning came to her for the
first time. It struck the gigantic oak right outside her window, setting
it ablaze for a moment, until the rain came and the flames were lost
in a hissing fizzle of steam and smoke. She lay still the whole time,
fingering the satin border of a pink blanket, which would eventually
fray from an excess of touch.

Outside the wide-open windows the rain washes her memory
away. I put my hand on her belly, and she rolls over and looks at me.
There is no surprise in her eyes. It is as though she expected me to
be here, and is pleased. Or perhaps she knew the whole time that I

was there, and was stringing me along, the way some humans can, in spite of their naive appearance. I stroke the soft skin on her belly, feel the sharp bones of her hips, move my hand up the centre of her rib cage and let it rest between her breasts. She reaches her hand up behind my head and pulls me toward her. If she is surprised that my body has weight the way a human woman's body does, she doesn't say anything. Her mouth opens, revealing the first hollow of her body. Her tongue is small and pointed. Her breath comes from a warm place inside the earth. We fly close to the ground and let the thunder come back.

The Women Wash Lentils

Carole Maso

When they are French, which they often are, especially in bed they say: *dérangement*. When they are French, and this is Paris, which it often is—so beautiful, so light-dappled, such light—the window opening up onto everything, everything: the tree-lined boulevard, the stars, the Tour Eiffel, she says, it's like a cliché, only beautiful: *croissant, vin rouge, fromage,* French poodles, polka dots. When they are French.

She says *mon bénitier, ma chagatte, mon abricot* into the ear of the woman until they are dizzy and mad for each other, having gone with surrender, with abandon to the place the language takes them, until they can't bear it one more minute—until—until—

When she is French, and she slowly opens the legs of the woman she also opens a book and reads:

> I picture lovers on the beach in Antibes. They are perfect in their black bathing suits, next to the blue-green water, under the hot sun. On their lips "*l'amour*," on their lips "*Cote d'Azur*." Dark glasses, Day-Glo, Picasso. They are lost in the long syllables of desire. The elongated shape of the afternoon.

And the woman says, that's beautiful and read me more and do a little more of that too. And the French doors.

When they are French, which they often are, at least one of them, especially in bed, they say: *la mer*. They say: *dérangement*.

Ocean. Sea. Deranged sea. And they read from *The Book of Oysters,*

which is also known as *The Book of Dreams:* "The oyster craves salt."
When they are dizzy and mad and delirious for each other, when her
lip devours the pulsing oyster of the woman, they read from *The
Book of Dreams:*

> To think of life is to think of oysters, all year round, almost
> as if you could hear all those millions of them breathing
> when the tide is out...The concentration of shore space
> and human effort toward the one single and singular end
> has a quality of dreams. *"Tout le monde fait ça ici."*

And the women dream oysters in their singing beds...And they
make their own bed sing.

They'll notice at some point, sometimes during and sometimes after
and once and awhile before, a phrase will come to them. Mysteriously,
or an image in the rose light: two women washing lentils.

When a phrase comes to them, or a picture, in their delirium,
their bodies mysteriously writing, inventing, making things up for
this, panting, pulsing, to near this throb and bliss and gorgeous-
ness, perfection. When they are in Paris. They ate like geniuses
together. They are like artists with each other. During lovemaking,
or just after, they see the most incredible things. *Ouvrez le livre.*
She reads:

> Every tree bears fruit here. All afternoon we eat plums,
> figs.
> "It's my birthday," she says.
> I sing her the birthday song, off-key. She laughs. "You are
> so lovely," I say. She is eighteen.

When they are dizzy and mad for each other in the moment just
before they are about to come, she stops and reads:

> I suck the dark fruit of our oblivion. Something opens that
> cannot be closed. And I am swollen with it, and I am

soaked in it. "You are so delicious," I say.

"*Et toi!*" We are floating. I cannot say what ripens in me.

And they are floating. They gaze out the ripe window, the passage from inside to out, and outside to in, and they dream of the fertile oyster beds in the tentative last light, and at the edge of the bed the tide pulls out. Making a sucking sound.

Oh my God, they're gorgeous, the women: washing lentils, as light comes and goes.

In the twilight. When they're French...

In the passage between day and night. The transition. In the uncertain hour. In the time, you who are French, speak, and I am able to attach a meaning to what you've whispered, as you approach me for the first time at the airport. And you smile and wait. *Je vous ai apporté des bonbons.*

I want you in the liminal stage. In the in-between place. It means in a doorway, in a dawn. When the lights go out, but before the performance begins. In the most vulnerable, in the most tentative. In the place where one thing is about to change into another. In the hovering.

The window seat suddenly bereft of cat. Through the half-light, two women washing lentils.

I want you when I am still on the airplane flying here—before I am aware of your existence; I am still dreaming you, imagining you, fantasizing this: our delirious oystering.

And you now between my legs.

Closing *The Oyster Book*, which is also *The Book of Desires*. In the egg you expel in sleep. In the slur of sleep. In the egg your brain releases, yearning—in the liminal space. Legs akimbo. In the moment of—in our fertile bed.

My hand before your legs open. My hand hovering near but not on you, all desire, before I begin, *commencer*, to open you, fuck you so gently in every possible way, in every type of day and weather, and then after that—

In the moment before this forever, when I am still innocent.

Before this *dérangement*.

Before your lips, which will never leave my body. Permanent, shuddered. Before you say with your lips, whisper, *mon bénitier;* I want you then.

In the liminal space. In the hanging, gorgeous, strange place between poetry and prose.

Oh—

My teeth raking your fertile bed.

Thoroughly. A thoroughness.

And the women read about edible oysters.

And the women dream.

She speaks of her childhood in the country. I'd like to have you then—when we're so young we haven't become anything yet. Eating chocolate. Making a *tarte aux pommes avec ta mère.* Picking flowers.

And the women dream poppies.

Inhale—staggered—dizzied:

Your hand hovering near but not on me. Or my mouth—you can feel my breath on your beautiful, beating—and yet I have not yet taken you in. The sensation of sucking in advance.

When they're so young they haven't done anything yet. I am just a student getting off a plane from America and you—your boyfriend has just left with his *famille* for the sea, *en vacance.*

It's August, Paris, the streets are deserted. I see you immediately. Your beau is gone. The world bereft of boyfriend—let's call him Jacques. Little *pauvre.* And we meet on the hot and empty *rue Anne-Christine* in August. The *rue sans Jacques.*

They're so young they haven't become anything. And neither of them has ever been with a woman yet, I say, slowly opening her legs. And they know they're already lost. They know once they start they'll never stop.

In the moment before they are together for the first time.

In the moment before they even imagine it. But then they imagine it. It occurs to them, without too much trouble at all. They saw it in a film once or maybe a dream. Or after reading from *The Book of Oysters.*

In the liminal space, the uncertain hour, where they hover in between being one kind of person and another. They breathe deeply, savoring all.

A dream of sucking, akimbo.

They've been up there so long—for an eternity; really fucking— they can't believe it—

And they're up there for days. She looking out onto the city she has never been in—from afar—all beauty, promise, shining—she looks out as the woman delirious—*you are beautiful,* she whispers, manages to stutter.

They've been living on fruit—apricots, figs, and cheese and wine—never moving from the bed—it's a cliché, but it's delicious: *baguette, fromage, vin rouge.*

A sign at the end of the bed says: *Bar—Crêperie—Dégustation D'Huîtres.* They're all over the place—first in the bed of the sea, then a field of poppies, then, then…all of Paris, all of France, and dreams of you…oyster beds…tasting.

When they're really fucking, they're all over the place. (Pink, gleaming.)

She reads from *The White Book,* or *The First Book of Desire:*

> Only our lovemaking could relieve the pain and longing that each had created in the other. The warm liquid our bodies gave up changed the atmosphere. It was smelly and dreamy and we floated in the world our sorrow made. We explored long into the day every curve, every contour of it.
> "Speak only in French," I told her.
> "Say nothing but with your eyes," she said.
> "Don't move or I'll stop."

They sigh.

When they're up there in the apartment, it's for an eternity and they're really making love and they're lost, and they're losing their way, and they never find their way back really. They're losing touch— they'll need to brush up on the language being spoken out there, where they left off…another life…lifetimes ago…really fucking…

It's French out there but with a twist.

She opens *The Book of Slang*. She reads: "Vagina may be called *le abricot*—the apricot. *Le barbuhe*—the bearded one. *Le bijou de famille*—the family jewel. *La bonbonnière. La chagatte.*"

And she reads from *The White Book*, which is sometimes called *The Fourth Book of Desire:*

> In the morning an old woman brings deux café cremès, deux croissants.
>
> She comes in quickly slows up and smiles. She has seen stranger things than two naked women in a small bed together. The room smells familiar. There's a warm breeze.
>
> "I want you."
>
> Each word a boat.
>
> "I want you to examine." And we begin again the elaborate seduction of sadness and language.

When they are in love with language, as they always are when they are French, they explore each word, as they explore each other.

They're so young—she hasn't become a writer yet, hasn't opened yet one large artist's book, the one who has come from America, on the plane. And the other, she has not yet once stepped into the House of Chanel.

Her impossibly long legs—

And the women dream.

And they read from *The White Book*, which is sometimes called *The Fourth Book of Desire:*

> I kiss her shoulder, part her lovely legs, sail across the perfect surface of skin, sweetly.
>
> "Please," I whisper.
>
> And she says, "Complacencies of the peignoir, and late coffee and oranges in a sunny chair." We make love to each lovely line.

And they're in love with language all over again.

And I'd like to do with any sentence what I'm about to do to you…

I'd like to do a lot more than just *italicize* desire. Elongation of the phrase. Your long limbs in the afternoon light. Your legs akimbo.

Anne-Christine. Marie-Claire.

I'd like to do a lot more with your name than just hyphenate it.

As I set you off by commas, *ma chagatte,* that's my Javanese cat. *Ma petite crevasse. Ma boîte à ouvrage.* My little work box. Let me suck. Work you harder. *Dégustation D'Huitres.*

Language and its weight on us. Like my hands all over your body. My little work box. It emits heat and light. It buzzes, it hums, *ma chagatte.* It purrs.

—Stop.

—No,

—I'd like to do a lot more than just hyphenate it. I'd like to swallow it. Feed my tongue on it a long time. Feel you on my tongue. Staggered. Suck the oblivion of your name.

Where language in you once again performs an amazing and unlikely feat.

I turn her over and over,

Because she is French, while she fucks she'd like to be read to. She is in love with literature, literary Javanese cat wrapped around my mouth. And I raise my head and I read into her:

> Beached on the hypnotic, lilting lip of a sweet—of a sweet,
> of a young nymph's clitoris, Sappho sings the world deliri-
> ous…Haloed rosy—
> *May I say*
> *I think no girl*
> *that sees the sun*
> *will ever equal you in skill.*

Words dripping down and she howls.

We stagger, stutter, shudder.

We pick up *The Book of Slang* for the day we will go out. Read to me, she begs. She's insatiable. She loves my American accent in French. Really? *Oui j'adore ça.* Really? No?

Yes, read to me. *J'adore ça.*

"Note," I read from the book, "that many of the following slang synonyms for *pimp* are, oddly, types of fish: Le *hareng* (herring), *le merlan* (whiting), *le brochet* (pike), *le hareng saur* (smoked herring).

Oh, the thousand pleasures of this world—in French, in English— lustrous, glistening. Gleaming.

I'd like to do a lot more with this sentence than just...

Than just offset it with commas, suspend it in space on its own line and admire it. Having touched it once—escaping. Having once felt it on my tongue—but now—no longer mine...To

have you...Suspended like that...Still.

Still. Language sends them into a delirium. They open a book. They open each other. They open another book. Listen:

> "Un petit gout, s'il vous plait." Her robe falls open. Her body gives off an extraordinary light. She seems to glisten. She touches my neck again. She applies just the slightest pressure. Her touch tells me she wants more. She wants my mouth on her breast. I touch her road belly. She nods. She wants my mouth to descend to that triangle, its luxurious dark. And she too needs a small taste. She grows. She grows wild. She turns from a brown horse into a white one. I pull her magnificent mane. Press open her thighs. Ride into light. I savor the brilliant, the blinding, the gleaming—

—If you could do anything in the world what would you want to do?

—To write someday our erotic *études*.

—If you could be with anyone?

—I'd be with you.

—If you could live anywhere?
—Right here. In Paris.

In the half-light, in the liminal space, suspended, hovering...
On the verge...
In the vulnerable place where you are so beautiful and squirming,
so—(pink flowers). My hand hovering. My breath on you.
—Can you feel my breath on you?
Good. Where you are so beautiful and in the state of becoming—
squirming there like that, begging for more or for reprieve.
Reeling. A stranding:
I read to you. My hand hovering, my hand near—but only near...
In the moment before I touch you: the theater darkened, the thrill
of your gorgeous unknown, the thrill of the possible, dizzy. In that
moment, where we gasp, the breath reversed—a place I love, a place
I fear.
In the space between light and dark. In the space between day and
night. In the cleft of your breasts. In the crevice, the cleavage. In the
vulnerable, in the tender cleft between, in the lovely center of this
sparkling...beauty—beauty. This utter twilight. In the place between
light and dark. In the place between poetry and prose.
And I take out *The Book of Slang* in the gap (*repeindre sa grille en
rouge*) between language and meaning (to repaint one's grill red;
that is, to have one's period, to menstruate). In the gap between
touch and speech, in the vulnerable, in the open, in the tender, in the
silence which constantly changes, in the dark which constantly
changes, in the tender, in the uncertain—lovely glistening center.
Changing.
You who live *dans la maison tire-bouchon*. You of the corkscrew
house, that's of the lesbian world, my corkscrew.
Teaching each other slang in the place between—open your—in
the twilight. Put your arms up, hold onto the bedpost now and close
your eyes.
On this darkened stage before everything is played out.
Hovering, hanging above—in the promise—suspended in air—and

the book—before you fuck me.

Once again desire has caught you off guard.

Read me more: And I climb on top of her and straddle her hips and read to her from *The Fourth Book:*

> "Women are so beautiful in their curiosity," I say; "their openness to everything. They are not like men."
> He turns away.
> It is a mistake to think that because our vocabularies are not large that we cannot hurt each other.
> I have gotten my hair cut so that now Lucien's and mine are the same length. He pulls my *cheveux longs.* "I like it when you do that I say."
> "What else do you like?"
> "Many things."
> "Like what?"
> "I like it when you pull my arms back, *comme ça,* like wings."
> "Tell me the names of the women."
> "What women?"
> "The names of the women you have loved."
> I look at him. He is blurry with pleasure.

Beautiful, invented one. Once again a hidden or unnoticed pattern existing in the world emerges through the magic of language and shows and shows us how to go. Read, she begs: and I straddle her mouth:

> "Go through the alphabet," he says.
> "*Oui?*"
> "*Commence avec A.*"
> "Okay," I say. "*A* is for Annalise."
> "*B*—Brett."
> "*C* would have to be Cynthia. She was my first girlfriend. We were in high school."

He smiles. A universe of women.

"*D*, let's see, *D* is for Dominique."

"*Dominique! Elle est française!*"

He's losing track of the letters...I pull his *cheveux longs*.

My delirious and passionate quest.

He gets up in the middle of the night to open the window.
I kiss him as he gets back into bed and we start again,
rotating this swollen, beautiful globe all night. *A. B. C. D.*
Slowly we raise the sun into the sky.

Beloved alphabet. She closes her eyes. In the extraordinary
space, the fragile space—in the place right before the heart breaks,
or the line—

In the space between letters, in the shape the white makes, the
fire, where the real word lives out we cannot see.

The women read from *The Book of Oysters,* which is also known as
The Book of Dreams:

> You can't define it. Music or color of the sea are easier to
> describe than the taste of one of these Amoricaines, which
> has been lifted, turned, rebedded, taught to close its
> mouth while traveling, culled, sorted, kept a while in a rest
> home or "basin" between each change in domicile, raked,
> protected from its enemies and shifting sands, etc., for four
> or five years before it gets into your mouth.

For four or five years before it gets into your mouth.

In the space between fiction and essay...poetry. In the moment
before you fall into irretrievable sleep, I take you, and you, again,
you smiling and protesting with your eyes closed—bleary and feverish having already descended—exhausted by our lovemaking,
lan guage making, speechless—exhausted, beautiful, invented
one...into dreams...ripening darkness. Our first night together.

It was in the airport Charles De Gaulle. She, sleeping now, held a
sign with a name on it, and I agreed, Yes, that is me, and we went.

—I will show you a kind of Paris...Paradise...

In the place between sleep and dream. In the movement from waking to sleep, as you fall...Paris...Paradise...into dream.

Into dream. Between the event and its movement into story. Between the event and its many formalizations in the mind. Before the metaphor. Between the act and the language, I love you. In the space between affection or attraction and then maybe love. Because this is France, after all. *Je t'adore.* Between the language and the act—when I'm just talking you through it—what I'd like to do.

Listen to this—from *The Book of Slang:*

To have a crush on: *faire des yeux de merlan frites,* or literally, to make fried marlin eyes at one another. To make goo-goo eyes.

In the space between the act and the language. My hand dripping, sticky, trying to keep up—scribbling—to get the words as close as possible, blurring hand, burning—I want you. And you put your hand just there, *comme ça,* and—a little harder, a little quicker and I find away to say *Oh la la*—or something like that—not much, and we're rising and falling. Your breast now in my mouth, your—

And we're rising and falling. In the doorway. The passage from one room to another...dripping. Goo-goo eyes.

It's a Saturday afternoon in Paris. August. The streets deserted. The streets quiet.

You are like a dream. All of Paris asleep. In the space where I lose, I lose—through no fault of either of us—in the unstable space and I try to call up—in the space between wakefulness and sleep, between sleep and dream—where language falters—

lentil...holy water...

God, you were—you are—on the plane away already, so beautiful, *très belle,* so hot—Let's cool off a little—salve, you were—

holy water basin

In the precious hours—such

dérangement and—

Our delirious oystering...A straddling, a culling.

See them in the distance, in the place still within the reach of your eye—but barely, barely...The women washing lentils.

You were lovely, *dérangement*. Wildness. Disappearing.

In the body's chasms. Lost in the body's chasms. The swell of you. The shape of your loveliness. All that was beautiful, as the words fail and a particularly lovely darkness comes on...

You once longed for a place where language was never the seed of doubt. But not now—no more—no. The sentence barely within your reach and glistening...impossible to get to. The sentence hovering, suspended.

Sexy.

Sexy one. Trembling. Such *dérangement*. Hip. Ripe lip. Hover.

Hips hovering toward the breast. Your mouth at my wrist. And the way the space keeps changing:

Your Javanese cat, your *chagatte,* feeding on my mouth. Or me grooming it...furred

...licking...*crevasse, petite crevasse.*

Between the language and the meaning.

The shape of the gap, the empty place—let it stand that way: the hips hovering...the breasts.

Outside the world passes. They pick up their *Book of Slang* to keep up. Paris is glisten and oyster and cherish—she'll have to take her word for it. They read from the book. Your breasts are: *les lolos* (little milk pitchers), *les amortisseurs,* those little shock absorbers. *Blagues à tabac, boites à lait...*

In the shape of the gap. In the gap between your gorgeous vulva and an apricot, or a box for bonbons.

In the shape of the gap. Hovering. Your lips but not quite. Your lips about to say—but not quite...

In the silence. In the moment, in the linger between this and that. Between experience: imaginative, sexual, or just out there in Paris for a promenade someday, and its thousand transformations.

She picks up the book. She picks up the book: she picks up the book. The listener waiting. In the moment before words escape the lips of the reader. In anticipation. The place where anything might still be possible.

Another view in the mind, that oyster, reveals:

He folds over the pillow and puts it under my lower back. I am raised toward him and he lowers his magnificent head to me and we meet each other halfway. His long hair is draped over my swollen belly.

"*Sel de mer,*" he says.

"*Oui.* I am salty. Soon there will be blood."

This excites him. We imagine together the blood that is to come. I tell him a story about the ruby jewels hidden deep within the kingdom.

Your lips at my lips. Your mouth painted red. From *The Book of Slang:* To menstruate—*avoir ses cardinales, avoir ses coquelicots, avoir son drapeau-rouge, avoir ses anglais, avoir de la visite, avoir ses ours.* That is, to have one's cardinals, to have one's red poppies, to have one's red flag, to have one's English, to have visitors, to have one's bears.

To receive one's cousins. To repaint one's grill red.

And she reads from *The First Book of Desire:*

The city sparkles like a jewel in the sun. The snow is blindingly white. She is smiling. She is bathed in apricot. The poem is complete. It is true: the world is a cathedral of light.

In the moment before she gets off the plane, in the moment before she ever sees her, in the liminal space, suspended, a woman dreams: Paris.

In the moment before she'll follow her anywhere. Descend those dark steps. Go down with her.

The woman shudders imagining, in the moment before she gets off the plane and onto—She stands at the gate holding a sign, and the sign says, *Mademoiselle Huitres,* and the one still flying, still in motion, in the airport of Charles De Gaulle, says, Yes, that is who she is.

And the woman smiles and agrees *oui,* yes.

Paris is glistening, gorgeous, golden, *formidable;* you'll have to take my word for it, she says, whisking her off—we'll not be seeing much of Paris...Between the words and what they mean—and the one who is French is already dragging her nails gently down her arm and she is already sighing and gasping for breath. It takes one sentence.

Drageur: to cruise.

Avoir un chien pour toi: to have a crush on.

—You won't, I regret, be seeing much of Paris...Unless—

Already they are inside the French doors, French windows, cat, baguette—a kind of shorthand. *Vin rouge, fromage,* yes.

And she is already dragging her long nails, but gently, so that the other woman can hardly feel them at all yet. She shudders in that amazing space. You won't be seeing much of Paris, *ma poule, ma petite, ma poupoule, ma biche, ma bonbonne.*

Unless we call your body Paris, my body, Paris, your mouth, Paris, your hair. Your feet are Paris, and your thighs, *mon coco, mon lapin, ma louloutte, mon poisson, mimi, chouchoutte...*are Paris. Your legs are Paris.

In their language long-legged Paris glistens. In their language Paris throbs. Its streets are wet and hot in August. It's lit up from within and radiant. And she arches her back, and she says, Ah! The Arc de Triumph! In their language games/love games/sex games: they say: Javanese cat and oyster gleam and Paris. Oh God and the Seine! The beautiful river flowing through them.

And she remembers the time before all this: on a plane, drawn to a woman or a city she has dreamt but does not know, and may never know, may never meet. Despite the urgency, the shifting, the wish...Bliss...

Having flown from the night, and now returned to the night.

In the transitional moment, in the moment—it's only a moment, between night and night,

Your body suspended in want, the mouth—the hand hovering. I feel your breath.

I can feel your breath. In the moment between night and night— in the hours in-between. Its half-light lapping against the darkness on each side.

Lapping and how we love each other there—on every side. In the transitional space between clothed and unclothed, unclothed and clothed. Night and night.

She taking one item at a time off me. One item at a time...piece by piece...delirious...

Once again desire has caught us off guard.

And the French girl with her accessories—so many *accoutrements*—there's so much to take off, slowly—in the corkscrew house, where I love you. Slowly, piece by piece—it seems we'll never get there—but that's okay.

And she's French and she's aching for it but she says: *lentement. And regarde: le bijou de famille.*

If they ever dress again she'd like to wear the watch called Piaget. A *clochard, les gants.* She'd like to wear the French woman's silk stockings. Her lipstick. In our blur. In the blurring between me and you. If they ever dress again. If they ever get up again.

The Seine...

Lentil to lentil and washing...

In the place between—

Like the thrill and longing of learning another language, a second language—or a slang, delighted. In the attempt to speak—on the verge of fluency—

They slowly begin to dress each other. And with each piece another act of love is initiated. And a reading from one of the five books of desire. Until they are fully clothed—and rubbing up against each other. And ready to stage a scene in the room. The one is holding a sign that says, what? maybe, Corkscrew House, or— and the other one volunteers, how about—*Mlle. Chagatte*—maybe that. In the airport of Charles De Gaulle. But they keep passing each other—

(once again sadness has caught you off guard)

—keep just missing one another—as they might have, of course, passing each other by moments—having never known each other for even one night.

On the verge of meeting—but not. And they weep wondering

what else, who else in this whole wide gorgeous world they miss. Will miss.

They are girls all of a sudden, waiting. One in Paterson. One in Paris. Waiting. And now at the edge of the bed: a field of poppies.

They shudder and open *The White Book of Desire* to make love to. To make love by.

Meanwhile, outside, Paris passes. They pick up their *Book of Slang* to keep up:

barbu m. (lit): the bearded one

bénitier m. (lit): holy water basin

qui est de la maison tire-bouchon (lit): who is of the corkscrew house, or the lesbian world

lentille f. clitoris (lit): lentil

éplucheuse de lentilles f. (lit): lentil washer

voir les anges (lit): to see the angels; in other words, to have an orgasm.

In other words.

Flying on the plane, mouthing Paris, and the women of France— it's a vague, still hazy, delicious, indulgent, gorgeous, and she opens her—the perfume of it—the imagination.

Lovely, glistening center.

Opening, and the one who would show her everything, opening.

Lifting a glass of good Bordeaux to one's thirst.

Lifting her hips.

Her lips uplifted to her thirst and vice versa.

Getting the, getting the mouth around the language of her thirst she reads:

> She is standing under the great clock in Grand Central Station and she is waiting for me...She is dangerously happy. The day is beautiful. There has never been a more perfect time to be alive, she thinks. There is no life more perfect than her own. And she is right.

And following her from Grand Central Terminal, or is it Charles

De Gaulle? And following her (in that moment—pink flowers—*les fleurs*) beauty, truth, liberty, desire—before either of us knows our lives, or knows each other—or know that one will ever acknowledge the other—even smile, even lift our eyes—

Let alone—

Let alone—this:

The pink flower of your breasts; having imagined, having lifted— opening

My eyes. In the space between seeing you and having you. Between imagining and seeing you. Between seeing you and you seeing me—and you looking back.

In the spaces of longing which last a lifetime.

the women the howl the song

In the longing that never ends. The lust. In the spaces forever between me and you. After she, after I return to New York. Even after—

Even after—

In the ocean between night and day, word and word, between you and me. In the liminal space—between English and French, language and meaning, poetry and prose, in the suspended space between you and me. In the sexual space. In the space between (pink) your breast. In the space (pink) between your mouth (rose) (descending) and my *abricot*. A light fuzz.

The women wash lentils.

In the space between stars, in the mysterious sexual space between the howl and the music, between the dream and "I'm right here"— your beautiful skin. *Je suis là.* I'm right here.

Look—in the rosy light, do you see what I see, now on the horizon: the women washing lentils in the twilight ocean.

She picks up *The Fourth Book of Desire,* which is sometimes called *The Book of Good-bye* and reads:

> He sucks on his middle finger. She watches. She has no underwear on; he knows that. He presses his finger to her beating—"Rosebud," he says.

They sigh and open *The Book of Slang:*

To swing back and forth, to be bisexual—*marcher à voile et vapeur*—literally, to work by sail and by steam.

In our sex talk, in our language games, in our slang, in our read to me, in all the ways we found to speak, in all the ways we found to live.

Come here and I will do your parsley (gladly).

In the interstices of desire. In the space between birth and death. In the reach.

All the places we found joy. All the ways we found despite everything—to live. The place in my brain where I imagined you, dear future, dear potential—and loved you—

In the time before we were anything we wanted to be. Oh sweet *être*. Oh lovely yet to be.

She has not yet written one erotic *étude,* one white book. She has not even opened her large artist's notebook.

She reads from *The First Book of Desire,* one last time. In the place of your inception, in the place of your conception, the wandering, longing for the egg, the idea becoming words, the feeling finding patterns, shapes in language wandering on to the white page—or the screen.

All the pleasure you've brought.

Between the place of your conception and the place where I put the final period. In the instant between, in the time before we are anything we want to be yet—(not even the large book)—and good-bye. In the fleeting space between birth and death. Beloved alphabet.

The child draws the letter A.

Between what I say to you in English and what I say to you in French. In the interval between what is said and the translation.

Between what I do to you and what I do to the sentence…breathing hard…

Ecstatic alphabet.

In the interstices. In the liminal space. My lentil and yours. So much pleasure…In the reach. Open your French doors.

In the lust that constantly changes, but never ends. In the ocean and the desire that never end.

In the light streaming through the French doors. The halo around your body: aureole. Between the god and the light—the interstice. Our desire. Our desire for everything: miracles, the sea...

> Intimations of the ages of man, some piercing intuition of the sea and all its weeds and breezes shiver you a split second from that little stimulus on your palate. You are eating the sea, that's it, only the sensation of a gulp of sea water has been wafted out of it by some sorcery, and are on the verge of remembering you don't know what, mermaids, or the sudden smell of kelp on the ebb tide, or...

A sucking sound as the tide pulls out.

And how now it seems, the window ledge, the world bereft of cat and music, word—the boulevard blacked out—this odd emptying (quite suddenly)—

In the uncertain moment between what you say and what I understand—it could be anything.

The shape of empty space, page. Don't be afraid, let it stand that way a moment: the hip hovering toward the desiring mouth. Or she on the airplane right before the imagination floods and transform—her—in that moment before there's anything at all—the brain at rest for a moment, perception kept at bay. For a moment—that peace. And how she tried from time to time to get that back with a bottle of good Bordeaux or a dark afternoon with a beautiful stranger.

The world emptying, blacking out, in the staggering.

In the lapse. In the passage. In the gap.

In the limbo, in the continuum, between the god and the light, the women wash lentils.

Me moving toward trying to understand you. Toward understanding you. I pick up *The Book of Slang*. In the gap between *il y a du monar au balcon* or "there are people on the balcony," and a woman with large breasts. In the gap between having one's period and repainting one's grill red. In the joyful, mysterious passage to metaphor.

In the passage between dream and word, dream and your body. In the gasp. Your body trembling, moving, alive. In the tentative beautiful uncertain. In the half-light. The darkness lapping and the women. In the half-light, where you will always be my *abricot* my *bonbonnière,* my Javanese cat. In the time between a Javanese cat and I love you. If we're lucky. In the time between I love you and good-bye.

Give me your red poppies. Give me your tomatoes, your cardinals. Give me your bears. Do you have visitors? Have you received your cousins?

In our corkscrew house. Let's have a dog. We'll make fried marlin eyes at each other for a lifetime…I've got the fever of a horse.

Let us wash together our rosy lentils. In the dusk. In the dark. We'll live on oysters there, and sea snails. The darkness lapping at us.

In the precious moments before I have even an intimation, even an inkling that I will one day have to say good-bye.

One day soon have to say good-bye. Between the night and the night.

And the suction of the plane. And our mouths like infants, sucking in the time before.

I have seen the angels.

For the rest of her life she will contemplate this bed where flowers bloomed and urge was fed. Where poppies bled. In the gap, in the passage, in the wordless place how gorgeous: in Paris. And seen from afar, from the edge of the conscious world, the women now drifting, dreaming, reading. The women, gorging on oysters. In the twilight. The woman dissolving. In the night and glisten and holy water basin.

At the exact moment, at the precise moment where longing, where love, where desire, where ache becomes the story of two women meeting in Paris in the perfect light of the mind. In oyster light.

I have seen the angels:

Look, out there, on the horizon, washing lentils.

R for Ricura

Amelia Maria de la Luz Montes

Using the alphabet is a good way to guess who will be my first. I whisper *A* for Antonia, *B* for Beto, *C* for Carmen, *D* for Daniel, *E* for Esmeralda, and *F* for, *F* for…Federico? But Federico is my cousin. People who have sex with first cousins have defective babies…skip to *G*. *G* for Gabriela. Yes. Perfect. Gabriela like an angel. But maybe Gabriela won't be the one. I close my eyes and pretend Jesucristo is looming above me with golden letters, outwitting my guesses. I close my eyes tighter, thinking maybe I'll see another letter like *L* or *M* and then it'll be Lena or Marina who'll be the first. Oh, what if this person's name is stupid like Manny. I'd hate a Manny to touch me. Maybe *P*. *P* for Pepita. Pepita will be my first. Pepita, the Spanish-language tour guide at Disneyland who followed me out of Adventureland and asked if I would meet her after work, after her tour ended at eight o'clock. I did.

Underneath the covers, I feel the bones of my rib cage. One, two, three, and then from hard bones to soft, spongy stomach. I move my hands further to find the hips like little knobs and then down to the triangle. "Triangle of love," says María Luisa to everyone in the locker room after drill team practice. "That's what it's called," she says. And everyone believes María Luisa because María Luisa has done it. At our freshman camping trip two summers ago, it was María Luisa who opened the window without a shirt on, not even her bra.

I notice sounds in the hallway. The light that comes through the bottom crack of the door partially darkens, then moves. My hands quickly reappear above the covers. Mom's footsteps clip along the wooden floor, then stop. She clicks off the light. The outline of the door disappears. I hear her two rooms away in the kitchen. My hands slowly ease back under the sheets.

It's habit, I suppose. Ever since I can remember, my mother has always warned against hands underneath covers. I didn't understand why and she wouldn't explain. So I made up a story about hands needing to be heard and not seen—because under the covers, I can hear them. It was María Luisa who told everyone that she liked keeping her hands under the covers.

"It feels good," she told Andrea. "There's nothing wrong with it."

María Luisa was always so bold like that. After the camping trip, people looked at María Luisa differently, like special. She walked different too, swaying her hips around. One time she walked into chemistry class late, wearing a really low-cut shirt. Even Mrs. Raymond stopped lecturing. She looked like she was going to ask María Luisa something even though her hand was still pointing to the equation on the board. Mrs. Raymond's mouth seemed to shape a word, but no sound came out. She watched María Luisa sit down like we all did and then she cleared her throat and kept talking.

"María Luisa is stacked!" Charlie Lockman whispered to Antonio Cruz in biology class.

"She's hot," he answered back.

I was in the desk right in front of them, leaning over my books, trying to look interested in what the teacher was saying. Their comments were like warm air on my back making my underarms feel wet and sticky. I wanted to move my hand under my arm to prevent what felt like sweat creeping down my blouse, but I couldn't move. I couldn't stop thinking about María Luisa and what she looked like when she opened the window, her fleshy arms holding up the creaky glass, the sudden breeze making her soft, ample nipples into hard knots. At the time, I couldn't understand my wish to be one of the football players below, to run up the stairs, hug her away from the window, and kiss her.

"Hot," Antonio said.

Antonio left St. Ignatius High just a few months ago. They say he got caught with pot. I think of him whispering in my ear "You're hot" while María Luisa laughs at me, holding the letter A in front of my face. "Antonio," she whispers. "María Luisa," I whisper back. My hands trace up past the hips, the sinking stomach, and the bony cage of ribs. Above them my breasts are softer, rounder, with a little knot at the top. But they're not as big like María Luisa's—they don't point upward like hers either. Not by a long shot. "Not by a long shot" is what the football players at school say when they want to act cool.

I think of Pepita—how she moved her hands right over my shirt when she was kissing me. She moved her hands softly over them, then pressed just a little.

Pepita is someone my mother does not like. I tried to tell her a little bit about Pepita, but she was quickly unhappy.

"She's too old and she's not Mexican."

"Mom, she's only twenty-three and she's Cuban—that's close enough!"

"She knows too much," she said, arranging my long hair in a twist.

I stepped back from her fussing with my hair, swept it up and behind me. "What does that mean, Mom? You've never met her."

"She's twenty-three—you're sixteen. She knows too much," she crossed her arms, holding herself tightly.

"I'm almost seventeen—almost ready to graduate!"

My mother thinks that anyone older than seventeen is not good for me. She also warns me that passionate love is like lighting a match. "It doesn't last. First you light the match and there's no turning back. Then when the passion is gone, they leave you."

"Well, maybe I'll leave them first," I say, knowing my mom won't listen.

She has old ways of thinking about love and lovers. She believes this because she grew up in Mexico, where the man she was going to marry was killed—hit by a car. He was her age and they had grown up together. "It was a perfect love," she said. Then when she came to this country, she married my much older father, who was already married to somebody else. She didn't even know—she just thought he worked long hours. A year later, he told my mother it was hard to love two women at the same time and left her. "He learned a lesson at my expense," she said every time she told the story. She thinks that whatever happened to her happens to everyone, no matter who you are or where you are.

My fingertips press down on the soft skin of my thighs.

"Rosario Arguello and Cecilia Villa Rubia have been together for years, Mom," I remember telling her that day. "And Rosario is much older than Cecilia."

"They're exceptions."

Everybody is an exception. Lately, she tells me that men and women over twenty are especially dangerous. That's why she let me go out with Victor Lopez last month. He was safe, she had said, but it must have been the exception. He stopped the car a block away from my house expecting me to have sex with him in the back of his car. He didn't even ask, he just expected. I walked home at 12:30 A.M.—the exception to Victor Lopez's safe reputation.

"I had to slap him to get him off me, Mom," I said.

"So he turned out just like all the rest," my mother shrugged. "Now you'll know what to do next time it happens."

She had thought because Victor Lopez was my age that he would behave.

"You put him in his place," she told me. "You taught him that his behavior was not fine with you. You taught him."

I didn't teach him anything, I think to myself as the palms of my hand flatten down against my thighs. The reason I slapped him was because I like him as a friend but I'm not very attracted to him—I mean, not enough for him to put his hands on me. I think of Pepita and I get a very different feeling. My mother says that older men and women will take advantage of me. They won't respect me. This is what I don't understand. My mother lets me go out with Victor, who acts like I'm going to give him anything he wants, and then there's Pepita, who's gentle and not rough.

Clipped steps approach the hallway. My hands move up and out from the covers. I clasp them together like in fourth grade in Sister

Joan's room—like when she told us our hands should fit together to look round and lovely like the world. My mom's steps disappear. It's quiet and I'm sleepy.

☐   ☐   ☐

"Someone's knocking!" I say. I'm pacing up and down the hallway next to the living room.

"Mom, aren't you going to answer it?" I can see her at the front window, peering through the curtain for the longest time—looking and looking.

"Mom, aren't you going to get it?"

She looks at me, her face old and frayed like the side of the yellow curtain in her hands.

"Open the door!" I whisper.

My mother rubs her hands against her apron, takes it off, throws it over the sofa, and smooshes her hair once, twice.

You look fine, Mom, I whisper to myself.

Pepita stands behind the screen door, holding the neck of her cello in one hand and a long-stemmed rose in the other.

"Good evening, Mrs. Castillo. I'm Pepita," she says, smiling.

She's got crooked teeth, I think to myself. *Mom will tell me she's got crooked teeth.*

"Hello," my mom says, and opens the screen door. Her eyes trace all six feet of her while the corners of her mouth twist in a rigid frown.

"This is for you," Pepita says, handing my mother the rose.

My mother looks uncomfortable, her hands rubbing against her apron. *Take the rose, Mom,* I think to myself.

"Thank you, Pepita," she says, taking the rose and moving toward the kitchen. "Let me get a vase."

My mother is obviously bewildered. She doesn't even offer her a seat and now she's there alone. When Victor Lopez was here, she gave him something to drink right away and sat with him.

Pepita doesn't wait for her. She plops herself down on the couch and positions the cello between her legs. She calls toward the kitchen, "Mrs. Castillo—I dedicate this song to you."

Too fast. She moves too fast is what my mother will probably say. She comes back while Pepita thumbs the strings, adjusts and tunes the large key-like chords. My mom walks slowly past her. She's carrying the large ceramic vase in both her hands with Pepita's rose sticking out from under her arm. She leans over the coffee table, puts the vase down, takes the rose and haphazardly lets it fall in the water. That vase is too big. *Mom, sit down,* I whisper, wanting to yell the words.

She stands in front of the coffee table and watches Pepita take out the bow and finger the chords for a moment. She straightens up and begins to play. Pepita's eyes close tightly, her forehead wrinkles, her mouth slightly opens. She sways with each stroke of the bow. Her long fingers strain tightly up and down the neck, the notes low and sad. She's playing something that sounds Mexican mixed with another rhythm I've never heard.

I watch my mom's eyes follow the movement of the bow. I think of my mother in Mexico when she was my age. I wonder if my father ever serenaded her. She looks at the rose leaning to the side of the much bigger vase. Finally, she sinks slowly into the chair in front of Pepita.

"That's one of my favorites," Pepita sighs. Her eyes slowly open. "For you," she points the bow at my mother.

"Thank you," my mother says, smiling for the first time.

"That was beautiful, Pepita." I come out of the hallway.

Pepita stands up. "Hello, Ricura."

"Something to drink?" my mother offers. "Lemonade, iced tea?"

"Iced tea would be great," Pepita's eyes stay on me.

I want her to touch me just the way my fingers pressed against my thighs last night. I want to feel her hands move over my shirt again, but the sound of my mother taking glasses off the cupboard shelf keeps me near the hallway. I feel stupidly shy. "Hi," I say.

Pepita smiles, winks. She carefully leans the cello against the wall by the door. I can hear ice being taken out of the freezer. Pepita stands up and leans toward the kitchen, listening. She looks at me and shrugs—like saying to me, *So what—you can come near me.* I move next to the cello, next to Pepita. Clink goes the ice into the glasses. Clink again, and Pepita leans toward me, kisses me softly. We kiss again once more, deeply, but then I hear my mother putting the ice back in the freezer and I gently push her back. "Not here!" I whisper.

"Not here," she repeats, smoothing her bangs. She sits back down on the couch and takes her first look around.

I wish we had new draperies—a new carpet instead of this stained brown thing. There's a fake turn-of-the-century painting against the wall. It shows a large hall with many dancers swirling around in colorful skirts, some of the men in fancy bowler hats and black berets. Pepita seems interested in it. She gets up and walks to the print inspecting the dancers.

She points to one of the couples. "They're like us," she smiles.

"What do you mean?"

"Dancing close, almost kissing," her arms open toward me.

If my mom saw her do that, she wouldn't like it. She wouldn't want any sort of contact, but I can't help it. I walk over to her and we kiss again.

Then she takes the statue of Coatlicue sitting on the end table just below the picture. "Fascinating," she says, lifting the statue and then looking up again at the painting.

"Is there a connection?" I ask.

"I don't know. They're both old," she laughs. "The painting reminds me of old Cuba—what my parents described their dances were like."

"The statue's an Aztec goddess—Coatlicue," I offer.

"It's eerie but beautiful." She traces the snakes that make up the skirt of the statue, then fingers the neck and head. "The skirt is amazing—so many snakes."

She leans over again to kiss me but this time I push her away. I can hear my mother placing the drinks on the tray. I walk toward the sofa and sit.

"Here we are," my mother announces.

She hands us our drinks, takes hers, and sits watching both of us. Her tan pumps are scuffed at the heel. She keeps tapping them together while taking short sips of tea. There's this silence I don't like—it's an embarrassing kind of silence—like I wish my mom would take a class in social conversation or something. I can't stand all this staring she does. Suddenly, out of the blue she says, "Ricura must be back by midnight."

"No problem, Mrs. Castillo," Pepita's voice hits a high note on the "illo" of Castillo.

Mom is eyeing Pepita again and it makes me nervous.

"Where did you two meet?"

"Mom," I say. "I told you where we met."

Pepita seems to relax the more I feel tension. She swings her arm on the side of the couch. "At Disneyland. About a month ago."

"Remember, Mom—when I went with Carmela and Susan to Disneyland? I told you." I can feel my face getting red.

"Yes, you did. And you work at Disneyland, Pepita?"

"Part-time. I give tours around the park in Spanish."

"Yes, the tour guides. They all wear those skirts and riding hats." My mother sounds authoritative.

Pepita smiles. Her front teeth are just a bit crooked. It makes her look distinctive—unique. "When it's cold, we have uniform pants as well."

"Oh yes, I remember," my mother takes a drink of her tea.

Now she remembers.

"Disneyland pays my tuition for school and music lessons," Pepita continues to smile. "Keeps me busy."

"And your parents?"

"I still live with them. They're not too happy about that, but I'm still going to school."

"Well, children living at home is a blessing," she smiles, her head tilts to the side.

"They tried to kick me out at eighteen, but I just wouldn't go."

My mother's smile disappears. She looks at the skinny stem of the rose in the wide neck of the vase. I look at my watch. "We're going to be late, Pepita. The movie starts soon."

My mom puts her arm around me before I go, but I gently move her arm away.

"Be good," she whispers. "*Que Dios te bendiga.*"

"Yes, Mom."

She moves closer to kiss me, but I look back toward Pepita and quickly walk out the door.

When we're finally at the car and Pepita is putting the cello in the back seat, she asks, "Why did you lie and say we were going to a movie?"

I cross my arms. My mother is still watching us from the front door so I keep my voice down. "You don't know my mom, Pepita. I know what I'm doing."

"Okay," she sighs. "I just always think it's better to tell the truth."

"Well, it wouldn't work here, Pepita."

"Why not?"

"I can't tell her I'm going to be at your friend's condo with you when your friend isn't there."

"Why not?"

"She won't like it."

"I told my parents where I was going."

"That's nice. My mom won't understand, okay? Let's not talk about this anymore."

"Okay, okay."

☐   ☐   ☐

There are windows everywhere in the condominium. I want to be daring and take off my shirt and bra and open one of the windows. But the yellow curtain makes me think of my mother. Her face, twisted in a rigid frown. I turn away from the window. Then is when I notice the steps leading up the stairs.

"What's up there?" I ask.

"Oh, go ahead and look around," she comes up close behind me. "Make yourself at home."

I have never walked on what Pepita calls shag carpeting. The upstairs is all shag—a cool blue color and thick so that every step is like walking on soft wool newly fluffed. The bed is king-size and has a built-in stereo system for a headboard. There are mirrors on the front and back walls. I notice my hair is kind of frizzy here, my lips pale like my mother's lips. I twist them down, and it makes me look more like her. I shape them into a wide smile and my mother's image disappears. When I look to the side of me, I can see how long my hair is getting—almost to my waist. At least my hair is way different from my mom's short, tight curls. Pepita's timer is beeping. She's taking something out of the oven. I feel like I should go help her, but I don't move toward the door. Instead I slowly unbutton my shirt. I loosen my bra and watch my round nipples crinkle into cold little dots. I want to remember to keep smiling.

"Did you try the stereo up there?" Pepita calls from the kitchen.

I cover my breasts with my hands and tiptoe to the door. "Not yet."

"It has a really great sound."

I walk to the mirror again. I can hear Pepita taking something out of the oven. My hands move my breasts close together and against the cold mirror.

"Did you notice the lighting?" she yells.

"No. I just haven't got there yet."

"It's really great. I can show you that from down here."

"Okay!" I look up to the mirror and look behind me and just then the lights dim to a muted pink color. My face looks different in this light but familiar. My mother's eyes and lips. I look above me and down and I feel surrounded. I don't feel like smiling.

"You like it?" Pepita calls.

I don't answer but instead quickly snap the clasp of my bra and button my shirt.

"Dinner is served!" Pepita calls.

I close my eyes at the doorway leading out of the bedroom. The doorknob is round and smooth, and I hold on to it tightly.

"Ricura! Come down."

I take a deep breath. "Okay."

☐   ☐   ☐

There are two goblets on the table next to two large plates filled with all kinds of foods that look somewhat familiar.

"*Picadillo, platano y moros* for *mi mujer*," she says and bends down to serve me wine. I watch the deep-red liquid splash luxuriously against the sides of the goblet.

When she goes back to the kitchen, I take the matches from the table and light the candles one, two, three, four. "Got any more candles?"

"Yeah, there are more in the drawer next to the silverware."

While Pepita explains how she combines black beans and rice together to make what she calls *Moros y Cristianos*, I place different-sized candles around the living room and light each one. The flickers of each flame create long willowy shapes against the walls and curtains. I laugh.

"What's so funny?" Pepita calls from the kitchen.

"It's like Disneyland in here—like the Blue Bayou with all the candles and the shadows."

"Don't remind me of work."

"How can that be work? It's the *happiest place on Earth*, right?" I laugh again.

"Yeah, right. Now let me show you the happiest place—right here, right now, eating this *picadillo* I made you." Pepita takes her fork and slowly feeds me.

The tastes of garlic, bell pepper, raisins, and olives fill my mouth. "Wow, that's good."

"I never go wrong with this recipe," she smiles, scooping the mixture onto her fork. "Mmm, another success!"

Then she takes a small slice of banana and offers it to me. "I've been wanting to cook this plantain for you—it's the perfect season for plantain—so fresh."

Its taste is a wonderful mix of cinnamon and nutmeg. "What are all these ingredients in the banana?"

"Rum and sherry really are what you need in making a good

platano," Pepita moves her chair right next to mine. "Of course, don't forget the cinnamon," she moves closer. "The brown sugar." She slides her fingers through the hair covering my ear and kisses my neck. "The nutmeg."

I can feel a tiny rippling effect tingling through to the other side of my shoulder.

"Goose bumps," she whispers, and kisses me again. She pulls me gently to the floor, and I feel her hands over my blouse again, her long legs wrapped around mine. She is warm on top of me then under me and over me again. I hold her tightly, opening my arms wider to feel the pressure of her body. Then she pulls me up. She unbuttons my blouse and unzippers my jeans.

"Wait," I say.

She looks at me with half opened eyes. "What? What's the matter?"

"Wait" is all I can think of to say. I fumble with my open blouse. "Wait."

"Okay. Okay," she traces the side of my cheek. "We can take it slow."

I close my eyes and travel my fingertips across her shirt, over the muscles of her shoulders and up to her neck. Her skin here is taut and thick, not like Victor—so skinny. Oh why did I have to think of Victor right now. It just makes me think of my mother. My mother who's probably holding those yellowed curtains, looking and looking out the window. Looking for me. Her eyes are right here. It's because she'd always say things to me like *I'm with you wherever you go* or *Your mother knows everything because she has eyes in the back of her head.*

Pepita kisses me once more and offers her hand. We get up and there's this awkward silence like when we were at my house.

"I know what we need," she finally says.

"What?"

"Music."

While she disappears upstairs, I eat more of the *picadillo*. It's getting cold.

"Do you like *danzon?*"

Danzon? What does she mean by that? "*Danzon* what?"

"You know, like what I played at your house—Cuban music."

"Yeah, that's great."

"Eat up!" she says, quickly running downstairs.

"I just wanted to wait for you."

"Well—what do you think of the music?"

The sounds of drums with violins fill the room. "It sort of sounds Mexican, but then different," I say. "I like it."

"It's an older type of Cuban music. I like the old music. I always wonder what life was like in Cuba long ago." She leans over me, takes an olive from my *picadillo,* and offers it to me. I take a bite, my lips touching her fingers.

I pick up familiar rhythms, melodies. "It really does sound Mexican."

"It does except for the congas. We have more African influence, I think." She sits and we eat. The tension from when we were kissing on the floor is gone. I feel more comfortable. Maybe it's the music. I watch the way she eats so intensely. She really likes her food—the way she scoops it up, closes her eyes, tastes every bite.

"Did your mom teach you how to cook?"

"Oh, no—are you kidding?" she laughs, her mouth half full. "She never cooks."

"Well, what got you into cooking?"

Pepita likes talking with either a piece of *platano* on her fork or an olive in her hand. She waves it around. "Cooking just happened. There was this job opening at a Denny's—the one on Venice and Sunset? Anyway, they needed a cook for their graveyard shift. I lied and said I knew how to cook and I got the job."

"Graveyard shift?"

"Yeah," she takes a bite of the olive. "I like staying up at night— and at night it's not as busy."

"You must have learned to cook—real fast," I laugh.

"Real fast." She smiles. "So then at home, I started experimenting with recipes from Cuba. Do you cook?"

"A little. My mom is the one who's the great cook." I hesitate, then take a fast bite of *picadillo*. "So, I really like this music."

"Your mother is very nice," she says.

I don't answer.

"You kind of look like her."

I put my fork down and take a long drink of the wine. It's warm and somewhat bitter. I take another mouthful of *picadillo* and then another long drink.

Pepita continues to eat silently. She looks up every so often and smiles. She points to my empty goblet. "More?"

"No thanks, Pepita. But that was delicious, really delicious." I mean it. I've never had *picadillo* with black beans and sweet plantain. Never.

Pepita moves close again. "Did you like that?" she whispers.

"I think it was the most wonderful meal. I mean it."

My hands fiddle with the napkin on my lap. She takes it and puts it on the table. She kisses my hair, fingers my long strands, kisses my forehead. I look up and our lips meet lightly at first. We keep kissing while she slowly unbuttons her shirt, lets it fall away. She's not wearing a bra. I think about how she's bold, like María Luisa—bold. Pepita tries my buttons again, pulling me down on the floor again. And then her hand finally inside my shirt, my nipple—hard and warm. I help her slip off my shirt, my bra. We move on top, under, over—my hands on her soft, smooth breasts, so delicate when the rest of her body feels tough, strong. This time, I'm the one who unzips my jeans and guides her hand past my waist. With both hands, she encourages my pants down to my knees. It feels good to feel her palms on my belly, on my "triangle of love," and I laugh softly. Her fingers find their way inside and inside, and she's doing things I never even tried on myself and they surprise me, my body. My body is doing—feeling like I've never felt before—like I'm going to get out of control and if I let go, let go—what will happen? She has me in her fingers, in her soft and pulsing fingers—or is it me who is pulsing? I kiss her hard and feel my breath escape me, feel my breasts expand against hers—so warm and soft. I look up in the candlelight,

and the ceiling is dancing with shadows, the yellow curtains catching
the light—yellow. I see myself in the mirrors upstairs, in my own
bed. I see my hands inside the covers doing what she's doing. I see
myself. I see myself and I can't. I just can't let her do it yet. Not yet.

I feel Pepita's breathing interrupted. "What's the matter?"
she says.

I don't answer at first. Then it comes out. "I'd better go home."

"Why?" Her brown eyes look translucent in this light.

I check my watch. "It's already ten thirty."

"We have a whole hour left."

"I can't. Take me home." I'm just about to cry but I don't
know why.

She looks at me and shakes her head. "You Catholic Mexican
girls," she says, gets up, and grabs her shirt.

"That was a mean thing to say." I get up quickly. "That was really mean, Pepita."

She starts putting on her shirt.

"I just need some time." I look away so she won't know I'm
brushing away a tear. "I'm only sixteen. You're twenty-three. You've
had lots of chances to experiment. Give me a chance," I blurt out.

"Look. I'm sorry," she says. "It's just that we were having such a
good time."

"Yeah, we can try again. I just need to go home right now."

"Don't worry so much," she tries to hug me, but I just
stand there.

"Just take me home."

"Okay, okay. I'll take you home."

The worst thing is driving because I live in Santa Fe Springs—all
the way on the other side of town. Thirty minutes of silence. I stare
at signs, read license plate numbers, notice that tonight is a full
moon—that the moon looks painted as we zoom along. I notice how
the 5 freeway road needs to be smoothed out. There's just too many
bumps—uneven paving that makes the car tires clunk every few feet.
Pepita just stares at the road, never looking at me, and every time I
think of saying something, it just seems too stupid to say.

"Good night," Pepita says quietly after she walks me to the door. She offers her hand. No hug, no kiss—just a handshake.

"Good night, Pepita. Thanks for dinner."

I watch her car pull away and disappear.

My watch tells me it's a bit past eleven. I turn to the door and already see my mom through the window—her face framed in curtains. She tries to hug me when I enter, but I walk past her toward my bedroom.

"The movie must have ended early," she follows me down the hall.

"Yes," I bite my lip. "It was short."

"I'm very pleased with her, Ricura. She seems like a very respectful person."

"She's nice, Mom," I throw my jacket on the bed and take off my watch.

"In fact, I'm delighted. I approve."

I throw the watch down on the bed. "I don't care if you approve or what you think, Mother."

"What?" my mother says. She's standing just behind the doorway, one hand on her hip. "You've never spoken this way." Now both hands are on her hips. "What kind of talk is that?"

"Leave me alone, Mother. I'll decide if I want to go out with her again." I slam the door to my room and fall on the bed crying.

The door immediately opens. "Ricura, what is the matter with you? Did something happen?"

"I really just want to be alone, Mother, okay?"

"Are you sure?"

"Very sure. Just leave me alone." My mother has tears in her eyes. I've never talked back to her—never—but I can't help it right now.

"Okay, Ricura," she sighs. "Okay."

"Look, Mom, I'm sorry I yelled."

She wipes her cheek with the back of her hand and closes the door. I fall back on the bed.

☐　　　☐　　　☐

My eyes open wide to darkness. I look around and notice the top of my dresser—the clock's neon glow-in-the-dark numbers that tell me it's three A.M. and I still have my clothes on. There's a lock on the door that I've never used. Slowly, I get up, hold the knob, and turn the lock. I unbutton my blouse and remember the way my breasts looked in the mirror. I think of Pepita as I unzip my pants. I get under the cool covers and pretend my hands are Pepita's soft hands. They are all over me, warming me. Pepita kissing me—filling me with the tastes of olive and raisin. I think of Pepita on top of me and me on top of her, remembering her whispers—"cinnamon, nutmeg"—how her bangs always fall over her eyes, her crooked teeth and the way her eyes shut tight when she glides the bow over cello strings. I reach down, down—feel muscles flex then relax, and faintly tremble. I see the faint light of the street lamp through the window, flickering and flickering. The moon's light makes soft shadows on the curtains, bluish-gray shadows of branches and leaves from the elm just outside. I close my eyes and feel my body strain up by itself, without my control, up, up by itself all tense and lifting, and I see the moon like a large O and O and O, round and round so neatly circular, every line perfectly curved. Every shadow dances on my bed. I laugh and slither way under the covers, curl myself up—my hands inside, inside, warm and wet.

Shani Mootoo

Sarah gave birth to her first child ten months after the marriage, and a couple of years later she was pregnant again. Chandin thought often of Lavinia, but his love for her had soured and mostly he felt betrayal. He was a dispassionate husband to Sarah, though he enjoyed observing his two daughters, albeit from a distance. He was composed and diligent performing his duties as Reverend Thoroughly's interpreter and field assistant. Yet he often felt chained to both the church and the Thoroughlys, and impotent to reverse the path his life had taken since the day the reverend made that trip to his parents' quarters.

Even when news came from the Wetlands that Lavinia had broken off her engagement, Chandin could only think with curdling cynicism, *I knew this would result! I could have told her that it would not have lasted!* As long as she stayed in the Wetlands, he would be able to keep at bay his unquenchable desire for her and his ferocious hatred, not of her but of the effect she wielded. But a crisis would arise, he knew, if he were to come face to face with her again—if, that is, she were to one day return to the island of Lantanacamara.

Before Lavinia returned to live in Lantanacamara, Pohpoh's parents seldom spoke to one another unless it was absolutely necessary. Sarah, whose reserved nature did not suit an occupation in the church, occupied herself grinding spices downstairs in the yard, which was cooler than the kitchen, or weeding the front yard once the sun had gone behind the house, or washing clothing.

Then one day without warning, even to her parents, she returned. Everything changed overnight. Chandin had not seen her, merely heard of her arrival, yet he clearly brightened. His children were surprised and pleased when he pointed out butterflies and flowering weeds, and purple and mandarin in the sunset sky. His colleagues noticed that he was now quick to enjoy other's wit and humour.

Still, he was shy to visit the Thoroughlys' house. Sarah returned home one afternoon to say that she had gone to pay her respects to Lavinia and that Lavinia was to visit them within the week. Chandin was like an excited child. He returned home the next day with a modest chandelier, and paid a man to install it in the drawing room. He paid another to put two coats of whitewash on his weathered mudra house. He bought a small imported rug for the living room. Out came his white shirts and trousers. He had Sarah bleach, starch, and press them. He bought himself an expensive straw hat with a narrow velvet band, imported from the Shivering Northern Wetlands and purported by the retailer to be the season's top Wetlandish fashion statement. He began to dress impeccably, to speak with the accent and strut with the airs of the Wetlanders he once again seemed to so admire.

Chandin woke unusually early the day Lavinia was expected. He complained a little to Sarah about feeling unfit and lethargic, and decided to take a walk up Hill Side. He returned after the children had awakened, just as Sarah finished preparing breakfast. He was in great spirits. He complimented his wife on the meal, and, after eating, he cleared off the table and, to Sarah's surprise, passed the broom across the drawing room and kitchen floors. He then swept the front and back porches and stairs. Inside he arranged and straightened the furniture. He went out on the front porch and re-entered the house, imagining what a visitor would see on first entering. He stood on the porch again, and looked in and admired his chandelier.

Lunchtime passed and Lavinia had not arrived. Trying not to show his nervousness that she might not come, Chandin lay in the hammock on the back porch and rocked. He thought about his wife and felt strangely distant from her, unrelated to her, as if a thick veil had dropped between them. His children's skin seemed suddenly too dark and their manner of talking crude. He wanted to remove himself from his wife and his children but knew it was impossible.

Lavinia arrived around tea time. She seemed genuinely happy to see Chandin. She showed him the presents she had brought for his children, and though he appreciated the gesture, it unsettled him: She seemed too willing to acknowledge his married state. He took two kitchen chairs out on the front porch and invited her to sit with him, while he had Sarah make a pot of tea. When Lavinia motioned to help, he quickly said, "She has learned to make a good pot. Let her do it and you come sit with me. Tell me everything that has happened since we last saw each other." He put his arm on her shoulder to guide her to the porch. He patted her shoulder in large, visible gestures, hoping to come across as brotherly.

When Pohpoh and Asha, playing out in the backyard, realized that the much anticipated Aunt Lavinia had arrived, they pelted up the back stairs. Hearing their excited entrance, Lavinia rushed toward them and, in the midst of the commotion, tea ended up being served in the kitchen, much to Chandin's disappointment. When Lavinia gave them the presents—books of Wetlandish nursery rhymes and folk tales—they asked her to read aloud right there and then, and a bond instantly formed.

Lavinia was so taken with the children that Chandin, unable to chat quietly alone with her, felt she had once again dismissed him. He watched peevishly from the back verandah as she was willingly led on a tour of the yard by the eager children. Sarah ambled alongside, grinning at their excitement. By the time the visit ended, Chandin could already feel the familiar sting of Lavinia's unattainability.

Much to his relief, Lavinia and Sarah rekindled their friendship, and Lavinia visited often. The hours between visits tended to be filled with tension in the Ramchandin household. Asha or Pohpoh, unable to stand the waiting, would sometimes ask for Lavinia to come along on excursions to the beach or river. Pohpoh noticed on these occasions that both her parents would relax. Soon Chandin became bolder, initiating outings he knew well would be of interest to the adventurous Lavinia. She never turned an offer down. When Sarah began to extend her own invitations, Chandin became sullen.

"She and I knew each other long before I married you. I wanted to marry her before I really knew you. I am not in the least comfortable that she and you are so close," Pohpoh heard her father shout one night.

"But you and she grow up like sister and brother. You couldn't marry she."

"This is utterly ridiculous. You know very well that she is not my sister. And another thing, is this how you speak with Lavinia?"

"What you mean?"

"Why don't you speak as you were taught in school? It is appalling that the educated wife of a man like myself refuses to exercise her knowledge. It just doesn't look good. What on earth would Lavinia herself think?"

"If you still so concerned with she, why didn't you wait until she returned from abroad to marry? You and I married now, boy. Ask her if she still interested in you. Ask her. Besides she never correcting how I speak. Is only you who always correcting me."

On Saturdays, when Chandin spent the day with Reverend Thoroughly going over school and church business, Lavinia would head over in her buggy to the Ramchandin house. Sometimes she arrived with her long golden hair in knots and tangles whipped up in the windy ride, her basket filled with candies and sweet-smelling potpourris from her grandmothers in the shivering Northern Wetlands. Other times she came with her hair piled in an untidy clump on top of her head, strands dangling in her smiling face, carrying the gramophone she had brought from the Wetlands. She would play the little disks all day, and the children would dance and prance and laugh until they were sputtering with glee in the drawing room.

Lavinia loved the freedom and wildness in Sarah's garden, so unlike her mother's well-ordered, colour-coordinated beds. She brought clippings and whole plants ripped from Mrs. Thoroughly's garden, the fresh, rich dirt still under her fingernails. She brought flame ixoras for Sarah and one memorable day she arrived with cactus plants, one each for Pohpoh and Asha. "Cereus," she called them, pronounced like the bright, fuzzy star, a climbing succulent whose leaves and trunk were ragged and unsightly until they bloomed.

"Only once a year," she said. "The flowers will offer their exquisite elegance for one short, precious night." She took them out into the yard and made a production of choosing the best planting spot. In the roots of one of the cacti was entwined a large, bulbous periwinkle snail in a gold-and-buff shell. Pohpoh insisted she must have the shell for an ornament. Aunt Lavinia held her back from prying the live snail from its shell, urging her to wait until it died and shed its housing naturally.

"Killing snails amounts to courting bad luck, sweetheart," she said, narrowing her eyes and shaking her head. "But let me tell you a little secret. Protect a living snail and when it dies, it doesn't forget. Snails, like most things in nature, have long memories. A snail's soul, which is invisible, mind you, will come back after it has died, looking for its old home. It will have grown bigger and stronger, and will hover around its old stomping grounds, guarding and protecting you in return—as long as you protected it first. Just wait until you find some naturally emptied shells, honey. And this is what you do: Display them nicely so they can be spotted by the floating souls of the snails that once occupied them. You press them into the earth—around a bed of plants or just make pretty patterns—and you, my sweet Pohpoh, and your Mama and Asha, and everyone whom you love will be ensured the fullest protection of the benevolent forces in the universe."

Aunt Lavinia winked at her. Pohpoh giggled at the whole idea and at Lavinia's telling. Sarah smiled and shook her head, for she too enjoyed the many tales that Lavinia seemed able to spin in an instant.

"Just you wait," Aunt Lavinia, enjoying the encouragement, continued, "just be patient. You will have your collection. But I'll tell you another thing: Recently emptied snail shells can have the most unpleasant, most nauseating smell—especially a bunch of them. You must make sure to boil all empty shells before you can keep them as ornaments. Boil them in plenty of water, for a long time, until the water has almost evaporated from the pot. And another thing: Salt, lots of salt in the water is a must.

During the week Sarah and Lavinia would make trips in the buggy to other towns or the market. Pohpoh and Asha enjoyed these outings. They stopped to play on the swings in El Dorado Park and for things to eat, and Aunt Lavinia was sure to shower them with pendants and charms for their hair. Lavinia commanded the buggy herself. Unknown to Chandin, she taught Sarah to handle it too, but Sarah knew better than to be seen taking the reins until she was past their village and deep into the cane fields, out of sight of the other villagers. Chandin admired things in Lavinia that he would have been ashamed to have his wife do. In the fields between towns Sarah would drive until Aunt Lavinia shouted out to stop. Aunt Lavinia would stand on the seat of the buggy or hop off onto the unpaved country trails, uncaring that the ground underfoot might be muddy or treacherous, and she would pull out her Eastman Brownie camera and click away. Before they reached the town again, Lavinia would once again take the reins.

Aunt Lavinia continued to visit but the Saturday trips to town and market gradually came to an end. It seemed to the children that their Mama and Aunt Lavinia were wanting to conduct all their visits indoors, or only as far outdoors as the backyard. There used to be a photograph of Mama leaning back against the kitchen sink, facing the camera. Perhaps it was only the photograph that caused Pohpoh to later imagine that Aunt Lavinia had also stood there with Mama, because she had an indelible impression of them both leaning on the narrow sink basin, their sides pressed tightly together. The image stayed in Pohpoh's mind, fortified with a memory of Mama trying to send her and Asha out to play, and of Pohpoh feeling something was being concealed. She had a vague memory of leaving the kitchen, noisily descending the back stairs, and then surprising them by returning quietly for candy. She crept upstairs and stood outside the kitchen listening. It frustrated her that Mama and Aunt Lavinia seldom spoke anymore except in soft, abbreviated sentences. They seemed to communicate more with their eyes, and with long looks.

Pohpoh's heart leapt when she saw the tips of Aunt Lavinia's fingers grasping Mama's waist. She understood something in that instant but save for a flash of an image of her father's face in her mind, she had no words to describe what she suddenly realized was their secret. She looked again. She tried not to let her eyes rest too long on Aunt Lavinia's fingers. Aunt Lavinia removed her hand and walked over to Pohpoh. Pohpoh stood frozen, sensing she had been caught and fearing the consequences. Aunt Lavinia squatted in front of her and took Pohpoh's face in her hands. Pohpoh inhaled lavender and remembered the little packages of potpourri.

Lavinia spoke gently to her. "Pohpoh, your mama is my very best friend. You have a very special mama. And you and Asha are very, very special. You're the best little children I have ever known. I wish you were my own children. I love the three of you very much." Pohpoh was unable to respond. But from that day on, she spent Aunt Lavinia's visits listening anxiously for her father. Whenever Mama and Aunt Lavinia did not seem to hear him return she would bound noisily up the stairs or barge in on them. At first, Aunt Lavinia did not leave until Chandin returned home and she had spent some token minutes with him. But when Chandin started complaining to Sarah that Lavinia was losing interest in him even as her brother, she began leaving before he was due.

Chandin passed the school holidays traveling throughout the island with Reverend Thoroughly dressed in white shirt, trousers and hat—like the minister—and spreading the Gospel and converting field labourers to Christianity. Aunt Lavinia and Sarah spent most of those days in the sewing room downstairs. They no longer tried to conceal their closeness from Pohpoh and Asha. The girls now woke early, anxious to see Aunt Lavinia, who still played games with them, chased them around the yard, and braided flowers, seeds, and feathers into their hair. She made them garlands that tinkled with the shells of dead snails that she boiled first to dull the fetidness. After a night's rain, when the clay soil was well-watered, Aunt Lavinia would gather a mound of the slippery earth, carry it to a bench next to the sewing room and teach them to mould baskets the size of her palm and fill the baskets with clay eggs.

Even with her back to them, Pohpoh was aware of Aunt Lavinia and Mama down by the mudra tree whispering and giggling to each other, or Aunt Lavinia and Mama down in the sewing room—Aunt Lavinia and Mama sitting on the sofa bed down there, Mama leaning into Aunt Lavinia's arms—or Aunt Lavinia braiding Mama's hair or standing behind Mama with her hands wrapped protectively around Mama's waist. Pohpoh turned her head away when she saw them facing each other once, and she felt them come together and hug. She imagined them kissing. She imagined Papa finding them kissing.

One day during the holidays Papa hired a hansom and driver to take the family and Aunt Lavinia to the beach. Aunt Lavinia and Mama sat on one side of the carriage and Papa, Pohpoh and Asha sat on the opposite side. Pohpoh detected an unusual hardness in Papa's face, and she lurched across, placing herself between Mama and Lavinia. She leaned against Aunt Lavinia, took her hands into her own and occupied them in one game after another. Asha slept sprawled on the vacated seat. Mama looked in silence at the fields and houses scattered in the countryside. As the moments ticked by, Pohpoh was conscious of her father staring at her mother as if he were seeing her for the first time.

Mama and Aunt Lavinia did not go into the water. They walked the beach while Papa sat in the surf with Pohpoh clinging to his back, trying unsuccessfully to distract him. Asha sat on his outstretched knees. His body washed from side to side with the push and pull of each wave, yet he seemed always to keep Mama and Aunt Lavinia in sight. His children jabbered incessantly, but he seemed to hardly hear what they were saying.

After the children's swim, Aunt Lavinia took out her camera. She took a picture of Mama and Papa, and then several of Pohpoh with

Mama, Asha with Mama, Mama alone, Mama with both children. Pohpoh asked to be allowed to take one of Mama, Papa, and Aunt Lavinia together by the water's edge. Papa got an idea from Pohpoh, grabbed the camera with playful force from Lavinia and told Pohpoh and Asha to stand aside. He watched through the lens. In the midst of their laughter and frivolity, he did not fail to see Lavinia place herself behind Mama, and he saw Mama press herself against Lavinia. Through the lens he watched carefully and saw Lavinia's hands rest tenderly on Mama's waist. He saw it all only because, that day, he intended to. And Pohpoh watched him as he did.

On the ride home, no one spoke. Even though the salt water, slapping waves, tangy sea breeze, and play had made Pohpoh sleepy, she forced herself to stay awake for the entire trip. Had it not been for the wheels of the buggy crunching the stone and dried earth beneath, and the horses' hooves clopping along steadily, the speechlessness would have been unbearably loud.

That night, after the lights were put out, Pohpoh lay in bed staring at the pomerac tree outside her open window. She listened hard but all that came from her parents' room were quiet, indistinguishable exchanges. Abruptly, there was silence.

Next morning she awakened with a start, angry at herself for having fallen asleep. She was terrified that she might have missed the outcome of her father's discovery, but he had already headed out to the schoolhouse. The only sign that something might have transpired was that Mama blinked her eyes rapidly until Aunt Lavinia arrived. She sent the children out of the house, and they too spoke in clipped, hushed voices. Pohpoh feigned sullenness so that Asha would prefer not to play with her, then she sat on the back stairs, pretending to scratch at the wood with a fingernail while straining her ears. Aunt Lavinia as usual spoke far more audibly than Mama. Pohpoh was unable to catch the full conversation, but the snippets that floated down were enough for her to understand.

"We have no choice but to make a decision." There was a pause and then Aunt Lavinia said, "Don't worry. Please don't worry about that. I have known that at some time in my life I would have to face it. It looks like the time has come." Pohpoh could tell that her mother responded but was unable to hear anything distinct.

"I will leave them a note partially explaining, and then I will write them in detail once we're there. But they will never accept any of this, and if they learn of it beforehand, they will separate us at once…Look, Sarah, either we do it now or we will never be able to. There would be no point for me in living if I was unable to see you every single day of my life."

Another pause. Pohpoh heard little of what Mama said.

"They are every bit a part of our lives. I too want them with us, no less than you. We will *never* be parted from the children. I promise you that."

Again Mama's words were inaudible.

"It is, dear. But I have access now to my inheritance. What better use to put it to than taking you and the children some place where we can be a family, where we will never be separated. Ah, my sweet, don't be afraid. Sarah dearest, tell me, is this what you want or shall we stop all of this at once?"

This time Pohpoh heard her mother. "Yes, yes, of course. As long as the children can be with us, I want to go far, far away with you, someplace where we can be together."

"Then I will get the passages. I will get them. I will arrange it all. We will be able to be together within the next few days. We can sleep at night and hold each other and…"

Mama did not go to the gate to see Aunt Lavinia off as she had in the past. Pohpoh suddenly felt very grown-up. She also felt weak and dizzy, knowing that she and her sister and her mother were going to go away—where she could not imagine—without her father. While she had no desire to tell him, she knew she was holding a terrifying secret.

For the next few days Pohpoh shivered even in the sunshine, while Asha sweated in her ignorance. She withdrew from Asha and began to collect things in a little bag. She gathered seeds and shells from the garden. She carefully snapped a leaf off the cereus plant, which was thriving but had not yet blossomed. She was determined one day to see the spectacular blossoms that Aunt Lavinia had described so rapturously. When the white sap stopped flowing like blood from the snapped-off end, she wrapped the leaf in a handkerchief, also a present from Aunt Lavinia, and placed it in her bag.

During the next days, Aunt Lavinia did not visit. Mama and Papa avoided each other's eyes, but it was noticeable even to Papa how busy Mama kept herself, and how much attention she was paying to getting meals on time, to cleaning up and straightening the house.

Then the day arrived. It was a cool morning. Rain had fallen all night and only recently let up. Insects were clamouring. Pohpoh saw the signs early that Aunt Lavinia would be coming. Once Papa was out of the house, Mama dressed in clothes she might have chosen for a special church event. She insisted on dressing Pohpoh and Asha, even though both were capable of readying themselves. When Mama slid the new dresses off their hangers, Pohpoh knew they had been chosen a while ago, for the garments had been pressed and placed in the cupboard for easy access. She made them wear their fancy shoes and new socks. There was such urgency in Mama's actions that neither child protested or asked questions. Pohpoh wondered if Asha also understood what was happening, for she noticed how unusually agreeable and attentive she was to Mama's every wish.

Aunt Lavinia arrived before they had finished their breakfast. The children were startled, but Mama didn't seem at all surprised, even though Aunt Lavinia had entered through the back gate, one that was used so seldom it had all but grown over with brambles. Neither did Mama seem interested that she had brought the buggy and horse all the way into the backyard instead of parking in front as usual. Pohpoh noticed that even though bright sunshine had followed the night's long rain, the buggy was fully covered. She observed too that Mama and Aunt Lavinia regarded each other with a strained formality.

Then Aunt Lavinia spoke quietly and urgently to Mama. "He has already gone off with my father. But I don't know how long they will be gone. We'd better hurry." Mama didn't move but held her hands up as if uncertain. Aunt Lavinia moved closer. Mama instantly backed away.

"You manage all the passages? The ship sailing today self? Look how it rain last night. It won't postpone, Lavinia, eh? It don't have another sailing for months, right?"

Aunt Lavinia stood still. She bit her lower lip. Then she very calmly but firmly said, "This is the last sailing before the rains. We must hurry, my sweetest."

Mama became unfrozen and began clearing off the table

"Are the things in the sewing room?" Aunt Lavinia asked. Mama nodded and Aunt Lavinia bolted downstairs and started hauling boxes and trunks up into the drawing room, then down the back stairs and out to the buggy. Her shoes squeaked sharply with each step in the wet earth. Insects carried on their ruckus.

Pohpoh watched from a distance. There were already two trunks atop the buggy strapped down with thick leather belts. She wondered where Aunt Lavinia got such strength. Asha followed Aunt Lavinia down the narrow stairs to the sewing room. Pohpoh could hear her asking Aunt Lavinia questions—what this was for and what that was for—and for the first time Aunt Lavinia was too preoccupied to answer carefully. Her tone was unindulgent and oddly sharp, and so the questions, obtuse and pointless, kept coming, as though answers were not what Asha really needed. Pohpoh stood in the doorway between the verandah and the kitchen and watched Mama busily closing windows and gathering photographs off the walls. Then Aunt Lavinia came up the back stairs and said it was time, and they must leave at once if they intended to make the sailing.

It was only then that Mama, holding the children's velvet hats in her band, pulled Asha and Pohpoh close, stooped down to face them and whispered, as though there were someone else in the room who should not hear.

"We going on a long trip, far away. We going with Aunt Lavinia on a boat. For a long time. Papa doesn't know. Is a surprise. I pack up all your things. Everything pack up." She placed a hat on each child's head. She bit her lip and blinked her eyes rapidly as she pulled firmly on the ribbons and tied a bow, first under Asha's chin and then Pohpoh's.

"Now I want you to go like nice girls quiet-quiet inside the buggy. You have to sit down and stay quiet-quiet until we get far away, you hear me? Okay now go, quickly. Aunt Lavinia will take you downstairs."

Aunt Lavinia placed her hands protectively on their shoulders and ushered them down the back stairs. At the bottom they waited for Mama. The sun had suddenly come out, and the wet leaves on the trees and shrubs were glistening. Mama stood on the top stair, looked around at the yard and then, with a deep breath, ran down.

Just as they entered the buggy Pohpoh remembered her bag with all the seeds and the shells and the cereus cutting.

"My bag, my bag. I have to get my bag." She ran toward the steps shouting.

Mama and Aunt Lavinia tried to grab her, but she was already ascending the back stairs. Aunt Lavinia headed after her and suddenly stopped. Pohpoh came to a halt, for she too heard footsteps.

"Come on. Pohpoh, come now! Come here!" Aunt Lavinia snapped an urgent whisper.

Pohpoh froze in terror. Her father had returned. Unsuspecting, he had strolled up the front stairs and across the verandah, had already unlocked the front door and was walking through the drawing room toward her.

Pohpoh stood still, unable to breathe, the whole world turning black around her. She saw her father hesitate, the cock of his head and the sudden twist of his body revealing he had noticed that pictures were missing from the walls, that the curtains were drawn, that the house was uncommonly tidy. She imagined what he was seeing—things cleared away or cleared out. She heard his unsure footsteps walk to the bedroom he shared with Mama.

Aunt Lavinia no longer whispered. "Pohpoh, Pohpoh," she called out sharply. She tried to grab Pohpoh's hand when she heard Chandin cry, "Sarah!" The nervousness in his voice made her pull back. When he called the second time, his voice was unrecognizable.

Chandin swept through the kitchen and onto the back verandah. Aunt Lavinia backed down the stairs in haste. He saw Pohpoh and ran past her. She turned to watch him, but the sun had caught on the jagged edge of the porch's iron roof and the spot dazzled like a blinding star. She heard her father descending the stairs, two, three at a time. She heard everyone shouting at once. She heard her father screaming, her mother screaming, and Aunt Lavinia's voice, suddenly deep and raspy, shouting her name and Asha's. She heard Asha screaming.

It was Asha she heard most clearly, "No! No! No! Pohpoh! Pohpoh, Pohpoh. I want Pohpoh. No! I want Pohpoh." Then she heard the buggy rolling swiftly through the yard. She lay in a puddle on the floor of the verandah, her nose against the damp wood floor, shutting out the sounds. She covered her eyes with both hands.

It seemed as though hours passed before her father dragged Asha, heaving with incessant dry sobs, up the stairs. He stood on the verandah in his Wetlandish whites, and not until the sound of the horse and buggy had completely died out did he move. He kicked the banister again and again, first with his right foot, then with his left. He hobbled into the house. The two children huddled on the verandah floor, unsure and terrified. He seemed oblivious to their presence. They watched as he swiped at the kitchen counter, sending pots and pans and cutlery crashing to the floor, clanging and spinning. Asha began a soundless, fitful crying. Pohpoh held her breath and covered her mouth. Her eyes missed nothing. Plates and cups and glasses shattered all over the kitchen floor. Her father tore through the house smashing ornaments. Asha and Pohpoh turned to face whichever direction he took, keeping him locked in their sight. He thundered into his bedroom, kicking and banging the walls. They heard the drawers of the armoire being yanked out. Pohpoh knew he was seeing emptiness. He came out with a tin, thundered into the kitchen, banged the container on the table. He rifled through photographs, pitching some on the floor. Those of his wife or Lavinia Thoroughly he crumpled into a ball, then spat on, all the while crying and making growling sounds. His children cried even more seeing him cry.

His task so blinded him that he did not notice Pohpoh tiptoe to her room. She walked straight to her Bible, which sat on the table where she and Asha did their homework. She shook the Bible and out fell a photograph. Her heart beat rapidly. It was the one of Aunt Lavinia and Mama that her father had taken at the beach not long before. She shoved it in her pocket and, holding her breath, made her way toward the verandah.

Her father's skin and hair were drenched in sweat. He staggered as though drunk and threw the crumpled photographs into the kitchen sink. He struck a match on the windowsill and dropped it. It did not take long for the little flames to become one large one. The flame leapt up from the sink, burning blue and orange. Black smoke tumbled upwards and flecks of blackened ash sputtered throughout the kitchen.

This Early

Mei Ng

It is morning, and I reach for the brass candlestick by the bed and scrape the wax that dripped down last night. Soon there is a small white pile and for a moment I almost believe it's shredded coconut and want to eat it. I'd be done much quicker if I would just get up and get a knife from the kitchen, but I'm not in a hurry. Besides, it doesn't seem right when other people are downstairs chipping away at the icy sidewalk, the frozen steps. All that noise and they've hardly made a dent.

You call to say you're on the way. We hang up quickly as though we can't wait. I brush the wax from my fingers and put the kettle on. Waiting for water to boil is something I don't do. I gather up the garlic skins from the floor; fill the salt shaker, eat a few cashews. There is hardly anything in the refrigerator: a couple of old yams, some lemons, a green pepper that's only starting to cave in on itself. It makes you nervous that I keep so little food in the house.

You walk quickly to my apartment, our morning bagels tucked inside your jacket, close to your body. When you get here, they are still warm so that the butter melts. We both hate margarine. You say, "What if there's a big storm and I can't make it over here, what will you eat?" You've known me a week, but already you know how I hate going out in the mornings.

I try to explain that it only looks like I have no food. In an emergency, I could whip something up. When there's too much food in the fridge I get edgy, afraid I won't get around to it. It's like I'm always waiting for food to go bad so I can throw it out already.

I wait for the water to really get going before I make the tea. I make your cup first; you like strong tea. I let it steep, then add lots of lemon, lots of honey. Then I make my tea with your old tea bag. I take my tea light, like old ladies at the diner. If it's too strong, I can't sleep at night.

You show me pictures from your trip to China. For a white girl, you look pretty good in your red imperial robe and headpiece, standing by the palace. You hold your neck very still so the headpiece doesn't tilt you over. It's heavier than it looks. You tell me you are angry at your mother for not teaching you Italian, that all you have left is lots of ways to cook pasta and a big family. I tell you my second language is Spanish, not Chinese. As I look at the photo of you by the Great Wall, I remember that your boyfriend is Asian, too, and I wonder if you've got some fetish thing going on. But then you are talking and touching my arm at the same time, and I think: Everyone's going to China these days, it doesn't mean anything. Me? No, I've never been.

The phone rings. The machine clicks on and then there's my father's voice in my room. "Hello, Daisy? Did you go out yet? It's slippery out there. I almost fell down when I go out to shovel. You be careful when you go down your stair," he says. Then he's quiet but doesn't hang up right away like there's something else he wants to say but can't remember what it is. He clears his throat, then it sounds like he's trying to hang up but can't quite fit the phone back together again.

"Was that your father? He sounds sweet," you say.

"My father? Sweet? I guess so," I say, because there isn't enough time to explain him. It would take all day, all night even, and you like to get back early.

My bagel is too big and doughy, each bit seems a lot of work. You don't eat your bagel either. We cover our plates with napkins and tell each other how we normally eat, tons and tons. We're just not hungry right now. Maybe later.

We say something about the weather, about how important the right boots are. You are not looking at me, you are talking and looking down at the floor. The more you touch my arm, the faster you talk. Your mouth is moving and I am looking at it.

Later that afternoon, we are on the couch, its velvet worn almost smooth as your skin. You tell me you've never done anything like this before. Outside, it sounds like everyone on the block is chopping ice. There is still so much to break up and push away.

My wrist is thin next to yours. Your arms just a little bigger than mine. I ask you if you work out, and you say only at your job, emptying bags of ice into the bin, reaching for bottles on the upper shelf. You say you hate all the people who come to drink in the afternoon but when they don't come, you miss them.

I ask about the scar on your arm near the curve of your elbow. It's so light you can hardly see it anymore. I put my lips to it as you tell me, "I used to clean my grandmother's chandelier. Her eyes were huge behind her glasses, but still she couldn't see so good. Her hand was always moving on the table, reaching for things she couldn't see. One day when I was cleaning, I moved too close to one of the bulbs. I'm always burning myself." I show you my hands, all the little scars. I don't have to worry about burns, but keep me away from glass.

You say you want a picture of me to take with you. I bring out my shoebox, and you pick the one of me in my orange sun hat, running on the beach. It's hard to tell what direction I'm running in.

You put the picture in your bag, then pile on all the layers again—you are well-prepared for winter. I hate socks and hats, I can stay in for days. I wonder if I'm getting like my father. He doesn't like to go out of the house, doesn't like putting on shoes, says they hurt his feet. He still dresses every day in a white shirt and neatly pressed pants, but on his feet are those old gladiator slippers.

"What are you doing for the rest of the night?" you ask me.

"Oh, I don't know," I say. "This and that."

"Are you going to read, cook dinner, go out?" you say. You are completely dressed and it's hot in my apartment. I see that you don't want to think of me just sitting here in the same position all night.

"Yeah, I think I'll read, make a little dinner," I say, so you can leave. I listen to your boots going down the stairs, then out the door. There is no sound as you make your way down the icy stairs. I listen for the gate opening and closing, then start chipping away at the wax again. I am working faster now, digging with my nails. There is more ice out there than anyone is used to.

I saw someone fall yesterday. She got to the corner and slid off the curb. Her legs folded under her, and she crumpled gently as though she were tired of walking and just wanted a little rest before going on.

I call home. I want to ask my mother how to make her sea bass with black bean sauce. Not that I have the ingredients, but just listening to how she makes it would be enough. My mother always gave me the best bits. After she drizzled the sesame oil over the top, she'd remove the backbone with her chopsticks. She would check to see if there were any little bones left, then she'd put a good piece in my bowl.

My father answers the phone. He says "Your mother?" like he doesn't know who I'm talking about. "She went shopping. Again. It's been four hours since she left the house. She took the cart with her. The refrigerator is so full you can't fit anything else in it. There's food all over the house. She buy, buy, buy, then she forget about it. How much can two old people eat?"

The next morning when you come over, it is the same with the bagels. We butter them but don't eat them. Today we don't talk about the weather. Today you're the one to say, "Let's sit on the couch where it's more comfortable." We start ever so slowly.

"I don't know what to do. Help me—you've done this before, yes?" you say.

Have I touched you before—here, and here? No, but I've wanted to for a long time. I don't say this to you.

"Yes? With other women?" you say.

"A little, just a little. A long time ago," I say. I don't want you to think I know what I'm doing either.

Afterward, we are finally hungry. You have dinner plans in a couple of hours, but you want to eat now. Even though it's only afternoon, I cook those two steaks that I had in the freezer. Sweet potato fries and a salad. See, didn't I tell you I had food?

I watch you cutting into your steak, and you're not the least bit squeamish. You take yours medium rare. All that blood. You tell me you don't want to hurt your boyfriend's feelings. He is a nice man, you tell me, easy to be with. He shaves before coming to bed so as not to bristle you. You don't know whether to tell him or not. I wonder whether you will eat two dinners.

It is time for you to leave, but we both want another cup of tea. I rinse the cups from breakfast and make your tea first. You drink it so dark. How can you sleep at night? You tell me to use a new bag for myself, but isn't it just a waste if I take it light anyway?

At my mother's house, she makes tea in the old blue-and-white pot that she's had forever. If you want it light, you take the first cup. If you want it darker, you have to wait a little longer. I used to have a teapot. It was ivory-colored, squat and small. First the knob on the lid fell off. Then the spout got chipped and finally the handle. I saved the pieces for awhile, meaning to glue them back together.

Downstairs, there are kids going door to door, with shovels over their shoulders. "Shovel your walk, mister? Just three dollars for the whole sidewalk. The steps too." People have taken to using axes and hammers like they are angry.

It is dark and I light a candle. Just one. The wax doesn't start falling right away. It collects at the top, then pours down all at once. Tomorrow there will be white dots stuck to the floor.

When you tell him about me, he doesn't seem to mind too much. "It's just kissing, isn't it?" he says. With him it's easy, you tell me, he's the boy and you're the girl. You've had lots of practice and you're good at it. When I come to see you at your job, tending bar, I see how much money the men leave on the counter.

It would be mean to leave your boyfriend when he hasn't done anything wrong. He's sweet, you tell me, a nice man. It's not that I think you're lying. I've known lots of nice men; I was married to one. Daniel would cook brown rice for me even though he hated the smell, said it smelled like mouse droppings. But he could never get it quite right. I would tell him to use more water, cook it over a slow flame. But somehow, it was always too hard. I had to put it back in the pot, add more water and cook it some more. But I would kiss him when I did this so he wouldn't feel bad.

You don't tell your boyfriend what you tell me, that when we're together, you don't have to be the girl, the woman; you don't have to be all the women on billboards smiling with their mouths open, their eyes closed. You don't have to hold in your stomach. You can just be a plain old person. This is scary to you; you're not sure how to do this.

One afternoon you say you will brush my hair for me. You brush slowly, starting at the bottom and working your way up. I can tell from the way you hold the brush that you've had long hair before. Now your hair is cut close to your head. As you pull the brush down my back, I remember that Daniel would brush my hair. After a while he could do it like you are doing now, but in the beginning he'd try to undo the knots in one stroke and ended up pulling my hair out. As you brush, slow and steady, I start to cry. You do not stop.

I had a friend once in the sixth grade. Her name was Marianne Shirts and there was no television in her house. I would sleep over, wearing one of her nightgowns that seemed softer than mine, and I would brush her hair a hundred times before we went to bed. After we got under the covers we would practice kissing. At first her tongue was a surprise, something I wouldn't have thought of myself. Then after a while, our nightgowns would ride up to our waists and our bare legs touching was another surprise. I was afraid that I would like practicing too much, that I would like it better than the real thing. One night when Marianne turned to me and said Wanna practice, I made myself say no thanks, like she had offered me a hot chocolate or a peanut butter cookie. I stayed up all night watching her eyes move back and forth under her lids.

After you leave, my mother calls me. First, pick a sea bass with clear eyes, not cloudy. When you get home, wash it in cold water, inside and out. Make sure there aren't any scales left on it. Soak the black beans in some warm water. Put the fish in a bowl, chop garlic, scallion, and ginger. Pour a little soy sauce on it, not too much. Then, steam it until it's done, maybe twenty minutes. Heat some peanut oil in a pan until it's very hot, but not smoky, add a few drops of sesame, pour it on top. Watch out for small bones.

Sometimes in the evenings, you go into your kitchen to call me. I hold the phone close to my ear; you are talking softly. I wonder what your kitchen looks like, and I imagine you leaning your head against wallpaper that was pretty when it was new, but it is faded now and buckled in spots. I'm sure that in reality the walls are painted a pale-yellow, and I try to imagine that, but I'm too busy wondering what your boyfriend is doing while you're whispering in the kitchen.

I know I can't ask you to wait for me, you say.

But wait for you? I say.

□   □   □

You have known your boyfriend for three years, but now he feels alien to you. You say that sometimes when you are in bed with him, you close your eyes and pretend it's me. This is not much consolation. When you tell him you want to keep seeing me, he says, "Sure, why not?" but then he gets real quiet. You ask him what he's thinking and he says, "Should we catch a movie tonight, or just stay in?" Later when he fucks you, he does it rough and you like it at first. Afterward, he says, "You shouldn't lead that woman on like that."

I would like to ask you why you keep my picture in your lingerie drawer. You tell me it makes you happy whenever you go to put on your bra and there's my face. The picture of you is by my bed. Next to the one of my mother. The one where she's sixteen and her face is smooth and white as the inside of a bowl. Her face isn't really white, that's just powder. It's the picture that made my father go all the way across the ocean in a boat called The Wilson, of all things.

"Ma, did you love him then?"

"Nah, I thought he was mean, he looked like a gangster."

"Did you grow to love him, Ma?"

"Love? Chinese people don't believe in love."

□   □   □

It is night and all the shutters are closed. I think of you, and even my teeth ache with wanting. I wait for the sound of chopping to stop, but there is so much ice. It's stupid to start waiting for spring this early.

Wrecks

Achy Obejas

I have to be sure I have the right insurance: that is, collision as well as liability. I simply can't afford not to be able to pay for whatever car repairs I might need, and I'm afraid that sooner or later (and probably sooner) I'm going to be sitting in a mechanic's waiting room, right there next to the Coke machine and the faded road maps, flipping through some weathered copy of *Time* or *Popular Mechanics*, waiting to be told what my insurance will and won't cover.

This is very important to me right now because I always have an automobile accident after a breakup, and Sandra, my lover of five years, just left me for some babe who lives in San Francisco, the promised land of fruit and nuts. We were one of those couples everyone envied—good-looking, funny, successful—so I'm still trying to figure out how this happened, and why. Sandra's dark, jealous, and birdlike, as impatient and breathtaking as a nestling, and the new babe is tall and wooden. I know I shouldn't dwell on it—it's not good for me, but I *know* they don't fit.

Since Sandra moved out on me in order to pump up her phone bill and become a free and frequent flyer, I've been trying to take the bus and train everywhere: to work, to the post office, even to the grocery store, which I hate doing because, since I can't carry ten bags of stuff with the same ease with which I can pack them into the VW, I end up having to do some shopping every time I leave the house. Since I'm trying to be environmentally conscious and use paper bags, which don't have handles, this is doubly tough on the five-block walk from the store to my apartment.

The last time this happened was about seven years ago. It had been three-and-a-half years of utter hell with Loretta, but I still couldn't believe she'd really left, so in my grief and disbelief I wrapped my car around a tree in a south Chicago suburb. I did it the minute Loretta left for Los Angeles, a city in which no one is actually born but to which millions are drawn like moths to a fire. Loretta was lithe, a singer with an immense and angry voice. I'd always thought we shared a cosmic connection of some sort: After all, we fought and fucked like minks. But she said she had to go because she'd imagined women would be kinder than men, and my sarcasm was wearing on her sense of sisterhood.

To make matters worse, after I'd wrapped my car around the tree, I refused to believe it was inoperable, so I did my damnedest to start it, sending the fan blades tearing through the radiator, which had been pushed up a good six inches. The entire mess cost me around two thousand dollars, including the towing fee back to the city; I should have just chucked the car—a beat-up mustard-colored Dodge Valiant—but I didn't. I just kept going. So did Loretta, who married the corporate lawyer for Hughes Aircraft. They have two daughters now, one inexplicably named after me. I confess, it does give me comfort: It's evidence of sorts that I had an effect on that girl after all.

Before that, when Doris left me for membership in a lesbian separatist living collective somewhere in the hills of Arkansas, I made a point of not seeing the steel post holding up the chain around one of Chicago's lakefront parks. I knew Doris and I had problems living together—she smoked with the same fatal simmer of an arsoned building, leaving powdery ash sculptures everywhere, but it seemed extreme that my nagging should drive her to repentance in a place where no cigarettes, polyester, or dairy products are allowed.

After Doris left, I'd wanted just to drive leisurely and miserably through the park, which was—wisely, I suppose—closed for the winter. I just wanted to get a look at the lake, frozen with the waves mid roll. I knew they'd remind me of all those little ash tubes, gray and mindless, that Doris had left around the house. But I never made it to the lakefront. I ended up sliding on some ice on the road and sort of hopping onto one of the little posts that held up the keep-out chain, ramming the post through the transmission of my car and causing total vehicular loss. Ultimately, I didn't mind so much. I hadn't yet noticed car accidents as a post-relationship pattern, and I'd never much liked that car anyway, a green-and-white Gremlin that looked like a pimp shoe.

To be honest, I think the whole accident/relationship thing really started after a brief affair with a former sportswriter for the *Chicago Sun-Times* whom everybody thinks is bisexual but who is really a lesbian. She'd cover Bulls games by watching them in her peripheral vision on TV while lying on top of me on her bed. After she moved to Washington, D.C., to cover society happenings, I ran my old Chevy van into the line of taxis waiting across the street from the *Sun-Times* building, giving the domino theory a whole new twist.

I don't drive anything as lethal as a van now, but rather my more benign, if not just plain cartoonish, VW bug, one of the original Beetles, red and rusty, but still dependable. Of course, I don't actually drive it much these days, since I'm convinced that getting behind the wheel will be eventually, inevitably, disastrous.

□   □   □

The fact is, I can't stay away from cars when I'm heartbroken. Even when I tell myself I shouldn't drive, I end up hanging out at fancy used-car lots, where they use terms like "vintage" and "pre-owned," just staring at those fine machines and dreaming about getaways.

A few days after Sandra left, I saw a 1956 vanilla-colored Porsche 356, the same kind of car in which Jimmy Dean spun right out of this world, and I swear I would have sold my mother to get it. But my mother's dead, Sandra was gone, and with her, every technological gadget I might ever have hocked for more than a hundred dollars, so I didn't have much with which to bargain with the devil, much less a car salesman.

So I just balanced my two paper bags full of groceries and stared at the Porsche. I touched it a few times until, finally, one of the sales guys came out to the showroom and told me to go home. He said I looked like I was going to cry and offered to get me a cab, which he even paid for. That was very nice, but not as nice as driving myself would have been. The thing about cabs is that even if you're rich enough to pay the meter, they still have their limits.

And the idea after a breakup, of course, is to have no limits. I think that's why I like the notion of cars when I'm going through emotional angst. They provide this very cool, very American answer to pain: Even if you follow all the right directions from Chicago to San Francisco, all you need is one wrong turn—one little fuckup—and you wind up in Mississippi, where there are no lesbians. It's so inevitable that you may as well enjoy the ride—the wind in your hair; the truck-stop waitresses who've always been curious but have never been with other women other than in their fantasy letters about threesomes to *Penthouse Forum;* the radio blasting away with great rock 'n' roll songs, then great tear-jerking country and western songs, and then, when the tinny static stuff comes on while you're daredeviling through the swamps, you can always pop on a Philip Glass tape and think yourself really courageous.

I'm no fool, though. I know all this romantic posturing about wide-open spaces, the adventurous South, and on-the-road possibilities; all these images and metaphors for freedom are inspired by men, jaded men like Jack Kerouac—that repressed homosexual who never really found love and died a pathetic mess of a human being. It's all a cover-up for just one thing: desperation.

I know from personal experience that, ultimately, no matter how many road maps I study, how many pairs of lacy underwear I pack for travel, how many times I tell myself that there are girls with Creole accents just waiting for me in New Orleans or Miami, all I'm going to do is drive around my ex-lover's house and have an accident. Sandra may pine for San Francisco, but she only lives one block away from me now. That's how crazy this is.

☐   ☐   ☐

Of course, I've seen a therapist about this, but all I remember is that she recommended I not see *Fatal Attraction,* which offended me terribly because, as a lesbian and a feminist, I would *never* resort to that sort of thing. Instead, I drive around and around and around Sandra's building, like a crazy windup toy that's *too* wound up and careens off into the furniture. I always want to throw up, but I don't—my stomach knots up and short-circuits the whole idea. It's like everything else about her and me: one false start after another.

We met through a mutual friend, a woman we were both crushed out on but who didn't want either of us. It took Sandra and me two dates to kiss, which is pretty typical by lesbian standards but a little slow by mine. By the time we made it to bed, it was more formality than desire: We already knew we were completely incompatible and went through it, I think, just so we could say we had.

Six months later we were both still prowling performing-arts spaces and foreign-movie houses as single lesbians. When we ran into each other again, we both seemed to glow with the right aura, kiss with lips that fit perfectly into each other's mouths, and make love with complementary rhythms. At first, even though it was very nice, I thought that it would be not a casual affair, but a *transient* relationship; I just wasn't sure we'd fall in love. But after another six months, even though I still had doubts about our romantic possibilities, she'd packed her little pointy boots, her Cuisinart, and her cats and resettled them in my Uptown apartment.

That didn't quite work out, though. She wanted more closet space. She didn't like the posters I had on the walls. She thought my Mexican rugs were cheap. So after six months we moved into another apartment, one that was ours from the start, in which no decision could be made without the other's approval. It should have been suffocating, but it wasn't. There was a funny comfort, an uncanny understanding to the way our furniture fit together and our clothes began to match.

Of course, there still were little problems. I liked to stay up until the wee hours; she was up before dawn. I liked rock; she liked salsa. I liked sex in public places; she considered it an adventure to do it in our own kitchen. But slowly, almost imperceptibly, we began to behave in ways that said we wanted to be together for a long, long time: My clothes no longer rested on the exercycle, but got hung up at night; her dishes didn't sit for days but got washed as soon as she finished her meals. I opened a savings account; she named me as her spouse on her American Express and got me a card.

If life was too mundane to be heaven, it didn't matter; it was heaven on Earth, or heaven enough. We had a long, train-like apartment with so much light we had to cover our eyes when we woke up. And on Sunday mornings, sitting in bed reading the paper while drinking coffee and soaking in Sandra's sleepy musk, I was as happy as I might ever have been.

It's true, I could never tell her about my weird Catholicism, or the way my heart hurt from pleasure sometimes, but I could confess to her my foulest fears, my most awful memories, and I knew they'd be safe. I don't know what she couldn't tell me, but I know no one had ever listened to her with quite the same rapture, or held her as fiercely when she was afraid. I know because she told me so, and to this day I believe her about these things.

All of that changed when Sandra took a business trip to San Francisco. She has told me what happened during that week a million times now, but even though I know too well how one thing led to another, I still don't see how—I don't understand why suddenly we didn't make sense, and why *they* did. She explained it by telling me she realized she wasn't in love with me anymore, and that she hadn't been for a long time. She talked about smoking cigarettes for the first time in years, and enjoying it; about walking on the beach; about going to bed at the same time every night with this new babe. She has told me far more than I ever wanted to know about what happened, but try as she might, she's been unable to make me understand how the gears stopped working for us, how the machinery went rusty without our knowing, and how one day the motor simply wouldn't turn over.

When it finally happened—when it became inevitable—I thought that, after five years together, the splitting would be agonizing. I worried about all the everyday things I might have lost sense of; I wondered, really, if I might not walk into walls or the middle of traffic, like a mental patient who thinks she wants freedom but really wants only to be out of the dark and into the light.

I feared the division of our possessions more than anything, not because they were so many but because they were so few and so precious. We were professionals, though, as efficient as the keenest of lawyers: cool, rational, shamelessly unsentimental. We went through the business of furniture without argument, and then we did the same with the dishes and kitchen appliances. After that, the few items of clothing that might have been debatable fell right into place with one or the other's wardrobe, almost as if they—and not we—knew instinctively where they belonged. Her CDs and my CDs gathered in perfect, separate piles.

Even the photo albums were simple to divide. We peeled back the plastic pages and plucked each image, one by one, laughing, and sometimes crying (actually, Sandra didn't cry; she hasn't cried once during this whole thing), remembering our trips to Santa Fe, and to Mexico City, and the good times in Tulsa. I was struck by how few pictures there were of *us*, but how many of her, standing beside this or that interesting tourist site; and of me, driving with that crazy look in my eyes, or leaning happily against the fender of a rented roadster. I always made us rent sports cars, no matter how inconvenient for luggage or sleeping, because there's nothing like driving at night, very fast, very sure, in a car that does absolutely everything you want it to. I think it's patriotic as hell. And I look corn-fed in those pictures, all of which she kept.

When I visit Sandra now, her cats eye me as if I were some long-lost relative, funny uncle, or divorced parent. It takes them a while to remember me, and I never know if they're reflecting her or acting on their own. I envy them nonetheless, their little brains, and that they get to sleep with her every night. The trouble is, most of the time—not all of the time, not when I'm out dancing with friends or watching TV—I still want her and our life back. I still want to go on long rides with her with the windows open, the radio blasting. I still want her to tell me stories, to fall asleep with her head in my lap while I drive. It's true that I didn't ever really know where we were going, but we *were* going, and it was steady, and it mattered. The trip itself was always as vital, as sunny, and as difficult as wherever we might end up.

Now, whenever I drive by, I look up at Sandra's apartment. I don't stare. I don't lunge out the window. I'm very subtle, the picture of calm. I check my gas gauge. I check my heat vents. I check my mirrors and hope no one has noticed that this is my millionth time around the block and I'm wearing a groove into the street. Actually, I never have any idea of how many times I've gone around the block. I lose track; I *really* lose track. I get lost, not on the street but inside my own head. Then I get fucking terrified that someone will see me when I'm trying to be casual about checking my mirrors and that they won't believe me, they won't buy my act, and maybe they'll call the cops or the neighborhood crime watch.

I always imagine that I do it right, though: I reach outside the car to adjust my sideview mirror, and then, right at that moment, I look up—casually, of course, to see if Sandra's light is on, if the cats are poised on the windowsill. I hope that maybe, just maybe, she'll pick that same moment to interrupt the flickering of the TV light with a few steps across the window frame, to the kitchen for more scotch or coffee, or to the bedroom to get her robe because it's cold and she misses me, or maybe, just maybe, to come to the damn window to look for me because she knows—I mean, she just absolutely knows— that I'm here, adjusting my mirrors outside her window, and needing her.

But, of course, it never works out that way. I don't see anything, or if I do it's all in a split second, an instant, that harrowing and fragile crack between the past and the future. I lose momentary control of the car, threaten the life of some neighborhood kid with the shrill of brakes and screaming car horns, and then drive as fast and far away as I possibly can—to the lake, to the Loop, to Kankakee—anywhere, just as long as I can hide my shame and panic when I get there.

When Sandra first left, my friend Lourdes kept up my spirits by saying stupid things. "Women," she declared, cozy in the bosom of a seven-year relationship with a woman who is both a cook and a carpenter. "You can't live with 'em, and you can't live without 'em." I thought this was particularly insensitive of her, kind of arrogant actually, but so blatantly dumb that it never failed to get at least one demented, disfigured laugh out of me.

One day, as I contemplated buying materials for a hex to cause California to fall off the Earth and thus eliminate all chances of happiness for Sandra and her new babe, Lourdes came up with what then seemed like an epiphany.

"You don't need any of this *santéria* stuff," she said. "You're a good egg: You just need a good chick to lay you."

I took her advice. I went on a sex binge, although it was difficult because I don't like to spend the night in a stranger's home, and I felt it was too soon to bring anybody to my home where the bed had been *our* bed, Sandra's and my cozy little love nest. So instead, I took girls out to Montrose Harbor, to the concrete circle that overlooks the lake and the best, most brilliant view of the city skyline. Even for natives, this can be breathtaking. We looked at the skyscrapers, at the long circuits of car lights on Lake Shore Drive, and at the way the sky divides into layers of blue and gray and pink, depending on the temperature, the pollution, and the cloud formations.

But instead of staring at clouds and trying to make sense of their shapes, we stared at the frozen waves and the little pieces of ice—all looking suspiciously like California floating out into the ocean—and tried to make sense of the terribly awkward situation we had put ourselves in. Inevitably, though, we would make love in my VW, an idea I successfully sold to each girl with the promise of "lesbianizing" high school necking experiences.

The first time was pretty hard. I came up breathless, convinced that I was surely doomed, that whatever drool I was wiping off my chin had just sealed the absolute hopelessness of any potential recovery of my relationship with Sandra. I realized then that every time I closed my eyes, I kept hoping to open them to one of those safe

Sunday mornings in bed with Sandra, our bodies tangled together, the cats on either side of us purring. I stared off into the darkness of the lake outside my car window, watched the rats skip between the fogged cars around us, and hyperventilated. I don't think I'd ever felt so alone in my life.

Then I noticed the girl I was with. I wish I could say I felt guilty for not remembering her until that moment, for having blanked her out so completely, but I didn't. Instead, I felt a kind of relief, a strange connection with all the other wretched souls of the Earth— whether they were reckless macho men or women—who woke up from their own selfish pain and suddenly realized they were about to inflict it on an innocent bystander whose only desire was love, or comfort, or maybe even something as simple as fun.

When I finally looked at this girl, I didn't know what the hell was going on, but it was pretty clear that she didn't need or want to hear my hellish confessions. She was fine, suffering not one little shrapnel of guilt or regret, popping a tape into the VW's stereo, singing along, offering me more cheap wine. I wanted to say: *Don't you realize what we've just done?* But she just kept singing, perfectly at home there with her elbow in my stomach and my breast crushed by her shoulder.

I knew I'd hit bottom when I realized what I really wanted was to confess to Sandra what I'd done, and to beg forgiveness for this and any other transgression, real or imagined. I wanted to explain to the girl in my car that this could never, ever, happen again because, for heaven's sake, I was an unhappily-processing-my-primary-relationship-lesbian, and this, this thing that had just happened between us—which was, of course, beautiful and powerful and just plain great—was still, well, *adultery.* As soon as I dropped her off, I had every intention of going home to that long train-like apartment, kicking out any strangers who might have wandered in, and throwing myself at Sandra's mercy.

But I didn't say anything, and I didn't do anything either. I stared out the car window, thinking the city looked extraordinarily innocent, and I eventually came to my senses. I moaned a few times, then forgave myself for the temporary insanity that let me forget the block of cozy bungalows that now exists between my mailbox and Sandra's, that we'd need marriage as a precondition for adultery, and that lesbians can only have, at best, a pseudo-marriage. I told the girl I was pseudo-separated, and surely headed for pseudo-divorce. Nonetheless, she never went out with me again, although she did buy me a scale-model VW and attached a very charming note thanking me for helping her remember how much fun it used to be to park.

I've been back to Montrose Harbor numerous times since, but when I got her note I rubbed my tender muscles, climbed into my very real VW, and started doing circles around the block.

□   □   □

I know exactly when the accidents will happen. I also know that, short of being tossed around and bruised by the steering wheel and shoulder belt, I won't be seriously hurt. And I know, as sure as I know that when I find true love again I will forget all of this misery and dive headfirst into it, that the next time—the very next time I get behind the wheel—I will experience my post-Sandra accident.

That's why I've been taking public transportation. It's why I've bought insurance, not in a conscientious way but in a totally ignorant, sure-to-be-exploited way. I simply filled out a form I found tucked into the weekly *Chicago Reader* and sent it off with a sixty-dollar down payment to a company whose phone number spells I-N-S-U-R-E-D. I don't know what came over me; I just know that I needed insurance right there and then.

When I told Lourdes, she suggested that if I *know* the accident is imminent, and that if having the accident is the only way out of this post-Sandra depression, then maybe I need to just get it over with and run over a newspaper boy, ram a mailbox, or hit a station wagon filled with suburbanites. She said that maybe by avoiding the accident I'm delaying the healing process, sidestepping the very idea that Sandra and I are as dead as disco.

Just yesterday I went over to Sandra's—an official visit to drop off a few things she'd forgotten in the move (a bottle of contact lens solution, a box of postcards, and a couple of pairs of cotton panties, all carried over in a paper grocery bag)—and for a few minutes everything seemed fine between us. We hugged when I arrived and, although she seemed smaller in my arms than ever before, her skin was as familiar and painful as ever.

Still, we talked without effort, laughed without embarrassment. It was almost like old times. Then the phone rang. Even before Sandra's answering machine picked it up, we both knew it was San Francisco calling. We stood there, listening to the whir of the tape, the click, and then the voice that has replaced mine at those times when only whispers matter.

I know I was lucky: Sandra picked up the phone and very carefully said she'd call back in a bit, that we were chatting. She could have gloated; she could have smirked; she could have laughed nervously. All of that might have fit. But she didn't. She did everything the sensitive-relationship manuals say to do: She exhibited patience, grace, and even gave me a little squeeze on the arm and a wet little peck on my cheek. She looked as sad and understanding as if she were my best friend, not the woman who'd dumped me. There was no question in my mind she was *trying*.

But it didn't matter. I'd already clenched my teeth, my fists, all of my muscles, and there was nothing that could loosen them up again.

I still haven't been able to get the episode out of my mind. And that's the part I don't understand. I know I've accepted the situation. I know that to go back would require a blinding absolution on both our parts, of which we're both totally incapable. I'm not asking for another chance. I've accepted we're over. I've even accepted, on some deep and awful level, that we are and will be with others. What I want is an answer of another sort: How long will this nag at me? How long will it hurt?

□   □   □

I've decided to take Lourdes' advice again, so I'm driving my car and looking for trouble. I'm listening to new tapes, tapes I bought on a lark at the 7-Eleven around the corner from my apartment. The place was blazing in fluorescence, humming right along when I went in, moved aside the little American flags that hung from the shelves, and picked out every third tape across the top row. I wound up with some heavy metal, Loretta Lynn, and a collection of the Archies' greatest hits, but I will survive all of their flaws and find beauty in them if it kills me.

My new insurance card is in the back pocket of my jeans. I've got a tall, cool take-out Coke between my legs, and I'm pressing down on the accelerator and singing along whenever possible with Metallica. I'm in complete control. I pass a Jeep on Montrose Avenue, right at the intersection with Broadway, and leave behind a mess of pedestrians waving their fists in the air. At Marine Drive I shift and laugh, sending a man in a raincoat chasing after his frightened dog on the perfect lawn around Lake Shore Drive. I'm in the fourth lane, and my radio is so damn loud I can't hear my own voice singing along. My hair whips all over my face, a crazy dance of snakes. Before I know it, I'm leaning hard, away from the S-curve, rounding up to the Loop, and I realize I'm running out of prime city concrete.

I'm thinking, *Yeah, the interstate looks good,* and I change lanes and climb the entrance ramp off Lake Shore Drive to I-55, pumping the VW, sure that everything I need will be taken care of in a matter of miles, even before the tape turns itself over. I'm thinking, *Yeah, San Francisco; I could drive there in a straight line if I wanted to.* I'm thinking all this, thinking crazy, murderous thoughts when everything—absolutely everything—comes to a dead halt right there on the entrance ramp, right there in front of me, in one overwhelming wall of excruciating sound and light. I feel my head graze the windshield, like some kind of slow-motion heavenly knocking—immediate and exquisite and over with before I know what's actually happened.

But I'm fine, and nothing has happened. Nothing, that is, except

that the belt has practically cut my shoulder with the sheer force of
how I descended on the brakes, all one hundred and twenty pounds
of me, as soon as I saw the red lights going wild in front of my face.
I stopped on a dime—*on a dime*. The guy behind me landed on his
horn, releasing one long, petulant whine. I sneered at him in the
mirror but he threw his hands in the air to apologize, and I realized
I had to forgive him, I had no other choice. The guy behind him,
I'm sure, kissed his bumper. I don't know after that. I look in the
mirror again, but there's no sign of the end to this loose, dangerous
train of cars on the ramp, all stopped for god-knows-what.

I jerk on the emergency brake, unbuckle, rub my shoulder, and
leap out of the VW to find, literally, less than an inch between me
and the car in front of me, a black BMW from which a gaggle of
preschoolers improbably scatters. There are lights everywhere: red
and terrible white lights from all the cars, blue lights threatening
epileptic seizures from a cop car that's backing up on the shoulder of
the interstate. I try to cover my eyes from all the glare and notice a
stream of liquid running between my shoes and down the ramp's
incline: green antifreeze, water maybe, with a thread of something
vivid and red that looks like blood. My shoes are soaked with it
before I can move.

I walk up, maneuvering from small child to small child, all of
them curious and straining to get a look at what's under the wheel
of the BMW. A woman's voice tells them not to look, causing every
one of them to stare even more intently. "Wow," says one, his eyes
as wide as saucers. "Disgusting," says another, her face greenish. A
man in a dark trench coat is pacing right in front of the car. "Oh my
god," he says. "Oh my god," over and over and over again. He has
a perfect haircut and his lower lip curls like he's about to cry. I can't
see anything except that the liquid flowing down the concrete ramp
is almost black now. The lights are so bright, and everything's so
confusing.

"Did the dog belong to anybody here?" asks one of the cops,
averting his gaze from the scene of the crime.

I look at the colossal mangled heap under the BMW's wheel and make out a blondish mutt, one eye like blue glass, the other black with blood from the ruptured sclera. His huge body is torn apart, and he looks like the devil. He's wearing no tags, no collar, nothing. His hair is soaked with dirt and all the liquids pouring from the car's engine.

"It's my dog," I lie, reaching out tentatively to the still warm paw, as open as a catcher's mitt.

"Well, what was he doing on the highway?" asks the same cop. "How come he doesn't have a collar? I mean, I'm really sorry and everything but…Jesus…you got any identification, huh?"

I pat my jacket for my wallet, not finding it, finally reach back to my jeans pocket, pull out my insurance card, and hand it to the cop. His partner, as faceless as he is, directs traffic around my Bug and the BMW. Since I'm squatting, the headlights blaze right into my face, and for an instant I feel like a criminal caught in some horrible act. One of the preschoolers, a little girl with a stammer, tells me she's real sorry her dad ran over my dog. I just stare at her, and she backs off, bumping right into the cop.

"You know this won't pay for the dog, right?" the cop says, handing me back my insurance card. "I mean, you're still responsible for whatever damage to his car, but I don't think you can get anything on the dog."

"She's irreplaceable," I tell him, and let go of the demon mutt's paw. I stand up and cover my eyes. The cop, who thinks I'm crying, squeezes my shoulder.

Now the cop's partner is in the squad car, making noises on the police radio. The squad's blue lights keep going around and around and around. The man in the trench coat, who can't seem to meet my eyes, keeps apologizing to me. "I'm sorry; I'm really sorry," he says, biting his lip until it finally bleeds. I squeeze his shoulder, and we make out a police report together. I think I'm going to owe him some money, but he says no, that he killed my dog, that he can't take my money for what little damage the dog may have done to his car. We're talking hundreds, maybe thousands of dollars here, but he insists.

Just my luck, I think, *I've stumbled upon the last Good Samaritan in the universe, and driving a BMW no less.* I can barely keep from laughing.

☐   ☐   ☐

When I get back in the VW, I check my emergency brake, my gas gauge, then I look in the mirror. My face is smudged and wet, a strange combination of dirt, sweat and, maybe, tears. I really don't know. I sit in silence for a while, just watching the cars go around me and the BMW. I watch them disappear, not so much into the flow of traffic as into the night, beyond the slope of I-55, into the long line of boarded-up houses and old factories, neglected lawns, and loose dogs around the interstate.

I remember seeing Sandra for the first time, dressed in black, somber, and a little scared, and making her laugh. I have no idea what it was I said. It's all behind me now.

Eventually, a huge blue city truck pulls up, followed by a tow truck. The city workers, all men with rough voices whose breath I can see, scrape the dog from under the BMW and hook the car to the tow truck. They hose down the concrete as the man in the trench coat and his family climb into a taxi. Before the taxi's off the ramp, the water has frozen, and workers are sprinkling salt over it. Finally, it's just me and the cops on the ramp. They turn off their blue lights, flick on their turn signal, and wait for me to mainstream into traffic.

Caravan

Gerry Gomez Pearlberg

I am furious at my girlfriend today. Going over and over in my head not the things she said but the things she didn't, abscesses that cut me to the quick. When I am mad at my girlfriend, I do what everybody does: I try to erase her from my mind. From the streets I walk. From the sky above. From the bars we always go to, which I am passing now. Dark bars where we buy each other drinks and recline on Egyptian pillows, kissing, her hand sliding up my shirt, even as she apologizes for her lack of restraint in a heterosexual public place—"forgetting" herself, as she likes to say.

I am trying to forget her too, but it isn't easy when you have a famous girlfriend, because then she's everywhere, the whole world is perpetually memorizing her, she is remembered by newsstands, TV sets, the very atmosphere. Case in point: I'm walking past a bookstore, the window stocked with good ideas I didn't come up with: books by cagey girls in acrid dialects, 'zines for adherents of this or that psychosexual persuasion, slickly packaged audiocassettes of long-dead poets reading their poetry live. And there, a magazine with my girlfriend's picture on the cover—and then another, and another, and another. High up on the very top shelf, glaring down at me. Glossy and inevitable.

My girlfriend is famous and that makes her look more real from the outside in than from the inside out. When I see a photo of her on the cover of a magazine—which is often—I am amazed at how definite she looks. How on the page there is a beginning, a middle, and an end to her. And yet, in real life I cannot escape her because there is no end to her—she is everywhere, larger than life, and this is the defining element of her life's elixir, Fame.

She shines on the covers of those slick magazines, and it's more than the effect of paper treated with chemical compounds. Her desire to shine becomes incarnate on the page. She glows and is beautiful, like a 1950s rawhide lamp, the kind with stenciled cowgirls and laced-up edges. When her full body is shown, her legs dangle boldly off the sides of chaise longues, swimming pools, and queen-sized beds, like smooth souvenirs floating far from the shallows of time. It is, in part, her hourglass figure for which she is so well-loved. The way she holds time by the scruff of its neck, shaking it to bits in the jaws of her extraordinary self-confidence in the potency of physical being.

I am amazed at how definite she looks on the page because in my heart she is an umbra, her suggestiveness her allure. Like a magic trick, the secret's all in the wrist: She does not insist, she implies. *Embodies.* On the page she seems realer than she has ever seemed in my arms, my shower, my bed. Perhaps that's what happens when light hits glossy paper. Perhaps it's all that light refracting back from her image, so precisely framed. It gives her a dimension distinctly lacking in our interactions; a sense of permanence, finality.

☐   ☐   ☐

In the beginning, Darka undid me. On our first date, we met at a seedy bar on the fragrant edge of the City. We had barely touched our lips to the salted rims of our cocktail glasses when she leaned toward me and whispered, "I want to enjoy your body and all its ramifications."

Her tongue was a stallion of muscle galloping across my river. Her breath in my ear a book I could not open. Who could have known that would be our metaphor? And why are books so often the metaphor?—Good Book, Open Book. I once heard the story of a lover spurned, who not only read her boyfriend's journal, but actually wrote in it—not concealing her invasion of privacy so much as formalizing it. She crossed out whole sections of his diary, rewrote the stories she did not want to hear, adjusted his syntax, and annotated his margins with her own interpretations of the truth of the matter. The Real Story, Whole Story, Story Thus Far.

Darka was wearing old fashion earrings, clip-ons encrusted with faux jewels of powder-puff pink and incision-red, the kind that transform the outer ear into a stardust ballroom, a glimmering arcade of music and dance. A whirlpool of skin guards the secret corridor in which love's hot breath blows and whispers are entrusted, and the earlobe becomes a velveteen love seat, a magnificent parlor of ardor and perfume. My grandmother had such earrings. She called them "costume jewelry." In that phrase was the suggestion of a ruse or charade. And grand seduction. Darka was wearing shiny earrings, those old fashion clip-ons encrusted with faux jewels of viscous-pink and decision-red. She wore them that first evening. I never saw them again.

That night at the bar, our bodies were infused with time. The sexiest song in the world was playing: Ella Fitzgerald's swooning rendition of "Caravan." Neither of us wanted the first kiss to end; we knew it would be all downhill from there. So it was only after a long, long time that she broke away—as she put it—"to visit the powder room." I waited for her on my bar stool, feeling off-kilter without the pressure of her body spilled against me like a ladder. I'd grown accustomed to the texture of her flesh, addicted within moments.

Time passed. She did not return for what seemed forever. She did not return at all. I decided to go after her. I paid for our drinks, grabbed my jacket, and dashed down the long spiral staircase—perpetuity incarnate—that she had disappeared into. There was a long, slate-colored corridor at the foot of the stairs. It twisted and turned, a viaduct. I followed it. Through the narrow streets of ancient Chinese cities, along the paralyzing catwalks of industrial capitalism's end-stage fortresses, across the claustrophobic caverns where naked bat pups by the thousands clung to the ceiling like lumpy pink wallpaper, chirping for their milky mothers' return. For what seemed forever I walked, crawled, climbed, pursued.

There, at the end, in a little arena, was Darka, splayed out on a chartreuse velvet couch with goat-horn feet, drunkenly gorgeous, a flagrant Cleopatra.

And there, on my knees, I caressed her, by the gate to the Ladies' Room, that great Forbidden City. Made love to her again and again with parts of the body I didn't know I had. Like a movie star, she returned only the favor of her presence in my arms. But her moans collected in my eardrums, riveting themselves to my spinal column like a liquid string of black barnacles. Her flesh smooth against my fingers, a pink pearl bubble bath—slippery, feminine, deliciously short-lived. She was a genie in the lamplight, a genie inverted—rub her the wrong way, and she'd surely disappear.

We went to the corner and hailed a cab. Inside that dark cradle, she leaned down to retrieve a fallen jewel and bit my thigh brutally hard. Then laughed when a gasp escaped me. The bite left a bruise the shape of a semicolon, suggesting more to follow. "Why have a segue when you can have a non sequitur?", that bruise seemed to say. I studied it every day for a week and was sad when it faded, end of an era.

On every corner we sped past stood the statues of the New Plague. The plague that zapped people while they hurried to work, ran out for groceries, took out the trash. But mostly on their way to work. They'd stop in their tracks, just up and die, like pillars of salt, X marks the spot. And like an evil spell in a fairy tail, touching or attempting to move their statued bodies would unleash so potent a hailstorm of bad luck and furies upon the interlopers that before long the corpses were simply left where they stood—in peace, as it were. Odd term, "up and died," isn't it? And how the passage of time renders old expressions new.

In this City of Statues our bodies sought each other out. She took me back to her place though I hardly knew her, except from magazines and the Big Screen, mid morning infomercials, and late-night appearances as everybody else's Special Guest. I knew what she looked like on the glossy page, on newsprint matte, on billboards, in Garamond #3, in 16-millimeter, and Panavision. The body looks different from each of these vantage points, but I wanted her in every conceivable dimension, first through fifth. And every position. Every proposition I made her, she accepted with glee.

In real life, up close, she was pure, unadulterated Technicolor. One hundred percent Red reds, one hundred percent Blue blues. Her colors popped out of themselves, *saturated*. Something about her whispered, *1957*. She was an anagram of seduction. And I a glass of water into which she lowered her smooth red stems.

□   □   □

What becomes a legend most? she asked.
A sexy, dangerous woman.

What becomes a legend most? she asked.
The one who makes love to your body, but not to you.

What becomes a legend most? she asked.
You do. You do. You do.

□   □   □

Fame, while commonly perceived as an acquisition, gift, or achievement, is actually an accumulation of losses. First you lose your privacy. Your face and body become public property. Next, you lose your friends. You lose the privilege of honest speech; anything you say can be used against you. You lose perspective on yourself, then humility, and ultimately, heart. In time you become a vessel, an open secret for pouring other secrets into.

□   □   □

Secrets are a dime a dozen, but here's a word that's gone out of style:
INTEGRITY
That first night together, while she lay sleeping, I thought about

how some words you just want to reach out and touch, to make a part of your life. INTEGRITY is a range of great mountains: difficult to attain. I remember encountering the Himalayas for the first time. It was like meeting a famous person—the way those mountains went on and on, the way they shone in the day and glowed in the dark, the way their faces were etched in blue shadow, and how differently they appeared from every vantage point. But there was one important difference: Meeting them in person wasn't a bit anticlimactic; it was the experience of a lifetime. There are thrilling experiences—like encountering a star of stage and screen—that you can embellish upon and mythologize. And there is mythic experience—like being in the presence of a great mountain—that does not fit within the confines of language, and is best left to swelter and swell in the personal canals of memory and nostalgia.

☐   ☐   ☐

Sometimes I feel I am being watched by them. The city is claustrophobic with the dead and their memories. It's true what they say about the dead taking their secrets with them, but no one ever mentions how many of our secrets they take as well. City of a Thousand Watchers. A thousand listeners and thinkers and rememberers. I do not believe, as many do, that the statued dead are angels in our midst, put there to help or judge us. But I do believe they are watching, with aching comprehension.

Sometimes I long to be witnessed, sad and unadorned. So I visit Cyclone's statue. Lay flowers at her feet. Or just stand nearby, watching and being watched. The expression on her face seems different every time. Sometimes sinister, sometimes serene. Sometimes familiar, or a dialect of fear. Cyclone was my lover. The plague overcame her near the movie theatre. I like to watch the crowds coming out of the movie, parting to either side of her. Making way for her. My Cyclone, like so many others, halted in time.

☐   ☐   ☐

Each succeeding love is a paradoxical culmination of the laws of chemistry and physics: greater in mass and volume, less stable than the one before. I love Darka more than all the others combined, and so differently from how I've loved the others. But each time is so different as to be virtually unrecognizable from the time before. After biting my thigh she said, *Your heart needs no lifeboat; it's dying to drown.*

☐   ☐   ☐

For the second time, I am on my way to see her, wearing my Walkman, riding the rails. Speeding uptown to a girl named Uncertainty. When I am certain of her, the invisible timer in my heart will click, and I will be compelled to move on. That is my pathology; love having become not a form of hope but a gorgeous futility, like gunning the engine on the Möbius Strip. But tonight I am the picture of earnest pursuit, on my way to her on a magic carpet of unadulterated desire. I am standing between the subway cars, dancing, listening to music and the howling wheels upon the ancient tracks, leaning into the fast black wind of the tunnel, wondering how it can possibly be that in Spanish, this word—*el túnel*—takes the masculine form.

Sometimes the train sidles up alongside another—a local, perhaps, or one that will split off at the next station in another direction—and like a glimpse into a parallel universe I see my fellow riders sitting and reading, napping, or staring blankly into the empty spaces that are fast becoming the fragments of their own accumulating lives. Not one of them is on their way to see her. Not one will kiss those lips tonight in the candlelight, not one will touch her there, and there. I am listening to music and howling into the darkness that I wouldn't trade these gifts, the gift of my life for any of theirs, for immortality, or heroism, or for anything I could name. I am grateful for this night, for the lurching subway cars that catapult me toward her, along the underground of this harsh, handsome city of cigarillos and peppermint sticks, manhole covers imported from India, alligator rumors in the slime—and women who wear the caps of matadors, reducing leather dykes, lathering butches, bulls, and bulldaggers like myself to their most essential tinctures: skin and horn and bated breath. I am grateful for such women, like the one I am careening toward. And for this, my night, advancing through the dark chasm between the well-lit cars' glistening slide show of normalcy's demise.

□   □   □

"Know what makes a whip crack?" Darka asked, and of course I didn't.

"The momentum of the tip as it breaks the sound barrier. That's the kind of speed I want to come at you with."

"Breakneck?" I asked.

"Oh, my poor baby. Breakneck is just the half of it," she purred, her intentions glistening through her black lace underwear, a socket of bioluminescence.

□   □   □

Where I live, there is a distant bridge that only appears at night, a piece of rock candy. I do not know its name, but long to lay lips upon it. I imagine my mouth will stick there, as if to dry ice, and that in time I will be absorbed into its catenaries and suspenders, made whole and nocturnal and useful at last.

□   □   □

She sleeps like a statue, still as a stone. I lie beside her and listen to her breathe. It is an obsession, wondering when it will cease. I listen to my own breath and bloodstream, the sounds of the world entering my eardrums. There is a part of me that is always awaiting the end: the end of the sounds within, the bloodstream's thrum, the ample humps of breath. And the end of the sounds outside, the world pouring in.

I watch Darka sleep and imagine her dreaming of her hero, Max Factor. To make it shimmer on the silver screen, Max Factor sprinkled gold dust in Marlene Dietrich's hair. For the sake of modesty, Max Factor created fur pants for the chimpanzees in Tarzan to wear. To make him more memorable, Max Factor created the famous ring around the eye of Petie, the dog in Spanky's Gang. Hollywood created the dreams on which our lives are based, and recycles them now, endlessly. For this reason, she is fond of telling me, fame and glamour—not adventure and honor—are what we long to reach out and embrace. I wonder what she reaches for in dreams, where all things are equal: a cyclone, a lion, a kiss, cologne. I wonder what the famous dream of, residing as they do in a world where stars are made and ground to dust and made again, through ruthless pressure, like diamonds.

I watch her sleep. How far she has gone from me. Drifting, a statue floating on a river. An impossibility, this dead-weight buoyancy in the ecosystem of sleep, where Darka's body is a cool marble canoe, parting the smoke-grey reeds, pushing the limits of surface tension.

◻   ◻   ◻

Every gift she gave me was a dream sequence, strange and absorbing. Like the Animal Drawing course she signed me up for at The Museum of Natural History. I remember the first class, wandering the Hall of Mammals late at night, long after the museum had closed, the sound of our footsteps echoing in the shadow of an enormous sperm whale suspended from the ceiling. How that strangely lit hall evoked for me the sensation of the first time one kisses a lover after having begun, almost imperceptibly, to fall in love with her: thrilling and desolate.

The overhead lights were off, but achingly bright fluorescence emanated from each of the mammal dioramas, like a series of slides projected at equidistant intervals along the wall. Within those boxed perimeters of light, water buffalos, orangutans, a herd of giraffes, and other once warm-blooded creatures were poised for all eternity in habitats crudely reproduced in plaster and paint. In places the walls—on which were rendered desert backgrounds, or jungles, or plains—were cracked and chipping, a ruination of faith. I remember thinking that the world's most enervating loneliness must surely reside in the dust-filmed frames of those exquisite creatures, and how much *this* sensation precisely mirrored those produced at a love affair's end.

The teacher had us pause to sketch a pride of lions in the Hall of African Mammals. A fallen aura of pulverized plaster illuminated the male lion's overblown mane. It made me think of a Nepali legend I'd once heard about a king who'd ordered the creation of great stone lions to guard his domain. They stood in pairs, potent and enormous, at the gate of every temple and palace. In ritual ceremonies, the king's priests were instructed to imbue these lions with "life." But the king, cowering from what he himself had wrought, grew fearful of these empowered stones, and ordered that they be placed in chains to ensure that they would never turn against him. Hence, the ancient lions of Nepal are bound forever in chains of stone.

I'll never forget what the Animal Drawing Teacher said on the very first night of class. He was discussing spined animals, as compared to invertebrates like insects, clams, and snails. He pointed out that virtually all vertebrates—a vast category of living things—have a spine from which legs, and in some cases arms or fins or wings, extend outward so that whether the creature is a biped or a quadruped, the fundamental "design" is remarkably constant. "Biologically speaking," he observed, "we have infinitely more in common with a bear, a bat, a shrew, and a whale than the surface details—mere variations on a theme—might suggest."

If this is true—and I believe it is—how can she and I be so infinitely far apart?

◻   ◻   ◻

Whereas once her cunt perched on my outstretched finger like a little wet sparrow, all heartbeat and hidden heat, now my heart has slipped from inside me and into her open, unsuspecting hand. She does me so perfectly that when she is finished I pull her up to lay upon me, my heart outside of me, stretched along my skin like a wet suit, shimmering. She is on top of me with her eyes closed, her hand still penetrating me, and I am watching her. Her eyes are always closed when she makes love to me, or, rather, to my body.

"Look at me," I say, wishing I didn't have to ask. And when she does, her stare is so intense and scrutinizing, her eyes so dark and empty, it makes me shudder. Dislodges something inside me I didn't even know was there.

"I'm going to cry," I say, as the tears begin rising.

She holds me with a tenderness that is entirely new. And I begin a silent cry, stifled like a moan passed into a pillow, and then I am sobbing, tears skating down my cheeks, infusing the pillow of stifled moans. Her hand is still inside me, still nursing the wetness there, and realizing this makes me cry harder, I who have never cried during lovemaking.

"Why are you crying?" she whispers. Her soft cheek, that smell I love, the flavor of her are pressed against my ear so that I can taste and smell her with my earlobe. *Why are you crying?* she wants to know.

I am crying because you don't love me, I think, *from the frustration of making love to you and knowing you don't love me.*

Instead I say, "Because I miss Cyclone."

Instead I say, "Because I'm exhausted."

Instead I say, "Because you move me."

Instead I say, "I really don't know."

I wonder what she expects to hear. Does she suspect and dread the truthful answer? Or crave it?

She pulls out of me and we fall asleep, locked in each other's arms. In a dream she tells me, "Being in love is like being in an airplane. A marvelous takeoff, full of expectancy and new sensations. Once in the air, the view alternates between exquisite and desolate. One anticipates glorious arrivals, face pressed against the window. Then the flight becomes bumpy, hazardous, frightening. The crew will refer to this as 'turbulence.' There is a long period of uncertainty, when prayers you didn't think you remembered find themselves crammed in your throat, along with your heart. At last the plane descends. The wheels touch the runway, and there is relief bordering on ecstasy. The passengers applaud. The plane bursts into flames."

In the morning, well before sunrise, I wake up beside her apathetic body, a warm loaf of sweet deviled bread. She is sleeping with her face turned away from me, as she always does and always will, a movie star with her eye makeup still on. I'd never kissed a girl with eye makeup until her. So much I never knew. Her back to me, her makeup and cologne, parted lips and attitude. Beyond asleep: oblivion personified. It's what makes a star: the capacity to suggest so much more than you actually are.

I reach around in front of her, touching her nipples almost imperceptibly, as if trying out a Ouija board. When she moans, I know I've reached the spirit world. It is precisely this implausible contact I seek with her, as if to speak to the phantom of her deepest passions, the ghost of who she was before disappointment rendered her so remote. What is it about this emptiness that draws me? The desert's apparent desolation and the subtle riches therein? The sheer enormity of its scope and mystery? Waking up to her is an adventure, every night a narrative. Unpredictable as a candelabra plunged underwater, a shipwreck submerged in flames.

She moans herself awake, nipples stiffening in my fingers, and for a moment I feel like a victor, except I'm not sure what I've won. Or that I *have* won. Or that there is even such a thing as winning. What does one long for in the desert? Water. Shelter. A fire at night. A variation in the landscape. The most fundamental of elements. Even a mirage seems too much to hope for. Even the intimacy of off-Broadway.

With her I found that Orgasm could mean Epiphany. The very first time we got into bed together she spoke about the holiness of lovemaking between women, the irony of our stigmatization. She made it quite clear that it was nothing personal, that she was simply articulating a general principle: that what our bodies did together encompassed—and was encompassed by—the sacred. "*Wine, flesh, fish, women, and sexual congress: These are the fivefold boons that remove all sin.*" So say the practitioners of Tantrism, and rightly so.

When Darka fucked me, she fucked my heart, drawing her hand in and out of that membrane shallow, my hollow squid, my squirt gun, my gumshoe chiton. And my heart rose through my porous flesh, enshrouding me like gelatin. Her knuckles chafing at my heart, chafing against it, was an epiphany, and that epiphany made me weep: *That nothing—save sex—would ever be right between us. That I might never find love again. That I, and all my friends and lovers, would die someday. That loneliness would be the chandelier, half-lit, illuminating the path toward a nostalgic yellow future without Darka in my arms.*

Sandoval the poet wrote, "Nostalgia is porous."

□   □   □

Sometimes I wonder what would happen if Darka disappeared one day as Cyclone did. How could I rescue her disappearance from her famousness? The famous never disappear; in the eyes of the world, they intensify. Death is merely an enhancement. How would I reconcile the intensified, famous Darka from the disappeared Darka who drifts to sleep in my bed each night, who is warm if not real, tangible if not actual?

I kiss her while she sleeps, but she is still as stone. I caress her, but she doesn't stir, a lioness battened down. I leave my lips upon her like a sugar maple leaf drifted down upon a bridge of sugary ice. I am trying to get somewhere, trying to get somewhere with her, but where? I want to retrieve her from her drifting, to awaken her or something within her. To offer and receive a kind of recognition that only lovers give. Is it simply a matter of reassuring myself of her warm presence, her blunt existence? Or attempting entry into an even more desolate landscape, like a searchlight skidding across enemy territory? What do I expect to find there? A crimson polygraph, set to stun? A turbulent creature enchained by stone? A queen-size bed where Pleasure and Time sleep with their backs to one another? Or a porous passage back to that first kiss in the bar—our one great moment of certainty: the sure sensation of her leg touching mine, a bruise soon to be embedded like a jewel in my thigh.

The Twelve Dancing Princesses

Robin Podolsky

The soldier was no longer young, and he was tired. He arrived at the palace, his tattered uniform soiled with the blood of old wounds and dusty from the road, with a knife and a pistol at his belt and a small pack slung over his shoulders. In the pack were a tin cup, spoon and plate, a flint, powder, bullets, and a cloak of invisibility. The cloak had been given to him by an old woman he had met in a wood into which he had run, bleeding and sick, in order to escape a battle.

The old woman had healed his wounds and nursed him until he was strong. She had given him the cloak when he told her that he was tired of war and afraid that if the king's guard seized him, they would make him fight again.

Once on the road, the soldier kept his back to the king's palace, hoping to see it no more. Then one night at a clamorous and sooty inn, over a deck of cards and a pitcher of ale, he heard talk that made him change his mind. One of the cardsharps—a man who more than once had tried to introduce his own deck into the play in place of the landlord's—moved and spoke with the unmistakable airs of a courtier, although his manners, like his once-fine clothes, had grown shabby from neglect. It was he who told the soldier that the king had promised one of his twelve daughters and the inheritance of all his kingdom to the man who could steal a certain secret from the princesses. That very next morning, the soldier set off for the king's palace. Upon arriving, he presented himself to the court at once.

When the king took the soldier's measure, he thought that here, finally, was a man ruthless, selfish, and dispassionate enough to do what must be done without falling under the sway of the princesses' charms. Pleased, he told the soldier how things were.

The king had twelve daughters, and the princesses were the most beautiful and charming women in all the land. Yet none of them had ever married. Each of them, even the youngest, had suitors from far and wide; kings and princes, poets and pirates, the richest of merchants, the boldest of rakes. And none of the princesses, not even the oldest, would give any of her admirers the time of day.

That was only half of the mystery. What most puzzled and angered the king was this: Every night his daughters would go to bed early, disdaining the social life of the court. And every morning they would sleep so deeply that they could not be aroused, exhausted as if they had reveled until dawn. And every afternoon, each of them would require new shoes, because the ones that she had worn the day before were so used up that the bottoms were full of holes.

When the king made his offer to the soldier, it was everything the fellow he'd met at the inn had told him it would be. The man who discovered and could prove what the princesses did at night would be rewarded with marriage to the princess of his choice and would inherit the kingdom upon the death of the king. However, there was another part to the king's proposition, something that the man who had told the soldier of the reward had neglected to mention.

Any man who attempted the task of exposing the princesses and failed would be put to death. A special graveyard outside the castle moat had been cleared out of the woods just to contain the failed suitors of the twelve princesses.

The soldier agreed to the king's terms. That night he was conducted to a small room, directly outside of the princesses' sleeping chamber, where their twelve beds stood side by side. The only door through which the princesses could leave the palace was locked behind him, but the door between his room and the princesses' was left open.

The soldier made himself as comfortable as he could in the little room's only chair, an uncushioned affair of wooden slats. After he had settled himself, the king's oldest daughter, clad in a simple nightdress and woolen robe, her long, red hair in a single braid down her back, let herself into the soldier's chamber. Without a word, she bowed and offered the soldier a glass of wine. He returned her bow and drank while she watched and smiled upon him with a kind of contemptuous affection and, perhaps, a bit of pity. When the oldest princess had left, the soldier quickly unstrapped the sponge he had tied beneath his beard to absorb any drink that he was offered.

Guessing that the wine had been drugged, the soldier feigned sleep. Sure enough, the king's youngest daughter peered into the little room to check on him.

"Well," the soldier heard the oldest daughter say, "isn't he unconscious just like the others?"

"It appears as though he is," replied the youngest princess, " but still, I feel that something is wrong. Something bad could happen to us tonight, some great misfortune from which we may never recover."

"You're always predicting things," said the oldest princess, "but if any of your prophecies have ever come true, it must be in some very subtle way that the rest of us don't understand."

The youngest princess said nothing more. From his chair outside the princesses' room, the soldier heard drawers open and shut and a great deal of movement and giggling. He heard footsteps moving away from him, toward the far end of the princesses' room.

The soldier threw on his cloak of invisibility and stepped into the princesses' chamber. There he saw all twelve princesses gorgeously dressed and ornamented with sparkling jewels, brilliant feathers and flowers that spoke to the soldier with their insinuating perfumes.

The oldest princess, in a gown that clung to her like a thousand spider webs spun of gold, her ruddy hair arrayed about her like a cape, stood by her bed, striking it with a staff. Instantly it sank into the ground, leaving a staircase as it went. Oldest to youngest, the twelve princesses descended the stairs; the soldier, wrapped in his cloak, following closely behind.

The youngest princess was sheathed in a dress that flowed over her body and fell about her feet like a mountain spring dancing with new rain. The sparkling stuff got under the soldier's boots and, by mistake, he stepped hard on the youngest princess' gown as he followed her down the stairs. "Someone is behind me!" she shrieked.

All the princesses turned to look, but saw no one. "There's nobody there," said the oldest princess. "You're always imagining things."

The youngest princess said nothing more. The princesses and the invisible soldier reached the bottom of the stairs, where the oldest princess' bed stood like a sentinel with its brass posts. The steps had taken them down to a quay at the edge of a broad, fast-flowing underground river.

All around were trees that looked as though they were made of silver and the leaves sparkled with diamonds. So that, later, he could prove to the king that what he told him was the truth, the soldier wrapped his hand in the cloak of invisibility and snapped off a silver twig with one shining diamond leaf at the end. It cracked with a resonant clang, like the peal of a silver bell.

The youngest princess started. "What was that?" she cried.

All the other princesses turned to look. In their giddy excitement and all their talk among themselves, they had heard nothing. "Will you calm down?" the oldest princess said. "You're a bundle of nerves tonight."

Down the river floated twelve slender boats with beautifully curved prows, and in each boat was a princess as lovely as any of the king's twelve daughters. As the boats pulled up to the dock, a princess got into each and began to help row the boat downstream.

Trailing the youngest princess closely, the soldier managed to follow her into a boat. In that boat was a princess in a doublet of velvet and lace fine enough for the king himself. She and the youngest princess embraced joyfully before they began to row.

"How heavy the boat is tonight!" said the youngest princess.

"It's only because we're impatient to get to where we're going," said the princess she loved. "I thought today would never be over." And they rowed hard to keep up with the others.

As the boats made their way downstream under the magical trees that glittered in some mysterious, ambient light, they were joined by others. Some of the boats carried princess couples, as happy as the twelve sisters and their companions. Others carried pairs of princes who were equally pleased with each other's company.

The landscape changed. After they left the silver forest, they came to a forest of gold in which the leaves of the trees glowed with pearls. Again, the soldier managed to break off a twig. Again, the youngest princess started at the noise that no one else seemed to hear.

They entered a forest of bronze, where the leaves were bright with rubies. Once again the soldier seized a twig and the youngest princess jumped at the deep sound. "What was that?" she cried.

Everyone looked at her. "Will you stop it?" said her oldest sister. "You're getting on everybody's nerves."

After that the youngest sister was silent, and her beloved princess stroked her hair and comforted her until, like the others, their boat docked at a pier next to a fine palace with banners and pennants flying, all lit up from within. The couples arose from their boats and went inside, the invisible soldier following close behind. Once more the youngest sister felt someone step on her dress, but she said nothing.

The princesses and princes entered the palace, which was resplendent beyond compare. The great ballroom was ablaze with the light of a thousand torches. The food was plentiful and delicious, and all found it satisfying though it felt in the stomach like nothing at all. The wines and punches made everyone cheerful but affected their grace and lucidity not a whit, and the musicians conjured the most irresistible tunes that got into the company's feet and commanded them to dance. The princesses in each other's arms, the princes in each other's arms, and the occasional princess and prince in one another's arms whirled and skipped until their sweat ran freely and the laughter that came from their bellies without a trace of decorum was loud and free.

There were hallways and rooms furnished in velvets and silks, in crystal and brocade, in leather and chains, where the couples could retire to enjoy each other's company alone, or not. There were gardens and atriums where night-blooming flowers panted their heavy fragrances into the night air and made visitors happy that the grounds were strewn with hammocks, slings and chaise lounges and with pools that invited a midnight swim.

The soldier had never seen anything like it. He tried to feel happy because he had found out the princesses' secret and he had proof and was unlikely to be caught before his work was done. But helplessly, he felt rising inside him a great, heavy grief. He watched the youngest princess, her fears forgotten, laughing with joy, undulating on the dance floor with her winsome love, their eyes locked, their pelvises not touching, but moving in unison nonetheless. He watched the oldest princess as she sat fascinated on a couch by the words of another princess whose many braids fell over her full breasts and shone with mirrors and bright beads from within the folds of her deep-purple gown. The oldest princess' face was smooth and alive, her hand locked in that of the lovely storyteller and pressed to the speaker's heart. The soldier imagined what it would be to have a wife whom he had robbed of her life's greatest joy. He tried not to watch the princes. They irritated him like scraps of memory that, refusing to harden into pictures or words, attach themselves to certain situations and flutter, agitating the air. The soldier watched the ball and thought and wasn't pleased.

☐   ☐   ☐

There were two more unseen guests at the great dance. From deep in a wood far away, by means that are best not talked about, two watchers observed all that proceeded. They were the old woman who had given the soldier his cloak of invisibility and the princesses' half-sister, born on the wrong side of the blanket, the Inevitable Thirteenth.

"Interesting," said the old woman, "most especially the subterranean dialogue between younger and older."

"Perhaps the younger sister's power makes the old one nervous," said the Inevitable Thirteenth.

"Perhaps the youngest will never be reconciled to the older one's power until she challenges it," replied the Old Woman dryly. "You know," she went on, with the smallest of chuckles that conjured, for an instant, the kind of witch that some people might expect her to be, "sooner or later, some rebellion against the Mother is, well...inevitable."

Her companion said nothing, and the old woman went on. "For instance, this story we're linked to shunts us into the broadest and most conventional channels of patriarchal power by the invocation of tropes that signify entry into and then rejection of the chthonic domain—in this case, the queer underground standing for the unchanging underworld, home of the devouring mother. Through the oldest sister's sabotage, unconscious or deliberate, of the adolescent paradise, that eternal glittering romance her sisters still cling to, the reader is pulled from the seductive allure of the underworld, is taught in fact that a condition of enjoying such phantasies is an eventual surrender to the normative, the everyday. Look at all that sparkle and reflection, the jewels like mirrors and the paired princesses and princes—none of our precious children may be commoners, after all, or stuck with the responsibility to rule—it shrieks with the narcissism of the *puella* and *puer,* the eternal child. To be followed, of course, by expulsion into adulthood and the heterosexual union—the inescapable triumph of the Father's Law."

"Compulsory heterosexuality. And death," said the Inevitable Thirteenth.

"And taxes," said the Old Woman. "The oldest sister wants to take her place as queen. She wants to be a mother herself. She wants change. And, like it or not, if she wants those things, it means some kind of accommodation with the phallocentric matrix of power that represents what we call daily life. It also means an embrace of the kind of ruthless power that the soldier represents, the killer within us all. She has to kill her childhood and betray her sisters—the maidens—to become the mother she's ready to be."

"Nice blend of Jung and Lacan you wound up with," said the Inevitable Thirteenth, "quite a serenity cocktail. Let's see how it all turns out after the happy ending, shall we?"

By means that are best not talked about, the watchers peered into the skein of stories that was the princesses and their lovers, all the other princesses and princes at the ball, the soldier and the king, and all the people of the land. Backward and forward through what we call time, the watchers traced the shining filaments of all their possible choices and consequent lives, unraveling the various strands. One thread, the one picked out long ago by the Grimm brothers as that which they most wanted to display, had been decorated so brightly that it outshone all the rest. To follow the line of that story, the soldier returns in safety, exposes the princesses, is believed and marries, of course, the oldest, the one who shushed her younger sister's fears. Then the thread grows dim. The Brothers Grimm never went on to say what happened to the youngest, to the other sisters or even to the happy couple after they were wed.

Entering the web of story, the watchers found that thread that was the youngest sister, the slimmest strand that shone with a pulsing, fevered glow. They saw that she never recovered from her sister's betrayal, from the loss of her own handsome princess, her one true love.

They watched the youngest sister surrender to madness, the only truth she could cling to, screaming out her visions and dreams to a world that dared not believe her. They saw three forced marriages fail after each of the grooms, youngest sons of kings with whom her father wanted very much to be allied, sickened suddenly and died inexplicable, painless deaths. They saw the youngest sister walled up, finally, by her father's order in a tower that had no entrance; watched her long, golden hair trail down the tower's walls, as she hauled up on ropes the water and bread that was her only sustenance, crying for a witch to climb that dazzling rope of hair and release her from her loneliness and rage. None came. They watched as she died, burned alive in her tower by villagers after an especially bad winter when their crops failed, watched while her father's guards stood by, having no orders to save her.

They watched the ten middle sisters who, married to the middle sons of kings with whom their father wished to be allied, went on to live longish, comfortable, and moderately pleasant lives and were never again quite so quick as they'd been when they danced and sweated under torchlight with the princesses they'd loved and the princes who were the only brothers they'd ever known. Toward their own daughters there would be mistrust, sometimes hatred, mixed with love. There would an affair of a soothing mirror that encouraged vanity and spite, a poisoned apple, there would be a spinning wheel, a long sleep, mutilated feet and glass slippers...oh, it would go on and on.

Finally, they found the strand of story that was the oldest princess, a tough, flexible, lustrous wire. They watched as the oldest sister welcomed, for a time, the sun on her face and the company of people she'd never met. They watched the grace and power with which she conducted the court as her father aged, and they watched her joy when she had a child, a beautiful girl. They watched as, after the death of the old king and the ascendance of the soldier to the throne, the oldest sister's power waned as she saw little of the sun, only endless rites of courtly courtesy under the torches of her husband's palace. They watched her boredom turn to bitterness and then impotent horror when she saw that her husband, the king, was still the drunken, ruthless soldier he had, with some interesting lapses, been before. She spent many nights alone in her sleeping chamber, in which her husband had the bed bolted to the wall. The king began to spend altogether too much time in his daughter's room, watchful and jealous lest she find some means to escape to the underworld and find sisters and brothers there.

"The teller is the tale and the tale, the teller," said the Old Woman. "Don't you think you're taking a one-dimensional view of all this?"

"And your view of the queer underground?" asked the Inevitable Thirteenth. "An edifice of adolescent romance that must be abandoned in order to grow up? Whose story is that anyway?"

"Are you not bitter," the old woman asked, "thrust out of the palace and into the wild?"

"And you," the Inevitable Thirteenth replied, "are you not bitter?

Abandoned as well, given the most meager respect, laced with not a little fear, because, finally, they don't desire you and you're still alive? Having to show the merest shadow of your power, known as an eccentric, a crank, a harmless old bat who just happens to have on occasion the most marvelous gifts lying around, like a cloak of invisibility that they accept as their due with the most perfunctory of thanks? Are you not bitter? But at whom? Maybe more than a little sour toward those of us who might not be so quick to fade into obscurity and who might not keep doing nice things for people who just don't appreciate it?"

"The word 'strident' is overused these days," mused the Old Woman. "However..."

"All right." The Inevitable Thirteenth settled down. "Let's watch some more. They might surprise us, all of them."

☐   ☐   ☐

The torch flames snapped, the couples danced, the room breathed perfume and sweat and lust. Music and laughter grew wild, the drums spoke louder, and it seemed as though the moans and yells that filled the far-off rooms and gardens could be heard in the ballroom's great din. When he could stand no more, the soldier made a choice.

"Let her decide," he decided.

The soldier threw off his cloak and walked toward the oldest princess, his worn, rough form surrounded by spreading waves of silence as he moved across the floor. The oldest princess met his eyes. Facing him where she sat, she released her companion's hand, but not before pressing a kiss into the smooth palm.

When he reached her, the soldier bowed, more abruptly than he had meant to. "Will you dance, Lady?" he invited, extending his hand.

The oldest princess looked at him gravely, without fear. She looked at the lovely and beguiling princess at her side, who was also the oldest of her own sisters, a woman whose words had begun to make the oldest sister feel that, even in the underworld, life can wild-ly, unpredictably change. She looked at her youngest sister, who had torn loose from her partner's embrace and was standing before her at the soldier's side, breathing hard.

The youngest sister could not yet see what the watchers had seen, she could not know just how things might turn out. But the feelings that seized her were exactly those she would have felt if she had known, to the last detail, what the watchers knew. She stared at the oldest princess, outrage and terror erasing her prettiness, marking her face with traces of the beauty it would someday achieve.

The oldest princess realized that she was not tired of her sisters after all. She was tired of sameness. She had wanted something new to happen. She did miss sunlight. She wondered about having a child, about how it would feel to reign in a court that was known to all the world. For the soldier, she felt something that approached and fell short of desire; a strange fellowship. She saw that he was as tired as she. She saw, also, that she was seeing the best of him then that she would ever see if they spent all the rest of their days together.

Meeting her affectionate, distant gaze, the soldier felt more weary and sad than ever. He remembered another pair of eyes that had, for a while, looked at him as the princess looked at the woman at her side until, one day, they turned from him in terror and disgust. Facing the princess, the soldier felt a deep regret for what he had become. He knew that, if she let him, he would still betray her secret and all would be destroyed. He hoped that she was stronger than he could be.

□   □   □

"Do you really think," asked the Old Woman, "that the Father's Law can be evaded by an act of willful refusal? Don't you see the futility of a phantasmic rejection of phallocentrism that depends upon that very regime for the terms of its own relevance? What do you suppose can be accomplished here?"

"I suppose," said the Inevitable Thirteenth, "that the possibilities are endless in any direction. The princess, married, might still escape the castle. Or the princesses and princes of the underworld might find their way above ground by another route, one that doesn't trap them in the father's palace. Or there may be more to the magic underworld than we have seen. All kinds of change may yet be possible. No, I don't think we can simply refuse the terms which, even now, construct our questions. But we can build a new thing, even if the stuff we build it with is old."

"The poor soldier," sighed the Old Woman, remembering the terrified, shivering boy he'd been when fever laid him low. "Can he build a new thing?"

"He could have once," said the Inevitable Thirteenth, "but from some acts, we don't get to come back. Remember, he's been the king's soldier for a long time."

"They made him," said the Old Woman.

"Yes," said the Inevitable Thirteenth. "But he's an example of what I mean when I say that there always is some kind of choice. It was the king, finally, who decreed the soldier's fate, but the soldier signed the decree when he bargained with a man who would sell his children and kill anyone who couldn't give him his way. Everything has consequences."

"For all of us," said the Old Woman, drawing her shawl about her in the cold, free vastness of the forest where few who were not desperate or lost ever came.

"Yes," said the Inevitable Thirteenth, moving closer and kissing her cheek.

The soldier's heart beat quickly as the oldest princess rose to her feet.

"Of course, handsome soldier," she said, "I'll dance with you." The soldier's face and that of the youngest princess were twin masks of despair.

"But first," said the oldest princess, leading him toward the buffet, "you really must allow me to refresh you with a glass of wine. It's a very special vintage, made by ourselves, for particular occasions."

She drew, from under the table, a sealed, dark bottle. Uncorked and poured, the wine was blood-red. It had been given to the oldest princess, just in case of intruders, long before—given to her by an old woman whom she'd met in a wood.

They almost smiled at each other as the soldier accepted the glass from her hand. "From the looks of you, you'd better drink it all," she said. "Poor man, you're nearly dead on your feet."

Excerpt from The Pagoda

Patricia Powell

The next day, he awoke close to four and looked out the window by his bed and saw that the ground was damp, that it must've rained overnight, though the rosebush below and the green clusters of banana trees beyond looked more wilted and exhausted and depleted of sap. He awoke close to four and was alarmed at how easy it was to grow slothful, especially now that he no longer had the shop. Aging terrified him, and each morning, with microscopic eyes, he examined the obscene warts that were once sweet and innocent moles. With thudding chest, he listened gravely to the gurgling juices fermenting in his system and knocked repeatedly on his wrists, measuring the deep pulsation of his heart. Grazing with two fingers and a simmering brow, he studied intently those joints that had a tendency to crick or tingle or twitch; bruises that had crystallized into festering chancres; pieces of his flesh that had either petrified or pulped.

And when there was nothing, he whistled as he washed and sang in off-key notes and yawned with astonishing vigor that bespoke an interior calm. But if there was anything as there had been several years ago, the lump that cemented his left breast, he plunged into a strange and complicated self that absorbed him completely. He stopped eating and talking. He suffered. He locked the shop, crept into bed and drew the thick red curtains, blackening the room. He refused to see the quack doctors with their hard and battered black bags, allowing not even Miss Sylvie to breathe on him. And each morning, with cautious fingers, he nursed the lump, mollifying it with the exotic oils and herbal potions he had sent Dulcie all over the countryside to procure, which drenched the room with fetid odors. When the lump finally dissolved, the crumbling-alabaster look disappeared from his face, and the crinkles round his eyes straightened, and he regained his sprightly walk and boisterous laugh and he offered credit and free rum at the shop for one whole week straight.

That afternoon, he snorted and splashed and whistled in the tub of tepid bathwater, sprinkled with perfumed leaves and the bark of great trees. He trimmed the sides of his beard near his ears and blackened the tufts of gray. He waxed his false whiskers and curled the pointed edges thoughtfully. He oiled his hair and powdered his skin and perfumed his throat. Back in his room, in the open door of his wardrobe, he rummaged among the clothes Miss Sylvie had passed on to him from her first marriage but that he rarely wore: slinky and shimmering silk shirts, striped cottons and twilled linens. He parted sharp lines of gray and black suits, and one by one, in slow meditative gestures, turned over shiny pairs of shoes—tasseled brown loungers—inspecting their leather, the cushioned interior that wrapped the feet in velvet, bringing them slowly to his nostrils, then looking off with glass eyes as if seduced by the slender and straightforward curve of heel.

He tried on a gray checked suit, but the cloth scratched and he exchanged it. He tied his neck with a silk scarf and scowled at the profusion of colors that knotted his throat. As he walked toward the clatter of their voices, he caught glimpses of himself in the many gilded mirrors lining the walls. His forehead worried, and he straightened it at once, composing his face into an expression of calm, of steely determination. He fretted at the large slabs of orange in his suit and at the silk bordering his neck, which made him claustrophobic. He glanced in the open door of Miss Sylvie's guest room, his eyes settling on the half empty glass of water on her night table and hardening at once at the sight of the indentations of their heads on the pillows, the tousled white sheets bedraggled from their wild night of lovemaking, and he could still sniff the sweat and perfume that clung to the hot, damp air. The closer he approached, the uglier he looked and the more he worried about the task he was to undertake.

They were there, the two, out on the veranda, sitting together on the couch with their backs to him. They drank tea, hot and sweet, that Dulcie had prepared, and he saw that the red outline of Whitley's lips still lingered on the sharp white rim of the cup. Miss Sylvie's eyes were closed, her head thrown back, the lighted pipe on her lips. Whitley's great white arm shouldered the couch, the fingers lost in the warm ringlets at the base of Miss Sylvie's neck. Not knowing how to chop up this closeness between them, this intimacy, Lowe paused in the entrance and listened to the low, worried tones of Whitley's voice complain about the rioting and rebellious Negroes, the spontaneous acts of disorder and chaos and anarchy exploding all over the countryside, at the ineptness of the police to protect them—*them*, the porcelain alabaster people who for decades through marriage tried to bleach stains of black Africa from their skins. She talked about the severe shortages and soaring prices, the government-imposed rationing. She talked about injustices and of unfair imprisonment, which Lowe remembered had been a frequent topic of conversation on the lips of the men at the shop. Before they burned it down!

He hated how they ignored him, how they pretended not to have heard his steps, not to have inhaled his persistent perfume. He coughed and cleared his throat, pulling up his trousers, which were tight and made it difficult for him to breathe deeply, difficult to move with ease, for the lack of room in the short crotch chafed him. Still no one moved. He shoved both hands in his pockets, intending to jingle the coins there, but there was nothing except his folded white handkerchief, bordered with his initials. He coughed again, blowing his nose furiously into the handkerchief, but as there was no phlegm, the noise was not impressive. He sounded only as if he were wheezing.

Finally Whitley looked up, and he saw irritation crouched there in her eyes, red and wrapped with kohl, and in the poise of her stiff, white neck with the hair hanging loose and in supple waves on top of the square shoulders. Her eyes then lurched away, and he could tell she was thinking of what to order him to do so he would disappear, but he was not dark-skinned, he was not of the African peoples, not mixed-race, not Indian, not low-class white—he was Chinese, different altogether, his people were immigrant merchants, were threatening the economic stability of her own alabaster people, so she said nothing at all, and her irritated eyes climbed back up to his composed face, and Lowe saw bitterness burnishing the horizons of her pupils, and he knew she was thinking of his relationship with Miss Sylvie, and he wanted badly to smile, for suddenly he felt a rush of strength.

Whitley turned away with a shift of her black curls and lifted, with ringed fingers that slightly shook, another stick of cigarette from the pack lying there on the wide, flat arms of the couch and brought it to her lips. With one quick scratch of match, Miss Sylvie lit the tip, and Lowe saw the misty outlines of somersaulting dogs, of flying snakes and swooping birds of assorted shapes swirling from her lips, rounded up and projected forward. He saw that her fingers no longer shook, that her eyes had taken on a glassy stare, that her jaws were no longer in tension, and even he relaxed just from watching.

He sank down into a nearby chair, defeated. Neither one looked at him. He tried not to stare at their fused shoulders and hips and thighs sitting there on the couch, not to stare at the smoke coiling from Miss Sylvie's soft lips, at the blackened rims of her eyes, which were swollen and red. Whitley's face too was wet. Lowe squeezed the handkerchief in his pocket, uncertain if he should offer it. Maybe they had had a fight. Maybe he was mad to try to come between them, to try and ask for what he wanted, to establish his rightful position there with Miss Sylvie. They both looked drugged with love, and neither one paid him the smallest regard. Whitley stroked her right knee with circular gestures, and from his seat he saw the muscles rotating in her back and shifting against the stretched fabric of her tall, white dress, which bellied over the tops of her shoes. He saw the curve of her cream calf sheathed in silk stockings as the rustle of muslin rode up her legs. He had tried so hard never to let himself feel so much turmoil and confusion. He had tried so hard all these years to bay his emotions.

"Everything all right here." The squawk of his voice embarrassed him. Still no one glanced his way, and he saw now in their long tender gestures, just in the way their massive shoulders slightly brushed, just in the way their plumb and angular bodies tilted, both facing the hills and gray sky; away from him, but turning so attentive and tranquil and yielding an arch, he knew that this was different from what he lived with Miss Sylvie. He knew that what was displayed here in front of him was some hot, deep, dark, searing thing. He knew that what was displayed here had nothing to do with how he awoke each morning to Miss Sylvie's humid palm on his throat, or her heavy hand thrown carelessly over his rounded stomach, the sole of a warm foot shifting restlessly in sleep on his calf. What was displayed here was sharper and wetter and hotter. He shuddered just from thinking of it.

Finally, Miss Sylvie spoke into the quiet. It was late afternoon and hazy; as if making up to rain again, the sky an iron blanket and the air still, no movements except for the tortured flies and mosquitoes that approached them, the gray buzzing of bees, of droning beetles, the leathery lizards that slithered by his chair and stopped at the squared toes of his shoes and stuck out a fiery orange tongue and nodded and slithered off again. There was the clink of porcelain cups settling into the circular bases of the saucers. The scratch of cloth from the slight movement of their legs. "Whitley want more. She want me to move there and live with her. And maybe she right. Things here drawing to a close now."

Lowe glanced quickly at both of them and at the dark, deep caves around their soft, sad eyes and the green forlornness blowing around them. He saw the great oblong shadows cast by their stout figures extended across the polished tile of the veranda. From the opposite slope of valley, deep in the green mass of banana grove, came the short and sharp and shrill call of birds. He felt a great fluttering in his chest and thought he wanted to cry. "So what you asking me for then, if you mind already set, what you asking?" He was barking at her, and in his mind he saw the image of the center diminishing, heard the waning cries of schoolchildren, an orchestra silenced and without musicians.

"Well, you asked, eh, Lowe, you asked."

His lips trembled. He wanted so hard not to be possessive, not to seem so weak in front of Whitley, but there was such a turmoil in his gut, such a deep tunneling, and his chest was constricted and he felt as if he could barely breathe. He rose from his chair and laced Miss Sylvie's high and glistening forehead, faced the top of the head that was beginning to thin and feather. "Look, you place is here with me. You hear that." He banged his hand against his shallow chest. "Not with this woman. This…" He was out of breath. He was frightened at the hysteria in his voice, at the cords standing out in his flushed neck, at the false, foolish quivering mustache he saw from the corners of his eyes. At his bared copper teeth that snapped up and down in his mouth. "Tell her to pack up and go now." He pointed at Whitley and took a step forward. "Tell her to go." A fugitive smile unsettled Whitley's face before it was immediately absorbed. Miss Sylvie didn't even blink. And Lowe, blushing all over and hot with shame, rushed almost tumbling to get away, his eyes full of tears, arms helpless by his sides, flailing around, searching for invisible exits, doors through which to escape. Inside the kitchen he brushed a stack of plates from a table with the sleeve of his hand. They crashed to the floor and he looked with surprised eyes at the destruction before him. Tears slid to his cheeks then, though he did not feel them at first. And that was when he thought of all those years between them.

□   □   □

How she arrived one morning with a colony of luminous gold butterflies frolicking round her head. It was late June, and the air vibrated with the odorous smells of blooming lignum vitae trees, and a horse-drawn cart rumbled to a halt at the mouth of the shop. It was still early, but the searing sun had already centered itself and was beginning to suck back early morning moisture that had glistened the backs of leaves and stalks of grass, wet the legs of trousers or the heels of shoes, and had left sweat on the panels of glass and arid stone sidings. The shop was empty, and Lowe was sweeping, cupping water from a chipped enamel dish perched on the counter and sprinkling the concrete, stifling the spiraling dust. Cecil leapt out, lean and angular in a frayed white frock coat and felt hat, and said, "Lowe, I bring a mother for the little girl." Then he disappeared underneath the canvas covering of the carriage.

Lowe swept, with trembling hands, sweat and dust clinging to his face and neck, the sun beating down on his temples and burning his white shirt. He worried. Admittedly, he was relieved. Finally the people would stop talking behind his back. Finally Liz would have decent company, and he would have help with her upbringing and with the shop that was slowly starting to prosper. But still he worried. For every time Cecil came, it disrupted the relationship he had built up with the villagers, who only came to distrust him again. Every time Cecil came, he was assaulted with the memories of the ship. The dank, dim quarters of Cecil's cabin with the cold white light pouring in through a porthole and the wooden panels glistening with charcoal sketches and watercolors; the loose, rough-cut sheets of brown paper scattered across the carpeted floor with illustrations; the scrawl of letters and words Cecil was teaching him.

He remembered rope wrenching into his narrow wrists; Cecil's footsteps hurrying with the enamel bowls of rice and the goblets of water for the baths; Cecil's frowsy smell filling up the room that was their home; his calloused hands rough on Lowe's shoulders, his breathing quick and sharp in Lowe's ears; Cecil's face buried in the back of Lowe's head; Cecil's teeth tight on the tip of his earlobe; Cecil's fingers buckling and unbuckling, buckling and unbuckling, and Lowe lying there, no image behind the expressionless eyes, no movements from the taut and tightened limbs, from the soft, thin shell, no movements save for a soft and precise singing from paper-thin lips, nothing save for a face of indelible calm.

And still Lowe worried. For what would be the price of the mother Cecil had brought? He knew Cecil enough by now. There were always strings with him. Always. Just six months ago, when Cecil last visited, he had been furious that there was no decent food to eat, just dusty tins of sardines and bully beef on wooden shelves; no place to sleep except in squalor, underneath the counter, on top of an old rattan mattress full of chiggers. Lowe had continued to wait on customers, whose pricked ears and wandering eyes betrayed their curiosity. He had continued to tally up their purchases with a steady hand and a precise arithmetic. But the edges of his eyes strayed. They followed the abrupt movements of Cecil's frenzied gestures: the way his fingers hooked and unhooked like cripples, the way he ground his teeth, rotated his jaw, and blinked often. He stank of rum and of sweat and of old and unwashed clothes and of day-old cigars. He swayed from drunkenness and from fatigue.

After the shop closed and it was just the three, Cecil paced and fidgeted. And Lowe, completely absorbed by the riot of unrest, lurched with Cecil's short, quick steps to the barred windows of the shop that looked out at the squalling rain, and back again to the locked door that faced the empty square, and back again to the barred windows that locked out at the silvery slant of persistent squalls. During all this, Cecil complained. He wanted to know where the profit was from the capital he'd given Lowe. One hundred pounds. If, like a damn fool, he was allowing those nigger people to eat him out and what kind of blasted Chinaman was he, anyway. What kind of blasted China businessman. This he said with laughter clacking through his false teeth.

Slowly, steadily, Lowe had begun to seethe. His eyes were muddy and his limbs blazed with the pounding fear. He opened his mouth and in an ostrich voice said, "Did you once ask me what I wanted when you bring me here? Did you know anything at all 'bout me when you throw me the bag of money and the shop key and left? Left me with the baby so weak and sick?" Lowe's stomach hardened, redolent with memories, even though down there, down there, he was moist.

One day Lowe awoke to the awful singing of sailors; to a wind swiftly collecting and burying their music, then replaying it. One day he awoke to a blinding sunlight, to a gush of sea air blowing in through an open porthole, to a washing and whirring of silver water and tumbling black cliffs. One day he opened his eyes and found his queue chopped off and lying flat on the floor, and Cecil was there plucking lice big as beans from his hair, the sides of which had been evenly trimmed, a deep part in the middle of his forehead. He saw too that his clothes, the padded jacket and half trousers, had been replaced with Cecil's khaki trousers; his striped shirt and white merino and woolen cardigan, his leather belt with a gleaming silver buckle, his cotton drawers and woolen socks; and a sturdy pair of boots that shimmered.

Scattered on the floor of the cabin were half-empty spools of thread and buttons of assorted colors, mounds of scraps left over from old trousers that had been gutted, then basted and stitched and hemmed and darted and reassembled. He saw fantastic slopes of wool and khaki and felt, saw the jagged jaws of scissors, and Cecil looking on with the frivolous fringes entangled in his red beard. With gesturing arms, he commanded Lowe to his feet, and Lowe picked himself up slowly on creaking arms, on wobbly blue legs still slightly swollen, and he staggered round, his head spinning.

Lowe didn't recognize himself, this melody of pain gushing through his limbs. He didn't recognize the clothes that rubbed roughly against his skin, he felt naked without the coil of hair, and in the mirror hung there on the wall he saw the stranger peering back at him, with weary eyes, and in front of him was Cecil, with the cords of thread in his fire hair, and lurking in the corners of Cecil's eyes a huge well of tenderness, which did not calm Lowe. He remembered a sharp curve of disappointment in his father's back when he turned thirteen and puberty struck. He remembered a weighed-down and weary neck hanging off his father's shoulders. He remembered a slope of resignation lurking there in the black hole of his face. And he looked again at the spotted-skinned man standing there, and he looked again at the trousers that veered over his legs and at the cardigan that draped along his shoulders, and he swung his head, which felt light without the cord of hair, and he knew he had crossed over again, that he had come to that place of uncertainty before and here he was again. But this time he wasn't sure of the outcome: He wasn't sure if he would make it to the island alive, or in one piece, whole. The stakes seemed greater somehow. The risks so much graver.

"Did you ask me if I wanted shop life?" Lowe yelled out into the darkened shop, nauseated with the memories. "Did you ask me if I wanted married life, wanted to have daughter?" His voice trembled; he held on to his stomach, which was extremely weak, and in his mind he located the metal bar leaning up against the counter by the trapdoor near the barred window. A metal bar he kept to wave dangerously at customers who got out of hand. "For who is to tell— maybe it wouldn't've turn like this," he cried. "Maybe it would've been different." He searched for possibilities and saw instead the old Chinese men with cracked faces and bleak, glassy eyes working out themselves on the plantations; he saw them swinging from trees with the imperial queues at their throats, leaning over shop counters, drowsy with sleep and from fatigue yet weighing out the bags of sugar, serving the glasses of rum. He'd only known when he left China that he'd had to leave. There was the intuition driving him to live. Plus, his father had betrayed him under the guise of tradition, though his one gift had been the dreams with which he infected Lowe so he could fly. But still!

Lowe said it again, in a thin, clenched whisper: "Why you couldn't so much as ask me what I want? Eh, why?" Nobody had ever asked him. He had just lived out all their fantasies. There was his father, who used to dress Lowe the same way he dressed himself. There was his father, who used to pile up in Lowe's head all his broken-down dreams, and then it was Cecil's fantasies and his grand plans for both Lowe and Miss Sylvie, and now all of a sudden Lowe had turned into a bad businessman, a useless Chinaman. After he had turned concubine to Cecil onboard the ship. After he had raised Cecil's daughter. After he had been there, shackled to the shop. "Did you ever so much as ask me what I want?"

Cecil laughed, a harsh metallic din that revealed none of his teeth. "What you wanted, Lowe, to marry like a real woman and settle down. Is that?" He weaved closer and wavered there beneath Lowe's granite eyes. "You, the only Chinee woman on the island. Is that?

What you think they would have done with you? Miss China Doll. Miss China Porcelain. You know what them do with the Chinee women in British Guinea. In Cuba. In Trinidad? Bring them to whorehouse. Is that you wanted?" Cecil laughed again. A stiff, wooden laugh that betrayed no mirth, for it was bridled with so much bitterness, soaked with so much scorn. A laugh muddied with mockery. A laugh that clashed with the thin silver drops of rain pelting the zinc outside. "Is that you wanted, Lowe?" Cecil laughed again, and Lowe backed away, frightened by the smile in Cecil's teeth, the oily desire in Cecil's eyes, the rum on Cecil's breath, the trembling on Cecil's lips, Cecil's face shiny and bloated in the tilt of yellow glare from a fast-fading candle.

Lowe thought again of the cold, dark dank of the place, of the buckling fingers, and again of the metal bar behind the counter of the shop. Cecil's shop. But Cecil was quick; he lunged at Lowe, ripping open the front of his khaki shirt, tearing at the waist of the white band hiding Lowe's skinny woman's chest. "Is that you wanted? To live in house married like real woman? With husband and things? Servant and things? With five Chinee children running round? Petting the dog? Petting Blackie the dog?"

Lowe sprang, his fingers twisted on the pipe in Cecil's skinny throat, determined to unhook the Adam's apple, determined to tear the nasty grin from his face. Determined to shut him up forever. On the ship he'd been no match for Cecil. Not even after the fever had abated and he had regained strength, the rust had returned to his cheeks, the diarrhea had slowed, and he had been infected with the voracious appetite—the bowl after bowl of rice and stew and soup he devoured, stuffing his bloated cheeks, barely waiting even to swallow as grains fell from his oily lips back into the bowl on his chest, on the floor by his feet; the hunger that knew no bounds, had no stoppage, was insatiable. Even after his appetite was curbed he had been no match for Cecil, for there had always been the fear of the other men devouring him one by one, or in a pack, wolves. The fear of being thrown down below into that sewer of human waste with the other Chinese. And what if they discovered his differences— how they would've turned on him!

But now, now the fear was different, now the fear had turned, now he would kill Cecil and bury him there at the back of the shop. The villagers would help him, wouldn't they! They'd clear the site, they'd dig the hole, wouldn't they! After all, wasn't Cecil the common enemy?

Beneath Lowe's hands, Cecil battled for air. Beneath Lowe's hands, he struggled. But he was so light from fatigue, he was so unsteady from drunkenness. And against his thin, angular frame, Lowe's nostrils were just calling up all kinds of smells from the cabin, all kinds of oil and fish and salt and rotting smells. The cry of terrified and shrieking Chinese, who went wild with the heat of fire that broke out on board. How they screamed and stampeded with the rattling chains clamping their feet, and there were the howling sailors hurrying to remove the stout iron bars that bolted them in, to open up the hatchways that had been barricaded. There were the bubbling and blistered and charred and hissing and smoking Chinese bodies thrown overboard into the wrinkled black brow of the sea, into the jagged jaws of swirling sharks. And then there was just the iron blanket again that was the smooth sea. No winds. Just a slow-moving boat, a twisted knot on inky waters. But those days were gone now, and sure as rain, he would kill Cecil. Sure as rain, he would blot out the images furred in his throat and tear out the tongue, pluck out the eyes. He would stifle him to death, choke back the laugh down the rusty throat, for there was no love between them, nothing at all between them; a daughter, yes, but no love.

Liz's shriek startled them.

With a trembling hand, Lowe slowly unlocked his fingers, slowly released the thimble of neck, slowly collected his wits about him, slowly collected his calm, and Cecil staggered away into the night, coughing and holding his throat, and Lowe heard the timorous taps of his shoes sluicing into wet mud. That was six months ago. Now he was here with a mother for Liz, and the fluttering and luminescent butterflies curved halos round the carriage.

In the room at the back of the shop Lowe had built on since, Liz slept on a four-poster canopied bed with a sturdy mattress, and

Lowe's eyes, shifting with their movements, returned again and again to the door in the back where his daughter, Cecil's daughter, slept in the room. He hadn't taken tea yet, hadn't taken even a hunk of bread yet, and so mirages swam before him and he felt slightly faint. But still he swept, the bristles of his broom leveling the dirt pyramids of carpenter ants, crushing shiny white eggs that would later have emerged as nymphs. Still he swept, though the bristles of the broom traveled the same area over and over and dirtied again the neat spots he had just now cleared. Then Miss Sylvie alighted from the cart. A tall and stout and white-skinned woman, with a stole of fine yellow hair and a matching yellow skirt that swelled out from her tiny waist into a full-blown flower.

Cecil took her to the back of the shop and Lowe continued to sweep, nosing the bristles of the broom into corners long forgotten, turning it above his head, knocking down contortions of webbing that had formed in the corner of the roof. He tried not to listen to their mumbling, rumbling tones, and when the backdoor slammed shut, he stopped himself from wondering where they had gone. Several hours later they returned, neither spoke to him, and the carriage whisked them away again in a cloud of pebbles and dust.

□   □   □

The following weeks, cartloads of carpenters and masons and plumbers arrived daily. They felled trees, set fire to bush, and cleared the land of rocks, of broken bottles and garbage. They sawed and hammered and cut and laid pipes and gutters, and when midday approached, they laid down their tools and brushed the dirt from their dusty backsides and wiped their dripping faces with the loose tails of their shirts and slowly edged toward the shops, where business picked up. For as quickly as the crumbling shelves emptied, they were replenished. In the fire of the midday heat, the men crowded the shops and laughed and smoked and drank and ate with enormous vigor and dozed with their foaming mouths wide open on the upright wooden benches or outside underneath tight clusters of trees and awoke exactly one hour later to carry away wheelbarrows full of stones and mud and cement mix.

They lifted the trunks of trees and flung them on the columns of their shoulders, and the muscles in their forearms strained underneath the impossible weight, and the veins on the sides of their faces and in their necks reddened and bloated up into pipes. They paused often to wet their parched palates with the rotgut rum that they carried in flasks tucked safely away deep into boots and to roll and smoke the wet brown leaves of tobacco and other herbs growing wild in the fields, which turned their eyes wet and bloodied and glassy.

And still they worked with astonishing expedience. Holes were dug. Cement was poured to create a foundation. Wood poles were inserted. More cement. Concrete blocks. For weeks the district prospered. Contractors boarded with villagers, and the thin bellies of the underage girls swelled with pregnancy. Rum bars were packed Saturday nights, church pews on Sundays. The butcher slaughtered hogs and cows and goats. The price of eggs increased, and that of cow's milk. Several months later, the house stood grandly on the very pinnacle of the hill, its back nestled against a forest of rocks and trees and woods, while the veranda gazed down at the villagers' mud-and-wattle, thatch-roofed hovels and huts, and ambitious half-finished concrete houses lined up side by side amid hillside and empty swampland.

☐   ☐   ☐

Late one evening, the thunder of hooves filling the entire valley finally separated into the harsh rising pitch of one lone rider, a speck of black on the rim of a purple horizon, before the figure gradually swelled and then dismounted in a cloud of spiraling dust at the shop piazza. It was dusk, and the square was deserted, and the craven dogs slept close by in the short, thick grass across the road facing the shop.

Lowe and his daughter had just eaten, and he had nodded off on a stool behind the counter while Liz rattled to herself in a corner swarmed with the many wooden animals and assorted paper birds

customers had given her over the years. He had already boarded up
the windows to lock out the swelling night shadows. He awoke to
clods of horse shit licking the pavement and saw the woman standing there at the counter, watching him with a ripple of a grin splitting her flushed copper face. Lowe coughed and straightened his
shirt, brushing back his hair, which was recently trimmed, and swung
his trousers off his hips and up to his navel and closed up his face and
clashed his eyebrows together and tugged at the curling handles of
his mustache.

She ordered a beer, and he knocked off the foamy top and
watched her lean the bottle to her head while her long sleepy eyelids locked and the corners of her mouth leaked. She burped long
and deep, ordered another, and he wanted to laugh, for he had
never seen a woman quite like this one. She was tall and robust, with
full and heavy breasts that strained against the fabric of her jacket.
She removed the hat tied underneath her chin with ribbons and
rested it on the counter. A bundle of gold hair sprang out, and
Lowe saw that the nape of her neck was damp and the sides of her
face were deeply flushed from the hot winds that lashed her as she
rode. Sweat had dampened parts of her back and blotched the
underarms of her blouse.

Liz, by this time, had flown to the other side of the counter to
inspect the quivering flanks of the foaming white beast that was her
stallion and that was continuing to pile up loads of filth at the mouth
of his shop. Lowe listened to her voice, rumpled with affection as she
pressed Liz's hands against the slow-blinking eyes, the wide trembling jaws, the slender and handsome face. He saw the jutting blades
of Miss Sylvie's wide shoulders; the large bones of her hands, lined
with veins and scarred by rope burns; her cruel lips deep in flirtation,
the strong, even teeth; the jaw, big and brown with dust.

She had appeared right at that moment before nightfall, when the
colors were both vibrant and pitted with melancholy. It was the
moment, too, right before the forest released its symphony of
sounds, before the night stalkers descended on the square with their
beating pans and bellowing accordions, their appetites boundless for

drink. In that hour, right before the dying rays of the sun disappeared, she was more handsome, the smell of her sweat more tart, the stench of the decayed and abscessed molars more fervent, her smile more haunting; her pupils were more distended and dark, her deep voice rumbled with more resonance, her lips brooded.

She returned to the counter, with Liz, his daughter, beside her in love, and ordered a third bottle. They stood in the shop, their faces bathed in the scanty light by the leaping shadows, the front door of the shop opened onto the deserted square. He had not lit the hissing lamps yet. There were the glass shades still to be rinsed off and dried with newspaper, the kerosene to be poured out from the oil drum and funneled into the spouting mouths of the lamps. Wicks to be trimmed. Still he did not move. And outside there was the swiftly approaching night, which carried the smell of storms. Through the glass doors of the display case, there was the silvery reflection of the slow-creeping moon grinning in the eyes of needles that sat in boxes on low shelves, glimmering on the piles of silk and cotton, embroidering the rings of ruffled white lace. There was the distant knot of stars, the echoing cry of a pack of swallows as they fluttered noisily in a circle over the darkening square.

She nursed the beer, straightening and folding her fingers, and talked quietly to Liz, and he saw the meandering movements of her fingers, some with flat, broad ribbons of gold. He wondered if she had married before and if she'd given birth. She seemed so vigorous with strength, so bold and brassy in her gestures, yet her eyes carried a dullness so intense he tried not to meet them. He wondered what Cecil had told her about him, Lowe, and what had been her response. He wondered what the parenting arrangements would be exactly, what they would entail. And then he brushed the thoughts aside, for they troubled him too much. There seemed to be no ending whatsoever to the masquerade. The layers just seemed to pile up more or harden. Furthermore, there were still the glasses to be rinsed, the rum to be watered and measured out into flasks and half flasks, the jugs to be filled up with water and drops of lime juice, the caps and bottles of beers and stouts to be polished so they winked at customers from their shelves. Still he lingered.

"Is funny," she finally addressed Lowe, without a smile, and in a voice loaded down with despair. And her eyes, he noticed, without wanting to, seemed lost, and the corners were wrinkled with worry. "But I been dreaming 'bout you for years. You and me and Liz in that white house on top of the hill overlooking the district. Strange, ain't it? For two full years." Then she was gone, her bill left there on the counter, fluttering from the sudden onslaught of wind, and Liz jumping up and down on the pavement and crying and waving after the figure that had hoisted to the saddle and was galloping up the hill at a conquering pace. Lowe was irritated. The shop had plummeted into darkness, and he couldn't find matches to light the lamps. Plus, there were the packs of cigarettes to be separated into sticks, tobacco to be cut up into feet and inches. There were the daytime accounts to be sorted and tallied and recorded and hidden away, and loose change put out in the till to assist in the night's transactions. There was the piazza to be swept clean of sweetie wrappers and the hardened black butts of cigarettes, and still there were thoughts lurking there and the worry of what would happen now, what would he have to pay out now, how much, now, to this woman whom Cecil had sent to mother Liz. And what was this nonsense about dreams!

He stormed outside to yell at Liz to get inside at once and stop acting the blasted fool and saw that the world was completely black and engulfed by the deafening racket of crickets. Inside, there were the counters still to be wiped down with soap and warm water, two- and three-pound bags of sugar and of rice to be weighed out and wrapped in brown paper, Liz to be tidied and bye-byed and put to bed, the firewood in the kitchen at the back to be doused with hot water, the dishes and pots scrubbed and turned down.

☐   ☐   ☐

Every day for the next two months Miss Sylvie sent a note by way of either Dulcie, the housekeeper, a tall dark-skinned woman who carried a suffering face and dragged behind her one slow foot, or

Dulcie's son, Omar, imploring Lowe to join them for dinner. And each day he crumpled the note and burned it in the fire that cooked his meals, cursing the audacity of these porcelain alabaster people to want to control his life so thoroughly and completely. Plus, he didn't like the air about them. The son, Omar, was sullen and restless, and he paced the four corners of the shop and watched Lowe with hooded eyes. He made Lowe uneasy, as did the mother, who seemed resigned to some great tribulation that exhausted her and caused her to produce the longest and most profound sighs, which made even Lowe shudder. Omar made Lowe think of his father. But unlike his father, who had little by little and over the years neatly and tightly folded over his disappointments into tremendous fantasies and had molded Lowe as well into something both unrecognizable and foreign, Omar wore his disappointments unsheathed. The villagers called him hostile and cantankerous and they kept out of his way, claiming that he didn't smell good, he had blood on his hands and guilt written all over his forehead. About the old lady, Dulcie, though, they seemed more curious and cautious, almost more reverent, as if trying to discern who exactly she was, for in some way she seemed vaguely familiar.

But each time Lowe watched Miss Sylvie's invitation curling up into flames, he worried. For there was Liz going on three, and he didn't know whom to ask about a decent school just in case the villagers took it to mean their government schools and one-room classes weren't good enough. There was Liz going on three, with no real mother, just a woman who had given birth and was now playing at being a man, on a West Indian island full up of brown people swiftly growing more and more infuriated with their economic status and the snail's pace at which change seemed to be approaching and what they considered to be the opportunities the government was doling out to his Chinese people. There was Liz going on three, with no real family, no future, no guidance, no homeland, no country; no people, nothing.

Wednesday evening Lowe locked shop early, tidied Liz and himself, and meandered slowly up the hill, the chills of the evening falling briskly around them. There was no moon, no stars, and the zigzag path of dry grass, thick and straight, which had been trodden down by feet, stretched out ahead of them, a blue-black cape. There were dogs, but none of them barked. People passed in groups of twos and threes, but no one said hello. He had never seen the house, and he hissed his teeth at its glowing white splendor ahead, complained to himself at its excessiveness in that small, hot district and worried at the leap he would have to make from shop life to that. For the people would never trust him now. Here he was Chinese, and here he was cohabiting with this white-skinned woman, Miss Sylvie, and here he was now living in the biggest house in the district with a dark-skinned maid and a dark-skinned yard boy. How to explain to the villagers when the very way he and Miss Sylvie lived up there in that house bore stark resemblance to a history and a way of life he did not live through but had heard as a story unfolding so many times at the shop he felt close to it. How to show them that he hadn't changed, wasn't changing, was still the Lowe they knew, he wasn't emulating the behavior of the ruling class even if it seemed that way, it was only that he wanted something better for Liz. And wouldn't any mother want the same for her child if she could?

Miss Sylvie, as if expecting them, was waiting at the head of the table with a smiling face that wrinkled up the corners of her eyes. They ate in silence, Dulcie wordlessly waiting on them with a stiff and wooden face, with a set of gestures precise and mechanical. Did they know everything? Lowe wondered. Had Cecil told them? And the arrangements, he worried, what would they be? Sitting stiffly at the other end of the table in a white shirt made even more gleaming by the single lamp illuminating the room, he watched Miss Sylvie fuss over Liz, cutting up her food into small neat squares, indulging her in extra portions of sweets, puckering up her lips and contorting her face into comical gestures so Liz would smile. And Liz did smile, and would sometimes even burst out into a laughter so gleeful it frightened Lowe, for she was always so solemn. Still, he kept his eyes flared on the pearls jumping about on Miss Sylvie's jutting collarbone and on the lamp-lit flashes of her teeth. He darted furtive glances at the tendrils loose from the upsweep of hair and falling into her forehead and along the temples and cheeks soaked in the diminishing light.

He listened to the tines of his fork scraping the plate, to the clanking knife sawing through meat, detaching flesh and bringing into his trembling lips. He could not taste. He listened to his masticating teeth before the pink tongue rolled bolus back into the gaping hole of his throat. There was the gulping swallow of juice sliding into esophagus, the protesting gaggle of a distended stomach. He had left his body again. Still, he stared straight ahead, his eyes expressionless as they traveled up and down the weakly illuminated paintings that covered the walls, barely distinguishing the cylinder of shapes: the soft crisscross straw of hat, a pointed tip of a European nose, a white vertical line of ship, a square edge of canvas sail, gleaming enamel of eyes in black face, the blue-green oil of water, a yellow plume of foam.

Crouched on a couch in the solemn drawing room, he absorbed the slow, steady swings of a pendulum clock and heard Miss Sylvie's and Liz's feverish exchange as they prepared for bed. He had never heard Liz so talkative. Always she was so sullen and pensive. He thought to get jealous, and then he stopped. A pair of white pajamas, starched and crisp, lay folded on top of the enormous pillows that crowded the great canopied bed of his room. But that night he did not wash, though Dulcie had left a goblet of warm water on the stand, though he was dirty and weary. He tripped over the rug at his feet and knocked off the night table a glass vase of white lilies, which crashed noisily to the floor, and he wrapped himself up at once and stood there cocked and waiting, but when the unending silence continued, he began to pick up the pieces, and they gashed and bloodied his hands. That night, he blew out the lamp and eased underneath the cool sheets and pushed his head deep into the soft feathers of his pillow and slept soundly. All next day, he was resolved never to return, but as evening fell and business ran slow, he locked up early again and he and Liz picked out their way slowly in the darkness up to the house, a flickering torch their only guide in that hot, still, black night with not even a breath of air, not even the rustling wings of bats.

One night, he had a dream that Miss Sylvie had come to his bed, and when he woke up he was frightened to find her lying there next to him and even more alarmed to find that his spindly arm was trapped underneath her wide shoulders, and he tried to remove it at once, though stealthily so as not to wake her. It was impossible, though she slept without peace, with outstretched arms and churning fingers, with a face gashed by nightmares and a heaving chest that sometimes produced a deep rattle from her throat. Thin strands of yellow hair swiveled off her freckled cheeks and the fragile limb that was her brown throat. He had never seen a beauty quite like this, and so close up to him and so overwhelmingly feminine and ripe and bursting it confused him. Frightened him, really. Even the way she smelled, as if frothing, and there was the taste of her sweat firing out from the barbs of bush that were her underarms.

It was early morning, and streaks of light were already peering in through the chinks in the red velvet curtain, and outside he could hear the stirring call of cocks and the response of other cocks from deep down in the valley on the other side of the rolling gray hill, and he heard too the warbling of swallows, the cooing of doves, the crying of chickadees, the whirring of hummingbirds, more cock calls. Slowly he turned his head so as to make out the location of his shoes on the rug near the door that would lead him down the hall, past the neighboring room, the gilded frames of handsome and romantic landscapes of regions he did not know, the low, narrow chest of drawers, the well-made bed with unruffled sheets and balloon pillows, past the window that looked out at the kitchen, and then the door, finally the door that would bring him escape. It was too much, this…this…didn't even know what to call it, his yearning was so furious.

She cleared her throat, and Lowe saw that a rectangle of sun had hoisted across the room and leaned into her face and that she was wide awake and watching him with amused eyes still drugged by sleep, and he immediately freed his thin, white arm that had long gone dead. He lurched toward his shoes, and she stopped him with the narrative of how she had been married since she was fifteen and within months after the dreams started coming her husband fell off his horse and broke his neck.

"But every night it was your face I keep seeing," she told Lowe, in a voice touched with tenderness. "How that to happen so?" she whispered, tracing the bones of his cheeks with the pads of her fingers, running them along the rugged lines of his lips, gently removing the black band of hair that lay there, circling the eyes and the curve of his nostrils, all the while singing the music of idle words, minuets about beauty. "Is the same round face with the one eye slightly bigger and the same mouth with the lips so full and pink and with the top one a little longer, the same teeth at the front caved in slightly. My husband used to travel, and I thought maybe it was his sketches that brought the dreams night after night. But it was you, you ownself. For two years."

Lowe fretted under her touch, his body stiff and unmoving, his breath barely able to escape his wildly beating heart, his roaring head. She knew! So then where the hell were the shoes! For if he could slip slightly to the right he would be free of her cream thigh sheathed in black garter that was the stumbling block in his path, he would be ready at the side of the bed and on the floor with the tap-tap of nimble feet down the darkened corridors with only creases of light to guide him through the maze of rooms, past the office with an untidy desk cluttered with papers, short squat chairs and a plush rug—the glimmering edges of a scrubbed floor. With her eyes closed, and with the steaming flesh, she straddled him. His great swooping copper bird with the dazzled gaze, the frenzied admiration, repeating her prosody of love.

Yet underneath her hands, plying his body, awakening it, her attentive fingers listening to it for harmony, there was only discord, for his body would not obey, would not dance, was not flexible and yielding, had no discipline. Above him, there was only the broiling cauldron of sky, a streak of light across a suction sea, a glittering dusk, an unreflecting mirror. Her butterfly kisses feathered his throat, and he was drenched in his own sweat and the fragrances of oils and perfumes, the harsh, wet smell of tobacco, that clung to her skin. He felt her wet lips on his wide-open eye, on his sweep of lashes, on a perturbed forehead. A nibble on the lobe of an ear. A stab to the center of the throat with a pointed pink tongue. An ocean of moans. Hers? And then steps silent as a priest's on the rug and wood floors, to his little room at the back of the shop. The naked and unpainted concrete walls of his shop. The shimmering zinc roofs. The awful singing of men. The cracked laughter of men. Laughs deep with disappointments, muddied with mockery, bridled with bitterness. The wooden shelves tiered to the white ceiling with boxed and tinned goods.

There were her teeth tight on the buttons of his shirt, picking them off, one by one. From the hollow of his throat to the thimble of his navel, she roamed with the freckled tongue, with a bow and with a nod. She removed the strips of cloth that banded the chest and swallowed at once the knobby red nipples. She murmured into his chest. She knew! She murmured into his belly. She knew! He continued to lie there dead, columns of tears leaking out the wrinkled corners of his eyes. There were only teeth and hard bites and spread legs and splayed fingers and darting tongue, a valley of breasts, a whirlpool of desire, a feverish breathlessness, a profuse talk of love, words racing and running and leaping, tumbling overhead; there was the chaos of phrases, a dark loamy earth, and Miss Sylvie at his feet, picking off socks, a warm mouth, a gaping cave, swallowing one by one, then the whole bunch, crumpled up.

A gasp for air. His? Fingers on the cracked leather of belt, on the hook of trousers, then on the buttons, and frenzied fingers rummaging into the square white band of his drawers, and scrambling up again to wrestle with a wrinkled shirt the color of khaki, then down again, swimming into the white waist and plunging in, a pointed tip of European nose, a taste, finger by finger, then the whole fist crammed in. A ship. A square canvas edge of sail. A checkered oilcloth and the strange curve of flesh. Haggard breathing. Cecil's! The galloping rhythm of tongue, taste of brine on lips, a raised arm with torn wrist, a vague twilight and dreamy eyes gripped by the drug of sleep. A molten sky. An auspicious moon. A sweltering market-place. A circling shark with a murderous tail. A leaning body full of erratic gestures, the undulation of limbs, the crunching of figures, the movement of light. Lowe could not retain the sequence from the chaos.

And so it continued for all those years, Miss Sylvie returning again and again to their room after spending weeks or months at a time with Whitley, who came to visit and who satiated the passion that she must have sought only in Lowe. And Lowe not moving, not rising to her touch or to touch her, not returning her kisses, her pro-nouncements of love; just lying there numb all those years, for each time, all he could think of was the dark dank of the place, a flash of bruised light, a pair of pliers, an unleashed fury, a strange curve of flesh, and those shoes ripping through rooms, past the varnished wood of the table, the marbled chests. Secretly and in his heart he yearned for her embrace, and often he wished he could simply small himself up into her lap and sleep there. But always she wanted more. He heard it in her frenzied breathing, he could smell it like danger on her skin, he could taste it at the back of his throat, and it was always there in the pressure of her fingers kneading him. He didn't feel as if he had agency, as if he had voice. For who is to say she wouldn't fold up her fantasies into him and turn him further into something he wasn't, as his father had done and then Cecil? And who is to say she wouldn't abandon him once her mission was accomplished. Who is to say!

And so Lowe just lay there prostrate, so overwhelmed by his fear, allowing Miss Sylvie to love him those nights after Cecil had come and left again, those nights after Whitley had gone, those nights after Liz had gone to sleep and, later, after she had eloped with the car-penter and escaped the convent school, which only as an exception admitted the children of the Chinese and those of the porcelain alabasters, those nights after the store had prospered and he had expanded and met Kywing, those nights when it was just the two of them, just the two of them and the dark and impenetrable night.

And for all those years Lowe had never wanted to touch her in that way, never wanted to love her in that way, never wanted to stroke the lines on her forehead or the ones by the corners of her eyes and lips. For who is to say what he would have raised up in her! He had never wanted to touch the mole on her back or the one on the right side of her neck, never wanted to inspect the insides of her legs or thighs, never wanted to fondle her nipple, never wanted to possess her body or snatch her from the claws of that woman, never wanted to kiss her parted lips or the smooth column of throat, never wanted to smell her perfumed skin or to taste her sea-salt silkiness, never wanted to travel inside her, never wanted to crawl or push, never wanted, never wanted till that moment. For at that moment he was a child not so afraid of death, and of darkness and of solitude. At that moment he was a child full up of innocence, ebullient with faith.

Excerpt from Rat Bohemia

Sarah Schulman

Last summer the mayor of New York decided to cut back on rat extermination. He also cut back on streetlights. As a result, night increasingly meant these dark outline of buildings surrounded by the scampering of eighteen-inch varmints. Ten million of them at least. My best friend, Killer, and I spent a lot of nights that summer just walking around because we didn't have any money. I was saying I was saving up to move out of New York, and Killer hadn't had a job in two years. She came over every night to eat and then we'd take a walk. She'd forgotten how to even look for a job. She'd forgotten how to sound employable on the telephone. One day I glanced over her shoulder at the Help Wanted pages of *The New York Times*, only it wasn't what you'd call *pages*. It was more like half a column. One Saturday we saw a kid get shot in front of the Unique Clothing Store Going Out of Business Sale, and the next day we watched a guy go crazy and throw glass bottles at people for twenty minutes. I've always wanted to shoot rats.

Killer and I are hard-core New Yorkers. But when we were kids the only homeless person you'd ever see would be a wino on the Bowery or an occasional bag lady. You never saw anyone sleeping on a subway car unless they were coming home from the night shift. The streets were not covered with urine then. That was considered impolite. There have always been rats, though. I remember as a teenager watching them run around on the subway tracks waiting for the Seven train to get me out of Jackson Heights. But mostly when I was a kid, rats were something that bit babies in a mythical, faraway ghetto. You never saw them hanging out in the middle-class sections of Queens.

An average rat litter is twenty-two little ones, and they can reproduce at the rate of six litters a year. Sometime in the 1980s I started to see them scampering regularly in the playgrounds of Central Park. Reagan had just become president and I held him directly responsible. Rat infestation felt like something the U.S. government should really have been able to handle. That's when I started thinking about getting a gun and shooting each one of them on sight. Picking them off the way hillbillies shoot squirrels.

That guy, last Sunday, who was throwing glass bottles? All he cared about was himself. His personal expression was more important to him than other people's eyes. That's the kind of attitude that makes this town a dangerous place to live. You never know when it can hit. The shooting in front of the Unique was more reasonable. It was just a bunch of friends killing each other. Don't have friends like that and it will never happen to you.

Every morning I go over to the old Veterans Administration building on West Twenty-fifth Street and wait on line to go through the metal detectors. The lobby walls are covered with these old World War II murals of soldiers getting fitted for artificial legs by nurses in starched caps. The women lift up the Veterans' new legs and demonstrate how to use them. Once I make it through, I have to ride up in the elevators with all the wacked-out veterans scratching and getting into fights. Then I get off at the seventeenth floor, where there is the Food and Hunger Hotline office, and walk past them to my office. Then I sign in at Pest Control and waste about half the day unless I get sent out on a job.

When I'm sitting in Pest Control, hanging out, waiting, I pay close attention to the goings-on at Food and Hunger. I want to see everything I can. Everything. I want to be a witness to my own time because I have a sneaking suspicion that I'm gonna live a lot longer than most of the people I meet. If I'm gonna be the only one still around to say what happened, I'd better pay close attention now.

Killer usually stops by the office at ten for coffee and peanut butter sandwiches. Then she checks in at a couple of restaurants to see if they need any prep cooks. I know for a fact that they're only hiring

Mexicans and Israelis. Everybody knows Americans aren't good for restaurant work. They want to talk on the phone in between high salaries and free meals. In the meantime, she's living on forty dollars a week from watering plants for a couple of offices and boutiques. The rest gets paid by the bed-and-breakfast guests she hustles at those four-dollar cappuccino places. Mostly Swiss people or Germans. They think it's quaint. She gives them a bed and then tells them to make their own breakfast. Then she comes to the office to eat some of mine. We've been living on this schedule for a long time already. It is one big, fat habit. You know one thing I don't like about homeless people? They ask you for a light and then hold on to your lighter for forty-five minutes blabbing on and on about some misfortune. The whole thing is designed to make it seem that they don't realize that they've got your lighter. But the fact is, they know they've got it.

Killer was brought up to be a racist. One night I went over to her place to watch TV and her parents brought over some food. Next thing you know the news came on and it was all "nigger" this and "nigger" that. Her parents had these sharp teeth whenever they said that word. They scrunched up the skin around their eyes. It wasn't said calmly. Killer knows better, but when she gets emotional, that's what she falls back on. Like one time some Puerto Rican guy was beating up his kid in the hallway, and Killer said, "Look at that low-rent over there."

"Shut up," I said. "You haven't had a job in two years. If you had enough patience to stand in line you'd be on welfare yourself."

"I'd be on welfare if it wasn't for the strength of the Eurodollar," she said as some blond couple rolled over in the bed. That was the way she looked at things.

God, that summer was hot. There's that way Puerto Rican girls sit close together on the stoops. They have skinny arms and those ten-dollar pink dresses. They smile and wear their hair long with a headband.

Every day homeless people come into Food and Hunger looking for food, but they only get Contact Cards. I gave Killer one of those cards, but she said the food they advertised wasn't nutritious.

One time, before breakfast, Killer walked me to work, but she wanted to stop off at the Xerox store on Tenth Street that was run by some Moonies. They were clean-cut peculiar and wore polyester pants up to their necks.

"They give away free bread and free Chinese buns," she said.

When we walked in it was kind of slow and real hot. It stunk of Xerox fluid. The polyesters had a few day-olds sitting on the counter and a bag of day-old buns.

"Don't eat it," I said. "It's old pork."

"Hi, Killer," they said, handing her two loaves. Then they turned to me. "What about you?"

"I don't need free food," I said.

"Look," Killer whispered. "Take it. I need it. I'll give you a fresh one later for your birthday."

"Okay. No, wait. I don't want bread for my birthday. I want a colander."

"Do you think I need a professional portfolio?" she asked.

Killer was still thinking about jobs.

"How is everything going?" Killer asked the Moonies, remembering to be gracious.

"We're having problems with rats," they said.

That woke me up.

"Do you have big ones?" I asked. "One-pounders?"

"Yep," they said.

"Did you put out poison?" Killer asked.

"Poison doesn't work," they said. "They're too strong. Besides, if you kill one that way it's just gonna stink up your place and bring maggots."

"Did you try traps?" Killer asked, trying to cut me off because she knew what I was about to recommend.

"Traps don't work," I said, ignoring her. "The rats are too smart. They spring the traps and get the bait."

"What about walk-in traps?" one of the Moonies asked.

"Too expensive," I said. "Doesn't work on a massive scale."

"Well, what do you suggest?" he asked.

"You gotta shoot 'em," I said. "You gotta get 'em one by one."

☐   ☐   ☐

The reason that all of this background information had been on my mind was because I spent most of last summer thinking about the fact that, frankly, I have not made as much of my life as I would have liked. I have never learned how to achieve. That's why I've been saving up to move out of New York. Florida might be nice. Learn how to drive. Go swimming.

Working this job is a real downer except when we go out for the kill. That's the best. But in the meantime, I have to sit here with the crew from Food and Hunger and listen to them make small talk. Especially that Mrs. Sabrina Santiago. She almost always has a city-worker attitude and therefore kicks my butt psychologically and regularly. Everything is about her territory and her ability to lord it over me. But she has nothing to brag about since she moves real slow and wouldn't say "How are you?" if it was worth a million dollars in food stamps. These types of relationships and social encounters are what have made me question my life.

Killer and I talk about this all of the time, about how we are going to better ourselves. The problem with Killer is that she's a pretender. She pretends that something is going to happen when nothing is ever going to happen. Then, when it's over, she pretends that something did happen when actually it was nothing. I love Killer. I don't mean to judge her, but I have to.

Mrs. Santiago called me from across the hall and asked if I would messenger something over to the computer store on Forty-third Street. Now, I knew that she was supposed to bring that over herself because Food and Hunger doesn't have the kind of money to buy a messenger service. I also know that Mrs. Santiago lives in Bushwick, Brooklyn, which is in the opposite direction from Forty-third Street. So out of the kindness of my heart I said yes. Then she made me stand there, freezing my butt off in that central air conditioning, while she chats away on the phone for forty-five minutes. City worker.

Of course, I'm eavesdropping because I've got nothing else to do, and the whole conversation seems to be about these storerooms filled with flour that the City got ahold of. But all of this flour doesn't do hungry people any good because most of them don't know how to bake bread. Or, if they do know, they've got no place to make it. Especially if you are a person with a substance abuse problem. You will never find the time to make bread. Therefore, all this potential food was sitting there going to waste. Mrs. Santiago was suggesting on the phone that they could get all the new prisoners in all the new jails to learn how to bake bread and they could bake up all this flour and distribute it already made. She was suggesting that in the future when they build prisons, they could include bread baking facilities and kill two birds with one stone.

By the time she actually handed me the package and I got downstairs, I found out that Killer had been waiting around in the lobby because both detectors broke down and everyone was being searched by hand.

"Fuck that," I said, and we both set off for the computer store.

Unfortunately, we decided to take the subway, which promptly got stopped between stations.

"Fuck that," I said.

After about ten minutes the conductor's voice came on over the PA system.

"Attention, passengers. Due to a police shooting at the next station we have been temporarily delayed. But we will now proceed with caution.

"Proceed with caution?" Killer said. "What is this, *Stagecoach*?"

"What are we going to do?" I asked.

"Look," she said. "When we pull into the next station, duck behind the seats. You gotta get lower than the bench in case the bullets come through the window."

So when the train eased into the next stop we ducked. But we both kept sticking our heads up to peek because we wanted to see what was going on. Sure enough, the place was swarming with cops and a bunch of medical personnel, all looking very tired and over-

worked. Then the guy across the aisle from us started to have a psy-
chotic episode. He started meowing. At the next stop, Killer and I
got off the train.

"Killer," I said as we walked uptown. "Tell me something. What the
fuck are we doing? What are we doing with our lives? I think about this
all the time now, and I can't figure out what category I'm in."

"Category?"

"Yeah, I mean, I don't have any money, but I'm not *poor*. I have
aspirations, but they're spiritual ones, not careers. I look around at
how people are really living, and I can't identify. But when I turn on
the TV I don't understand that either. What the hell is going on,
Killer?" I asked. "Who the hell do we think we are?"

"We're bohemians," she said.

"What?"

"We're bohemians. We don't have those dominant-culture values."

"We're bohemians?" I meekly asked.

"Yeah," she answered. "Ever heard of it?"

"Of course," I answered indignantly. "It's people who go to foreign movies."

I was identifying already.

"Look, in the past there were decade-specific names," Killer said.
"Like hippies, beatniks, New Age, punks or Communists."

"What do we call them now?"

"That's the whole thing," Killer said, her black hair flapping carelessly against her green skin. "Nowadays it's not generational.
Bohemians aren't grouped by clothes or sex or age. Nowadays it's
just a state of mind. Anyone with a different idea is in."

We were standing by the front door of the computer store, and
Killer obviously wasn't planning to enter. So we stayed out on the
sidewalk and discussed existence like any New Yorker would do in
our place. We were outside in that inside kind of way. There's weather and a sky at the top of the corridor. The walls were made of buildings and streets ran on like cracks in the plaster.

"But what about turn on, tune in, drop out, Socialism, and other
social outcast stuff?"

"Listen," Killer said. "In the fifties, the Beats, those guys were so all-American. They could sit around and ponder aesthetic questions, but a cup of coffee cost a nickel. Nowadays with the economy the way it is, you can't drop out or you'll be homeless. You gotta function to be a boho. You have to meet the system head-on at least once in a while and that meeting, Rita, is very brutal. Nowadays you have to pay a very high price to become a bohemian."

The Great Baptism

Jane Thurmond

There is a time in my memory when my age is not measured in years. "Before the flood" or "after the flood" suffices. Days convert to watermarks, distances calculated from the lapping surface of the lake to the roofs of houses. The flood must have come when I was nine. I've determined this by the watery memory of my possessions washing out my upstairs window—my birthday tea set bobbed by and Tiny Tears reached for me as I was dragged by my father toward the chimney. And then, of course, there are the people that I knew before the flood whom I would never see again.

For months Mother called the flood the Great Baptism because, at first, it put us on the path to a better life. My own baptism happened in the church before the flood, but I was never better for it.

Eternal Life Baptist Church was saved from total destruction by the slope of the earth, but after the flood, when most of the survivors moved away and businesses shut down, the church followed. Last summer I made the trip back to see what was left. Eternal Life Baptist still stood. When I pried open its rotted walnut doors I could still hear the echoing microphone, the gallant choir and the gentle sloshing of water. Not water from the flood, but baptismal water. Yet when I think of how baptism feels, it's something like a flood. Or like falling off a dock with a dress on, the skirt billowing up around you as you sink. There comes an instant when you must choose whether you will punch against the preacher or simply lean back and trust the weight of his hand, strapped across your gaping mouth, blocking the water.

When my mother was twelve, she was baptized in a river. On the bank she stood in starched white lace, orange mud oozing around

her ankles, until she was led into the water by the preacher in his
soggy suit. She promised herself an indoor ceremony for me.

Perhaps she chose Eternal Life simply because of its baptistery,
which loomed like a large fish tank implanted in the wall high above
where the choir stood. Facing the choir, we sat in stiff pine pews, our
necks hinged back, lulled by our aquarium view. In a blue sea of
organ chords we drifted with the waves on the other side of the glass
and watched the preacher push the heads under, watched the elegant
legs float up. Behind ripples and splashes swayed swirling aqua tile.
Above the water line, the tile burst into a bright mosaic sky where
two enormous hands, God's hands, reached down as if they could
scoop us all right up to heaven.

When I was eight my mother's wish was realized—me and the
preacher chest-deep in water, lit up from underneath so we were
glowing.

Baptism is supposed to save you. That's the good part. The bad
part is that it doesn't change you; it doesn't suddenly make you do
right.

☐   ☐   ☐

Our town was perched on a limestone rise overlooking a narrow
lake as smooth and green as a chalkboard. We lived in one of the
split-levels built along the bank by the oil company and provided as
part of Dad's pay. That's when they were still in love, before he started traveling. Each night sweets followed pungent platters of food set
on crocheted trivets. Dad would hunch over his dinner, his hair
falling across his forehead, one arm encircling his plate, and consume
helping after helping of my mother's dishes. Mom would round the
counter, drying her hands on her rickracked apron, and she'd reach
for Dad's cheeks, bobbing his head back and forth. "Judy Ann," she
cooed, "who's the *best* father in the world?" I sang back, "My dad."
Sometimes we'd wrestle on the living room carpet or they'd spin
around the pink stone patio, pretending it was a ballroom.

One summer night Mom was out playing the organ for church

choir practice while Dad worked late. I rocked alone on the patio glider, listening to neighbors' lives open up through lit windows that fell in yellow rectangles on the water. Across the inlet, the church steeple shot up with its stained-glass window the size of the moon. Through the colored glass, music melted over the tops of trees. Lights flickered like blue flames across the lake. Someone over there was splitting wood. Coyotes moaned and dogs barked back. Fireflies darted through darkness. The seniors had just graduated, and the engines of their cars droned up and down Lake Avenue. Whooping boys and squealing girls kept time with the even squeak of my glider. I climbed down to the street and walked while the music calmed the whole town. Cars slowed, drivers straining out windows. People stopped on sidewalks to sit under trees and gaze out over the lake and listen. Sometimes there would be a long prelude of organ chords, and I'd call across the water, "That's my mom."

When I wandered past the corner park I heard someone humming, and turned toward the monkey bars, where I found a girl hanging upside down. She stopped singing when she saw me. "Is it always this hot here?" she said, her arms dangling in the dark.

I leaned in close and squinted. "Who's there? Do I know you?"

"You know me only if you met me in the last few days," she said, swinging from her knees. "I just moved into a house down River Road. Our furniture filled up three pickup trucks. They're *still* unloading."

I climbed a few rungs to get a closer look. Her yellow hair fell like an undone bolt of silk. Her cheeks were dark, reddened with blood settled in her head.

"My name is Judy Ann Wiggins," I said.

"Laura Leigh," she announced, sticking out a hand for me to shake. "Porter's my last name now. Before that, in Idaho, it was Villanueva, and before that it was McDougal, in Montana."

"Why does it keep changing?" I asked.

"Mom keeps changing husbands and houses. After each wedding she sits my brothers and me around the kitchen table, passes out paper and pencils, and we practice our new names. P-O-R-T-E-R," she recited. "This one's easier than the others."

Leaves high in the elm trees shuddered. The chorus swelled. I pointed to the steeple. "Listen for the organ. The person playing it is my mom." The music had captured me again and I climbed down. "See you around, Laura Leigh." I waved and walked backwards, watching the tangle of arms and legs and bars fade into the shadows.

"Hey, kid," she called. "What grade will you be in come September?"

"Fourth, and my name's Judy Ann."

"I'm older than you are, Judy Ann," she sang, then hummed along again with my mother's music.

Before I knew it I was down at the church in the blackness of the balcony, sitting with my feet up on the seat like I'd never do in a Sunday dress. No one even saw me. No one knew. Chandeliers brightened the rows below. The choir roared above the steady tap of the director's stick against his metal music stand. My mother bowed toward her sheet music, her fingers crawling over the keys, her feet dancing on the foot pedals. I leaned my head back and listened until their hymnbooks thumped shut, the organ lid snapped and everyone shuffled outside toward the café. The chandeliers finally faded and the door slammed, leaving me alone with the rafters swelling and creaking in the dark. And then, more than ever, the baptistery was a blue square of light, beckoning me like the doorway to heaven.

Heat engulfed me and sweat wet my back. My bangs dampened against my forehead. Is it always this hot? Laura Leigh had asked me this, and I had never answered. Now all I could think of was yes, yes. I wilted as I gazed at the baptistery until it occurred to me that I could be up there swimming.

I pulled myself from the bench, tiptoed down the balcony stairs and slowly walked the center aisle, scanning every seat. Chandeliers barely swayed, creaking from the arched ceiling. The smell of newly laid carpet rose around my feet. At the preacher's podium I turned and faced the empty pews to be certain I was alone, then slipped through the door to the tunnel that climbed to the choir loft and above to the baptistery. On all fours I felt my way up the stairs until

I stumbled onto Reverend Culpepper's thick-soled shoes stashed on a shelf and his baptismal gown hanging from a hook.

When I realized where I had ended up, I crouched close to the cement floor, recalling the last time I was there, for my own baptism. I had been ordered to change out of my Sunday clothes near this very spot, in the dressing room next to the reverend's. Behind the drawn curtain I had folded my sailor dress, stuffed my socks into my patent leather shoes, and slipped the gown that he had tossed me over my head. I smoothed out the creases and stood motionless in the center of the dressing room, listening for the others to emerge in their gowns. Instead, from the stall next to me, I heard the reverend's pants unzip, saw them drop and bunch around his feet. I imagined him in his shorts. His chalky knees. The little hairs curling against his chest. He cleared his throat and scratched.

Stretching the gown toward my ankles, I had struggled to hide myself entirely with cotton so thin my nipples showed through. Finally, I filed out with the others, folding my arms across my chest, and had waited in line for my sins to be cleansed away.

I rolled on my back and opened my eyes wide to remind myself I was alone. My face felt cool against the cement. I stood and slipped out of my shirt and shorts. In my underwear, I crept to the edge, then slid into the tile-lined tub of water.

Pretending to perform for a large audience, I staged my own water ballet. I rocketed up, slicing the surface with a twist, my toes pointed, my hands pressed against my thighs. I jackknifed underwater, every muscle straining for balance and grace. My stiffened arms spiraled up. The waves sloshed and broke against the tile. Underwater flips, handstands, floating on my back.

No one came in. No one saw. I pressed my face against the glass and stared out into the church to check. Nothing. Only rows and rows of pews. Dark aisles. Just me in my private pool. A seal slipping under water.

So this became my secret. Nightly, I continued to swim.

Don't let me mislead you into thinking I led a lonely life. Before the flood I had friends on every corner. On warm summer nights as

I walked home from the church, children dodged in and out of shadows, racing under streetlights clicking with june bugs, calling to me from games of kick-the-can. I recognized their hula hoops spinning from dark yards, the *shush* of their Slinkies, and I'd wave their way, tossing my damp hair.

Weeks later, in a game of hide-and-seek, I met Laura Leigh again, hidden behind a house in a maze of hedges. Soon we were spending entire days together. She was from a large family, farther down River Road where the earth swelled with the bare roots of trees. Although she had passed her eleventh birthday she was smaller than me. Her two brothers, three stepbrothers, and Mr. Porter were rarely home. She could never guess the day of the week because, for her, summer days all seemed the same. No one left her house for work on weekdays, and Sunday was a day no more special than the rest. At their kitchen table her mother sat like a statue, examining a deck of cards stacked and restacked in a never-ending game of solitaire. Through a cloud of smoke, she gazed up at us from her scorepad and took another sip of scotch. "Bring Mama somethin' sweet," she slurred as we passed, tapping her cigarette into an ashtray that overflowed onto the linoleum.

Some nights Laura Leigh slept over. We'd lie in my wide bed and count the stars Dad had painted on the ceiling with phosphorescent paint. Big Dipper, Seven Sisters, an oversized North Star. From piles of stuffed animals we contemplated the universe. I imagined heaven on the other side of the ceiling. Who ended up there and who didn't was as clear to me then as the differences in the sun and the moon. You were either saved or you weren't—as easy as an instant under water. In Sunday school–teacher fashion, I recalled the topics of my Sunday lessons, explaining to Laura Leigh the features of heaven and hell. But soon I would learn that, baptized or not, I would do unforgivable things that even a flood's undoing could not wash away. A flood I saw coming because of the bats.

One evening, just before sunset, Laura Leigh spotted my father's binoculars sitting on a shelf. Soon we were perched on the patio, staring at the bridge at the far end of the lake. Tiny cars crossed silently through the lenses. Beneath the bridge the water glowed like stained glass. "There they are!" she finally cried, thrusting the binoculars to my face. I peered through the lenses until I spotted a colony of thousands of bats spiraling upward from under the bridge. They swirled up like a pillar of smoke, then dispersed to specks in the purple sky.

"The bats feed every night," Laura Leigh explained. "They'll return to the bridge when the sun comes up." She slipped the binoculars back inside their case. "I've got another secret that I'll trade for one of yours." I nodded. We hadn't yet told each other everything. She leaned close to my ear. "Those bats were only the beginning of mine. Follow me."

We took the road along the lake past her house, under a moon so bright we cast long-legged shadows that slipped in and out of trees. Gravel crunched under our boat shoes. She led me to a metal shed nearly covered over with vines and pushed the door open, yanked me inside, then sealed the door behind us. I stood in the dark, trying to identify the musty smell. Laura Leigh's hands fumbled until an old Christmas candle in the melting shape of an angel lit up the room. She pointed up to the corner of the shed, and I squinted in the dim light until I spotted a bat hanging upside down from a dowel. Its face had the look of a tiny newborn calf, with a mouth as pink as my mother's lipstick, its nostrils like pin pricks, its eyes two black beads, its head crowned with oversize ears. Its wings fell like portions of a split parasol.

Laura Leigh stepped on a stool and stretched her arm up. The bat squeaked and bared its tiny teeth. "Her name is Barb. She can't see us, so she's afraid. After she smells me and realizes who I am, she won't bite." Laura Leigh slowly turned with the bat hanging from her finger. Barb was as small as the palm of her hand. "Judy Ann, open that jar of bugs," she ordered. "Grab hold of a moth. Now, put it close to her nose." Barb grabbed the beating moth with one claw-like thumb, covered half her own body with a cloaked wing and ate. I ducked as Barb flew above her bowl of water, lapping with her tiny tongue, wings a brown blur.

"Did you get her from the bridge?" I asked.

"My brother caught a bunch in a net. Barb's the last one. The others died or got away, but Barb's stayed on for weeks." Laura Leigh blew out the candle, and we stood silently in the dark. She added in a whisper, "I've thought about letting her go, but she depends on me."

Once outside Laura Leigh poked me with her index finger. "Now it's your turn. Tell me a secret."

I trotted ahead. "Follow me," I said over my shoulder.

The breeze coming off the lake had stopped completely and after running to the church, even the outside air felt stuffed up and soupy. When we pushed open the sculpted doors, Laura Leigh glowed in the blue shaft of light from the baptistery, her blond hair tinged green. I slipped my arm around her shoulders and coaxed her up the aisle, past the podium, until she stumbled through the secret door. "You're going to love this," I promised, as we climbed through the tunnel, up the stairs and emerged, finally, at the edge of the water.

"Well, this is it. Welcome to my private pool," I said, unbuttoning my shirt.

She twisted her hair around her hand. "You're kidding, aren't you? What if we get caught?"

I draped my clothes across the back of a chair. "Don't worry," I said, "No one's here. I've been doing this for weeks."

Peering over her shoulder into the darkness, she undressed while I floated on my back. I pushed the air from my lungs and lay on the bottom of the pool. When I came up for breath she had perched at the edge, filling her chest until her ribs resembled the fine bones in Barb's fanlike wings. As Laura Leigh stepped into the water, her cheeks grew pinker and her lips drew into a perfect "o." When she ducked her head under, a halo remained on the surface of the water until she popped back through it slick and smiling.

"I'll show you what it's like to be baptized," I said, my left hand pressed between the wings of her bony back, my right palm raised and facing the glass. "I baptize you in the name of the Father and of the Son and of the Holy Spirit. Amen." Then just like Reverend

Culpepper, I pressed my hand over her mouth and nose, and pushed her head under. Her legs floated up. She didn't fight. Laura Leigh came up laughing, like people sometimes do with a real preacher, happy that they're safe now, saved.

I performed my newest water ballet. My triple floppy. My five-way splash. She turned three somersaults underwater without coming up for air. We sank and rose up pressed together, and then, without thinking, we clutched each other and kissed. Like we'd seen on TV. Like my mom and dad. The water slapped and churned. I pulled her toward me and we kissed again. "Let's try it this way," she said, arching my back over her arm, dipping her shoulders to meet mine. My legs slipped up, and I started to laugh, until I heard a bump from the pews in the dark. We lurched forward and peered out into the church.

"Don't stop," came a choked voice muffled through the glass and sloshing water. "Kiss again." I sank back and looked at Laura Leigh. The color had drained from her face. Again, the voice ordered, "Judy Ann, do it. If you don't, everyone will know about your little swims."

Our limbs stiffened, but I obeyed. When we kissed for him our mouths were hard. Our bony chests bumped underwater, and our eyes blinked back the beginnings of tears.

When I heard the faraway click of the door to the tunnel, I let go of Laura Leigh. "He's coming," I whispered. "Let's get out of here." But she couldn't move, so I grabbed her arm and pulled. But she slipped away under the shadow of the man reaching for her. I can't fault myself for trying to escape. She lost her nerve. She wouldn't run.

I clamored down the stairs in the dark, bumping against the banister, then sprinted up the aisle. When I looked back, the baptismal tank was empty except for water churning against the glass.

Outside I crouched with no clothes behind the azaleas. My pulse pounded in my neck. Even in the still heat, goose bumps spread across my arms. In the distance children laughed, but the church was quiet. The cold stone wall supported my spine.

I slowly counted backwards from 100, sang songs to myself, and studied leaves on all the branches before me until the door finally opened and Laura Leigh stepped out, fully dressed, her blouse blotched with water. She stood on the top step examining her arms and legs as if she were checking to see if they were still attached. When I whistled she jerked her head my way. "It's me," I whispered. She came over carrying my clothes and threw them across the hedge.

"Why didn't you stick by me?" she cried. Her eyebrows were drawn together, setting a deep crease in her forehead.

I was silent for a while before I answered. "I didn't have my clothes." Slowly, I pulled on my shirt. "Besides, no one can find out about the swimming. We would have gotten caught."

"*He* would have gotten caught," Laura Leigh whispered between her teeth. Muscles in her cheeks tightened and squared her face.

I stopped dressing and studied her. "What did he do?"

She shrugged her shoulders. "You know," she said, letting her arms go limp at her sides. "You should have helped."

My breath choked in my throat. "Did he hurt you?"

"What do you think?" she said, pressing her palms against her eyes.

"Who was it? Have you seen him before?"

"I don't know anybody in this lousy town." She backed away. "Not even you."

As I wrestled with the buttons on my shirt, she turned and ran. A group of boys under the streetlight drop-kicked a football back and forth. The ball arched high until it slapped onto the sidewalk. Laura Leigh kept running as if she didn't notice. Her clumped hair thumped her back. My hair dampened the collar of my shirt. Zipping my shorts, I stepped into the church yard and the boys paused and waved, but I looked straight ahead and forced my legs to walk.

When I reached my house I stood in the yard. My father's silhouette slipped back and forth across the window. It was Saturday, his evening to putter around the house wearing a tool belt, fixing leaky faucets and tightening loose screws. Through a crack between curtains, I could see my mother on the couch reading her Sunday school lesson. I entered through the back door, a smile plastered across my face, as if this were any other summer evening. "Good night," I said, kissing their tender cheeks, and ran up to my bed.

I pulled the soft sheets around my neck and faced heaven. The four walls fell away. The painted stars began to move until I couldn't tell if I was looking at the ceiling or the sky. I grappled with what I could or should have done. I sifted through whispered stories I had heard while sitting on dark curbs or gathered with my friends on the school ground. My face grimaced again in disbelief, recalling girls giggling through sordid stories. They illustrated with their hands, stroking their own bodies, or drew impossible pictures in soft sand.

I sorted through this gibberish again and again, trying to make sense of the deep crease in Laura Leigh's forehead that had sliced through the darkness. The stories followed me into my dreams. I slept twisted and trapped in sheets.

☐   ☐   ☐

In church the next morning, as the sun streamed in on the rows of people filling every pew, I memorized the faces of the men as they bowed their heads in prayer, trying to figure which one. I listened to their voices in the lobby. I examined hands as the ushers passed offering plates brimming with dollar bills. From the balcony I studied Reverend Culpepper through binoculars, following him back and forth across the pulpit, focusing and refocusing my eyes.

After lunch I walked down River Road where Laura Leigh's mother sat in the open doorway. "I ain't seen her all day," she said without looking up. Every day that week I wandered past her house, peeking between leaves. I checked their dock and found one brother dangling his feet above the water and baiting a bamboo pole. "Not here," he said, shrugging his shoulders and shoving a hook into the brittle belly of a cricket. I walked to the shed, where I found Barb alone, silently hanging in her corner. Beneath her on the shelf, the angel candle was reduced to a small puddle of wax and a crisp wick that hardly held a flame.

A few days later at dusk, I stood on our patio thinking about Laura Leigh. My constantly churning stomach had lessened to flinches of nervousness. I tried to relax each night, pressing my eyes to Dad's binoculars, waiting until the gray spiral of bats emerged from under the bridge and circled and spread across the darkening sky. You might say I owe my life to the bats. Had I not watched for them, I would not have seen the wall of water burst through the bridge as the flapping wings emerged. I would not have shouted for my parents who ran outside in time to register the danger.

They dragged me by my shirt sleeves from the patio across the balcony, then boosted me to the roof. Water roiled around us. As we all teetered at the top, waves crashed against our house. My mother prayed aloud, her cheek pressed against the chimney. My father encircled us with his arms. We all shouted above the roaring waves. Beds and drawers and rooftops pummeled past. A car carried a howling cat. Tree trunks were tossed in the current like toothpicks. With each gasp for help that wrenched past, my father reached into the waves but came up empty-handed.

In a matter of hours our town shattered to pieces that scattered and finally settled in silt, like our next-door neighbor's chess set that floated through our kitchen window, popped open in the grand piano, and spilled and sank against the strings.

In the middle of the night, I woke up in the school gymnasium under dry blankets surrounded by rows of creaking cots. Wailing voices filtered through the bleachers from the doorway. My mother's dark hair spread across my bed where she rested, waiting for me to come alive from a fitful sleep.

A few hours later I awoke again. "No, I won't have it. We won't be separated. We're going with you," my mother said as she tightened a blanket around me. She carried me through the gymnasium behind my father to the company truck. We piled in and rumbled down a back road, washed over with water. My father hunched over the steering wheel, his clothes still caked with mud. My mother's breath frosted the side window. Her bruised and fragile fingers rested on my cheek. It was daybreak and the sun had drawn its first pink streaks across the horizon. The CB radio crackled with static. "Didn't Laura Leigh live somewhere out here?" my mother whispered. I sat up and tried to recognize what was left. We moved slowly, surveying the clogged path the flood had taken, crossing into pasture when the road swelled with water. "Survivors could be hanging on to anything," Dad said, his eyes darting from tree to tree. He pulled to a stop and examined every branch. I searched for waves of yellow hair.

"Hold on, would you look at that." Dad lifted me out of the car still bundled in a blanket and pointed across the water.

Bats were plummeting out of the sky toward the place where the bridge had been, nose-diving into nothing but splinters and air instead of the cool dark space below the bridge where they had left their children hanging upside down. "They'll have to find another home, like us," he said, rubbing his bristly cheek against my forehead.

I heard my mother sigh, "Poor little things. I always feel sorriest for the innocent animals. They don't know what a dam is. They can't understand a flood." She rolled down her window to get a better view. "There's a difference in being spared and being saved."

Back in town I watched the sun rise higher in the sky. The flood water looked dreamy, steaming in the heat. By the third day, no trace of high water remained, but the town was coated and clotted with mud. The summer sun dried this silt to dust, and the wind blew it into muted clouds that hung over the jumble of houses, branches, and upturned cars. Each day in the gymnasium, a miracle survivor appeared. Men sat on the edges of cots in mud-streaked waders, wads of tobacco puffing their cheeks, and swapped stories of daring rescues. Trips were organized to view the great gash in the dam. I walked up and down the streets, studying the faces of every child. I checked and rechecked lists of names, searching for Laura Leigh. Kids from the neighborhood wandered through the rubble, and I asked each of them if they had seen or heard. My parents and the other survivors sadly sifted through their belongings. An air of reverence hung over the town as the death toll rose.

Reverend Culpepper conducted daily services in the high school auditorium, where we clamored to make sense of the disaster that destroyed our town. From the back of the auditorium where I remained, the reverend shrank to the size of a moth. I sprawled on the cool linoleum and drew a picture of Noah's ark. Soggy animals bloomed from the butcher paper, paired on the deck of their fragile wooden ship. Hours passed. Under my stubby crayons, fog rolled in until all the animals' heads were draped in smudged gray clouds.

Within a week Dad had loaded a car with the little we had left. We coasted down Lake Avenue for one last look, then pulled out onto the main highway that paralleled River Road. Alone in the back seat I knelt on my knees, facing the rear window, and looked in awe for the last time at the tangled mass of uprooted trees with rowboats lodged in the branches. From the front seat my parents said their soft good-byes. "The world is recovering and so are we," Dad said, patting my mother's shoulder. Yet, we left without learning the fate of my friend. Watching the town disappear, I tried to find comfort in recalling her baptism. How she went under water without flinching, and the look on her face as she came up laughing.

The Arc of Plot

Terry Wolverton

A story is not the same as life, I warn my writing students. *Life,* I insist, *is plotless. Random. One thing happens, then another. Always another.*

My students look at me blankly, or slide their eyes down to the mottled tabletop, or shift their gaze to the yellow walls, which appear a little sickly under the fluorescent lights. The low whisper of the air conditioning fills the silence of the classroom. It's an unseasonably hot night for December, even in Los Angeles. Santa Ana winds have sent the temperatures into the low nineties all this week, igniting brushfires in the canyons and road rage on the crowded freeways. The winds sweep away the customary blanket of ochre smog, but leave us restless and dissatisfied. They animate the inner demons, intensify the shade of every mood. Melancholy deepens its blues; fury sparks in violent red; the gray of ennui threatens to swallow everything in sight.

Thirty minutes ago I was sitting in the parking lot with snot and tears streaming down my face, sobs shuddering in my chest. As gusts buffeted my little Honda, I wanted nothing so much as to turn the key in the ignition and drive away. I couldn't imagine how I would pull it together to face my class, put on the persona of calm authority, a loving coach for their creativity, and stand before them for two hours in that guise. But I am faithful to my obligations, so here I am, nose blown, my makeup restored.

We tell stories, I instruct the group, *to confer meaning. To give form to the shapelessness of life.*

I want them to appreciate the contrivance of plot—beginning, middle, end. I'm tired of stories that are too much like life: Something happens, then it stops; we don't know why.

I stand at the head of the long table around which thirteen students slump in folding chairs. Five men, eight women, mostly in their thirties. Some are drawn to this free weekly workshop at the Gay and Lesbian Center because they want to capture their lives on paper, but others come, week after week, because they need a reason to leave their charmless single apartments, their microwaved dinners in front of the TV, to have some place to go on a Wednesday night.

When I first began teaching, twenty years ago, I thought that working with adult students would mean that everyone would be motivated, disciplined, more like colleagues than students. What I've learned is that the habits of the grade school classroom are deeply ingrained; the challenge of learning still provokes anxiety, the suggestion of homework always elicits a groan. And the teacher is a figure of authority, to be worshipped or resisted, placated or undermined.

Rita has her head down on the desk, as if she's in kindergarten and it's nap time. Her face is turned away from me. Kevin has a magazine in his lap; my words compete for his attention with airbrushed bodies of nude musclemen. Ondine plays with the run that has laddered her lime-green tights, poking one finger through the hole in the threads, making it widen and spread.

A story is a record of change, I inform them. *We tell stories to make sense of change.*

Luis is bright and truculent. He scratches one big ear with the tip of his pen. I can see him puzzling over this concept, trying to think of a story in which no change occurs so that he can prove me wrong.

If there is no change, I continue, *you may have a great prose piece, but you haven't really got a story.*

Luis retracts the point of his pen and scowls, stymied. He sits up straighter in his chair, folds his AIDS-thin arms across his chest, resting his hands in his armpits.

Plot is the device we use to give shape to a story.

I pluck up a dry-erase marker and step to the white board to draw the shape of an arc with a long sweep of my arm. I label it "The Arc of Plot."

In life, I tell them, *shape is murky. How do we really know when something begins, or when it's truly over?* I trace again the curved line on the white board. *The arc of plot is the structure by which the change—and therefore the meaning—within a story is revealed.*

In blue marker, I draw a stick figure at the left-hand base of the arc. *It's the protagonist who undergoes the change. By taking action and confronting obstacles,* I make little Xs along the curve of the arc, *the protagonist arrives at the end of the story different than how she or he began.* The stick figure I draw at the right-hand base is green, not blue.

Ondine raises a languid hand, tipped with long acrylic nails painted a frosty celadon. They glow against her deep-brown skin. "Could you give us an example?" she asks. "What kind of change are you talking about?"

I sigh inwardly. My students want everything prepackaged, user-friendly. I sometimes wonder how they can manage to write when they seem so reluctant to think. I'm not usually impatient with them; maybe it's the wind that has me on edge. Mostly I sigh because I'm unprepared to respond.

"Uh, su-ure," I draw out the word, stalling. I furrow my forehead as if I am sifting through too many possibilities, considering and discarding. In fact, my brain is suddenly reduced to a state of preliteracy; I cannot remember the plot of a single story, novel, movie or play. I am blank as a newborn. Every eye in the room is focused on me as I try to conceal this.

"I know," I muster a false heartiness. "Let's make something up." This is always dangerous since I'm never quite sure what might pop out of my subconscious, or theirs, but in this moment I can think of no other option.

I take a brown marker and bisect the arc with two vertical lines so that it is divided into three segments. At the top of the board I write "Beginning," "Middle," "End" in the corresponding sections of the curve.

"So, who can tell me the six elements that belong in the beginning of a story?" The group looks at me with dull expressions, as if to deflect my question. They're not stupid, just loathe to be called on in class. "Rita?" I prod.

She does not sit up, but instead props her chin on cupped hands and asks, "Uh…a protagonist?"

"Bingo." Then, to the whole group, "So, help me out here—who is our protagonist?"

"She should be a writing teacher," Ginger shoots back with a smile full of mischief. She's got a gold ring in her pierced eyebrow, a silver stud in her tongue that I can sometimes glimpse when she speaks. I've wanted to ask her what it's like to kiss with that, but I wouldn't want her to get the wrong idea.

"Dark hair. Cool glasses. Early forties, but she dresses hip," Luis contributes from the other side of the table.

Should I be flattered? I suppose I asked for it. I want to pull the plug, steer this session in another direction, but it's too late. The best tactic is to appear unrattled.

"Okay," I agree, keeping my voice neutral, "our protagonist is a writing teacher in her early forties. What else do we need to set up the story?"

"We need to establish the setting," Kevin has closed the magazine. Everyone in the room, in fact, is more attentive, sensing the possibility for things to veer out of control.

"It's L.A., man, 1998," Ondine informs him. "City of Angels. City of cell phones. City of selling oranges at intersections to men on cell phones in shiny BMWs." She's a decent poet when she applies herself.

"Okay," I attempt to recap. "We've got our protagonist…"

"What's her name?" Henry wants to know. Still in his twenties, he's a beautiful Vietnamese boy, though his skin is pitted with acne. His stories are transparent autobiography, in which a young Asian man is always the tragic victim. No amount of gentle critique can persuade him from this stance.

"Her name is Terry!" Luis insists.

My students look at me, wonder how far I'll let this go. I wonder myself. "So our protagonist is Terry," I repeat, "and our setting is end-of-the-millennium Los Angeles. What other elements need to be in place?"

"What's her conflict?" This from Ginger. I gaze around the room, wait to see who will supply her with a dilemma to resolve.

If everything's fine, I've told them in the past, *there's no need for story, because there's no need for change.*

No one speaks; they're waiting for me. The moment stretches too long, frays. *What's her conflict?* I think to myself, trying to force my brain to turn away from its only thought, the one it's speeding toward like a bullet train. The careful little wall I keep between myself as teacher and the rest of my life begins to crumble, a few loose bricks breaking into bits at my feet.

"Let's say...I don't know...what if she's...uh...in love with some-one who can't love her back," I propose, trying my best to appear as if this idea has just popped unbidden out of my imagination. *They don't know much of anything about my life,* I reason.

"*Can't* love her back, or just doesn't love her back?" Rita queries. There's a bitterness in her voice to which I resonate. Her stories are always dark, caustic, and she's merciless on herself during critiques.

"Can't, I think" is what I answer. "There's more conflict that way, more dramatic possibility."

"So what's the name of this person you're in love with?" It's the first time tonight that Richard's spoken up. He's a quiet, serious man who writes odd, despairing little fables of modern life that are inex-plicably affecting.

"You mean, that *she's* in love with?" I correct him. I always insist that we talk about characters in the third person, no matter how much the writer declares them autobiographical. *When we write about ourselves,* I've told them, *we're always creating fiction.*

"Remember," I chuckle, "this is fiction." To my own ears this protest rings hollow. So I continue. "Let's call her Vivienne."

I invent for her a name that disguises her identity, her ethnicity. Even fictionally concealed, her image springs before my eyes, her shining dark curls, the Aztec planes of her face, her full lips. It shakes me. Even all these months later, I'm stunned at the ferocity with which hurt rakes my sternum like a clawed hand. My knees sway with momentary vertigo. All of a sudden I feel ripped open, here in front of my class. Can they tell?

"So, would she be considered the antagonist?" Rita is sitting up now, sipping from her Starbucks cup.

"Not in the beginning." A few more bricks clatter around me, raise a little red dust. For a moment I can't tell if I've spoken or only thought the words, but the students nod, appear satisfied. I feel as if any moment I might plunge into quicksand and sink from sight, but the teacher in me is brisk and efficient, keeps moving ahead with the lesson. "What other elements do we need?"

Kitt raises her hand. "The catalyst," she volunteers. "What sets the story in motion?"

I nod, add this to the white board. When I answer, I attempt to sound as if I'm crafting the story, inventing as I go. I have no way to know if anyone is fooled by this, but it allows me to continue.

"What if...before this heartbreak there was another?" I suggest. "Let's suppose that before this story begins, Terry was in a long-term relationship, like a lesbian marriage."

I'm relieved that no one in this class has been a student of mine for long. That's the beauty of a beginning class; it renews itself each year, like skin.

Ginger wags her hand at me. "How long?" she wants to know.

"Three years?" Kevin suggests with a gulp, as if that period were only slightly less than eternity.

"No," Rita snaps, "Longer than that. Like ten years or something."

"Shit!" This strains Kevin's considerable imagination.

"Of course, there were some problems," I continue, "just like in any relationship. But there was a bond, a commitment."

"Then one day her partner announces that she's in love with some secretary at work," Luis cuts in, "and—bam—the lesbian marriage is history." His mouth curls in a twisted smile, as if he takes perverse pleasure in the disaster he's just wreaked.

I could quibble about the details, but he's pretty much nailed it. It wasn't all that long ago—a year, a year and a half. I can remember days when I came in to teach sleepless and shell-shocked. I would stand before my classes scarcely able to construct a persona with which to interact with them. I disclosed more than I should have, unable to contain my grief, driven to seek comfort from any quarter. Those students were sympathetic and solicitous; they left me encouraging messages on my phone machine, shyly handed me greeting cards with inspirational messages and scrawled inducements to "hang in there." One sent me to her psychic, another brought flowers.

Some of the women students, the ones with whom I'd grown particularly close, came on moving day, carried my meager belongings—unmatched furniture, boxes of books, armloads of clothing, garbage bags stuffed with underwear—from my home where tall windows looked out onto lemon trees to the squat stucco house I had hastily rented. I gave myself over to their care, upending the roles of teacher and student. They made up my shabby bed, loaned me appliances, filled the house with lighted candles, and smudged the rooms with sticks of burning sage.

I am so grateful that none of them is in this class now. The students who sit before me have never witnessed the dust balls under my desk, nor seen me collapse on the kitchen linoleum to weep.

"So, the catalyst is the first loss," I pull myself out of my reverie and once more address the class. "Our protagonist is hurt, she's vulnerable. Everything she once thought solid has dissolved."

"Does that help to establish the stakes?" Richard wants to know.

"Absolutely." I quickly add "Stakes" to the white board.

"That's when Vivienne appears," Ondine declares, eager for the story to begin.

And she was like a miracle, calm as the earth, a stable foundation, crooning, "You can rest here. I'll be safe for you." A voice on the other end of the phone—"Call anytime," she offered—first thing in the morning as she got ready for work, or keeping me company late at night as I ate steamed shrimp and vegetables from the takeout Chinese deli. On moving day she took me to IKEA to buy a dresser so my underwear wouldn't have to stay in garbage bags; she navigated me through the crowded aisles, her hand on the small of my back. And how I leaned into that warm pressure, let it guide and steady me.

"How do they meet?" Kitt wonders. She's a pudgy woman with a child's face and a head full of blonde dreadlocks. She's always talking about what she wants to write, but I have yet to see her complete anything.

Ginger's got an idea about that. "I think Terry's known her for a long time," she proposes. "Vivienne's had her eye on Terry for years, and now she sees her chance."

I nod, as if this is only one more detail, a small complexity of plot. "That could heighten the stakes, because there's already a connection with Vivienne that Terry would want to preserve."

"And because they know each other," Rita interjects, "Terry lets her guard down more quickly than she would with a stranger."

What I won't tell them is that she was my student. For six years. One of my favorites—big talent, an original voice, a lot of attitude in the classroom. It would freak them out, and rightly so. I always insisted I would never get involved with a student, although I used to imagine it was a matter of their protection, rather than my own.

"So how do they get together?" Ginger is eager to know.

"They do a few things—go to the movies, have dinner, go to a reading, a play," I suggest. "Then Terry invites Vivienne to be her escort at a community fund-raiser, a formal dance."

"Whoa, dress-up!" Henry preens, and his face grows dreamy conjuring a vision of the scene. "Vivienne's in a black suit; she's stylin'. Terry's in a long black dress, like from the forties, all big shoulders and narrow waist."

I remember that night so vividly. Miles Davis' "Kind of Blue" on my stereo as she came to pick me up. She brought me a corsage, white roses, and I was so touched as she pinned it in my hair.

"And they dance together real close and steamy," Luis taunts.

"Cheek to cheek!" Ondine teases. "Is this the night when they do it?"

"Not yet," I caution. "We need some conflict to keep the story going. They dance, there's electricity, but Terry thinks it's way too soon for her to get involved. When Vivienne takes her home, she tries to kiss Terry, but Terry says no."

"Oh, that's cold," Luis protests, then adds, "but it does prolong the suspense."

Still, it occurs to me that maybe all of this is only prologue; maybe the true catalyst for the story is the night she lost her keys. One week after she'd slow-danced with me, that night I'd sent her home unkissed, she came to hear me give a reading, as she'd done faithfully all those years she'd been my student. Sometime during the reading her house and car keys disappeared. Afterward, we made a frantic search of the bookstore, retraced her steps from parking lot to entrance, shone a flashlight through her car windows—nothing.

I offered to help—how could I not, kind as she had been to me. I was willing to wait while she called a mobile locksmith, but she was rattled, wanted to wait until morning to deal with it. I would have driven her home, helped her break in, but—as she puzzled—how would she get back the next day?

That's how she ended up at my place, spending the night. Wearing my T-shirt. Wedged onto one side of my bed. Who was I kidding? Every nerve in my body alive to her nearness, the smell of her hair against my pillow. It was a hot night. An exquisite torture— my desire for her at war with my resolve not to transgress that boundary.

"So, does that introduce the central question?" Kitt inquires.

I blink at her for a moment, unable to recall the last words I spoke aloud. Despite the air conditioning, I am sweating, my back damp, underarms clammy, as if the hot wind blowing through the city streets had entered the building, swept its way down the halls, insinuated itself into this yellow room.

Kitt seems unaware of my hesitation. "Is it: 'Does Terry relent and get together with Vivienne?' "

"Or maybe," Ginger interjects, "the ex gets jealous and realizes she lost a good thing with Terry."

"That can't be it," Henry protests. "Don't you remember what she said about the conflict: 'The protagonist is in love with someone who can't love her back'?"

"I know!" Kevin volunteers. "Maybe Vivienne can't love her because she's from an alien culture that doesn't allow intergalactic romance." Kevin's stories are always filled with aliens and rocket ships and intergalactic sex.

"That's an interesting idea," I try not to sound dismissive, "but I think this story should be a little more realistic than that."

I scrawl "Central Question" on the board, the final element needed for the setup. "Remember how I've told you that in the beginning of a story we can think the central question is one thing, but as events unfold that question might actually change?"

In the beginning, my resistance had many reasons: It was too soon for me; she was my student. She didn't fit the profile of my imagined partner—someone whose ambitions burned bright as my own, someone who wanted a big life too. Later, though, I would grow to cherish the differences between us: the rich garden of her inner life, the dreams that bloomed like rare, exotic flowers; her capacity for comfort, a pleasure in everyday life, soothing as spiced milk. These qualities were a bed of fertile earth in which I could plant myself, in which I might grow.

I worried that I had too much power: I was older, her teacher. She confessed she'd had a crush on me the whole time she'd been in my classes. She showed me poems she'd written in that state of longing. She had snapshots of me on her refrigerator, her desk at work. I was moved, humbled; she'd carried these feelings for six years, coals kept kindled inside her heart. Could I ever care for her the same way? The first night we kissed she looked at me with eyes like dark lakes and said, "Don't hurt me."

"Initially," I answer my students, "we do wonder if they'll ever get together. Vivienne pursues her, but Terry has misgivings. Even after she succumbs, she still holds part of herself in reserve."

"So first we wonder if they're gonna do it, then we wonder if Terry is gonna be a bitch to Vivienne," Luis synopsizes.

Luis is pushing his luck; he knows I'll let him get away with it. To bust him for his insolence would only serve to narrow the gap between myself and the fictional Terry.

I ignore him. "All right," I challenge the group, "what happens next?"

"Despite herself, girlfriend's gonna fall in love with Vivienne," Ondine smiles, catching the tip of her tongue between her wide teeth, savoring this turn of events.

"Would that be a reversal?" Richard asks.

I've taught them that *a story cannot proceed too smoothly toward its conclusion. A protagonist may appear to be headed in one direction, then turn around and do the opposite.* Like that first night I kissed her, falling into the sweet abyss of her mouth. I kept insisting "I can't do this" right up until the moment I let her pull me into her arms.

"The more she fights it, the harder she falls," Ondine's eyes spark.

How hard I fell. My heart cracked open without thought for the consequences, as if lightning would never strike twice in the same place. The last years of my "marriage" I'd felt so neglected, unconsidered; now here was someone who seemed to notice everything I did and felt and needed. She remembered a pink sweater I'd worn once to class years earlier. She pestered me to lock my car door, fearful that someone might break in and hijack me. She paid a coworker to crochet me an afghan so I wouldn't be cold the nights I didn't see her. She brought me little household items—a colander, a new showerhead—that she'd observed I was missing; I felt like she was looking out for me.

Our first night together she ran a bath for me, lit the house with candles, brewed a cup of tea. Finally settled on her sheets, I nestled into her body, while she asked me how I wanted to be touched. *Here is someone who can really love me,* I told myself, and I could scarcely fathom my luck.

As I fell, I came to cherish everything about her: the curves of her hips, her stories of growing up with eight brothers and sisters, the look of relief and contentment that stole over her face when she ate something she really liked. I sent bouquets of flowers to her office, baked the cornbread with maple syrup she liked so well, soaped her hair in the shower, my fingers massaging her scalp.

A thousand times I've asked myself why I fell so deeply. I'd meant to be so careful, although at the time my only thought was for being careful with *her;* I thought I held all the cards. Once I stepped off the ledge, though, I began to plummet, no longer in control of how far or how fast the drop. In my marriage, I'd always held certain boundaries—habits or stances I refused to alter—ferocious about being true to myself. Perhaps I was determined not to make the same mistake; perhaps I was so shattered by that ending that I had no more boundaries to defend. Not only was I willing, I longed to let her change me.

"But," Rita interjects, pulling me back from my musing, "the minute Terry falls in love with her, Vivienne starts to pull back." Rita scowls at her fingernails, hands splayed on the tabletop. "*That's* a reversal."

I almost gasp. Could these students know more about me than I'd realized? Did they gossip about me when they went for coffee after class? Or is this a predictable twist, predictable to everyone but me?

"Oooh," Ondine winces, "That ain't right."

"Vivienne stops returning phone calls," Kevin expounds, "says she wants to date other people."

Ginger takes it a step further, "Terry runs into her coming out of the movies one night with a gorgeous blonde!"

It wasn't quite that bad. Still, nothing in the beginning of our relationship could have prepared me for her reversal. She, who had courted me so hard, began to retreat. She would no longer talk on the phone at night, insisting it disturbed her sleep. She would no longer see me during the week, and usually only one night on the weekends. Although she still swore she loved me, she began to say that it would never work out between us, that we should pull the plug. "I can break your heart now, or I can break it later," she said to me.

I grapple for an explanation. "Vivienne begins to be afraid. She finally gets something she wanted for a long time, and it terrifies her. She can't tolerate it. She flees."

"So, this is where the love interest becomes the antagonist?" Richard wonders.

"I suppose it is." My words betray a certain reluctance. "But remember, not every antagonist is a villain. They don't always intend to thwart or harm the protagonist. Often their actions are what make the protagonist change and grow."

Why do I defend her, make excuses? I can't bear for anyone to think ill of her.

"In her own story, Vivienne may not be a villain," Rita allows. "But in Terry's story, she sure the hell is!"

But I can't bring myself to see it that way. Maybe I try to tell myself her story to make my own less painful. In that story, she's a woman at war with herself, protagonist and antagonist in the same skin. The one who loves me, the one who cannot overcome her fear.

She tells a different version. She says, "It just didn't work out." She says, "We're too different." She says, "I just don't feel the same way about you." And what choice do I have but to believe her?

"So isn't this the point where the central question changes again?" Kevin asks.

"It sure is," Kitt answers. "Now it's: 'Is Terry going to lose Vivienne?' "

"And what happens to the stakes?" I query.

"They get heightened," Henry replies. "Is Terry gonna get dumped a second time? We're worried for her."

And with good reason. The answer to his question is, Of course, yes, but for the longest time I wouldn't see it. I wanted to live inside her story, my version of her story, to engage in her struggle; I believed that love could win out over fear. I thought if I could just hold still for long enough, she might learn to be safe with me. I comforted myself with the fact that she always came back. But then she always went away again, farther and farther, taking more with her each time.

I think about one August afternoon we visited the new aquarium in Long Beach. She'd stopped sleeping with me by then, but I awakened that morning to an E-mail from her. "I love you so much," it said, "and I'm looking forward to spending the day with you." An encouraging signal. We went to brunch beside the ocean, traded bites over a view of the sun-sparked waves. Our conversation was animated, momentarily purged of the strained moods and awkward silences that had come to punctuate our interactions.

Then we retreated from the midday glare into the cool darkness of the aquarium. We were like children, palms smudging the glass of the huge tanks—"Look at the colors on that one!" "Hey, check out this big guy." We were transported in that underwater world, however simulated. Her hand on the small of my back.

"Let's take a trip to the Sea of Cortez," I suggested. We used to always talk about where we would travel. She smiled, agreed. It was a plan for the future, our future, and I held it close. In the gift store she bought me a silver chain, a slave bracelet. She knelt there on the carpet, in front of all those families on their Sunday outings, to fasten it around my bare ankle. She told me it looked sexy.

Every moment that day spoke to our intimacy. Our dinner of fish tacos at a place we'd always liked to go, our stroll through the health food store, a remembered familiarity of shopping together. Back at her house, the evening waning, she encouraged me to stay a while, lie with her on her narrow couch. Her arms around me, my head on her shoulder. When I tilted my face up for a kiss, she pulled away. "I am not your lover," she insisted. "I can't do this with you."

"Then what is it you've been doing all day?" I demanded, tearful, incredulous. It all erupted then, each moment of that day detonating, leaving us both charred, ashes on our tongues. Some gate inside her clanged shut and I was left on the other side, howling to be let back in.

"This is a story with a long middle," I tell my students. "Sometimes Vivienne is right there, acting like a lover. But whenever they start to get close, Vivienne backs away again."

Kitt shakes her pale dreadlocks in sympathy. "Intermittent reinforcement," she frowns. "And Terry's stuck on that roller-coaster.

When Vivienne's in the picture, Terry's happy. When they're on the outs, she's miserable."

"She doesn't sleep. She gets real skinny. She cries every day," Ondine orchestrates each point with a sweep of her long fingers; her green nails flash across my field of vision.

Henry adds, "Yeah, and her friends get sick of her. It keeps going back and forth."

"But that makes it suspenseful," Richard argues. "There are all these twists and turns. We don't really know how it's going to turn out."

"It's not suspenseful," Rita growls. "It's goddamned predictable. There's only one way it can turn out."

"So why doesn't Terry just dump her?" Ondine wants to know.

"Maybe she really loves her," I suggest. "Maybe she believes that underneath it all, Vivienne loves her."

"That's not love," Luis insists.

"Maybe she can't dump Vivienne." There's an edge of hysteria to Rita's voice. "Maybe she's hooked. She keeps thinking if she just hangs in, she can win." Her eyes are beginning to tear. She swipes at them, a furious gesture, leaving trails of smudged eyeliner like bruises at each temple.

I have a sudden flash of understanding: She hasn't been reading my secret diaries, or eavesdropping on my therapy sessions. Rita's gone through something like this herself. Maybe she's still going through it.

"The best thing she could do is walk away," Ginger advises, like a "Dear Abby" with piercings. "That's what's gonna make Vivienne want her again."

How many times have I heard these same arguments from my friends? How many times did I collapse on their couches, across tables in uncountable restaurants, flooding out the latest episode of a saga that seemed like it would never end?

"The central question is changing again," Henry points out. "Now it's: 'How is Terry going to get free?'"

Ginger disagrees. "I think it's: 'How much can a girl take?'"

"Or," Richard suggests, " 'How does she survive this new loss?' "

"How many times can the question change in a story?" Kitt wants to know. Her round face bears a worried expression. "Won't the reader get frustrated at some point?"

Frustrated, yes. Sick to death of it, I think, but the teacher answers smoothly, "Not as long as each question proceeds from the one before."

"Okay," Luis challenges, "but how does the protagonist change? That's what you're supposed to be telling us." His black eyes bore straight into mine.

"Yeah," Ginger concurs, "I'm ready to smack her for being such a victim."

I've told my students that *between the middle and the end of a story, the protagonist must undergo a "Decisive Moment." We cannot sympathize with a protagonist who is solely the victim of outside events. The decisive moment is one in which the protagonist becomes the agent of her own change.*

So what is my decisive moment? It is exactly this question I've wrestled with for so long. I've done acupuncture, bodywork, yoga, and homeopathy. I've seen a psychic, read tarot cards, thrown the I Ching, consulted my astrological chart, burned candles at the full moon. I've cried every day for six months; I've spent thousands of dollars on therapy. I've unearthed the little girl in the lavender jumper, alone and waiting late into the night for her parents to come home from the bar. I've revisited the rebellious teenager, clutching a bottle of Cuervo and a smoldering joint. I've crooned to the woman abandoned by her lover of nine years. Still, the resolution of this story remains as elusive as the first time she said "I don't want to see you anymore."

"How do you think she changes?" I throw it back to the group. Feel free to play god, I want to tell them. See if you can make Terry do or feel what I haven't been able to.

"Girlfriend gets fed up with bouncin' on the end of someone else's yo-yo," Ondine wags one celadon-tipped finger. "She jumps that tired string."

"Yeah, she gets some self-respect, stands up for herself," Ginger echoes, her voice rising as if delivering an anthem.

Richard is thoughtful. "I think Vivienne finally pushes her too far. Maybe she goes back and forth one too many times, or maybe she does something especially awful, but it's the last straw."

"I know!" Henry exclaims, a bit too eagerly, "Maybe they have this major fight, and Terry punches her lights out."

Kevin breaks in, "Or else Terry's abducted by aliens, and she gets this really galactic view of the situation, and realizes that Vivienne's not the one for her anyway."

The group is electrified by their solutions to the protagonist's dilemma. It's part wish fulfillment, I'm sure, things they've fantasized doing but haven't, couldn't. That's some of what fiction does for us; we can portray ourselves as stronger, braver versions than in our ordinary flawed lives.

"Maybe she takes everything Vivienne ever gave her and makes a big bonfire!" Henry's eyes light up.

"No, no," Kitt objects. "She just says, 'Leave me the fuck alone, don't call, drop dead, have a nice life.' " She raises one arm in the air, snaps her fingers for punctuation.

"Then she gets a new haircut, drops ten pounds, and looks so fabulous that Vivienne eats her heart out," Ginger adds.

"And *then,* she meets someone terrific who falls madly in love with her," Kitt concludes, "and they live happily ever after."

"Wait a minute," I interrupt them. "Is that story believable?"

Luis shakes his head, but everyone else is saying, "Sure," "Hell, yeah," "Why not?" until Rita breaks in.

"What if she just can't change?" Rita asks, with such quiet intensity that everyone in the room quiets down. Her harsh tone has dissolved into a plea. Shoulders hunched, a flush burns on each cheek. She's gripping her spiral notebook so hard her knuckles have gone pale beneath her dusky skin. "I mean, I know she needs to for the story and all, but what if she can't?"

Her despair calls out to mine with the lure of children's voices on a summer afternoon. My misery wants to push open the screen door, snatching up a quarter for the ice cream truck, run out into the full light of day to join the others. Instead, like a child deformed and hideous, the secret shame of the household, it must stay confined to the dark and airless attic of my skin. It has no place in this classroom, yowling and spitting and drooling, making everyone embarrassed or afraid.

A story is not the same as life. My students want to craft an ending that ensures that not only will Terry be all right, she will triumph. She's come through a harrowing loss, but she's learned from it, grown stronger, is determined to love again. How can I blame them? It's what readers want from a story.

But in life, our protagonist goes on for a long time in that state of stunned grief, sleepwalking through trips to the grocery store, cross-town freeway commutes, her first trip to France, the workshops in which she assumes the persona of teacher, pretending to be someone with wisdom to offer. It is possible that she may never understand why this happened, or what she was meant to learn. Maybe she will spin forever in Vivienne's orbit, an unclaimed moon in weak gravity.

"If she can't change," I answer Rita softly, "then maybe the story isn't over yet."

And perhaps mine isn't either. My decision would never satisfy my students. I haven't stormed out, told her off, sought revenge, or thrown myself into someone else's arms; I haven't severed the bond. We still talk on the phone, go to dinner, the occasional movie, buy each other spontaneous gifts—a book, a shirt, a CD. In her story we are learning to be friends. In mine, I simply continue to love her, without hope of reciprocity. Sometimes this is almost enough; the rest of the time I tell myself that I am learning something about keeping my heart open. Sometimes hope still surfaces, like a blossom in a hostile season, all the more poignant for its evident impossibility.

This is what I hate about life, its messiness and ambiguity. Did my story begin with my breakup, with the first night I danced with "Vivienne," or was it the first moment she walked into class six years ago? And did it conclude when she said, "No more; I want to move on"? Or is it still to end in some future we have not yet lived and cannot even imagine?

"It's nine o'clock," Richard's quiet voice nudges me.

My eyes stray to the calm face of the clock on the yellow wall; its hands dictate our beginnings and endings here.

"We have to stop," I say apologetically. "Great work, everybody; I'm impressed. You're really starting to get this plot thing. See you next Wednesday."

My students stand and file out, letting in the heat from the hallway as they prop open the door. Rita is the first to go, out of the door like a shot, and I resist the urge to call after her. Kevin ambushes me with a question about the due date for another assignment— is it flexible?

It is Luis who lingers when everyone else is gone. "Are you all right?" he asks, and his voice is tender. And I realize that he understands the way that story and life can blur and blend together until boundaries dissolve. If I let him, he would wrap his bony arms around me, hug me to his too-thin frame. I could talk or not talk, cry or not cry. I see all of this offered in his black eyes.

What I've learned, though, one thing that Vivienne has taught me is that we cannot escape our roles in this drama. That no matter how astute my students, however deep the regard in which they hold me, I can be no more than a character in their lives, the beloved teacher, a fiction. I must always stand apart from them, never threaten to become too real. This is what they need from me. What she needs.

I look for a long time into Luis' eyes. "I'm fine," I tell him quietly, and he nods, once and then again.

"Take it easy," he says as he turns.

"You too," I call out, as the door closes behind him.

I gather my notebook, my file folders. I shut down the air conditioning, feel how quickly the heat takes the room in its thick embrace. All the energy I summoned to teach, the adrenaline of performance, drains from me now, leaving my body limp and numb.

For a moment I let myself collapse into one of the metal chairs. I expect my earlier tears to return, but they don't; there is only a hollow ache in my chest and the sound of wind against the roof.

Wearily, I hoist myself up, erase the white board, the arc of plot dissolving into fine particles of color that stick to my palms. I whisper her name, her real name, but no one hears.

Excerpt from Soul Kiss

Shay Youngblood

I set the bed on fire, then stand in the doorway watching it burn. The flame from the first match flickered, then died. The second match caught, then blazed before my eyes. I stare into the flames and see my mother's hands reaching out to me, the treacherous lump thickening in my throat as I reach for her. I've set the bed on fire. The bed where I dream Mama's dreams and sweat through her nightmares, running from her enemies. I stand in the doorway watching it burn. I miss my mama, but I don't want to. I am seven years old, and yesterday is today, tomorrow never comes.

Pushing me aside, Aunt Merleen grabs the white enamel pitcher of water that always sits on my bedside table. She dashes out the fire.

I hear Aunt Faith singing, "My bed. My beautiful bed." Sweet soprano.

Aunt Merleen just shakes her head to the tune of "Umph, umph. umph." Rumbling bass.

The smoke fills my ears and coats my tongue with sadness. The burning dreams fill up my lungs with longing.

"Is she dead?" I ask from the doorway, looking at Aunt Faith's tiny bare feet.

"No, child, she's not dead," Aunt Faith answers sadly.

Her answer smashes all hope against the wall. If she were dead I could stop waiting. If she were dead I could die too.

"Why did she leave me?" I scream at them and bang my head against the door frame over and over until Aunt Faith draws me up to her, holding my head against her belly. She lets me cry and scream for days into her soft, smoky apron. I don't ask about Mama again for a long time. I begin sleeping on a quilt on the hardwood floor that smells of lemon oil. I stop dreaming and begin to see shadows underneath the bed.

☐   ☐   ☐

One Sunday after visiting Grandma Gert, Aunt Faith tells Aunt Merleen to drop her off at the hospital to visit one of the sick members of the church. I am left alone with the stormy one. I follow her in through the backdoor of the house. I take off my shiny black church shoes and put them in their box by the backdoor. I put on the pink ballet slippers they have asked me to wear in the house. Then I drag the stepstool over to the kitchen sink, where I scrub my hands with Ivory liquid dish soap and a rough bristled brush just like they have taught me. I walk down the narrow carpeted hallway lined with framed poems and prayers and sit on the bottom step of the front stairs looking at the closed front door as if it will fly open and my mama will be standing there with her hands on her hips ready to take me away. I can almost see her soft, smooth hand beckoning me to her. That is what I pray for every Sunday, so I sit and wait and hope. Aunt Merleen ignores me mostly. When I hear her grumbling, something about the bed, I try not to, but I cry.

"You miss her, don't you?" Her voice is a thunderous whisper beside me.

I can't speak, but nod my head yes, wiping the tears away.

"Come on." Her bark is softer as she turns to walk away.

I look up to make sure she is speaking to me.

"Come on. I won't bite you." She is smiling a little.

I follow her into the kitchen. She hands me a pair of stiff blue overalls, a blue flannel boy's shirt, and a pair of black high-top sneakers. I drop the yellow girly Sunday dress to the slick linoleum floor and slip into a boy's world. Spring into summer, I get my hands dirty oiling screws from the lawn mower and planting rosebushes. My fingers become bloody from carving wooden birds and fish. I run. I climb trees. I throw rocks at tin cans. I am distracted from the pain that makes me want to set myself on fire. For many nights I sleep in my new boy's clothes, dreaming about my new life.

Aunt Merleen is hard on the outside, but I learn where she keeps her softness. She can't stand to see pain the way some people can't stand to see blood. I keep her secrets and she keeps mine.

Because she thinks most of the neighborhood children are thieves and future criminals she won't let me play with them. It is too far to play with the children I meet in Sunday school so I play alone, games I remember and ones I make up to pass the time. I read the books Aunt Faith buys for me and act out stories in front of the mirror. I am Cleopatra, Delilah, Mary Magdalene, and the Queen of Sheba, one after the other and all at once. I am also Harriet Tubman on the Underground Railroad and Frederick Douglass giving a speech, Mighty Mouse and Batman.

Across the railroad tracks are the government housing projects. From my bedroom window I watch the project children jump rope, play hopscotch in the dirt and dodgeball, and skate on the broken sidewalks. I imagine myself in their games, but I end up playing all by myself. All summer long I pretend that I am a boy, doing boy things, wearing boy clothes.

☐   ☐   ☐

School breaks our routine. On my first day at the red brick school down the street, I insist on wearing my boy's clothes.

"Little girls just don't wear pants to school," Aunt Faith says patiently, waiting for me to change my mind.

"Aunt Merleen wears pants all the time," I say, hooking my thumbs firmly in the shoulder straps of my overalls just as I have seen Aunt Merleen do when taking a break in her garden to consider the flowers, fruits, and vegetables of her labor.

"That's different. These are my work clothes. If I were going to school I'd wear school clothes." Aunt Merleen is taking her time with me, and I can tell she is getting weak because she starts pacing back and forth outside my bedroom in the hallway, trying to think up a good argument. I'd figured out how to soften them up so I could get my way. They hardly ever said no to anything I asked for. Pretty soon I figured I'd be driving the car to meet my mama at the train station.

"Pretty please?" I say, giving them the most pitiful look I can manage.

They both laugh and throw up their hands as if I have won this round.

"You've got your mama's ways. Get your sweater and your book satchel and let's go before you completely miss your first day at school," Aunt Merleen says as she walks heavily down the stairs. She is wearing a plain plaid shift dress I've never seen her wear before and a pair of run-over loafers she wears when she works in the garden. She drives me down the street to the school and walks me up to the door.

"Mind the teacher and do your best," she says, and opens the door to my classroom. She waves at the teacher from the top of the stairs and lets go of my hand. I look at the rows of solemn faces looking back at me. Only one face is smiling, a girl with a limp pink ribbon in her hair. By the time I look back Aunt Merleen is gone. From the moment I descend the stairs into the large basement classroom the teacher refuses to teach me; the children tease me and refuse to play with me because I am different. None of the other girls wear pants. They are all frilly girly-girls all tied up with satin ribbons. They call me names and throw rocks at me. I play alone on the monkey bars, making up words to songs. I want to cry, but I don't. The next day I wear one of the dresses Aunt Faith has remade for me, a navy-blue sailor dress with white buttons that float down the front. The dress reminds me of my mama.

I make friends with a girly-girl who wears flowered dresses and pale-pink ragged ribbons in her long, dark hair. She is a project girl. Her name is Joyous, but I call her Joy because she is always giggling even when there is nothing to laugh at. She is tongue-tied so she calls me Myra. I like the way she says it. In her mouth my name is an unexpected happiness. We become so close that when we come to a pole or a tree or an old tire in the road we always hold hands and

step around it together, on the same side. We know that it is bad luck
to split a pole. You always follow the person you love when you come
to an obstacle in the road. She comes with me to the big, white
house. I can tell that Aunt Merleen does not approve, but she does-
n't say anything, not even "good evening." Aunt Faith is nicer; she
gives us a plate of cookies dusted with powdered sugar and short
glasses of milk. I have to show Joy where to put her shoes and how
to put the pink ballet shoes over her socks and scrub her hands in the
sink until they are clean.

We play on the screened-in side porch which looks out onto the
garden. Joy tells me she is part Indian. I wonder which part. I tell
her that makes us sisters because my mama is part Cherokee. I tell
her that there is some Spanish in my blood too. To prove it, I teach
her some of the words my mother gave me.

Bonita...encaje...dulce...azul...musica...sueño...

We make dolls out of Aunt Faith's French magazines, Coke bottles, broken shoestrings, buttons, and glue. We fill the bottles with
sweet lemonade and color it with dye and drink it till our lips are the
color of blue roses and just as soft when she teaches me how to kiss.
And we kiss for hours; years go by and our lips and our eyes remain
closed, together. We discover other secret feelings in my bedroom
with the door closed. I like touching her closed eyes with my lips,
pressing my tongue in her belly button, brushing against her soft, fat
thighs with my cheeks. I hide crayons and nervous fingers between
her legs to see how far they will go. We hide under the bed playing
house, in the closet playing doctor. When we play Beach Blanket
Bingo under blankets thrown over chairs I am Frankie and she is
Annette. I am always in charge.

One day me and Joy are caught kissing. Her mother catches us, and
I become a girl again as if I have been a butterfly that becomes a rock.

"It's an abomination before God," her mother declares, and
makes us pray together on our knees on the dirty kitchen floor. Baby
Erica's crying competes with the TV on full volume from the next
room and mixes with our loud prayers for forgiveness. Her mother
chants scriptures into the sticky air for hours. Then she walks me

home. She walks three steps ahead of me wearing a sleeveless faded green shift that once zipped up the front but is now held together in two places with huge silver safety pins. Her blue flip-flops sound like wet hands slapping the pavement. The night claws at me, closing me in. Joy's mother walks me right up to the door of the big white house. I am so scared I start to cry before Nag can speak. But she speaks. She tells everything she knows and my future if I do not change my wicked ways. Aunt Merleen listens to Nag through the screen door. She tells me to come in the house, but does not invite Nag beyond the top step of the porch.

"You won't have to worry about her no more. She's not allowed down in the projects no way. Thank you for bringing her home. Good night, *Miss* Dyson." Aunt Merleen closes the door in her face. I can still hear Nag cursing us out on the porch in the dark.

"You late for supper," Aunt Merleen says, taking long strides down the hall to the kitchen. I follow her, wondering what she is going to do to me. She chooses each sentence carefully. "Your Aunt Faith is at choir rehearsal. She don't need to know about all this." She pauses, bites her lip, then says: "I told you not to play with them project children."

Aunt Merleen starts talking to the can of soup she is opening for my supper. "You ought to wait until you a little bit older to go around kissing. Kissing and all that is for grown folks." And that is the last word she says on the subject. A secret we keep from Aunt Faith. I spend hours in my room thinking of the day when I am older, when I am a butterfly and can start kissing girls again.

Me and the girly-girl are friends for a long time after this, but we never kiss on the lips again or find secret places to play on each other's bodies. We don't speak of those times, but I never forget them. I can't stop thinking about kissing. My friend the girly-girl encourages me to wear dresses. I look like I fit in, but I never do.

☐   ☐   ☐

"Where is my mama's suitcase?" I ask when I miss Mama so much my chest hurts from the pain. The two years I've waited for her seem like an unfair prison sentence. I am nine years old, and I feel that I have been very patient, but I have also grown curious. Answers to my questions are as scarce as answered prayers.

"We put it up for her," Aunt Faith says without looking up from her sewing.

"Could I see it? Maybe she left her address in there." I sit next to the piano unraveling a thread at the bottom of my shirt.

"Your mama don't have an address, baby. She's traveling."

"You heard from my mama?" I ask, wide-eyed. "When she coming to get me?"

"We didn't exactly hear from her," Aunt Faith says quietly.

"Reverend Wilson's son-in-law saw her in Atlanta last year. She said she'd send for you as soon as she could," Aunt Merleen says flatly from her chair, exchanging a look with Aunt Faith that says more than my ears will hear. She makes a great noise of turning the pages of the newspaper stretched out in front of her.

"What's she doing in Atlanta?" I keep picking at the threads. They fall on the carpet, making patterns like a cat's cradle.

"She was working, getting ready to go to Memphis, I think he said." Aunt Faith keeps moving the needle and thread in tight tiny stitches that will be invisible to the eye.

"She'll come back to get you when she can. In the meantime, ain't we doing all right? Why don't you read me one of them Simple stories by Langston Hughes. He write some funny stories, don't he?" Aunt Merleen quickly folds up her newspaper and talks fast like she is trying to hurry Mama out of my mind, but I'm not having it.

"Didn't she leave a address? I could write to her at the post office in Memphis. She probably waiting on a letter from me. Can I look in her suitcase?"

"There ain't nothing in that suitcase concern you. It's for your mama when she come back. Now leave it alone." Aunt Merleen's tone hits me in the stomach; I pick up the broken threads from the carpet and take them with me to my room to poke into the window screen like constellations in the sky. I refuse to let them see me cry.

I want to look for the suitcase, but I am never left alone in the house. I suspect they keep it in their bedroom, which I have only seen from the doorway next to the bathroom. It is a large room with neat twin beds made up with colorful patterned quilts. The beds are separated by a small night table. There is also a dark wood vanity beneath a smoky mirror, a matching chifforobe with a place for Aunt Faith's Sunday hats, and a tall chest of drawers. Aunt Merleen's shotgun lies like a sleeping soldier under her bed. Everything is in its place. A place for everything, but me. I am on the outside with my nose pressed to the window waiting for something that is mine.

☐   ☐   ☐

Indian summers and dog days go by. Holidays and birthdays pass as quietly as grass grows. Not one word from her. I am so mad at my mama for leaving me, I am not sure I can forgive her. Life is so difficult without her. At the Parent-Teachers Association meetings I am stuck sitting with Aunt Faith, who my teacher thinks is my grandmother. At church on Mother's Day Aunt Faith and Aunt Merleen wear white flowers pinned to their dresses because their mother is dead. I am forced to wear a red flower because my mother is alive, but I feel as if she is dead. I wish I could wear a pink satin rose for my mother because she is missing.

In school the other children tease me.

"Where's your mama?" they ask, as if they are interested.

Not waiting for an answer, some of them speculate.

"Maybe she's in jail." Everybody laughs, everybody but Dwight James, whose mama is in prison for killing his daddy because he beat her one time too many.

"Or at the welfare office trying to get some government cheeeeese." Their laughter is like a cloud of bees stinging me from all sides.

Before I can think of something smart to say back, another girl says, "I bet she ain't even got no mama." I learn to pretend that I am deaf to their insults. In two blinks I can grow cement in my ears.

If I focus on the color blue I can sometimes hear music in my head...*sweet*...*blue*...*music*.... The sky is all I need, or a page in a book or the hem of a skirt, as long as it is blue.

During library period, I excuse myself to go to the bathroom. The librarian, Miss Belton, is a graceful middle-aged woman who wears her hair in two thick black braids wrapped like coiled snakes on top of her head. She likes me, so I don't have to beg like some of the other students. She waves me out of the room, her hand caressing the air as delicate as a lady's handkerchief. The long wide hallway echoes with the sound of my footsteps. Two flights down in the basement, the girls bathroom is one big open room with a row of white porcelain toilets facing a row of white sinks and squares of chrome-framed mirrors. I am washing my hands in the sink. When I look up I see two upper-class girls come in. Sonya is the baddest girl in school. She is the biggest too. She has stayed back twice in the fourth grade. I think this is what has made her so mean. Her shadow Victoria is with her. Victoria does everything Sonya tells her. They beat up a girl after school one time and took her lunch money every day for a month before the girl's mama told the principal. Sonya got sent home for a week. She came back with a broken arm somebody said her brother gave her, and she was meaner than ever. When they see me they start laughing. I keep lathering my hands with the smooth bar of orange soap that smells like medicine. Sonya starts in on me.

"Look at her, looking in the mirror like she something." Her voice is tough and accusing.

Then Victoria gives me a shot. "Think you something don't you? Think you cute."

"And with a stupid name like Mariah Santos you must be Mexican or something."

"You Mexican Sand Toes? Is that why you think you so good?"

I blink twice, but I am so mad I can hear them through the cement in my ears. I look around, but I can't find the color blue. Even the sky is gray. I don't know what to say. Victoria pushes me against the sink. I am about to throw soap in her eyes when Joy comes in. Her skirt circles the air as she whirls around and stands in between them and me with both hands on her hips like she is Marshal Dillon on *Gunsmoke*. Like a hired assassin on *The Wild, Wild West*.

"You messing with my friend?" she says, puffing up like she's six feet tall instead of five feet even.

"What's it to you?" Sonya asks, taking a step forward.

"If you messing with my friend, you messing with me, and if you mess with me, my sister Nicky will kick your ass." Joy tosses her hair over her shoulder and stands her ground. Still life in motion. Sonya is the one to back down. Nicky is always in trouble for fighting at the junior high school, and rumor has it she bit a girl so hard you can still see the teeth marks on her face.

"Ain't nobody messing with you or your stuck-up little friend. Come on, Vic, let's go. It stinks in here," Sonya says, dismissing us with a wave of her hand as she leaves the bathroom.

When they leave I breathe again and let go of the sink. I am relieved I didn't have to fight the biggest girl in the school. I don't even know how to fight. No one has taught me how. Until then I'd never needed to defend myself with anything other than words. I don't know what to say. I want to kiss her, but the girly-girl steps away from me.

"I can't do that anymore. I'll get in trouble. My mama says we'll go to hell in a handbasket." She leans back against the sink and smiles.

"I'm sorry. I don't want you to go to hell." I stand awkwardly in the middle of the room, chewing on the side of my finger, not caring whether I go to hell or not.

"It's okay. You're still my friend to the end. You my girl, but you can't let people walk over you. I'm not always gonna come like Batman right on time to save your ass. If anybody mess with you, you pick up a brick or a rock or the biggest thing you can find, and before they can blink, you knock the hell out of the biggest one in the bunch and they'll leave you alone." She shows me how to use an empty Coke bottle as a weapon. Before we leave the bathroom she winks at me. I wink back just like she taught me two summers past.

When a girl twice my size says, "Hey, Santos, I saw your mama down on Eighth Street turning tricks at the gas station," I say, "You say that when I get back." I go back into the big white house and fill a Coke bottle with water. I drop a broken Alka-Seltzer in the water and watch it fizz. I go back outside and I yell at her, "Come over here and say that to my face. I'll burn your ass with this acid. I'll put your lights out." I throw the bottle at her. It sails through the air and lands a few feet from her dirty tennis shoes. She runs off yelling, "You crazy, Santos, you crazy. They ought to send you to Milledgeville." Nobody messed with me after that. I was left alone. Word got around fast: "Crazy Santos. The girl is mad."

My teachers at school reward my good behavior and excellent memory with straight A's, and I continue to set an example for the other students, which does not earn me many friends outside of class. Miss Belton lets me check out books on Mexico. I know I'm not supposed to deface a library book, but I cut out one of the colored maps so that I can sleep with it under my pillow. I dream of a different Mexican city and village each night, and in these dreams I walk the streets and dusty unpaved roads looking for my father, hoping he has found my mother and that they are waiting for me to join them so that together we can paint the sky blue.

I miss my friend the girly-girl. Her easy giggles and house games. Neicey only plays with me because my aunt gives her piano lessons and she has to wait for her father to pick her up in his taxi. We don't talk much. She is really stuck-up. She lives in a house in Randall Estates and goes to Catholic school even though her family is Baptist. After her Saturday morning lessons we play Candyland, Monopoly, or checkers until she hears her father ringing the doorbell. She doesn't even bother to say good-bye when he comes, just smooths down the folds of her velvet dress as if she has gotten dirty playing with me. My aunts think she is sweet, but a girl who cheats at checkers is low-class—I don't care where she goes to school.

Contributors

Dorothy Allison is the author of *Trash; The Women Who Hate Me; Skin: Essays on Sex, Class, and Literature; Two or Three Things I Know for Sure; Bastard Out of Carolina,* the acclaimed best-seller and a finalist for the National Book Award; and *Cavedweller,* for which she recently won the 1998 Lambda Literary Award for Lesbian Fiction.

Cynthia Bond is an artist, activist, and author. She is working on her first novel, *Ruby,* an excerpt of which was critically praised when it appeared in the anthology *Afrekete.* She has also edited an anthology of writing by gay and lesbian youth, *When the Bough Breaks.* She works as director of the Pedro Zamora Youth HIV Clinic at the Los Angeles Gay & Lesbian Center.

Beth Brant is a Bay of Quinte Mohawk from Tyendinaga Mohawk Territory in Ontario. She is the editor of *A Gathering of Spirit,* and author of *Mohawk Trail, Food & Spirits,* and *Writing as Witness.* The past recipient of an Ontario Arts Council Award, a Canada Council grant, and a National Endowment for the Arts fellowship, she is currently working on *Testimony From the Faithful,* a collection of essays about land and spirit. She lives in Michigan.

Poet/novelist/artist/xicanista **Ana Castillo** lives in her hometown of Chicago with her son. Her last project, *Goddess of the Americas/La Diosa de las Americas,* was published by Riverhead Books in October 1996. She recently finished a novel, *Peel My Love Like an Onion* (Doubleday, 1999), and a collection of poetry, *I Ask the Impossible.* Widely anthologized, she has also written for newspapers and magazines across the country on various topics, includ-

ing the murder of Tejano singer Selena and most recently on gender roles in the farmworkers movement (*Los Angeles Times,*
4/20/97). Castillo received an American Book Award for her first
novel, *The Mixquiahuala Letters.*

Elise D'Haene's fiction has appeared in several anthologies and
journals, including *Hers* and *Hers*[2] (Faber & Faber), edited by Terry
Wolverton and Robert Drake; *1999 Best American Erotica* (Simon &
Schuster), edited by Susie Bright; and *The Mammoth Book of Lesbian
Short Stories* (Carroll & Graf), edited by Emma Donoghue. Her first
novel, *Licking Our Wounds* (Permanent Press), won the Best Gay
and Lesbian Fiction Award at BookExpo America Small Press
Awards, Chicago, 1998. She lives in Los Angeles and New York with
her lover, Celeste, and their dog, Alf.

Born in Dublin in 1969, **Emma Donoghue** is an Irish writer who
lives in Canada. She has published novels (*Stir-fry, Hood*), fairy tales
(*Kissing the Witch*), drama (*Ladies and Gentlemen*), lesbian history
(*Passions Between Women; We Are Michael Field*), and anthologies
(*Poems Between Women; The Mammoth Book of Lesbian Short Stories*).

" 'The Fox on the Line' is one of a series of fact-based historical
fictions," Donoghue says. "The Irish journalist Frances Power
Cobbe (1822-1904)—'Fà' to her loved ones—and the Welsh sculptor Mary Charlotte Lloyd met in 1860 in Rome and lived together
in London from 1863. After the passing of the watered-down
Cruelty to Animals Act of 1876, Cobbe and Lloyd campaigned not
for reform but for a total ban on live animal testing—a cause yet to
be won. In 1884 they retired to Wales. When Mary Lloyd died in
1898, her will forbade Cobbe to 'commemorate her by any written
record'."

Emma Donoghue's vision of lesbian writing in the 21st century is
that lesbians will write about anything and anyone will write about
lesbians, thus making the business of defining and anthologizing
more delightfully impossible than ever.

Mary Gaitskill is the author of *Bad Behavior; Two Girls, Fat and Thin; and Because They Wanted to*. She lives in upstate New York.

Larissa Lai was born in La Jolla, Calif. She is currently based in Vancouver, British Columbia, where she works as a community organizer, writer, and critic. In 1995 she was the recipient of an Astraea Foundation Emerging Writers Award. Her novel, *When Fox Is a Thousand* (Press Gang Publishers, 1995), was nominated for the Chapters/Books in Canada First Novel Award in 1996. She recently spent an academic year as Canadian Writer-in-Residence with the Markin-Flanagan Distinguished Writers Programme at the University of Calgary. Her poetry, fiction, and nonfiction have appeared in numerous journals, including *Bamboo Ridge, West Coast Line, The Asian American Journal, CV2, Matrix, Room of One's Own, Estuaire,* and *absinthe;* as well as several anthologies, including *Many-Mouthed Birds, Pearls of Passion, Bringing It Home: Women Talk About Feminism in Their Lives, Eye Wuz Here,* and *Into the Fire: Asian American Prose.* Her articles and essays have appeared in *Kinesis, Fuse, Harbour, Rungh, Video re/View: The (best) Source for Critical Writings on Canadian Artists' Video, Canadian Literature,* as well as several exhibition catalogs. She is working on her second novel, *Salt Fish*.

Carole Maso is the author of *Ghost Dance, The Art Lover, Ava, The American Woman in the Chinese Hat,* and *Aureole*. She teaches at Brown University.

Amelia Maria de la Luz Montes teaches literature at the University of California, Santa Barbara, in the departments of Chicano and women's studies. Her credits include poetry and short stories in *UCLA Voices, Saguaro,* and *Hers*[3] (Farrar, Straus & Giroux). She is a Xicana writer and native of Los Angeles.

Of her story she writes, " 'R for Ricura' was inspired by Ana Castillo's essay 'La Macha: Toward an Erotic Whole Self' (*Massacre of the Dreamers*), in which Castillo argues for a woman's right to her own desires. Ricura lives in a world where fluidity in sexual identity is not an issue. I value Ricura's integrity—her willingness to explore sexuality and authority on her own terms."

Shani Mootoo was born in Ireland and grew up in Trinidad. A film-maker, videomaker, and visual artist, her paintings and photo-based works are exhibited internationally. She is also a published poet and the author of *Cereus Blooms at Night,* a novel, and *Out on Main Street,* a collection of stories. She is working on her second novel.

Mei Ng is the author of *Eating Chinese Food Naked* (Scribner, 1998). She was born in New York City and currently lives in Brooklyn.

Achy Obejas is the author of *We Came All the Way From Cuba So You Could Dress Like This?* (1994), a collection of short stories, and *Memory Mambo* (1996), a novel, both published by Cleis Press. She was born in Havana, Cuba.

Gerry Gomez Pearlberg is the author of *Marianne Faithfull's Cigarette* (Cleis) and the editor of *Queer Dog: Homo/Pup/Poetry* (Cleis), winner of a 1998 Firecracker Alternative Book Award.

Robin Podolsky is a writer who lives and works in Los Angeles. Her first book, tentatively titled *Queer Cosmopolis,* is forthcoming from New York University Press.

Of this story, she says, "As a child, I would cry over 'The Twelve Dancing Princesses.' Did the oldest sister betray her sisters on purpose? How could they forgive her if she did? What if the princesses didn't want to get married? And so on. My vehement reactions to the stories I read and viewed helped to push me toward writing. I like reclaiming and retelling popular myths to serve queer purposes—it's not as though someone can point to what 'really' happened. I believe that myths and folk stories will serve to see us into the next century so long as we're honest with ourselves about identity as artifact and we're not afraid to change."

Patricia Powell is the author of *Me Dying Trial, A Small Gathering of Bones,* and most recently *The Pagoda,* which won the Ferro-Grumley Prize for Best Lesbian Fiction. Powell is a Briggs-Copeland Lecturer in fiction at Harvard University.

Sarah Schulman is the author of seven novels: *Shimmer* (Avon, 1998); *Rat Bohemia* (Dutton, 1995), winner of the Ferro-Grumley Prize for lesbian fiction and a finalist for the Prix de Rome; *Empathy* (Dutton, 1992); *People in Trouble* (Dutton, 1990), winner of the Gregory Kolovakos Award for AIDS Fiction; *After Delores* (Dutton, 1988), winner of the American Library Association's Gay, Lesbian and Bisexual Book Award for fiction; *Girls, Visions, and Everything* (Seal, 1986); *The Sophie Horowitz Story* (Naiad, 1984); and two nonfiction books, *My American History: Lesbian and Gay Life During the Reagan/Bush Years* (Routledge, 1994), winner of the Gustavus Meyer Award for a Work Promoting Tolerance; and *Stagestruck: Theater, AIDS and the Marketing of Gay America* (Duke University Prize, 1999), winner of the American Library Association's Gay, Lesbian and Bisexual Book Award for nonfiction.

Jane Thurmond writes fiction and works as a graphic designer in Austin, Texas. Her short stories have appeared in various publications, including *The Iowa Review, The Austin Chronicle, Hers[1], Hers[3],* and *Indivisible.*

Terry Wolverton: See "About the Editors."

Shay Youngblood was born in Columbus, Ga., and received her BA from Clark Atlanta University and an MFA from Brown University. She is a playwright (*Shakin' the Mess Outta Misery* and *Talking Bones)* and the author of a novel, *Soul Kiss,* and a story collection, *The Big Mama Stories,* one of which was awarded a Pushcart Prize.

Terry Wolverton is the author of *Bailey's Beads,* a novel, and two collections of poetry, *Black Slip* and *Mystery Bruise.* Her fiction, poetry, essays, and dramatic texts have appeared in numerous literary publications, including *ZYZZYVA, Calyx,* and *Glimmer Train Stories,* and been widely anthologized. She has also edited several acclaimed literary compilations, including *Blood Whispers: L.A. Writers on AIDS* and, with Robert Drake, *Indivisible: New Short Fiction by West Coast Gay and Lesbian Writers,* and the Lambda Literary Award-winning series *His: Brilliant New Fiction by Gay Men* and *Hers: Brilliant New Fiction by Lesbians.* Since 1976 Terry has lived in Los Angeles, where she's been active in the feminist, gay and lesbian, and art communities. In 1997 she founded Writers At Work, a center for writing workshops and individual creative consultations. She is currently at work on two books: *Embers,* a novel in poems, and *Insurgent Muse,* a memoir to be published by City Lights Publishers.

Robert Drake is the author of *The Gay Canon: Great Books Every Gay Man Should Read* and the novel *The Man: A Hero for Our Time.* He is coeditor of the anthologies *Indivisible: New Short Fiction by West Coast Gay and Lesbian Writers,* and the Lambda Literary Award-winning series *His: Brilliant New Fiction by Gay Men* and *Hers: Brilliant New Fiction by Lesbians.* From 1986 to 1998 he earned his living as a literary agent, finding time to serve from 1993 to 1998 as book review editor for the *Baltimore Alternative* and teach writing at community colleges in Philadelphia and Anne Arundel County, Md., as well as The American University and St. John's College, where he received his MA in 1993. Born in

Portland, Maine, and raised in Charleston, W. Va., he was living in Ireland when he was beaten unconscious in a gay-bashing attack, sustaining severe trauma to the head. He is undergoing rehabilitation in Philadelphia.

Acknowledgments

The editors wish to thank Gwin Wheatley for incalculable editorial assistance and so much more, and Robin Podolsky for additional editorial assistance. We gratefully thank the authors, publishers, and agents who gave permission for the works to appear in this book. Finally, deep appreciation to John Talbot, and to Scott Brassart and Angela Brown for patience and support.

Credits